Hour of the Witch

Also by Chris Bohjalian
Available from Random House Large Print

The Guest Room
The Red Lotus

HOUR
of the
WITCH

A NOVEL

CHRIS
BOHJALIAN

RANDOM HOUSE
LARGE PRINT

Copyright © 2021 by Quaker Village Books LLC

All rights reserved. Published in the United States of America by Random House Large Print in association with Doubleday, a division of Penguin Random House LLC, New York.

Cover photograph © Magdalena Russocka / Trevillion Images

Cover design by John Fontana
Title page art © Morphart Creation / Shutterstock

The Library of Congress has established a Cataloging-in-Publication record for this title.

ISBN: 978-0-593-39651-3

www.penguinrandomhouse.com/
large-print-format-books

FIRST LARGE PRINT EDITION

Printed in the United States of America

10 9 8 7 6 5 4 3 2 1

This Large Print edition published in accord with the standards of the N.A.V.H.

For
Brian Lipson and Deborah Schneider,
for their patience, candor, counsel, and kindness

And once more for
Victoria,
forever my muse and inamorata

Dost dream of things beyond the moon,
And dost thou hope to dwell there soon?

—Anne Bradstreet

PROLOGUE

It was always possible that the Devil was present. Certainly, God was watching. And their Savior.

And so they were never completely alone. Not even when they might wander out toward the mud-flats or the salt marshes which, because they all but disappeared at high tide, they called the Back Bay, or they happened to scale the Trimountain— three separate hills, really, Cotton and Sentry and Beacon—they had virtually flattened as they moved the earth to create the jetties and wharves and foundations for the warehouses. Not even along the narrow neck that led to the mainland, or when they were in the woods (most definitely not when they were in the woods) on the far side of the slender spit.

They knew there was something with them when they were otherwise alone in their small, dark houses—the windows sometimes mere slits and often shuttered against the wind and the cold— and a man could write in his diary (his ledger, in essence, in which he would catalog the day's events and his state of mind in an effort to gauge whether he was among the elect), or a woman could scribble a few lines of poetry about the trees or the rivers or those astonishing sand dunes that rolled in the night like sea waves.

Sometimes the presence was frightening, especially if there were other indications that the Devil was at hand. But then there were those moments when it was comforting, and they, mere sheep to their divinity, felt the company of their shepherd. It was soothing, reassuring, breathtakingly beautiful.

Either way, more times than not, the women and men took consolation in the notion that there were explanations for a world that was so clearly inexplicable—and, usually, inexplicable in ways that were horrifying: a shallop with a dozen oarsmen disappearing beneath the water somewhere between the piers and the massive, anchored ship with its barrels of seasonings, its containers of gunpowder, its crates of pewter and porcelain and pillowbeers. That shallop vanished completely. One moment, sailors on the docks in the harbor could see it plainly. But then the clouds rolled in and the rains began, and the boat never emerged from the froth and the foam, and the bodies never were found.

Never.

Or that farmer who was gored through the stomach by a bull and took three days, every moment of which he was in agony, to die in his bedstead. How do you explain that? By the end of the ordeal, the feathers and cornhusks in the great bag beneath him were as red as the linen in which they were wrapped. Never had it taken a man so long to bleed out.

Three days. A number of biblical import.

But, still. Still.

How do you explain a husband who will break his wife's leg with a fireplace poker, and then chain her around the waist to the plow so she can't leave his property? And who then goes away? The woman waited a full day before she began to cry out.

How do you explain hurricanes that suck whole wharves into the sea, fires that spread from the hearth to the house and leave behind nothing but two blackened chimneys, how do you explain droughts and famines and floods? How do you explain babies who die and children who die and, yes, even old people who die?

Never did they ask the question **Why me?** In truth, they never even asked the more reasonable question **Why anyone?**

Because they knew. They knew what was out there in the wilds, and what was inside them that was, arguably, wilder still. Though good works could not in themselves change a thing—original sin was no fiction, predestination no fable—they might be a sign. A good sign. Sanctification followed justification.

And as for divorce . . . it happened. Rarely. But it did. It was possible. At least it was supposed to be. Mediation was always better than litigation, because this was, after all, a community of saints. At least that was the plan. There were the tangible grounds: Desertion. Destitution. Bigamy. Adultery (which was indeed a capital crime because of the Lord God's edicts in Leviticus and Deuteronomy, though no adulterer ever was actually hanged). Impotence. Cruelty.

It was a violent world, but still you weren't supposed to strike your spouse.

At least not without provocation.

Mary Deerfield knew all this, she knew it because God had given her an excellent mind—despite what her husband, Thomas, would tell her. And though brains hadn't helped Anne Hutchinson (Winthrop himself opined that her problem was that she meddled too much by trying to think like a man), and in later years brains most definitely would not help the score of women who would be hanged as witches in Salem, she knew intellectually she had done nothing wrong and didn't deserve to be hit like a brute animal. She wouldn't stand for it. It seemed that her mother and father, bless them, wouldn't demand that she stand for it, either.

The issue, of course, would not merely be his violence, nor would it boil down to a debate over what she said versus what he said. The wrack of their marriage was not solely his cruelty, and the divorce petition would be grounded by snares beyond her ken. Here, she realized, there were times when she would have been better off if she could have been alone but for the angels or her God, and—conversely—there were times when she would have given a very great deal for a witness that was human.

Because even for a mind as sharp as Mary Deerfield's, it was the recognition of her own mean desires and roiling demons where things began to grow muddy.

THE BOOK of the WIFE

. . . and so infidel-like he would call
me a whore and concoct the most wild
stories as to my behavior, and then
he would strike me in the name of
discipline as if I were an untutored child.

**—Petition for Divorce filed by Mary
Deerfield, from the Records and Files
of the Court of Assistants, Boston,
Massachusetts, 1662, Volume III**

One

There were two mistakes young men would make when they would first pick up a scythe: they would try to do all the work with their arms, and they would make their swathes far too wide. They would attack the grass, as if they thought it would get up and run away if they didn't kill it quickly. It would be their fathers or their uncles who would demonstrate how much better off they would be if they would put their backs into the motion too, swinging the snath in an almost indecent, leisurely, metronomical sway. Draw the blade back, hands on the nibs, as the right leg strides ahead; then cut— imagine that sickle moon is the tip of a pendulum on a tall clock—as the left leg walks forward. That was the way.

If the blade were sufficiently sharp, great tufts of grass would collapse around the metal as it advanced through the field, and their arms would not feel like anvils.

The first time that Mary Deerfield's husband hit her, she didn't relate the motion to scything: she was in too much pain and she was too surprised.

Her skin stung. It was the second time, half a year later, just before she turned twenty and just after the first anniversary of the day they were married, that she noted that he punched her the way a knowledgeable man would scythe. His arm swung effortlessly, the movement graceful and efficient. An arc. She fell against the pumpkin pine table, the pewter candlesticks toppled over, and the tankard of hard cider he had been drinking spilled onto the floor and into the trencher with their dinner. Still, however, she saw most clearly the image of the men scything—the details from her memory more concrete in her mind than even the way the cider was puddling that moment in the stewed pumpkin—and the wavelike rocking of their upper bodies and arms.

He called her a whore and she said he knew that she wasn't. He said he had seen her looking at other men, younger men, with lust in her gaze. She said this wasn't true, but she thought he was going to hit her again. And so she prepared herself for the blow, her shoulders scrunched against her neck and her hands before her face. But he didn't hit her. He was shaking with anger, unfounded though it was, and she hoped a good measure of guilt, but he didn't strike her again.

Instead he stomped out the door, saddled Sugar, a handsome eight-year-old gray gelding with a black mane, and he was gone. She placed her fingers on her cheek and wondered at its warmth. Blood gathering under the skin? There would be swelling, it was inevitable, and she was glad that they had been alone. She was dizzy with shame. She took his mug and held the cold pewter against the skin where he had hit her, and sat down in her chair. She contemplated a mystery: **How is it I am humiliated when I am alone? Does not humiliation demand an audience?**

※ ※

Four years later, Mary Deerfield's husband snored beside her in bed. In public, he was never a loud or offensive drunk, which was probably why he had never been fined or sent to the stocks. He kept his anger inside his home, and rarely (perhaps never) did he allow it to vent when their young servant girl, Catherine, was present or when his grown daughter would visit. Mary thought she heard the girl moving downstairs now, somewhere near the fireplace, but she couldn't be sure. It might have been the wind.

The poor girl's brother was dying. The boy was Catherine's twin, and he had always been more frail than his sister. The two of them were eighteen. He probably wasn't going to make it through the fall. Like her, he was indentured. Catherine said this evening that he had managed to nibble at his supper and keep down a little meat, but otherwise his complexion was bad and a few pieces of pork weren't going to prevent him from withering away.

When Mary's husband had returned tonight from the tavern, she had pretended she was asleep. He had stayed extra late. She had felt him looking at her, but she knew that he wasn't going to wake her to apologize for striking her earlier that evening. (And he certainly hadn't been watching her because he had been contemplating the idea they would couple. There wasn't a prayer of that, not after all he had probably drunk.) Over the years, a pattern had emerged. He'd drink, he'd hit her, and he'd go away to drink some more. The next day, he would say he was sorry. She presumed he would apologize in the morning for hitting her again tonight. He would insist on his own sinfulness before leaving for church. She recalled what they had squabbled about: the garden looked weedy and unruly, and he felt it reflected badly on him. At least that was how it began. She knew he had other demons that pricked him with tines as sharp as needles.

Thomas was forty-five, not twice her age, but close enough. She was his second wife, his first— the former Anne Drury—having died eight years ago, soon after Mary's own family had arrived in the colony, when Thomas's horse had kicked her in the jaw and snapped her neck. Thomas had shot the animal that night, even though it had been a docile beast until that terrible evening. He and Anne had

had three children together, two of whom had died young, but a third, Peregrine, was an adult now. The woman had married only weeks before Mary herself had wed Peregrine's father. Consequently, Mary had never lived under the same roof with her, and given the reality that the two were contemporaries, she was glad. After all, she was both Peregrine's stepmother and her peer: she couldn't imagine having to discipline someone almost her age. Peregrine was more like a stepsister than a stepdaughter, albeit a stepsister who, Mary suspected, didn't much like her for the simple reason that she wasn't Anne. Peregrine now had children of her own, which meant that Mary, though only twenty-four, was a grandmother. The idea on occasion left her doleful and reeling.

She closed her eyes and listened to the sounds of the autumn night. There were still leaves on the trees in the marketplace and the commons that hadn't been girdled, but soon those leaves, too, would fall, and there would probably be a killing frost as soon as the moon was full. It was well beyond half now. She touched the spot on her face where Thomas had hit her, aware that people might ask what had happened in the morning. Then, while conjuring a reason for the bruise that she could tell them, she fell into a deep sleep.

I know the taverns and ordinaries. That
is no secret and nothing for which I
need either this court's or the Lord's
forgiveness. But have I ever been fined
for too much drink? No. Hast thou ever
lashed me publicly for such offense?
Of course not. This court knows me,
it knows my mill. And, yes, though
there is evil within me and my heart is
inclined to sin; though I have reason
often to be ashamed before God; the
truth is that I have tried always to glorify
God in all things. Though I will have
many failures to answer for in the end,
my comportment toward my wife, Mary
Deerfield, will not be among them.

**—The Testimony of Thomas
Deerfield, from the Records and Files
of the Court of Assistants, Boston,
Massachusetts, 1662, Volume III**

Two

Mary Deerfield knew she was beautiful. Her eyes were delft blue, her skin as pale and smooth as the porcelain on which they occasionally dined back in England when she was a girl, and so there were moments when she worried that her conceit was a sign she should watch. It was not good to be prideful.

Still, as she dressed for church she was relieved to discover that Thomas had struck her just close enough to her ear that she could actually hide the bruise under her coif if she tied it snugly around her face. Early that summer, she'd had to tell her neighbors that she'd walked into a cloak peg in the night, and she had been teased for her clumsiness by everyone but her mother, who, Mary feared, suspected the real source of the black-and-blue mark.

Church today would begin at nine, end at noon, and resume at two. This had been a good summer, with enough rain and sun that the men had gotten in three cuttings of hay for the winter, and the crops in the fields had grown larger than she had ever seen them here in Massachusetts. There were pumpkins nearly the size of butter churns.

Today would be a service in which they needed to humble themselves before God and thank Him for their good fortune. The Devil had been noticeably absent, save, perhaps, for the death of the two babies on Marlborough Street and His visit to poor Catherine's dying brother. In all fairness, the pitiable William lived in a home in which everyone knew the family hadn't buried an ox bone in the foundation of the house when they had built it, or glazed any of the bricks in the chimney with salt. Some people had suggested that the babies' deaths were the work of witches, not the Devil, but Mary saw only hysteria in that sort of speculation. Babies died all the time. And there had been no women she had seen or heard about who had manifested possession. If the Devil was recruiting handmaidens that summer, it was to the southwest in Hartford.

The truth was, it had been a lovely summer and a most pleasant September. The mill her husband owned would be grinding flour and cornmeal throughout the autumn and into the winter, and that might keep him in good spirits. When he was busy, he was happy, and he would drink only as much cider and beer as he needed to quench his thirst. Last night, she told herself as she finished dressing for church, would be the last time for a long time. Months. He really didn't become drunk all that often. Soon enough he would wake, perhaps catch her gazing at her reflection or adjusting her collar or cuffs as they ate, and tease her gently

for her vanity. He'd apologize and once more thing
would be well.

Or, at least, well enough. Tolerable.

Downstairs she heard Catherine uncorking th
jug with the molasses and preparing their brea
fast. One last time she checked her coif to be su
that it hid her bruise, and then she went dov
the stairs—a luxury here that she didn't take
granted, since so many of her neighbors still I
mere ladders connecting their first and sec
floors—and through the parlor, before joining
girl in the kitchen.

"Good Sabbath to thee, Catherine," she saic

The girl smiled and bowed her head slightl
don't hear Master Deerfield," she said. "Is he w

"We'll hear him any minute. He's still aslee

She saw that Catherine had already latche
bedstead upright against the wall and set the
for breakfast. The girl didn't have her own cha
the way that she and Thomas did on the s
floor, but slept instead here in the kitchen an
The house, Mary knew, was impressive by I
standards—her husband was a miller, so it w
fitting—but it paled against the home in wh
had grown up in England. Here they had si>
on two floors, not including the cellar but
ing the storage room back of the kitchen. (
to stoop when she went back there, and it I
gotten to the point where Catherine knew
ner of the house better than she did.) T

a nice hall and a parlor and kitchen on the first floor, and two spacious chambers on the second. There was a massive fireplace linking the kitchen and hall, a second, smaller fireplace in the parlor, and even a modest fireplace in the chamber she shared with Thomas. She knew of no more than a dozen other homes with three fireplaces and three chimneys, and one belonged to the governor, one to the reverend at the First Church, and the others to especially wealthy Boston merchants and traders, including her father.

She continued to hope that someday she would have children who would sleep in that second chamber—the way Thomas's daughter from his first marriage had had her own room in the first house the man had built here—but she had understood for some time now this wasn't likely. After all, they'd been married over five years.

"It was a late night for him," Catherine said, referring to Thomas, and she was careful to allow no hint of disapproval to color her tone. But she never did. The girl rather fancied Thomas. Mary could see it in the way her cheeks sometimes grew flushed around him or the way she would hang on his words as if he were a pastor. She hovered over him and sometimes seemed to follow him like a well-trained dog.

"It was," Mary agreed, glancing at the pot over the fire, and pausing to savor the plaintive trilling of the mourning doves that had nested in the oak just

outside the kitchen window. They were continuing to coo when she heard Thomas waking, but Mary stopped listening to the birds so she could focus on the noises above her. Sometimes she could tell her husband's mood by the first sounds he would make in the morning. If his day began with a great contented stretch and yawn, he would remain in good spirits, at least through their midday dinner. If, on the other hand, his lungs were packed and he began either by coughing or spitting, then he would be ornery and she would find herself hoping that he would remain at the gristmill until the end of the afternoon when he returned home for supper.

She heard the thump of his feet hitting the hardwood floor, followed by a sound that could be likened to a great male cat purring: the low rumble that Thomas Deerfield would make when he would stand, drowsy and well pleased with his world, on a good morning.

She wanted to look at Catherine for the reassurance that the girl had heard it that way, too, but Thomas was a gentle patriarch around Catherine. The girl may have known that her master had a temper, but it couldn't have seemed extreme to her, and any discipline he exerted upon his wife in front of her was well within reason. Besides, Mary refused to acknowledge that her home's tranquility was really so fragile, and so she focused instead on taking the Psalter down from the shelf and finding one of the psalms with which Thomas liked to open their day.

She settled on a prayer and bookmarked the page, and left the volume beside the trencher she would share with her husband.

⁂

Thomas was dressed when he came downstairs, save for his moccasins and his cloak. She was about to speak—ask him how he had slept, whether he was feeling well, anything to ensure that he knew she had no plans to show him anything but deference while Catherine was present—when he came to her, placed one hand on her waist and his index finger upon her lips, and said, "Prithee, say nothing. I was in a foul temper last night and I took it out on thee. I am very, very sorry and I will ask my Lord to forgive me. Wilt thou as well?"

Then he kissed her forehead, and even through his mustache and beard she was surprised by how dry his lips had become in the night. She started to speak, but he shook his head and said to the girl by the fire, "Ah, Catherine, good Sabbath. How wise thou were last night to be visiting thy brother. I was a monster to this fine woman. A ghoul."

"I doubt that is possible, Master Deerfield."

"Oh, trust me: it is. It is and I was. I worked hard and then I drank much, and before I knew it, I was filled with demons. So, tell me about thy brother. How is he?"

"A little better, perhaps. He ate some."

Mary felt him loosening his grip on her waist, and she looked up and saw him smiling at her. He winked. He was still so handsome when he smiled. Then he turned his full attention on Catherine. "When was the last time that Dr. Pickering tended to him?"

"Friday, I believe."

"Was he purged?"

"Yes, sir. Purged and cupped."

"Maybe tomorrow he can be bled again. William is a strong lad."

"May it be so."

He glanced at the Psalter and said, "Oh, Mary, this is a fine choice. Lovely! Let us gather."

Catherine placed the pot with the mush directly on the table and joined them while Thomas read the psalm and prayed aloud. When he was through, he took a long swallow of beer and started to eat.

❧ ❦

In Plymouth, to the south, there had been a time when the Separatists had been called to their church by a drum. The congregation would assemble before the captain's home and march to the meetinghouse three abreast behind the drummer.

They hadn't done it that way in close to twenty-five years—not since the 1630s—but Mary never understood why anyone would approach church as if it were a military skirmish.

Here it was considerably more civilized. They had a bell in the steeple of the First Church, and the congregation didn't gather as if preparing for battle. They arrived, each with their families, as if they were still back in England, with the only real difference being that she and Thomas would separate at the door so he could sit with the men and she could sit with the women and the young children. This morning she sat beside her mother in the third pew on the left, along with Catherine and her mother's servant girls, Abigail Gathers and Hannah Dow.

She realized soon after the Reverend John Norton had begun his first prayer that today was not going to be a Sunday rich with either grateful ebullitions or penitential whimpering from the congregation. It was a more intellectual sermon, and people were responding accordingly. She herself was going to have a difficult time concentrating, and so she sat with her spine straight to try and remain focused. Still, her mind wandered, and she found herself glancing at the boys and girls. She would look at the families—separated by an aisle, yes, but still she would link the men with their wives and their children, because certainly God looked at the congregation that way. She would turn and glimpse the children in the pews behind her as they fidgeted, their mothers disciplining them with a whispered word or a small pinch, and she gazed at the downy curls that escaped from one young girl's bonnet.

She reminded herself that at twenty-four she was not so very far from being a young girl herself, even though she was a grandmother and married to a man whose beard looked always to be dusted with hoarfrost. Thomas's daughter, Peregrine, and her husband already had two children, including a girl just old enough to sit atop a horse if the animal was led to walk slowly.

By the time they were through with their scripture and psalms and had moved on to the sermon, she was staring transfixed at the women who were married and healthy and still young enough to bear children. She would watch as well the women her own age who were cradling their toddlers or their infants in their arms, such as Ruth Sewall, the birth of whose baby, Richard—a name too big, she thought, for a child so small—she had attended that summer. For a long moment, she found herself fixated upon Peregrine and her two little ones, and she felt her own mother grasping her hand and squeezing it, motioning with a nod to pay attention to the pastor.

It grew clear as the morning dragged on that today was going to be one of those Sundays where it would be all she could do to focus on the prophecies and the lessons, but she would try her best. She checked her coif to be sure that it was masking her bruise, took a deep breath, and watched the reverend with his sharp beard and long face, listening as he spoke today of merit-mongers and civil men who might be outwardly just and temperate and chaste, but who were deluding themselves if they thought a few good words could atone for their sins.

❧ ❦

Peregrine and her husband, a young carpenter with a complexion that showed the scars of a ferocious childhood battle with smallpox, and their children came for dinner between the church services. Her husband was named Jonathan Cooke, and though he was Mary's son-in-law, he was six months older than she was. She liked him and, along with her daughter-in-law, laughed heartily at his jokes about wild turkeys and lobsters and the other ridiculous-looking animals that were staples in their food here. Jonathan was handsome, with hair the color of sweet corn (**like mine,** Mary had thought when they were introduced) and a body that was tall and trim. She had seen him building a house that summer, working without his sleeves, and saw that his arms were browned by the sun and the hair there bleached almost white.

Jonathan had lived in the colony about as long as Mary, nine years now, but he continued to allow himself an occasional off-color jest, as if he were still in England. Mary didn't know if Peregrine had understood these sporadic double entendres when he had started to court her years ago, but now that she was a married woman, it was likely she did. Thomas worried that Jonathan lived beyond his means but agreed he was ambitious: someday he wanted a business of his own and carpenters working for him. Given the way the city was expanding, spreading in all directions but into the sea, that seemed possible.

Thomas included Catherine's brother, William, in his prayer before they ate, and Mary watched the servant girl nod her head silently. Neither Catherine nor William had yet joined the church, and while Catherine seemed to enjoy the service, Mary had heard people presume that William had only attended when he'd been well because it was the law. She felt an unexpected and undeniable ripple of pride in both her husband's eloquence and his generosity. There were some men today who knew William yet wouldn't have remembered to include him in their prayers.

"I thank thee," Catherine said when he was finished, and she looked at Thomas with gratitude.

"It's nothing. Really."

"No, sir. It was a—"

"I'm not a physician. It's all I can do for thy brother, but I am happy to do it. May the Lord yet show him mercy."

"Amen," Jonathan said, and he started to dig

with his spoon at the salmon that had been set before Peregrine and him, and to break off pieces into smaller bits for his children. Then he turned to Mary and asked, "Where is that bruise from? It looks like it must hurt."

"Oh, yes," Peregrine said, and she reached over and with the very tips of her fingers pushed the edge of the cotton cloth farther back behind Mary's ear. Mary might have stopped her—brushed her daughter-in-law's hand aside and said it was nothing, nothing at all—but she was stunned by the realization that her coif had loosened, and already her mind was reeling with prayer: **Prithee, God, let the ties have slackened only when I was helping Catherine to get dinner on the table and not while I was in church. Prithee, God . . .**

"Was it a fall?" her daughter-in-law was asking, and she looked over at the stairs that led to the chambers on the second floor.

"No," Mary said, wishing she had thought about this sooner. She couldn't possibly say she had bumped into a cloak peg again. Not a second time. No one would believe that. "It—"

"It was the spider," Thomas said, referring to their massive wrought-iron frying pan with legs. "It was my fault entirely. With Catherine gone last night with her brother, I made a feeble attempt at helping Mary get our supper. I bumped her with one of the struts when I lifted it—when I was trying to be of assistance."

"It's a wonder thou hast no burns," Jonathan said, incredulous though relieved.

"It wasn't hot," Mary reassured him, not exactly lying, she decided, because last night the spider honestly was cool. "We were just having a bit of pease pottage," she went on, "so I wasn't even heating the spider."

"Ah."

"Does it still hurt?" Thomas asked. "Tell me it doesn't."

"Oh, I was completely unaware that I even had a bruise," she said, and she took Thomas's hand and squeezed it. Then she released her grip and re-tied the cloth strings of the coif.

❧ ❧

In the night, Thomas climbed upon her and they made love, but as usual the sensations felt nothing like when she touched herself. She tried to fall asleep afterward when he was through and had started to slumber, and briefly she prayed for the miracle that somehow her womb would seize her husband's seed and she would be carrying her first child before the first snow. But she remained agitated, and she knew it would be impossible to fall asleep unless she finished the job her husband had started.

Mary was not troubled by the reality that when her husband was passed out beside her in their bedstead—occasionally drunk, always exhausted, sometimes a little of both—her body was such that she could pull up the shift in which she would sleep and satisfy herself. Nor was she particularly alarmed that the sensations—the shuddering waves of pleasure, the way her lids would grow heavy and she, too, would nod off—never occurred when her husband would mount her, heaving, and they would couple. She didn't even feel shame that what she was doing was somehow deviant, since her private little (and she would not use the word **habit,** because it wasn't, it wasn't, it **wasn't** a habit) discovery was the most pleasurable thing that she did these days with her life.

And it certainly wasn't why her husband had accused her of being a whore the other night. It wasn't why he had hit her. He hadn't any idea of what she knew now she could do. No one did, not a single human soul. No, her principal thought was her inability to decide whether this was a small gift from God because He had not given her a child, or a vice offered by the Devil that was going to keep her from conceiving. Ever.

On occasion, she wondered if this were a sign she was damned. The idea would occur to her on Saturdays when she would be boiling water so she could clean their clothes. It would cross her mind when she was tending the salad herbs in the garden or pouring hot wax or tallow into the pewter molds for the candles. It would come to her, alarming and unbidden, when she was mending a cloak or breeches or a shirt. Signs, after all, were everywhere; it was just a question of knowing how to read them.

And yet some nights long after sunset, even this fear was not sufficient to compel her to keep her hands between her nightcap and her pillow when she felt the urge: she would convince herself that she wasn't destined for Hell because in all other ways she led a good life. An exemplary life. And though she understood that works alone could not buy one's salvation, the fact that she wanted so desperately to behave well was a favorable indication.

Her hands between her legs, she thought of a boy back in England. He had gone to Cambridge and become an architect, and her father might have allowed her to marry him had her family not made the long voyage to Boston. Had the Devil put this fantasy into her head? She decided not, because the boy's face had been downright angelic, and she couldn't believe that even the Devil would dare to use such a pure face in his temptations.

As she finished, the bedstead creaked: the ropes underneath the mattress pulled the wooden joints against one another. She hoped Catherine was asleep downstairs, but if not, she would presume it was merely the master rolling over.

I am a raft of secrets, she thought, and she imagined herself on timbers from a shipwreck, the water around her endless in all directions.

The other night she had fantasized about her own son-in-law, Jonathan Cooke. When she had seen that fellow in her mind's eye, when she had heard his voice and seen his eyes and his lips, she had tried to shun him, to send the image away, because the idea that it was he she was thinking about when she did this elicited from her pangs of self-loathing that were almost unbearable. But only almost. What did her God think of her when she thought of Jonathan? How disgusted would Peregrine, her daughter-in-law, be?

She recalled a moment when she'd held one of Jonathan and Peregrine's daughters on her lap, and when he lifted the child back into his arms, their cheeks had brushed and their lips had neared. It had been accidental. It had to have been. As had the time when she had been wearing a skirt newly arrived from London, and after he offered a compliment that was nothing more than polite as they were starting down the street after church, his fingers had grazed her lower back. She had turned, a reflex, their eyes had met, and for a brief second she had felt a rush as if he were trying to tell her something. But then his gaze was elsewhere, and he was saying something to Thomas about a house he was building.

A line from one of Anne Bradstreet's poems dangled just beyond her memory's reach as she brought her fingers to the edge of her nightgown and dried them. It was a love poem her older neighbor had written to her husband, Simon, a man who for a time had been their governor, and she knew the inclusion of the verse in the book had embarrassed Anne. But the poet hadn't even known that her brother was going to have a book published when he'd taken a stack of her poems with him to England. He left in 1650, and returned to the colony the following year with the bound volumes.

The rhyme, Mary thought, was about how much Anne missed Simon when he was away on business, as he was frequently. It saddened her to know that she would never miss Thomas if he ever had to travel. It grieved her that despite the fact he was right beside her in their bed, asleep atop the feathers that were such a luxury in this strange, needy world, he wasn't even among the men whose images would fill her mind when she would reach between her legs and sate the mesmeric frenzy that some nights filled her soul.

She is a shameless, impious, and lustful woman. By her sins, she will not only pull down judgment from the Lord upon herself, but also upon the place where she lives.

—The Testimony of Goody Howland, from the Records and Files of the Court of Assistants, Boston, Massachusetts, 1662, Volume III

Three

When Mary and Catherine were done harvesting the last pumpkins and squash from their family garden on Monday morning, the two women went to Peter and Beth Howland's house to see Catherine's brother, William. Outside, a group of small children, boys and girls, were playing marbles, and Mary saw little Sara Howland had the most glorious yellow silk ribbon wrapped around her straw hat.

The shutters on the house were drawn, and the inside of the Howlands' home was dark, even though it was almost midday. Immediately Mary could smell William, despite the fact that Peter's wife, Beth, was boiling spinach and currants and leeks over the fire.

The physician hadn't arrived, and while Catherine ventured into the small room in the back in which her brother lay alone with his fever, Mary stood with Beth in the hall and showed the woman what she had brought.

"I have comfrey for his ruptures and sores," she began, "and dill from our garden."

"Dill?"

"It sometimes relieves the nausea. And mint to encourage his appetite."

"It will take more than mint to make him eat. And more than dill to keep him from vomiting," Beth insisted. She was tall and stout, at least ten years Mary's senior. She had three children and lost exactly that many more. She had piercing black eyes, beneath which, today, were deep, shadowy bags.

"Be that as it may, we do what we can," said Mary.

"Mary, thy simples—"

"My simples have helped others through many a sickness."

"Thy teacher was a witch."

"Constance Winston? She was not my teacher and she was not a witch. She **is** not a witch. She is . . ." And Mary heard her voice trailing off. She had first ventured out to the Boston Neck, to a side street near Gallows Hill, two years earlier, because she had heard rumors that the old woman there, Constance Winston, had cures for barren women. She and Thomas had been married not quite three years, and never once had her time of the month failed to arrive. Constance had suggested stinging nettles steeped in tea and, when that didn't succeed, oil of mandrakes. Neither had worked, and the vomiting from the mandrake tincture had briefly given Mary the hope that she was indeed with child, which had exacerbated her disappointment when her blood finally came. Still, Mary had visited the woman six or seven more times and had learned much about other simples. She hadn't seen Constance in over a year now, and felt a pang of guilt that so much time had passed since her last visit. It wasn't that Mary was so busy; she wasn't. It was that the woman's eccentricities had begun to seem more like cantankerousness. At least that was what Mary usually told herself. She speculated when she was most honest with herself, when she was alone in her bedchamber with her ledger, that she had become unnerved by the comments she had heard about Constance and the woman's friendship with the hanged witch Ann Hibbens. The gossips had begun to circle, and Mary didn't want to risk an association because of the dangers it posed, both to her reputation in this life and to her soul in the next.

"She is what?" Beth pressed Mary. "Just an old fool?"

"No, she is not that either. But she is neither my teacher nor my friend."

Beth waved her hand dismissively and said, "Fine. I care not. Do what thou likest, if it doesn't make the boy worse."

"Has he been up at all or does he sleep mostly?" Mary asked.

"Sometimes he mumbles a word or two, but I

don't believe he's been much awake since before church yesterday morning. I believe that was the last time."

Mary took this in. The boy probably was beyond the ministrations of comfrey and dill.

"He still has over five years left on his contract," Beth continued, shaking her head. "And he's been sickly for so long."

"It would be a great loss," Mary agreed.

"He's become like a big brother to the children. Especially the boys. They are very, very sad, the whole lot of them."

"And thou, too, I am sure."

"I am. I needed his hands. Peter needed his hands. He was—"

"Not was, not yet, prithee."

The goodwife sighed. "As thou wishest: he is an able servant. A godly man—albeit a sickly one. The cancers are everywhere up his arms now, and his body feels completely aflame. His forehead is like a skillet. I could sear on it."

"Thou soundest so angry. Thou—"

"I am angry!" she snapped, and Mary was grateful that the other woman was keeping her voice low so Catherine couldn't hear her. "We will lose good money on William, and much needed help."

"I'm sorry."

"Catherine is of the same stock. Thy family will see."

"Beth!"

"I do not mean to wish ill on thee."

"Yet thou didst."

"I did no such thing. I simply spoke a truth."

"Sometimes speaking—"

"Gives voice to our thoughts. Nothing more. Words aren't potions."

No, Mary thought, but they are spells. But she didn't say that. She knew that Beth Howland understood that, too. "I saw Sara outside just now," she said instead, changing the subject to the woman's six-year-old daughter because she didn't want to argue. "That's a lovely ribbon on her hat. I saw her with other children, but not her brothers. Are the boys about?"

"They're around somewhere. They may be down at the harbor, watching the ships. I wouldn't be surprised if Edward has gone to watch his father. That lad will be a cooper, too, I warrant. Born with an auger in one hand and a plane in the other."

They saw Catherine emerge from the room where her brother was lying, her face composed. She looked to Beth and asked, "Would there be another cloth, prithee? One I could use to wash William's brow?"

"Yes, of course," Beth answered, a ripple of exasperation in her voice. "I will get thee one."

While she led the servant girl to the blanket chest, Mary went to the front door and peered outside at the goodwife's daughter. The girl was still so little. When she laughed, Mary could see the gaps where her baby teeth had fallen out and her adult teeth were coming in. She had a lovely, infectious smile, Mary thought. When she giggled, the other children giggled with her.

If someday God gave her a child, Mary prayed that it would be a girl who would laugh like that and whom she could dress in straw hats with yellow silk ribbons.

Behind her, she heard Beth and Catherine bringing a cloth and a bowl of cool water into the sickroom, and she turned away from the children and joined them. There she dressed William's sores with comfrey, placed dill on his swollen tongue, and read to him from the almanac. Once his body shivered, but were it not for the occasional rise of the sheet above his chest, someone might have presumed that she was reading aloud to a corpse.

❧ ❧

Catherine did not return home with Mary that morning. She offered, but Mary saw that it was paining the girl to leave her brother in such evident weakness and discomfort. Besides, Beth needed to tend to her own family, not her dying indentured servant, and so Mary suggested that Catherine remain. She reassured her that she would prepare both dinner and supper, and she and Thomas would be fine.

The sun was still high when Thomas arrived, and there was a film of white dust from the mill on his doublet. He was moving with the careful bearing to which he resorted when he wanted to hide the reality that he had had too much to drink. It was a gait that reminded her of the marionettes she used to see when she was a child back in London. Her stomach lurched, a turbid little wave that caused her to pause with the heavy pot in her hands. It was a small miracle that he was capable of riding all the way from the North End without falling when he was like this, since he had to traverse the Mill Creek as well as the drawbridge at Hanover Street. She reminded herself that the vast majority of the time when he came home for dinner this way nothing unpleasant occurred. He'd probably had an extra pint or two with one of the farmers when he was cutting a deal. Or maybe the morning had been slow and he'd drunk with his own men or with the fellows who ran the sawmill next door.

When he saw she was alone, he asked where Catherine was. Mary answered that the girl was at the Howlands' with her brother. He nodded and sat down at the table near the fire.

"What did she leave us to eat?" he asked.

"We went straight from the garden to the Howlands, so she didn't leave us anything. But I boiled us a nice salad with the herbs we picked this morning, and we have bread I bought from Obadiah."

"No meat? No fish?"

"There wasn't time. But if thou wouldst like—"

"A man needs meat, Mary. Hast thou forgotten that?"

"Thomas, prithee."

"I asked thee a question," he said. He spoke carefully, enunciating each word, but no longer trying to rein in his frustration. His eyes narrowed. "Hast thou somehow forgotten that a man needs substantial food to do the work of the Lord?"

"Of course, I haven't. I just thought—"

"Thought? That is thy problem. Thou art always thinking. Never doing. Thy mind is like . . . what? It's like . . . cheese. It's softer even than most women's."

"There's no call for that."

He shook his head, his eyes reproachful though half shut with alcohol and annoyance, and sighed. "Maybe that's why thou art incapable of taking seed. The Lord God knows it's best not to strain a woman that has the mind of cheese. White meat."

"What wouldst thou have me do? Not allow Catherine to visit her brother?"

He seemed to think about this, his face growing flushed. He picked up the knife on the table and held it before him as if it were an unfamiliar animal. "I wouldst have thou put that pot down is what I would have. Sit," he commanded, and she couldn't read his tone. It had a hint of menace, but was this just because of the way he was holding the knife? She put down the pot and sat across from him in the chair in which Catherine usually sat.

"No," he said. "Sit beside thy husband."

She obeyed, but she never took her eyes off the knife. He ran his thumb over the edge of the blade. "'Tis not as sharp as I'd like. 'Tis not as sharp as it should be," he continued. "My fortune seems to be surrounded by all things dull."

"Thomas—"

"Silence thy carping tongue. Spare me." He tossed the knife onto the wooden table. "Even a beast of burden deserves a rest. I will eat thy boiled salad and bread. But tomorrow I will expect a man's dinner."

She had barely been breathing as she had waited to see where this was going. When she saw that at the moment, at least, he had no plans to strike her, she stood and retrieved the wrought-iron pot and placed it on the table, careful not to make it appear that in either defensiveness or fear she had slammed it onto the trivet. Then she ladled the cooked vegetables into the wooden trencher. He was watching her intently. She uncorked the beer and poured his tankard only half full, hoping that despite the force of his gaze he wouldn't notice. Then she sat down with him and waited for him to bless the food.

Finally, he spoke, but it wasn't to pray. "Why not the pewter?" he asked. "Why art thou serving me dinner in a trencher like I'm one of the hogs?"

She realized that the heat of his anger was but shielded momentarily by a cloud. He wasn't quite spent yet. "I am doing no such thing," she tried to explain. "Some days we use the pewter and some days we don't. Thou knowest that. I was in a hurry when I returned and I grabbed the first bowl I saw."

"It is one thing to eat our breakfast off the wood. But not dinner. At least not my dinner. I am a miller. Or hast thou forgotten that, too? Was that white meat behind thine eyes so absorbed with the demands of boiling a bloody carrot that thou forgot thy husband's calling? I think that's possible, Mary. Dost thou agree?"

"I'm sorry. I'm very sorry, Thomas. What more can I possibly say?"

"There's nothing to say. If thou art going to spend thy whole day taking care of everyone but—"

This was enough. She had been with their servant girl's dying brother and Goody Howland. She stood up as straight and tall as she could, and then, looking down upon him, said, "Thou art drink-drunk, and all I'm hearing is the hard cider and beer talking. If thou dost want the pewter, I will get thee pewter."

But before she could retrieve two plates from the cupboard in the parlor, he grabbed hold of her apron, causing her to stop short. "Thou mayest if thou want," he said, rising ominously from his chair. "But thou shan't be doing me any favors."

She thought he was about to hit her, and put her hands before her face.

"No," he said, "if my wife insists on spending all her days taking care of everyone but her husband, then I am going to dine at the tavern, where I shan't be expected to eat a boiled salad for my dinner, and they don't dish out ale like it's gold. A half mug? That is stingy. Awfully stingy. And no way for a wife to treat her husband."

He released her apron and she lowered her fingers from her face. He was, much to her surprise, smiling—but it was a mean smile, cold and cruel.

"Thou art like a child," he said, "a babe that knows it has misbehaved." He shook his head and she honestly believed that she had been spared. He was leaving and the storm had passed. But then he lifted her by her arms—she sometimes forgot how strong he was—pinning them to her sides, and hurled her into the bricks along the side of the fireplace. She protected her face with her hands, but her fingers and elbows and one of her knees cracked hard onto the blocks. From the floor she looked up at him. He picked up the trencher with their meal and dumped it upon her, the herbs and the sauce still hot, but not scalding. He sighed and shook his head in disgust.

"Such is God's creation: the boiled supper that is Mary Deerfield," he said. "Well, He made the snake and the ass, too. Why not make a woman with white meat for a brain?" He happened to notice for the first time the flour dust on his shoulders and sleeves, and brushed it away. Then he left the house without saying another word.

※ ※

Did other men treat their wives the way Thomas treated her? She knew they did not. What she could not parse was whether he acted as he did only because of his proclivities at the ordinaries (and at their house), or whether there was a deeper cause. Did he despise her because she was barren? Did he really believe that she was dull and his violence was tutelage? Was it something that was in him or— what might be worse—something that was in her?

After all, it seemed that he had never struck his first wife. Or, if he had, Peregrine had never said so. And she certainly seemed to harbor no ill will toward her father.

Still, as Mary cleaned up the mess and then cleaned up herself, she contemplated with sorrow and weariness the corruption that was eating away at her marriage.

We expect a man's government of his wife to be easy and gentle, and, when it is not, something is amiss.

—The Testimony of the Reverend John Norton, from the Records and Files of the Court of Assistants, Boston, Massachusetts, 1662, Volume III

Four

Mary Deerfield's mother did not dress the way she had in England—she brought only one of her satin gowns to the New World—but she did wear myriad shades of purple and green and gold, and in the summer and early fall, she hid the ties on her shoes with great rosettes of ribbon. She was a beautiful woman, like Mary, and though there was more white in her hair this autumn than there had been even the previous fall, it was still a largely bay mane that was shiny and thick. She was not tall, but her carriage was such that she could be formidable, and Mary believed that her lone disappointment in this world was the fact that only one of her children, Mary herself, had come with her husband and her to Boston. Charles and Giles were grown and had businesses to attend to in England. They chose not to uproot their blossoming families: their young wives and their infants. In Giles's case, there was already an estate with a sizable number of sheep and cattle and hogs. Mary, however, had not had a choice. She was only sixteen, and though clearly there were young men who soon enough would have become suitors—and appropriate suitors, at that—her father felt the New World was both a religious calling and a way to build upon an already impressive trading empire. (Mary suspected the latter was of more consequence, but she would never have said such a thing aloud and grew frightened when she imagined what such thoughts suggested about the state of her soul.)

In hindsight, Mary knew, all of those suitors would have been more fitting than a man such as Thomas, and the marriages more advantageous to her and to her family. But she didn't have so many choices here. They as a family didn't have so many choices here. Yes, there were more men than women in Boston, but either they had not joined the church or they were adventurers or they lacked the means and social rank to marry the daughter of James Burden.

Her mother stood before her now in her and Thomas's parlor in the middle of the morning in the middle of the week, days after Thomas had thrown her into the hearth, with a small bolt of the most extraordinary lace Mary had seen here in New England under her arm, and eight silver forks, each the size and rough shape of a spoon, in her hands. She understood instantly that a ship her father had been expecting had docked and that her mother was going to give her some of the lace, but she couldn't imagine what she was supposed to do with the forks. She and Thomas already had a pair of large, two-pronged carving forks, of course, one of which was silver. But these smaller versions with three prongs? She'd heard of these utensils with three tines and she knew they were tools of the Devil. She was considering saying something to that effect to her mother, when her mother anticipated what she was thinking, put the ivory lace down on the table so her daughter and Catherine could admire it, and said, "Governor Winthrop had a fork himself, my child."

"What for?"

Her mother raised an eyebrow and smiled. "He may not always have used it, but he didn't hide it. His son has it now."

"But why wouldst thou want to try such a thing? Why wouldst thou want me to?"

"Father says they are growing more common back home now."

"I rather doubt that. Back home now they have better things to do than invite temptation with the Devil's tines."

"A small trunk with some was just unloaded in Father's storehouse. People will use them, Mary, even here."

Mary was about to scoop up the forks and hand them back to her mother when Catherine put aside the lace and picked up a single one and made motions in the air as if she were spooning stew.

"Like this?" she asked.

"I believe that's the way," said Mary's mother. "It can also spear the meat to hold it in place."

"So, thou wouldst not put the knife down, then? One would move it to thine other hand for cutting?"

"I think so."

Mary watched her mother and Catherine grin at the notion. She couldn't believe it, her father importing forks! This time she didn't hesitate: she lifted the forks from the table and took the one in her servant girl's hand. "Thomas won't abide forks in this house and neither will I," she said, handing the silverware to her mother.

But her mother smiled at her in a fashion that was almost devilish and put them on the cupboard shelf. "Thou wilt come around, little dove. I promise thee. These are not inducements from Satan; they are but gifts from thy parents."

ఆ ఠ

Mary had errands in the city that afternoon, and though she hadn't a reason to walk as far as the wharves at the town cove, she did. She saw the anchored ship that had arrived with her father's consignments and stood there, inhaling the salt air and savoring the cool breeze off the ocean. There was a skin of sloke on the surface, and algae was clinging to the beams of the pier. The planks on the dock wobbled beneath her shoes, and like a small girl she allowed herself to rock back and forth on them as if this were a game.

Finally, she walked to the edge of the pier and gazed at the water in the harbor. She knew, because her father had told her, that a mere twenty years ago if she had knelt on this wood and run a net through the sea, she would have caught fish; if she had stood at the shore and bent down, with a single swipe she would have pulled from the sand a mussel or a clam. It took more work now. Not a lot, and certainly the fishing was easier here than in England, but the city was growing fast. Already the lobsters were gone from the salty channels just inside the beaches; a person had to wade out a bit now to catch them.

There was a shallop in the water, the oarsmen rowing the small craft in through the waves from a large schooner moored a quarter mile distant. There was another ship unloading at the next dock, and she—along with some little boys who seemed to have arrived out of nowhere—watched the sailors at work. The men were tanned and young, and though it was autumn and there was wind in the air, the sun was still high and the crates and casks were heavy, and so she could see the sweat on their faces and bare arms. She knew she had come here to watch them: this was the reason she had walked this far. But she didn't believe this was a sin or the men had been placed here as a temptation. Visiting the wharf was rather, she decided, like watching a hummingbird or a hawk or savoring the roses that grew through the stone wall at the edge of her vegetable garden. These men—the fellow with the blond, wild eyebrows or the one with the shoulders as broad as a barrel and a back that she just knew under his shirt was sleek and muscled and hairless—were made by God, too, and in her mind they were mere objects of beauty on which she might gaze for a moment before resuming her chores. She could admit to herself that what she experienced here was akin to lust, but she also reassured herself that it was not precisely that cancerous or venal.

Still, she understood that if someone ever did inquire why she was here, she would reply that she had come in search of her father or she was on her way to her father's storehouse. It wasn't the truth, but she knew that people could be petty and some would try to read more into her occasional forays here than was either accurate or appropriate.

❧ ❧

She did visit her father before going home, just in case. She doubted that anyone of consequence had seen her stroll here, but there was no reason to take chances with the gossips.

The storehouse was more crowded than usual because a ship's hull had just been emptied into it, and it was a potpourri of exotic scents: seasonings, of course, but also the smell of the massive bolts of calico, the books (musty from the voyage), and the rugs that had started to mildew at sea.

The building wasn't as tall as her grandfather's hay barn had been back in England—nothing here was, not yet, not even the brand-new Town House with its court and offices for the magistrates—but it was almost as wide and perhaps half as long. There were casement windows fifteen feet up the east and west walls, but her father also kept the southern doors open during the day, and a corridor of sunlight streamed inside, illuminating the massive containers of guns and glass, and all manner of tools made of iron: handsaws and hinges, wedges and padlocks, drawing knives, gimlets, gouges, hammers, andirons, fire shovels, pint pots, scythe blades, chisels . . .

It was amazing to her the service that her father—and men like her father, because he wasn't the only saint who had the resources to buy and sell goods at this magnitude—provided the colony. In the room, in the containers and casks and barrels stacked to the height of two men (the blocks of a giant child, she thought) were the skillets and spiders and kettles that would stock the newcomers' kitchens (and always, always there were new people coming) and the tools on which the farmers would depend. The chains. The plow blades. The spades. The axes that the men, tirelessly and aggressively, would swing to fell the forests, work that was endless because the woods stretched on . . . forever.

And there were bedsteads. There were chairs more ornate than could be manufactured by the woodworkers in Massachusetts. There were pistols with ivory handles and pistols with brass trim around the flashpans, and there were muskets and buttons and swords.

She saw her father in conversation with a group of businessmen. One of them was probably the ship's captain. When her father saw her standing in a swath of sunlight, he left them and came to her. She knew he wouldn't want her to hear the conversation, more because of the sailors' inability to restrain their language than because he thought her too demure to hear his business negotiations.

"Ah, little dove," he said. "I wasn't expecting thee."

"I didn't know I was coming when I left home. I had errands, and—"

"And thou were enticed by the treasures thou heard had arrived."

She knew he wasn't serious, at least not completely. His smile was so broad and mischievous that it made his beard—a small triangle on his chin—seem less severe. He was wearing cuffs that matched his collar today, a particularly sumptuous and detailed set that she suspected he had chosen to impress these men.

"No," she answered, returning his grin. "It takes more than a little calico or tiffany to tempt me."

"I'll be just a few more minutes," he said. "Canst thou wait?"

"I can."

"Good. There are new bodices and wings that girls thine age are wearing back in London. I also have two trunks of books."

She nodded and went to stand in the doorway, where she faced the warm sun with her eyes shut and smiled. Books. On occasion, Thomas had suggested that she read too much and from tomes that were inappropriate. Oh, but books had always been one of her pleasures. She thought herself most fortunate that moment, but then two questions caused her to pause: First, what did it mean that, on the one hand, Thomas often berated her for being dim and slow, but on the other could chastise her for reading? Second—and this was an enigma of far more consequence—what did it say about her soul that a few bits of fashionable silk or cotton cloth and some interesting books could make her content?

⹁ ⹂

Before leaving, she placed a petticoat, a bodice, and two books—Michael Wigglesworth's new poem inspired by Revelation and a collection of the psalms deemed most helpful in diverting the

Devil—into her basket, and thanked her father once again.

She considered how she never went to see her husband like this, but reassured herself that it wasn't a likely thing for her to do because she usually saw him at dinner and because there were considerably fewer surprises to be found in her husband's world of grains and powders than in her father's ever-changing empire of goods. Besides, it was a longer walk to the North End. The harbor? It was closer. It was just the right distance if one wanted to stretch one's legs.

But then a realization came to her, triggered in part by the way Thomas had no curiosity in any book but the Bible and the Psalter (and she doubted he actually had much interest even in them), and though she could push the idea from her mind, it lodged there like a stump too wide and strong to be evicted: she wanted to see as little of the man as she could. It wasn't that he hit her or, recently, had thrown her into the hearth. It was deeper. She really didn't like Thomas Deerfield. She didn't like anything about him. Some days, in fact, she loathed him.

❧ ❧

The city was crowded as she walked home with her basket of gifts from her father, and when she stepped around a dead bird she was nearly flattened by a pair of oxen pulling a cart along High Street. She jumped aside and the driver, a godless-looking man whom she instantly imagined quailing in some shadowy hovel on the Sabbath, yelled that she needed to be awake more and continued on his way. She had slop from the street now on her waistcoat and skirt, and knew either she would have to clean them before making supper or give them to Catherine to blot. Supper would be delayed if she didn't hurry, and it had been too nice a day to risk fouling Thomas's mood by failing to have his food waiting for him when he returned from the mill.

"Mistress!" she heard someone yell. "Prithee, wait!"

She turned, not supposing that she was the mistress being hailed, and saw a fellow her age dodging horses and people as he crossed the street, intent on catching her. He was balancing a basket of apples on his shoulder with one arm and carrying a book with the other. He was wearing baggy, open-kneed breeches and a coarse, hempen shirt. He was handsome, his cheekbones a ledge and his thick hair coal. She presumed he was a servant.

"Dirty sheep stealer, he was!" the fellow hissed when he was at her side. "A bloody scalawag! Did he hurt thee?"

"Hurt? Why would I be hurt?"

"I feared either the oxen had stomped thy foot or the cart had run into thee."

"No, neither occurred. I was splattered, that's all."

"It's getting as bad as London."

"Oh, it's not that bad."

"I hope that's true," he said, putting down the basket. "I know London. I know well how filthy that place can be—especially the part where I was lodging for a time." Then he handed her the book he was holding. "Thou dropped this when that cart nearly hit thee."

"I thank thee." The book was the lengthy poem about Judgment Day. There was an awkward moment when it seemed she would continue home. But she didn't.

"I have read this Wigglesworth," he told her. "**The Day of the Doom.**"

"Will I appreciate it?"

He smiled so broadly that she wondered if he was going to laugh. "They've printed great numbers in London, most of which they are exporting to New England. Dost thou appreciate the terrors of those destined for Hell? Then, yes. It is more sermon than poetry. A lot of cutoff hands."

The remark made her think of her son-in-law because it was the sort of thing someone was more likely to say in England than here. "How long hast thou lived in Boston?"

"Six months."

She was not surprised.

"There was still snow in the shade when our ship docked," he continued. "I grew up in Yarmouth. Fisherfolk: ina, mina, tethera, methera, pin." He raised his eyebrows and grinned mischievously.

"For whom dost thou work?"

"For Valentine Hill."

She nodded: the merchant was a friend of her father's, roughly his age, and just as blessed with good fortune.

"My father is James Burden," she said.

"I know the name, most certainly. And I can see thou just saw him." He nodded at her basket of treasures.

"I did. These are—"

"Trinkets is all," he said, finishing her sentence. "I understand. Mr. Hill's daughters are likely to greet the arriving ships, too."

"I was not greeting the ship. I was visiting my father."

"Forgive me, I meant no disrespect," he said, and though his voice was contrite, his eyes were amused. Once again she thought he might laugh.

"None was taken," she answered.

"Dost thou need an escort home?" He bowed slightly, a movement that would have been imperceptible had she not been looking right at him. "My name, should thou ever need me, is Henry Simmons."

"Why would I ever need thee, Henry Simmons?"

"Another incident with an oxcart, perhaps?"

"There shan't be another of those. I shall take care."

"I pray 'tis so," he said. "Now, I know thy father is James Burden. May I inquire: What is thy name?"

"Thou mayest." She waited a moment, teasing him. Finally, she said, "Mary Deerfield. My husband is Thomas Deerfield. He owns the largest gristmill in the North End." She wasn't precisely sure why she was telling this Henry Simmons that she was married and who her husband was and what he did. But she had the sense it was because there was something considerably more forward in this conversation than she was accustomed to.

"I hope thy new"—he glanced into the basket, and when he saw beside the books the petticoat and the bodice and the transparent tiffany silk, he looked away—"articles give thee good use."

"I thank thee for seeing to me," she replied.

"Oh, it was the most fun I've had since . . . since the Sabbath."

She turned, blushing, unsure whether she should be flattered or view the remark as the profanity it was, and when she did she was surprised to see that not more than a dozen yards away stood the ever judgmental Goody Howland. Mary paused because she had never run into the woman this close to the wharves, but the moment passed and she started toward her, pleased that she might have company on the walk home. Beth, however, was irked. She was scowling, her nose wrinkled as if the smell of the sea was distasteful to her, and then Mary understood that her neighbor was frowning at her.

"Beth, is something troubling thee? Has something happened to William?" she asked, wondering if Catherine's brother had just gone to either God or the Devil.

"William will die, but he hasn't died yet."

"Then what?"

The woman shook her head. "Thomas Deerfield is a good man. He deserves better than that sort of behavior from his wife."

"What sort of behavior? What was I doing?"

"I saw thee with that boy," she said, and she waved her hand dismissively at the servant with the apples, already across the street and on his way down the road. "How well dost thou know him?"

"I only just learned his name!"

"Thy relations seemed overly familiar."

"He was worried I'd been hit by a cart."

Beth sighed and stared out at the ocean. "It appeared to be something quite different."

"A pool of water will bend a straight stick. Thou knowest that. What thou saw—"

"I'm sure what thou art saying is true," Beth continued, interrupting her, and it was clear that Beth did not believe a word she had said. "I'm just peeved because of William. But I can give thee my guarantee: people will babble if thou dost continue to behave in such ways. We know what we have seen of thee of late. Dallying with the likes of that lad? I urge thee to be careful. Thou dost not want to dishonor thy Lord, thy husband, or thy family."

"My family—"

"Thomas, then. Will Catherine be by later?" she asked, changing the subject both because she didn't want to discuss this any longer and because she wanted to know what kind of help she could expect with her dying servant.

"She will, yes. I'll see to it," Mary answered.

"I thank thee," Beth said.

"Art thou going home? If so, we can walk together."

"I'm not. I have things to do," she said. "Good day." Then she turned and continued on her way without offering another word.

Cruelty may be defined as violence without provocation and discipline that is excessive.

—**The Remarks of Magistrate Richard Wilder, from the Records and Files of the Court of Assistants, Boston, Massachusetts, 1662, Volume III**

Five

Mary's daughter-in-law, Peregrine, was friendly with Rebeckah Cooper, but she wasn't quite as close to the young goodwife as Mary was. Mary considered Rebeckah her best friend. Still, the other two women had something in common Mary was unlikely to share with either: children. They each had two. And so Mary was not surprised when she visited Rebeckah and found Peregrine already there. The small yard in the front of the Cooper house was a chaotic and rather happy frenzy: four small children who, that moment, could not be corralled by their mothers. One of the women had made a circle from a vine and dangled it from a low tree branch, and the young ones were trying (and largely failing) to toss through it rags filled with dirt and tied into balls. Mostly they were running around the vine and tossing the rags at one another, shrieking with laughter.

"Mary," Rebeckah said when she saw her, "this is a treat!"

"I hope thou meant this pumpkin," she replied, and she handed her friend the gourd, which she had needed both arms to carry. She guessed it weighed easily twenty pounds. "I also have a recipe that one of my mother's servant girls invented. It was delicious."

"One of the girls? Abigail?" asked Peregrine.

Mary nodded. Then Peregrine looked at her, her eyes intense and narrow, and embraced her. "Thy bruise hast healed nicely," she said softly when their faces were close.

"What was that?" asked Rebeckah. "Didst thou have a bruise?"

Peregrine released her and took a step back, and Mary felt the other woman surveying her—all of her—in a fashion she could not decipher.

"Thomas was trying to help a few Saturdays distant and accidentally hit me with the spider," Mary told Rebeckah. "It was nothing."

"Where?"

"Thou canst not see it anymore. I'm fine."

Rebeckah pointed at her older child, her five-year-old son, who was holding one of the balls just beyond the reach of the three girls, as each of them kept jumping to try and snag it. "That lad? Conked me in the mouth with one of his father's tankards when he was carrying it to the bucket and I was bending down to get a spoon. I thought he had knocked out a tooth. Men and boys are a hazard in the kitchen," she said, and she laughed.

"They are," Mary agreed. She looked toward Peregrine, assuming that she would be laughing, too, but she wasn't. Maybe she hadn't heard Rebeckah or maybe she was focused solely on her older daughter, who couldn't reach that homemade ball and seemed to be on the verge of tears. But, still, Mary was surprised that the other woman wasn't even chuckling.

≈ ≈

The next day, Catherine was on the stone steps just outside their house with a bucket of ashes in her hands, and so she heard the noise before Mary. Mary was inside, using the afternoon to get Thomas's clean clothes mended.

"They're lashing a Quaker," she said to Mary, "come quick!"

As so she did. She stood at the edge of their yard and looked down the street with her servant. They watched as an older man—a fellow Thomas's age, Mary guessed—walked behind a cart pulled by an ox, his hands bound, a rope around his neck that linked him like a leash to the rear of the wagon. Behind him, one of the tithingmen whipped his bare back periodically.

"Look," Catherine continued, "they've let this one keep on his breeches and his shoes."

"No," she said. "Those women chose to be naked. At least one of them did. She insisted upon it."

"Now why would she have done something like that?"

Mary was about to explain that the woman had been protesting what she felt was the injustice of her prosecution—persecution, the Quaker had in fact said, initiating a war of semantics that only made the penalty more severe—and the hanging of that missionary woman named Dyer. Mary didn't, however, because she saw that among the small parade of gawkers behind the poor man was a group of half a dozen children, including two of Peter and Beth Howland's brood. She saw Sara, their little girl, and Edward, the younger of their two boys, and they were throwing gravel from the street a pebble or two at a time at the Quaker.

Mary put down the clothing in her arms and ran to the procession. She pushed past a woman she didn't know and grabbed the pair of young Howlands around their wrists, catching them both by surprise, and pulled them to the side of the road, where she stood with them before the house of Squire Willard.

"There is no call for that," she said to the children. "There is no call for that at all. I doubt the magistrates wanted thee to be stoning the poor man while he was being whipped."

Edward, a boy nearing ten, wrestled his arm from her and met her gaze. "But he's a Quaker," he said, "and he's probably a witch, too!"

"If he's a witch, then I wouldn't be vexing him further," she said.

Little Sara turned her face squarely upon her

brother and started to chant softly, "Edward will be hexed. Edward will be hexed. Edward will be—"

The boy punched the girl on her arm and she yelped, and so Mary, in turn, slapped the boy on his rump. "Thou art too old to hit her," she scolded him.

"Sara said—"

"I don't care what Sara said. Thou art old enough to know better than to be hitting thy sister, and thou art old enough to know better than to be throwing rocks at that man."

"They were pebbles," he insisted, as if that made it all right. Then he shook his head, desperately trying to hold back the tears, but it was a lost cause. Abruptly he was crying and his sister was sobbing with him, and the onlookers who'd come outside or glanced up from their dying, dwindling gardens now turned their attention from the Quaker—who was considerably farther down the block now, anyway, the blood and ripped flesh on his back making it look like a harlequin's doublet—to the weeping children.

"I think it's time to go home," Mary said to them. "I'll walk with thee."

Before she could turn them in the direction of their house and start with them on their way, she saw the door behind her open and Squire Willard emerge on the short path to the street. Isaac Willard was elderly but fit, a widower, and was known for walking with his cane back and forth from the carding mill he owned in the North End and along the Neck to Roxbury and the mainland.

"I'm going that way, Mary," he said, and he sounded cross. "I can return them home."

"I thank thee," she said, wondering at the suggestion of anger in his voice. She didn't believe he was the sort who would be annoyed by the sight of a Quaker being disciplined. Quite the opposite. Most likely, the punishment had his hearty approval.

"It's nothing," he said. "Come along, children."

And then, though they had gone no more than three or four steps, he stopped and turned back toward her.

"Mary, thou should not encourage babes such as these to disrespect the wisdom of the magistrates."

"I did nothing of the sort."

"I was at my window. I heard what thou said, and I saw that wallop thou bestowed upon young Edward. Now—"

"It was hardly a wallop."

"I agree it is better to be whipped than damned, but it is better still to be reasoned with."

She wanted to argue with him and defend her action, but she knew it would get back to Thomas if she did. And so she lowered her gaze and apologized. When she looked up, the boy was smirking at her, and he resembled more than a little the grotesque-looking face that had been carved onto the Rhenish pipkin from which she sometimes served stew.

❧ ☙

There were still pansies with flowers at the edge of the street and beside the steps to their house, and Mary stooped to deadhead them. She was agitated by the way Isaac Willard had disciplined her a moment ago, and she couldn't bring herself to return to her mending.

"Shall I start supper?" Catherine asked. The servant was still in the doorway.

"Yes, that would be fine. I'll be but a moment."

The girl went to the back of the house to retrieve some eggs, and Mary had just resumed her work on the flowers when she saw something metallic sparkle in the jumbled knot of green tendrils. She reached for it and came up with a fork, one of the small ones that, according to her mother, people were starting to use back in England. And though this looked to be one of the very forks that her mother had shown her last week, clearly it hadn't been dropped here by mistake: it had been driven tines first into the ground, so that less than an inch remained above the dirt. On a hunch she reached amidst the pansies on the opposite side of the stone step and rooted around with her fingers. Sure enough, there was a second fork there, too, pressed vertically into the ground like a post, on a line with the first. Once again, barely a thumbnail was aboveground.

She pulled it from the earth and looked at the two forks together. There were myriad ways to try and keep the Devil at bay, just as there were innumerable ways to invite Him into one's life. She feared this was an invitation, given the fact that everyone knew a three-tined fork was the Devil's instrument. Certainly, He wouldn't be deterred by a pair of them in the ground.

She brushed off the dirt and put them in the pocket of her apron, and wandered to the rear of the house where Catherine was already on her way inside with a wicker basket of eggs. She stepped around the chickens and caught up with her servant in the back doorway.

"I found something in the flowers in the dooryard," she said.

"Yes?"

"Something I believe was placed there with wicked design," she continued, watching the girl for a reaction. When she got none—at least nothing that Mary construed as a precursor to a confession—she pulled the forks from her apron, as if she were one of the street conjurers she'd seen from carriages when she'd been living in London. "These," she said, "were planted tines down in the dirt near the front door."

"Tines down, thou sayest?"

"Indeed."

Catherine's eyes grew a little wide now, a little alarmed. She studied the forks. "Whatever for?"

Mary shrugged. "Thou knowest nothing of this?"

"Of course not!"

"Thou didst not sow these like seeds or see someone else do such a thing?"

"I would have told thee if I had."

Mary nodded, unsure if her servant's indignation was genuine, but giving her the benefit of the doubt. Still, the air felt charged. "I do not want thee to have secrets from me," she told Catherine, "just as I will not be obscure in our companionship. There are already too many secrets in this world."

"I thank my mistress for that courtesy."

"But I cannot understand who would court such impiety. I cannot imagine who would invite the Devil in. I do not believe it was my mother—"

"No!"

"Or my father or Thomas. And so I am troubled."

"Yes, ma'am. I am, too."

Mary ran her thumb over the silver handles. "I heard a story the day after my father imported the forks of a man impaling the hand of his trencher mate with one of these. It happened back in England. In Farrenden."

"The worst things occur there. The Devil's playground."

"Perhaps I will tell Thomas. He may not know

who did this, but he might know why someone would."

"He is very wise," Catherine said, and they both went silent. Finally, Catherine raised her face to Mary and said, "We have so many eggs, should I make an Indian pudding?"

꒰ ꒱

In their bed in the dark, the candles extinguished, Thomas entered her, and she wished that he still believed this might result in a child and wasn't merely the remedy for the inner lip of his lust. But she knew that he, like everyone else, was convinced that she was barren. He moved atop her and grunted, and her mind wandered away from him. This time, however, it roamed not to other boys and men she had seen in her life, including her own son-in-law, Jonathan Cooke. Instead she saw a vision of Thomas's seed inside her—the infant the size of a raindrop—dying because there was no sustenance there. Nothing to which it might cling and take root. She imagined the deserts in Hebrews, Exodus, and Deuteronomy, and she saw her womb now the way she had heard different preachers describe those unfathomably arid, waterless worlds. **Barren.** A word, it seemed, for worlds and for women. Did Thomas's driblet-sized child shrivel inside her once its watery pond was gone, did the thing become as dry as old grain? A particle of inland sand? Or did something else happen to the minuscule baby? She had held Thomas's seed in her fingers when it had trickled down the insides of her thighs, wondering what this yield needed that she could not give it.

When Thomas was finished, he brushed a lock of her hair away from her eyes and felt the moistness on the side of her face.

"We have applied ourselves indeed," he said, and he laughed, mistaking her tears for sweat.

She nodded though he couldn't see her and then he rolled off her and lay on his side on the bedstead. Soon he would be asleep, the remnants of his exertions would stream from between her legs, and once more she would reach there with her fingers and take pleasure from the small gift the Lord had given her in lieu of the ability to conceive and bear a child.

Assuming, of course, this was a gift and not the root cause. She recalled once more the forks in the dooryard and Thomas's casual disregard of her concerns when she had broached them at supper. No doubt, he had said when she told him of her discovery, a child had done it. When she pressed him, asking where a child would have acquired three-tined forks, he suggested that perhaps her mother had dropped them and someone—anyone—had driven them accidentally into the ground with his boots. No deviltry to it, he had said, and not likely witchcraft. Still, she could see in his face a whisper of trepidation, as he, too, was chronicling in his mind who might wish ill fortune upon them.

When Thomas's breathing had slowed and the sound was nothing more than a small, scratchy whistle as he exhaled, she spread her legs once again and draped her hand lazily between them. She rubbed herself slowly with her fingers, but her mind kept returning to the two forks. For years now, she had prayed for a child and her prayers had been unanswered. In her prayers, she had made promises to the Lord that, sinner that she was, she knew she couldn't keep: She would be as obedient as God's truest saints, she would fast and pray, fast and pray, she would ignore the flesh and its pleasures. She would never again do . . . this.

She did not pray for a child because she feared that, without one, in her dotage she'd become a crone in a cottage: a woman such as Constance Winston. She did not pray for a child for Thomas: he was old and she wasn't even sure that he desired another baby. No, she prayed for a newborn because she wanted now to love a child the way that Thomas's first wife, Anne Drury, had loved Peregrine, and the way that child, now a woman, in turn loved her offspring.

All of her prayers, all her entreaties . . .

All they had brought forth from her was blood on the twenty-third or the twenty-fourth day instead of the twenty-eighth or the twenty-ninth. Blood sometimes twice between full moons—those nights in the month when they needed fewer candles because the sky was so light, and one could travel the evening streets before curfew without a lantern.

And now there were those forks. A small thing, yes, but the world was rich with small things that in truth were signs of great importance.

Without finishing, she pulled her shift back down over the tops of her legs and considered asking the Lord for something smaller than a child: to disclose, perhaps, who had left those forks in the dooryard, and why. But she didn't pray to God. She didn't pray to anyone or anything, at least not with a literal appeal. Instead she simply opened her eyes and her mind wide, allowing her desire to know who had planted the forks to waft from inside her into the night air, where soon enough it might settle like a dandelion seed upon the source. One never knew. And if, she decided, that origin was evil, so be it. Thy will be done. At least she would know.

But what if someone had planted the forks in the ground because that individual—whether witch or saint—knew something of the magic of conception and was answering her deepest cravings? What if the forks were part of a spell to give her the child she desired?

Yes, that was dabbling in something dangerous, too, but was it evil?

She made a decision: to further encourage the culprit—whether it was man or beast or Devil or witch—to reveal himself, she would return the forks to the dooryard. To their exact spot. She would do that as soon as Thomas had left for the mill in the morning.

Her last thought before sleep was that once the forks were back in the ground, she would look carefully at everyone around her, and she would remain at all times as alert as the sentries who stood watch atop Beacon Hill.

. . . which is why I know a fork can be a weapon most terrible.

—The Testimony of Mary Deerfield, from the Records and Files of the Court of Assistants, Boston, Massachusetts, 1662, Volume III

Six

It was young Edward Howland, the ten-year-old boy, who knocked on their door in the rain while she and Catherine were preparing breakfast and Thomas was upstairs getting dressed. The boy was nervous, and briefly Mary attributed his apprehension to the small spanking she had administered the other day. The child was breathless, rocking from one leg to the other, and his eyes were fixed on the ground. And while that might have been a factor in the boy's evident unease—he didn't have Squire Willard to serve as his protector now—she realized soon enough why Beth had sent him. William, Catherine's brother, either had died in the night or was going to pass before dinner, and Catherine should attend to him right away.

"Prithee, Catherine should come now," said the boy, after he had shared his mother's belief that no one was sure William would even be alive after breakfast.

Mary sent the boy home and informed Catherine that it was time and she would accompany her. Then she pulled on her cloak and told Thomas that she and Catherine were going to Peter Howland's and his breakfast was simmering in the spider. It was only out of habit and hope, but she also brought with her a basket of simples. One never knew what miracles the Lord might yet feel disposed to offer.

⁂

In addition to the herbs that Mary herself had administered and the prayers of the church, she knew what had been done to try and save William's life over the past month. He had been given a drink made of lemons—so very precious in Boston in autumn—and wormwood ground into salt in the hope that his vomiting could be stopped, and he had the ashes of an owl (feathers and all) blown down his throat to salve the burning there. He had the juice of a crayfish rubbed on his tongue. The physician, Dr. Roger Pickering, administered a drink made of eggs and fennel and rum, and gave him nutmeg and cardamom to try and ease the pain. Then he bled and cupped William. And when William began to bleed from inside his nose, the physician tied up spiders and toads in a rag and insisted the ailing patient inhale the fumes. After the toads had been boiled and dried and ground into dust, the healer took the fine powder and with a length of straw thrust it up William's nostrils. The bleeding stopped, and so he was purged and cupped once again.

And still the man grew weaker. The sores spread across his body from his neck and his arms, and his mind became addled.

Mary had continued to visit, one day bringing hops and another bearing sorrel, twice offering valerian for the pain (on both occasions the old rhyme came to her, **Valerian and dill will hinder a witch from her will**), but her remedies offered no more comfort than the doctor's. Prayer made Catherine feel better, and it probably would have made the rest of William's family feel better, too, but Catherine was the only family present here in Boston.

⊰ ⊱

Mary saw that the sores on William's arms and neck had started to ooze once again, and there were stains the color of rotten apples on the coverlet. For a second, she presumed that the boy had died in the time it had taken Edward to fetch them. He was lying on the bedstead with only his arms and his head atop the quilt, and the comforter atop his chest was as flat as the face of a pond. She touched his feet under the blanket and they were cold. Only when she felt heat radiating from his forehead like a warmed brick did she realize that he was alive. Still, she had to place her ear against his lips to hear the small, almost imperceptible whispers of his exhalations.

"We've sent for the minister," Beth said from the doorway, her arms crossed. "But I tend to doubt Reverend Norton himself will come. I expect an elder."

Mary stood back so Catherine could sit beside her brother and then went to the kitchen for a cloth. She dunked it in the cool water in the drum and was returning to William's bedstead when Beth stopped her.

"What dost thou really think that will accomplish?" she asked.

"It will make him more comfortable," she replied.

"He is beyond comfort. Let him go. Thou art only prolonging his pain."

"I will be content to let him go if that is the Lord's will. But there is no reason for him to suffer in the meantime."

"Suffer? Dost thou believe he feels anything anymore? Not ten minutes ago he wasn't even breathing. He—"

Mary looked beyond Beth into the shadows and the gloom, and then pushed past her.

"Mary—"

"I will see to him," she said. Then, concerned that she had sounded peevish, added, "Thou hast done more than anyone could have asked."

Catherine was holding one of her brother's hands, massaging the joints on his fingers, and telling him that she would write their father to inform him of all he had accomplished here in Boston: how much of his servitude he had worked off, how many friends he had made. She would share how the children in the Howland house had revered his son, and how much William would be missed.

Mary leaned over the bedstead and draped the cloth on his forehead, and then knelt on the floor beside the siblings. She hadn't been there long when the breathing, already shallow, stopped, and with neither a final spasm nor flinch William Stileman died.

༄ ༅

At supper that night, Thomas offered tales of the men who had brought their grains to the gristmill from Roxbury and Salem, and how high the water was in Mill Creek for this time of year. He was in fine spirits, and Mary had to remind him that William had passed. He scowled, but then looked to Catherine to express his condolences. A moment later, still pleasantly drink-drunk, he resumed his storytelling, and Catherine listened in a fashion that suggested either a patience beyond her years or a fondness that was inappropriate—and, given how little Mary thought of the man, undeserved.

And yet Catherine did like him. Her master. Mary could tell. But whether she saw in him a substitute for the father she had left behind in England or something more, Mary couldn't decide. He was old enough to be her father, a makeshift parent, but the girl didn't look at him quite that way. Oh, she was cognizant that he was married. And yet there was something in the girl's gaze that held within it an unmistakably amorous tinge. That did not mean the girl had adulterous designs. So, perhaps, it was not an affection that was improper. It was merely one that was unmerited and misguided, and that the girl could not fully restrain. A reflex.

Maybe it was reminiscent of the embers that seemed to exist between her and Jonathan Cooke but would never, ever be billowed into flame. Something harmless.

Mary glanced down at her trencher and imagined eating with one of those forks. She shook her head ever so slightly to clear her mind and returned her attention to her husband and Catherine. She knew that Peter and Beth Howland would not want to pay a stone carver to chisel a death's head for William, and so she had told the girl that her father would incur the costs of the burial. She had gone to see him immediately after the boy had died, and her father had agreed.

After dark, once they had gone upstairs and extinguished the candles, Mary lay on her bedstead beside Thomas a long while, and then said, "All we really knew of William was what Catherine told us. I wish we had known more. I wish we had spent more time with him before he grew ill."

Thomas said nothing, and she realized that he

had already fallen asleep. And although she had lain there for at least fifteen minutes, she was too restless to nod off, and so she climbed off the mattress, took one of the long tallow sticks from the table by the nightstand, and went downstairs. She stepped carefully around Catherine, who seemed to be sleeping as well, lit the candle with one of the last starry cinders in the fireplace, and went outside.

The moon was almost full, and the air felt as cool and damp as the ocean. Tonight for sure there would be the frost that would finish the gardens, and so tomorrow she and Catherine would be chopping the great browned pumpkin leaves into mulch. Down the street she heard horses and men laughing, and she guessed they were revelers on their way to or from the ordinaries. She presumed that Thomas would have gone out tonight, too, had he not had so much to drink on the way home. Was it also possible that he felt Catherine's pain and the way the household had been sobered by William's death? No, it wasn't. That wasn't Thomas.

Her feet were bare, but she wouldn't be outside long. She went to the spot where she had replanted the silver forks, and ran the tips of two fingers over the dirt there. She felt the very tops of the handles, and beside them something more. Something round and smooth. At first, she thought it was a stone, but when she pawed away the dirt beside it, she could tell it was wood. She pulled it from the ground and saw that it was a pestle, planted upright into the earth like the forks. It was not her pestle, however, she knew that right away, because this one had been made from a darker wood (and she was quite sure it was not merely the dirt that had given the pestle its bay cast), and she felt something carved into the handle. When she brought the candle flame to it, she saw that someone had sliced into the wood a trident: a three-pronged spear. She removed one of the two forks as if it were a carrot and compared it to the design on the pestle. It was a match.

Behind her she heard the door open, and there stood Catherine in her sleep shift.

"It was thee," Catherine said, her voice tremulous. "Thou accused me of placing the forks into the ground, but it was thee! Thou art the witch!"

"No! I—"

The servant girl took a step back. "What were thou planting by the light of the moon? What is thy spell?"

"It's a pestle," Mary answered, and she started toward Catherine, but Catherine retreated.

"Stay away!" she said. "Prithee! I mean thee no harm. I will keep thy secrets."

A bat swooped near them and chirped, and the two of them ducked. Tallow dripped onto the stones.

"I did not plant the forks, I was planting nothing tonight," Mary insisted.

"But thou were, I saw thee!" She started back

into the house, banging the door loudly against its frame. Mary followed her, the fork and the pestle in one hand and the candle in the other, and found the girl cowering beside the hearth.

"I beg thee, leave me be," she whimpered.

"Catherine, stand up," Mary told her. "Thou art behaving like a child."

As Catherine stood, her eyes grew wide. Mary could see that a revelation had come to her: "Thou killed my brother. Thou weren't assisting the physician with thy simples; thou were killing him."

"No!"

"Yes," she hissed. "Yes. That is the truth! Thou art a student of Constance Winston—"

"I haven't seen Constance Winston in months! Maybe a year!"

"But thou learned from her. Thou were her student. And now thou art a disciple of the Dark One!"

"I am no such thing! Thou knowest well that I—"

But the girl was no longer listening. She pushed past Mary and raced outside into the night.

"Catherine!" she called, but the servant was already in the yard. Mary couldn't imagine where the hysterical girl would go, but she was confident that she would return soon enough. What other choice had she?

Mary turned when she heard her husband lumbering down the stairs.

"What have we here?" he asked, his tone that of

an irritated patriarch or a father frustrated by his recalcitrant children. "Where is Catherine?"

Mary considered the girl's preposterous accusation. Then, her voice calm, she replied, "Catherine seems to believe that I'm a witch."

He nodded, seemingly relieved by the utter absurdity of the claim. "And why is that? I have seen no sign of possession."

"Because someone planted two forks and a pestle in our yard."

"The forks mated and birthed a pestle?" he wondered sarcastically.

"Someone is dabbling in something wicked."

He rubbed the back of his neck. He was annoyed he had been woken. He was irritated by the absence of his servant girl. "She needn't fret. Mary Deerfield is too simple to be a witch. My wife has too barren a womb to be a witch." Even though he was unhappy at having been disturbed in the night, this was not the response that Mary had expected. Instantly she grew wary.

"Thomas," she began carefully, "I know thou dost not actually believe I am simple. Why dost thou insist on such . . . such cruelty?"

He stood a little taller and gazed down at her. "Cruelty? I do not believe there is a man or woman in this city who views me as cruel. Most people? They think I'm docile as a fawn."

"They think no such—"

"Hold thy tongue and do not question what

people think of me. I have known the people of Boston as long as thou hast been alive."

"I'm sorry. I meant—"

"I know what thou meant." He sighed. "Mary, thou hast a soul that is much imperiled by pride. Thou believest too much in thine intellect as a woman. Thou . . ."

She almost asked him to go on, but she feared that he would view it as impertinence. And so she waited as the pause grew long. Finally, he continued, "Thou dost not appreciate or abide by the places the Lord God has allotted to us. To a man and his wife."

"I do," she said, hoping her tone conveyed a contriteness that she did not in fact feel.

"No. Not true," he said. He approached her and looked at the fork and the pestle in her hand. He took them from her and put them on the table. Then he took her candle from her and placed it in the candlestick.

"Didst thou plant these in the yard?" he asked, pointing at the items on the pumpkin pine.

"I did not."

He rubbed his eyes. "Well, then, let us see if thou art a witch. Shall we?"

Mary couldn't imagine what he was thinking. All that was clear was this: he was angry and tired and he was feeling particularly nasty. With his left hand he grabbed her left wrist and placed her hand flat on the table, palm down. He spread wide her fingers and lifted the fork. And instantly she understood his intentions and struggled to pull free, terrified, but it was too late.

"No, Thomas, no!" she begged, but he ignored her.

He slammed the fork, tines down, into the bones in the back of her hand. She shrieked in pain, her eyes shut and the backs of her lids awash in dancing light, and then she was sobbing and dizzy as the agony rippled up her arm and throughout her body. She felt the pain everywhere. Everywhere. When she opened her eyes, she opened her mouth, and she understood on some level that her face must have been a skeletal rictus, all aperture and torment.

He released her and clinically surveyed what he had done. The handle of the fork had bent before the tines had augered holes through or between the small bones there; she hadn't been pinned to the table. But when she lifted her hand, the blood ran down her arm like spilled wine, and she feared from the excruciating pain that the bones there were broken. She collapsed into the chair, utterly stunned both by her husband and by a throbbing pain more incapacitating than anything she had ever experienced.

"Well, thou dost seem to bleed, Mary. Thou dost seem to bleed plenty," Thomas said. "Thou bleedest monthly. So, I think we can conclude that my servant girl is mistaken and my wife with white meat for a brain is no witch. She may disregard her place in our Lord God's plan. She may have whorish thoughts. Oh, I see thee, Mary. I know thee. I see, too, that the fire needs raking. Once thou hast tended to that, clean thyself up. I hope this lesson is a seed that takes root. Because it is discipline applied as a lesson. It is pain applied with reason. Now, I am going back to bed."

Then he shook his head, proud of himself, and shambled up their stairs.

Gently she pressed the sleeve of her shift against the back of her hand, and then she pressed harder. It was a balancing act: she needed to stop the bleeding, but pressure exacerbated the pain. Little by little her mind cleared, and she resolved that when she could, she would indeed try and sleep. She would go upstairs and climb back into bed beside the beast. But in the morning, as soon as she and Catherine had made him his breakfast— assuming the girl returned—and he had left for the mill, she was going to pack a satchel and go live with her mother and father. Her father would know whether she should see a constable first or meet directly with a magistrate. But she had heard a word and she had heard stories. The word was **divorce.** Her husband was no saint, and as Mary watched the sleeve of her shift grow the color of cherries and felt the wetness against her skin, as she shivered against the pain, she resolved that she was going to divorce Thomas Deerfield.

I saw my mistress placing the Devil's tines into the earth, burying them, but for what purpose I cannot say.

—The Testimony of Catherine Stileman, from the Records and Files of the Court of Assistants, Boston, Massachusetts, 1662, Volume III

Seven

They had, she understood, crossed a river, and there was no going back. This attack was too brutal, too violent. Moreover, Thomas had been sober when he had smashed the fork tines first into her hand. It suggested a calculation that unnerved Mary. And his contention that it was educational? That he was saving her soul? This was frightening because it meant there was no longer safety even when he was not drink-drunk.

In the morning, he insisted on unwrapping the cloth and looking at the wound. It was starting to scab over and the three points from the fork were lost in the gelatinous, fragile poultice her body was forming atop the wound. A purple bruise spread out from the spot like a fan, a shape that was eerily reminiscent of the asters in the garden that only recently had been killed by the frost. It reached all the way from her knuckles to her wrist. She was aware of the way her heart was thumping in the wound. In the bones there that were broken.

"Thou wilt heal," he said to her. He didn't

apologize. Perhaps he, too, understood that the ground beneath them had been shaken. She said nothing in response. The throbbing pain had conspired with her anger to keep her awake most of the night, and the combination of her exhaustion and her discomfort left her weak.

He noticed that no one had started a fire and breakfast wasn't cooking. "I see Catherine hasn't returned yet," he observed.

"No."

"I suppose she has gone to the Howlands'. I rather doubt she has ventured out to join the savages or the praying Indians in the woods. She will be back. She owes me five years yet. She won't want to see that time extended. The law . . . well, she knows the law."

Mary did not view Goody Howland as especially generous of spirit, but she agreed it was likely that she had allowed Catherine to spend the night in what had been her late brother's bed. She was less sure how the woman or her husband, Peter, would respond to the girl's crazed accusations that her mistress was a witch. Beth didn't like her, this Mary knew; the goodwife had judged her harshly just the other day by the docks. The woman envied her because of her parents. And while envy was a mortal sin, it grew rampant in everyone's soul; it was but a dandelion, a weed that was unstoppable here and one learned to live with. It was a character flaw far less dire than the sort of mean streak that led a man to stab a fork into his wife's hand.

But then, where in the Commandments did the Lord God forbid a man from stabbing his wife? Murder was a sin; sticking a fork in one's wife was . . . what? Thomas claimed it was discipline. She wasn't even sure what the colony's law was when it came to a man's cruelty toward his wife.

She considered warming the spider and offering to make him breakfast. But the idea passed. It had been a reflex born of years of duty. She wondered if he expected her to start work on his meal.

Apparently, he didn't. "If Catherine is not back by dinner, come by the mill," he said. "I will go fetch her. I doubt Peter wants to feed her or buy her from me. She has, it would seem—rather like thee—a brain that is sorely addled." He shook his head and smirked. "Thou art many things, Mary. But I would not put **witch** upon thy ledger." Then he turned and left the house. Outside she heard him saddling his horse, and then he was gone.

❧ ❦

Mary considered going by the Howlands' herself that morning and seeing what nonsense the servant girl was spewing, but she experienced daggers of pain up her arm when she forced her hand through the sleeve of her waistcoat and pulled on her stockings. And so instead she walked directly to her parents' home. She would see her mother and then together they would approach her father. James Burden was friends with the governor and the magistrates, and would know precisely what to do to begin the process of divorcing Thomas Deerfield.

❧ ❧

"What has happened to thee?" her mother asked, her alarm evident when Mary removed the cloth that wound around her hand.

They were standing in the parlor, her parents' house among the most sumptuous in the colony. There was a tapestry on the wall of the English countryside—a meadow that was part of the family estate on which Mary's uncle still lived—and it was a reminder of how mannered even the wilds were in the Old World compared to this one. The stairway to the chambers on the second floor was wide and had a window along the steps. The cupboard was almost the length of a wall and decorated with fine plates, as was the lintel along the top of the hearth. On another wall there was a portrait of Mary's grandfather—an aristocrat Mary met when she was a child, but who had died before she had gotten to know him well—by William Dobson. There was a framed map of Boston and a second one of the New World. They even had two upholstered chairs that James had imported earlier that year; another six had been sold to the governor, an elder, and one of the magistrates.

Before Mary answered her mother's question, she asked where the servants were. Her parents had two, Abigail Gathers and Hannah Dow. The girls had arrived together the year before last, though they were nothing alike. Abigail was eighteen, tall and slender and talkative, and likely to find a suitor among the indentured soon; Hannah was seventeen, short and shy, and painfully uncomfortable around men. Abigail's intellect was manifest in the concoctions she created in the kitchen, such as the spices she had begun adding to the stewed pumpkin—the recipe that Mary had shared with Rebeckah Cooper.

"They are out back. Abigail is milking and Hannah is tending to the pigs," her mother told her. "Thou canst speak freely."

Mary took a deep breath and answered: "My husband took one of those forks thou brought to my house and tried to spear my hand to the table."

"He what?"

"He has been hitting me, too, Mother. I have told no one until now. But I can live with him no longer. I cannot live with a man who will take the Devil's tines to his wife."

"The bruise on thy face . . ."

"Yes. That bruise. And others."

They sat down at the table in the kitchen, and Priscilla Burden examined her daughter's hand clinically. "Let us put some wine on it. Then we'll make a poultice. We've ash in the hearth and some fat from last night's dinner."

"I believe the bone is broken."

"Thou canst not splint a hand. At least I can't. We'll visit the physician."

Mary nodded.

"How bad does it hurt?" her mother asked.

"Less than last night. But it pains me."

"I have valerian."

"Mother?"

Priscilla waited.

"When I told thee that I can no longer live with Thomas, I meant it."

Her mother stood and reached for a pewter bowl on the cupboard. She placed it on the table and uncorked a jug of red wine. "That wound is fresh. This might sting," she said, placing her daughter's hand in the bowl.

"I intend to divorce him," Mary continued.

"I don't know the law, little dove."

"Father will."

"But I do know that Joan Halsell tried to divorce George Halsell and lives with him still."

"Are they members of the church?"

"No. Neither's a saint. But I urge thee to think

carefully. The Lord—" her mother started to say, but stopped when her daughter flinched against the pain of the alcohol on the wound.

Mary exhaled and said, "This will be an issue for the magistrates, Mother, not the church elders."

"Perhaps. But there are still the gossips."

"Wouldst thou rather thy daughter was beaten by a brute or spoken of poorly by gossips? I tend to believe it is the latter."

"Dames such as those wound, too; it is with a slower poison, but one equally as hurtful in the end."

"So be it. I can bear their malice. I cannot bear his."

Her mother dried the wound with a towel. Her voice grew soft when she said, "I never thought thy marriage to Thomas Deerfield was a perfect arrangement. Thou wouldst have found a more suitable spouse had we remained in England. But I never thought him a brute. He wasn't known for striking Anne."

"Well," Mary said, "he is about to be known for striking me."

❧ ❧

James Burden's warehouse was adjacent to the customhouse, and he was just leaving as Mary and her mother arrived. Mary could see the alarm on her father's face; it wasn't that he was surprised by their visit, because Mary and her mother were frequent visitors. It was the wrap on her hand and the anxiety on her mother's face.

"Well, this is a joy," he began carefully as they stood outside the entrance, "but I can see there is more to this visit than most days. What has happened to thy hand, Mary?"

"My husband pretended it was a piece of meat he was planning to carve," she said. "We have just come from the physician." And then, as her father began to digest this remark, she provided the details there on the wide wooden planks of the wharf, as the men unloaded yet another ship that had just docked and three Indians arrived to trade the furs that filled their sled. By the time she had finished, his face had grown grave.

"We will see to this. I should beat the man myself."

"But thou wilt not," her mother said, her tone almost scolding.

"No, of course not. But this won't stand. I'm appalled. Let us go see Richard Wilder. He's both a friend and a magistrate."

Her mother looked wary. "Art thou sure this is the right course? I worry about the church. I think of the beadle and the elders and the reverend—"

"And I think of our daughter," her father said, snapping at her mother in a fashion that Mary could not recall from all of her years living with them in England or here in Massachusetts. "This is a civil issue. Marriage here is but a civil contract. Mary and Thomas were married by a magistrate, and I will see to it that they are divorced by a magistrate."

"Is that truly thy desire, Mary?" her mother asked. "Art thou certain?"

Mary knew that she was, but the magnitude of what she was proposing began to grow real. She thought of the reverend with his fierce eyes and his high forehead, his small, sharp beard. She thought of the congregation. She thought of what petty and cruel women such as Goody Howland would say. And she thought of the Lord. What would He say? Her resolve was starting to waver, but then farther down the pier she saw Henry Simmons— that fellow employed by Valentine Hill who had assisted her after she had nearly been run over by an oxcart—his hair the creosote-black she recalled and his eyes the color of sky berries in the first weeks of August. He was in a common jacket today and holding a ledger. She had presumed he was indentured to Hill, but perhaps he was something more: an employee or an apprentice. He noticed her just that moment and tipped his cap, smiling. And something about seeing him now struck her as a sign.

Her back stiffened and she said to her parents, "I haven't a doubt. I am firm in my resolve. My heart needs healing, too. The sooner we begin, the sooner it, along with my hand, can begin to mend."

No. Never. . . . I never saw my master
hit or hurt Mary Deerfield. Not
even once.

**—The Testimony of Catherine
Stileman, from the Records and Files
of the Court of Assistants, Boston,
Massachusetts, 1662, Volume III**

Eight

Mary Deerfield and her parents met with Richard Wilder at midday, before he left for dinner. They met the magistrate at the new building they called the Town House, the hulking wooden edifice only two years old that the community had constructed at the head of State Street. It was three stories tall with twin cupolas, great chimneys, and wide, gabled windows off the third floor. Around the cupolas was a railed walkway from which a person could appreciate the way the city, barely three decades old, was expanding in all directions from the sea. (A year earlier, Mary recalled, she and Thomas had stood on its new balcony, and she had observed that the Boston construction was like the tide coming in and never leaving. He had corrected her, saying that the tide brought only seaweed, dead lobsters, and the wood from swamped ships.) Outside in the square, the stocks were empty today, and the whipping platform was quiet. The sun was moving amidst drifting puffs of white fleece, the clouds' shadows spotting the cobblestones like puddles.

The Court of Assistants met on the second floor,

where there were two large chambers. The court was not in session today and the governor was gone, and so the building was quiet but for a few selectmen and a lone scrivener leaving off a written pleading for Richard Wilder. There were smaller rooms on that second floor, too, including one that was usually locked, where the magistrates kept paper, quills, ink, and penknives. Wilder had a key and brought them to that room so they could chat in private. There were shelves and pegs on the walls and a table in the center, but neither a bench nor a chair. On one shelf were three copies of **The Book of the General Lawes and Liberties Concerning the Inhabitants of the Massachusetts.**

The magistrate was a tall man, thin to the point of being gaunt, and he was bald but for a band of white stubble above his ears and along the back of his head. He was approaching sixty and had been in the colony almost from the beginning. He'd arrived in 1634, only four years after the first boats had come to Boston. Friends with both the governor and the deputy governor, Wilder had served on the Court of Assistants since 1650. He had a long face that seemed a match for the length of his body, and it was further accentuated by the fact he had neither a mustache nor a beard. He murmured that it was growing chilly and took his cloak from a peg on the wall and climbed inside it.

James Burden motioned at Mary's hand and asked her to tell Richard what Thomas had done to her. The magistrate listened, occasionally asking a question or requesting a clarification. When she was finished, Wilder turned to her father and said, "Forks? Three-tined forks? Why, James?"

"Thou must know that Governor Winthrop used one himself. There is nothing in the Bible forbidding them," he said. "Hast thou tried one?"

"I've not."

"I will send thee a set. My gift."

Mary felt her hand pulsating and growing warm, and wished there was a chair on which she could sit. Boston was nowhere near the size of London and she strolled its cobblestone streets all the time, but the walk to her parents' home and then the walk here had exhausted her. She wanted at the very least to lean against the wall with the pegs. She wasn't sure what to make of the idea that the magistrate's initial inquiries had been about her father's decision to import three-tined forks into Boston.

"We'll talk to the minister first," Wilder said. "My wife would not be pleased to have such a thing as a three-tined implement in our house without Reverend Norton's blessing."

"Yes, do," her father suggested. "He is a most godly and reasonable man."

"Tell me: who was the magistrate who married Thomas and thee?" Wilder asked Mary.

"Samuel Prower. He passed two years ago."

"I miss him. A good fellow."

"He was that," Mary agreed.

"A divorce is no easy task. I have seen but a handful in all my years here."

"And what were the circumstances?" her father asked.

Wilder took a long breath and rubbed his eyes. "The first was Elizabeth Luxford. That was in 1638, I believe. No, 1639. The year of the drought. Her husband, whose name escapes me, already had a wife back in England. The court granted Elizabeth her divorce, put her husband in the stocks, and fined him mightily. Then they sent him away. In 1644, the court granted Anne Clarke her request for divorce when her husband ran off—left the colony—to live in sin with another woman."

"And the others?" Mary asked.

"Since I've been on the court, we've ruled in the petitioner's case on the grounds of desertion or adultery: Margery Norman. Dorothy Peter. Dorcas Hall. And then there was that recent madness."

"George and Joan Halsell," Mary's mother said knowingly.

"Yes," he said. "Hast thou met them, Priscilla?"

"I have not. I know only what people say."

Wilder nodded. "I would have been surprised if thou kept company with the likes of them."

"Prithee, tell me," Mary said.

"A few years ago, Goody Halsell claimed her husband had been abusing himself with Hester Lug and being unclean with the woman. I, for one, believed her accusation. But the court ruled that George should continue to have and enjoy his wife, despite whatever sins he may have committed. They live together still."

"She must be miserable," her mother said.

"Most likely. The trial was quite a spectacle." The magistrate turned his gaze on Mary. "I presume thou knowest that thy trial in the Court of Assistants would be public as well."

"I do."

"But, it seems to me, thou hast grounds. Since I serve on that court, it would be improper for me to provide counsel, but I certainly see reason for such a petition. Thomas has beaten thee considerably. He has attacked thee, it would seem, without cause."

"Yes," Mary said, her tone growing adamant despite her weakness and pain, "I have never given him cause."

Her father looked at her, his eyes moving between her wounded hand and her face. Until this meeting with the magistrate, she had never told him the source of the bruise that had lived so long beneath her coif. She had only that morning confessed the truth to her mother. But had he intuited now what really had caused it? Had both her parents known all along? "Tell me, Richard," her father said. "Thou hast granted divorces for desertion and adultery. What of cruelty?"

"No. But that does not mean that thy daughter hast not motivation for such an extreme measure. A man may not lawfully strike his wife. The court will need proof of marital fault, but thy hand, Mary, and all who have seen it, suggests thou hast motivation for such a dire petition."

She nodded. She took comfort in the fact that Thomas had savaged her left hand and not her right. The magistrate must have noticed the way she had just glanced at the wrap on it. He smiled at her in a fashion that was reassuring. "Mary, thy father and mother are both reputable people and saints"—he said, and then winked at her father— "even if thy father is now trying to introduce a little deviltry into our dinners."

James rolled his eyes at the good-natured chiding.

"But," Wilder continued, "thy husband is also a man of good standing and reputation. He, too, is deemed a saint. And that means the trial will draw formidable attention."

"I can live with that. I cannot live with him."

"I assume thou wilt move in with thy parents during the trial?"

She looked at her parents. She hadn't asked. But already her father was nodding. "Yes," she answered.

"Then I will start the proceedings tomorrow. The Court of Assistants is scheduled to convene in two weeks, and the trial will occur then. Dost thou need a scrivener? Someone to take testimonies and assist with witnesses?"

"Who wouldst thou recommend, Richard?" her father asked. "I have used Charles Proper for my business pleadings."

"Proper is a good man. But in this case? Use Benjamin Hull. Very good at petitions of a more domestic nature. Keeps an office on the corner of High and Mill Streets. Studious fellow. Exacting to the point of eccentricity, but that's a gift, given his choice of calling."

"Very well," her father said.

"And always better a scrivener than an attorney. I know more and more people are resorting to those appalling advocates who twist and trick, but many of the magistrates still view them with justifiable disdain."

"I agree," said James.

Then the magistrate continued, his tone avuncular, "Mary, this is a step of great consequence. Just to be certain: wouldst thou prefer to think about this one more night?"

"I would not. I would like to go home and get some of my clothing, my diary, and my Bible, and then I would like to go to my parents'."

"Thomas is at the mill?"

"Or a tavern. I suppose he came home for dinner, and when he found the spider cold and the house empty, he went to eat elsewhere."

"What about thy girl?"

She paused. Finally, she could bear standing no longer, and so she leaned against the wall, apologizing as she did. Then she answered, "My girl ran off last night."

"Before or after Thomas stabbed thee with the fork?"

"Before."

"So she did not witness the attack?"

"She did not," Mary answered, and the alarm was visible on both of her parents' faces.

"Where is she now?" Wilder asked.

"I do not know. Perhaps she has come home. Perhaps she's there now. But I presume she went to Goody Howland's, where her brother was indentured until he died."

"Why did she leave?"

She started to shake her head. It was complicated and absurd: it all came round and round to those bloody forks. She felt herself sliding down to the floor and tried to muster the strength to stand, but it was gone, it was gone completely, subsumed by the throbbing in her hand and the fever that was rising up through her arm, and the anger and the frustration and the injustice and the fear. It was all just too much. And so she collapsed onto the wooden boards, and suddenly her mother and her father were kneeling beside her and the magistrate was gazing down at her, his face a mix of confusion and concern. She wanted a drink of water badly.

"Mary," her mother was telling her, "don't move. Just try and be still."

She nodded. The magistrate was unsure whether to ask her his question again. Finally, she said to them all, "My servant girl left because she thought I had buried some of those very forks in the ground. In the walkway to our door. She ran away because she thought I was using them as some sort of spell. She believes . . ."

She paused because it was all so ridiculous. So inane. She almost couldn't bear to speak the words.

"Go on," said the magistrate.

And so Mary did. "She ran away because she thought I was a witch," she said. Her mother, unsettled by all that had already occurred, glanced at her father, her face shaken and her eyes scared.

⚜ ⚜

When Mary and her parents returned to her home, there was no sign of Thomas or Catherine. The three of them went inside and saw that the hearth was cold and then, at her father's insistence, went back outside to the walkway.

"Show me where thou found the forks and the pestle," he said. And so Mary did. The marks where she had dug were still evident, the dirt in small piles.

"Thou told Richard that thou didst not place them there. Was that the truth?"

"Yes," she answered, her voice tremulous because she knew this was not precisely the case. She had not placed them there the first time. She had not placed the pestle there ever. But she had returned the forks to the earth, jamming them back into the dirt as if they were stakes. On the other hand, she understood the intent of her father's question. And so had she lied? Had she just sinned? She was unsure, but she feared that she had.

"But if thou hadst discovered the forks previously and confronted Catherine previously, why were thou out in the night with them?"

"James, stop interrogating our daughter," her mother said.

"I am only making sure we understand. The magistrates certainly will ask." Then he turned back to Mary and continued, "I do not mean to sound harsh, little dove."

"I understand," she said. And she realized that she must tell the truth now, wholly and completely, both for the sake of justice and for the sake of her soul. "I had replaced the forks where I had found them, hoping the person behind them would not know he had been discovered."

"Didst thou suspect witchcraft from the beginning?"

"I did," she said.

"Human or demon?" her father asked.

"Human."

"Mary," her mother said, her tone cautious, "I

know thou dost pine for children. Tell me: was this a spell of thy making?"

"Mother! What in the world have the Devil's tines to do with a child?"

"I wanted to be sure. That's all. I need to know my daughter has not been seduced by the Devil or His minions."

"It is thou who brought the forks to this house! It is thy husband who brought them to this city!"

Her father shook his head and said, "They are but utensils."

"Yes," her mother agreed.

"But," her father continued, "if thou, with all thy knowledge, could misconstrue their use and perceive them as a bauble dangled before us by Satan, anyone could. This matters because of what that servant girl believes. We all know that even the most nonsensical accusations have caused grievous injury."

"The harm caused by those forks begins and ends here," said Mary, and she raised her wounded hand, angry that her parents were losing sight of the real crime.

Her mother rubbed her back in a wide, gentle circle. Her father started toward the back of the house and the women followed him. They saw that the Devon was in desperate need of milking, and Priscilla grabbed a bucket and tended to the animal, while James spread grain for the chickens. Mary gazed at the vegetable garden, which was still not fully put to bed for the winter—there were those massive, brown pumpkin leaves, not yet converted into mulch—and at the section of their meadow with the tall poles where she and Thomas grew their hops. The twine was empty now, the hops having been harvested with the last of the vegetables.

Then Mary and her mother went inside and climbed the stairs to the second-floor chamber. They packed some clothing and the few items Mary wanted into her leather satchel. Her mother said she would carry her extra shoes. It didn't take long. For a moment, after Mary and her mother had retrieved her possessions, the two of them surveyed the small room.

"Reassure me, Mary," her mother said, her voice low. "I will ask but this one last time: Thou art not dabbling in witchcraft? True?"

"True," she replied, though a part of her grew frightened. Had she in fact replaced those forks in the ground because she hoped their presence might breathe life into her barren womb? Were they an offering to the Devil, a quid pro quo? **I offer my allegiance as a handmaiden and in return am granted a child?** She had endured so much last night, slept so little, her body wracked by pain, and been asked so many questions today that she just didn't know anymore, which caused her to fret further still about the state of her soul and her future in Heaven.

Before they left, Mary wrote a short note to

Thomas and placed it on the table where they ate, telling him where she was and that she wasn't returning. She noticed the pestle that she had pulled from the ground on the shelf. When her mother wasn't looking, she dropped it, too, into her satchel.

Mary Deerfield may be barren, yes, but is she unclean? I will not dissemble and suggest that I know. Only our Lord and Savior can say why she has never been with child.

—The Testimony of Physician Roger Pickering, from the Records and Files of the Court of Assistants, Boston, Massachusetts, 1662, Volume III

Nine

Mary offered to help her mother and Abigail, the older of her parents' two servants, prepare supper that night, but neither would allow it because of her hand. Her mother insisted that she rest while she stirred the succotash in the spider, adding a little butter and garlic, as it cooked. Abigail took the bread and venison from the oven and then began setting the table. Mary was relieved the Devil's tines were nowhere in evidence. Her parents' other servant, Hannah, was outside feeding the animals. It would be dark soon, and her father would be home from his warehouse. The three women chatted, though Mary alone was seated in one of the ladder-back chairs.

It was then that they heard a horse's hooves and, a moment later, boots on the walkway. Abigail went to open the door even before someone had rapped on the wood, and there stood Thomas.

He took off his hat and bowed before his mother-in-law and his wife. "Good evening, Priscilla," he said, and Mary was unsure what to make of his tone. It was almost bemused.

"Thomas," her mother murmured, little more than acknowledging his presence.

Then he turned to Mary and said, "Wouldst thou like to come home now? Art thou ready?"

Abigail looked at her mistress and asked if she should set an additional place at the table for Thomas. Before the woman could reply, however, Thomas answered, "If anything, Abigail, there will be one person fewer at the table. I believe my wife will accept my apologies and come home with me."

"Thou art apologizing for sticking the Devil's tines into my hand?" Mary asked him.

He sighed. "I did no such thing. That is the truth."

She raised her hand, which was still wrapped in cloth. "Here is the evidence. Thou canst not lie when the truth is this plain."

"It was the gooseneck on the teakettle, Mary."

For a moment she was dumbfounded by the brazenness of his lie. Finally, she gathered herself and asked, "Art thou saying thou plunged a teakettle spout into my hand?"

He rubbed his eyes. Then he dropped his arms to his sides and met her gaze. "I did not move quickly enough when thou tripped with the kettle. I should have caught thee. I am sorry. I will forever see thy tumble and the way the gooseneck gashed thy hand when thy body fell upon it. If I were a younger man, perhaps I would have been able to spare thee such pain. I beg thy forgiveness as only a sinner can."

"Art thou going to lie so shamelessly? Dost thou honestly expect me to return to the home of a brute and a liar?"

"I am grateful that the water was not scalding," he continued.

She was astonished by his temerity. Was he actually going to claim that she had tripped while carrying the kettle? "No," she said firmly. "That was not what happened at all." She saw Abigail glance at her mother; the girl was uncomfortable, unsure whether she should be present but unsure as well how to leave.

"Prithee, help Hannah with the animals," Mary's mother said to Abigail, and the servant, visibly relieved, left for the back of the house. Then Priscilla Burden looked at her son-in-law—a peer, really, in terms of age—and continued, "Thou art playing a dangerous game with thy soul."

"More dangerous, Priscilla, than thy husband bringing three-tined forks into our community? More dangerous than thy daughter using those Devil's tines for witchcraft? Thy family risks bringing down God's justifiable wrath upon all of Boston. I am but a man who hopes to bring home his wife, where God and magistrate alike know she belongs."

"We are all sinners, yes. But some of us are more loathsome than others," her mother said.

"I am no witch, Thomas," Mary added.

"Catherine seems to fear thou art."

"She is mistaken."

Thomas nodded. "I agree. I would not want thee back if I shared her beliefs. But, still, an accusation can weigh heavy."

"Even one from her?" asked Priscilla. "A servant with years left on her indenture?"

"The greatest sin is pride, Priscilla," Thomas said, his voice uncharacteristically ruminative. "We all know this. I have none. I know my frailties and my failures. I apologize with all my heart for the harsh words that on occasion I have said to thee, Mary. But, Priscilla, rest assured that I have never struck thy daughter and most certainly would I never attack her as she suggests with those Devil's temptations that thy husband insists on importing."

"I want thee to leave," Mary said to him, fighting hard against her tears. She wanted to say something, and she wanted to say it without visible lamentation—because she knew she would never regret the words she was about to speak. "I hope never to be alone with thee again."

"That is not thy right."

"It is when thou hast attacked me."

"Thou art my wife."

"And today thou art my husband. But that will change. Mark me, Thomas Deerfield, that will change."

"Think on that, Mary. I know thy mind is but . . ."

"But what? White meat?" she asked, finishing his sentence for him. "Is that not what thou believest?"

He smiled, his face the older but still handsome visage she recalled from days that now seemed as far distant as childhood. Then he shook his head and said, "I know thy mind is sharp and thou hast always been a fine helpmeet. I am grateful that thou hast been in my heart in the past, and I believe thou wilt lodge there again. I will leave thee tonight in the good care of thy parents."

She nodded and presumed they were done. But her mother, it seemed, had one more question for Thomas.

"Tell me, prithee," Priscilla asked. "Where is Catherine?"

"She is at my house. I presumed mistakenly that Mary would be returning home, and so I retrieved her from Peter Howland's. But since Mary is not coming back with me, I am unclear where Catherine will go."

"There are gossips," said Priscilla.

"I agree. Also, there are laws. I expect Peter and I will come to an accommodation where I will pay for Catherine's lodging in the evenings and she will return during the day to tend to the animals and cook and clean. I believe it will be a short-term accommodation, because I expect my wife will soon enough see the absurdity of her accusations and return home—where she belongs and where God expects her."

He put back on his hat and said good night. Then he climbed onto his horse and disappeared into the dusk that was falling upon the city by the sea.

�� ��

The next morning, Mary and her father met Benjamin Hull at his office, arriving there at the same moment as the scrivener. He was wearing a waterproof cloak of camlet that had been dyed red, and when he hung it in his office, Mary noted that his collar and cuffs were spotless, as white as the single cloud Mary had seen against the cold, blue sky as she and her father had walked there. The man's doublet was a lush green. There was nothing dowdy about the scrivener, including his black beard, which looked sculpted perfectly to his jawline and chin. Mary guessed that he was a decade older than she was.

The office was small, the walls whitewashed but barren. He had lined up his quills and inks as if they were soldiers on parade.

Hull opened the casement window, despite the chill, to allow more light into the room. Then he sat behind his desk, and they sat on the bench across from it. With great fastidiousness he flattened a piece of paper. Then he listened as they explained why they were there and how they were hoping he could assist them. When they were through, he sat forward and said, "Thou hast not told me of any witnesses to Thomas Deerfield's cruelty."

"There are witnesses to the things he has said to me," Mary said.

"Didst thou tell anyone after he beat thee?"

"My friend, Goodwife Cooper, noticed the bruises. So did my son-in-law, Jonathan Cooke."

"That's helpful."

James Burden leaned in and added, "Mary's mother and I did, too."

"And Goody Howland? Perhaps she commented upon them?"

"She may have seen them too, yes," said Mary. "But she is not likely to speak favorably of me."

The scrivener folded his hands on his desk. Then: "Thou hast given me little time. The court meets in less than two weeks."

"Wouldst thou proceed differently if there were a month or more?" her father asked.

"Art thou suggesting that we wait until the next session?"

"Perhaps," James said.

But the idea of having to endure this purgatory, married but not, was too much for Mary. She wanted her divorce and she wanted it now; she wanted to be free. "How much work is needed?" she asked the scrivener.

"I will need to take the testimony of the witnesses and be sure some are present when the magistrates hear thy petition. That means finding them and interviewing them."

"It is not a lengthy list."

"No," he agreed. "But it still takes time. There is, for instance, Catherine Stileman. There is Goody Cooper. There are the owners of the ordinaries where Thomas may have shown his tendencies to act badly when drink-drunk. That could be important, Mary, and it is an area I will pursue with vigor. I will also want to spend time with thy parents and thee to make sure that the court proceedings are not a mystery and thou art comfortable answering the magistrates' questions."

"I know Richard Wilder," said her father, and it sounded to Mary like a boast. Apparently, it did to the scrivener, too.

"Thou knowest him as a friend," said Benjamin Hull. "I doubt thou hast experienced him much as a magistrate."

❧ ❧

That night, Valentine Hill and his wife, Eleanor, came to supper, and Mary noticed that her mother did not have Abigail set the table with three-tined forks. They ate potatoes cooked in the hot coals and a wild turkey the girls roasted over the spit. Mary did not have much of an appetite, which she attributed in part to the way her life had abruptly grown unsettled and in part to the pain, which lingered in her hand. When she removed the dressing the doctor had placed on the wound the day before, the scabbing was unseemly and the bruise the color of blackberries.

Mary understood that Valentine and his wife were like her parents: wealthy and privileged in ways that few others were in Boston. The four of them knew John Endicott, the governor, well. They had pews close to the front of the First Church and often spoke with John Norton, the minister, directly about his sermons. But the Hills had hair that was entirely white, and Valentine had grown stout; Eleanor's nose was red and her fingers gnarled with age. They looked considerably older to Mary than her own parents, but she wondered if that was a delusion.

After they had prayed and Abigail and Hannah had served them, the men spoke of the ships that were arriving and of their contents, and Mary's mind wandered. Both her father and Valentine viewed their work as important to the colony, and the fact that it made them rich as proof of their sanctification. At one point, Eleanor Hill asked about the savages she had seen trading at the harbor that morning and wondered if the Indians from the praying towns might ever become commonplace. The men seemed uncomfortable with the prospect of Indians in a Boston church, but Eleanor persisted, until finally her husband smiled and said, "Thou dost sound as addled as our nephew. Henry, too, seems to give them credit for wits that God seems not to have bestowed upon them."

When Mary heard the name "Henry," she sat up a little straighter. "Henry Simmons?" she asked.

"Yes," said Valentine Hill, spooning a piece of potato into his mouth and chewing with relish. "My nephew. Eleanor's sister's son. He arrived this year from Yarmouth. How dost thou know him?"

"I know him little," she said. "But one day he helped me when an oxcart nearly ran me over. I presumed he was a servant."

Valentine shook his head. "His carriage is poor. But his mind is good. Excellent, in fact. Someday he may take over my business since we haven't sons ourselves—assuming his attitude improves."

"Were thou hurt by the oxcart?" her mother asked. "Thou said nothing of this."

"Because there was nothing to tell, Mother."

"But Valentine's nephew assisted thee."

She nodded.

"He's a good boy," said Valentine. "He is just too glib and too confident of his status in this world—and in the next. He is a bit of a leveler. Consorts with the damned and the poor and the savages."

Eleanor laughed. "Thou consorts with the savages! How much dost thou trade with them?"

"It is one thing to trade with them," Valentine corrected her. "It is quite another to misplace them in the Lord's hierarchy." He turned to Mary and said to her with the directness he was known for, "Thy father tells us thou dost plan to divorce Thomas."

"Yes," she said.

"He's a rich man. Thou could be a rich woman," Valentine said. "If the court were to rule in thy favor, thou wouldst receive one-third of his property. Thy estate would grow considerably."

"That is not why I am proceeding," she told him. She was offended he would bring up such a thing.

"No, of course not," he said. "I was only speaking of the law."

"I cannot imagine expecting Mary to return to a man who will stick a fork in his wife," Eleanor added, disgusted at the thought.

In truth, Mary could not conceive of such an outcome either. Already she was wondering what she would do when the divorce was official. What she was doing would have consequences; some she could anticipate, some she could not. It was rather like climbing aboard the ship back in England that was going to traverse the ocean. She had stared up at the rigging and the sails from the wharf and felt a mixture of awe at the adventure before her and trepidation when she contemplated the utter uncertainty of her future. She had not been nearly as frightened of the voyage as some—it was the storm on the thirteenth day that first suggested to her that the discomforts of the deceptively small vessel paled before its fragility against waves that crashed down upon the quarterdeck and rocked the ship like a baby's rattle—but neither had she experienced God's presence the way others had. Yet this divorce was otherwise very different: first of all, it was a choice she was making. She hadn't been given a say when she'd been a girl: her parents were going and, thus, so was she. Moreover, no one among her friends or family would judge her ill for following her Lord and accompanying her family to this new, more devout world. People would feel quite differently toward her after she had divorced Thomas Deerfield. That was clear.

But nothing else about her future was. Would she remain in Boston with her parents? Would she live alone nearby? Or, perhaps, would she return to England to live with one of her brothers?

No. Not that. She was but twenty-four. The Lord may not have planned children for her, but there was no reason to presume He had laid out for her a life of lonely spinsterhood. She would remarry and she would remarry here, among the godly and the saints. She would find a good man: she would not make the mistake she had made the first time. And it would not be hard: already the colony was so much larger than it was five years ago. In addition, as Valentine Hill had observed, her assets would be extensive. Her dowry, as it were, would include both her third from Thomas Deerfield and all that came with being a child—albeit, a daughter—of the renowned merchant James Burden.

Once again, her mind roamed to Henry Simmons, and when she thought of him she stopped worrying about tomorrow and the day after tomorrow and what would become of her. She stopped fretting and she even stopped thinking about her hand. The pain disappeared for a long, numinous moment, burned off like morning fog in the harbor.

"Mary?"

She looked at her mother. Everyone was staring at her. "Mary, where was thy mind?"

"I am sorry, Mother. What wast thou saying?"

"Valentine was asking: wouldst thou consider mediation? We have not spoken to the elders."

She turned to her parents' friend. "No. Thomas and I are beyond mediation."

"I could speak to Reverend Norton," he said. "If thou changest thy mind."

"So could my parents. So could I. But we shan't. That is not my desire."

"I expect, in that case, that he will come speak to thee."

"So be it. I shall stand my ground."

"Very well then," said Valentine Hill, ripping at a piece of the turkey with his fingers and thumb. Then, meeting no one's eyes, he murmured, "The way thou sometimes drift off, Mary. It is like thou art under a spell."

She is neither healer nor midwife. Her simples may not be of the Devil, but neither are they healing. Her teacher was that old woman who lives out by the Neck. And I believe no midwife would ever allow so barren a womb to be present at a birth.

—The Testimony of Physician Roger Pickering, from the Records and Files of the Court of Assistants, Boston, Massachusetts, 1662, Volume III

Ten

Mary sat with her mother at church, as she did every week, but Catherine chose this Sunday to sit instead in the furthest reaches of the sanctuary, a pew second from the rear and far from either Mary or Priscilla Burden. Though Catherine was living with the Howlands, she was not sitting with Beth: she was with a group of indentured girls from the city, all of them in their late teens, and Catherine may actually have been the oldest. Mary only spotted her when she happened to stretch her neck and turn around as the third hour of that morning's service was beginning. The servant girl was gazing at Thomas. Mary had not seen Catherine since she had raced from her house a few nights ago, moments before Thomas would try and impale his wife with a fork. But Mary had heard about Catherine's activities during the past week: the girl had told Goody Howland how she had seen Mary out in the night in the dooryard with the Devil's tines, and Beth Howland had told at least one (and probably more than one) of their mutual acquaintances. When Mary saw Rebeckah Cooper at the cobbler where both women were buying fall shoes—though Rebeckah was buying shoes for herself and her two children—her friend told her that Catherine had made some wild accusations to Beth. Beth, her friend insisted, believed the servant was a little hysterical herself, but was still suspicious of Mary. Rebeckah didn't think that either Beth or Catherine had plans to accuse her of witchcraft, but she speculated that this was only because they feared Mary's station in the colony and the clout of her family.

"Perhaps, also," Mary had added, "she will not make such an accusation because I am neither possessed nor a witch, and she knows this is the truth."

She saw Thomas glancing at her during the sermon, his face seeming to move with athletic skill from wistful to threatening. One moment it seemed that he missed her, his aging eyes imploring her to return. The next? His countenance was hard and mean, and she saw in him the man who one time had thrown her into the brick hearth. She saw as well his son-in-law, Jonathan, who was seated beside Thomas, and he was watching her, too. He had been working outside as a joiner on a new house, and his face was handsomely tanned. His wife, Peregrine, was but a few rows behind her. They were a beautiful couple. She was envious of Peregrine, she knew that, and she felt waves of both shame and desire, though she couldn't have said which had a more pronounced undertow. But it was clear that her life would be at once easier and more pleasant if she were to spend her days (and nights) with a man closer to her age and disposition such as Jonathan.

When the service broke for dinner and the worshippers began to exit the First Church for their midday meals, Mary parted from her mother and Abigail and Hannah, and started after Catherine. She mumbled as her excuse that she hoped to avoid Thomas, but her mother must have seen that there was more to her sudden exit: Thomas was making no effort at all to work his way toward them through the crowd.

Mary saw the girl starting down the street toward her old house to prepare her master his dinner, and so she picked up her pace and overtook her where the marketplace began to merge with the homes of the city's wealthier families.

"Good Sabbath to thee," she said to Catherine.

The girl looked at her, more annoyed than alarmed. But she was polite: "Good Sabbath," she replied, continuing to walk.

"The air is nippy this morning. Autumn has arrived."

"It has," the girl agreed.

"Is Thomas treating thee well? Are Goodman Howland and his wife?"

"Yes." Then Catherine noticed the way that Mary was wearing a glove on only her right hand,

and how the left was still wrapped in cloth, and said, "I heard of thy accident."

Mary shook her head. "Thou knowest it was no accident."

"With the kettle," the girl continued.

"With the Devil's tines," Mary corrected her, "and with thy master as the Devil's agent."

"Art thou accusing him of witchcraft?" Catherine may have been prone to overreaction, but she was not dim. She had heard the sarcasm in Mary's tone and was responding in kind. Nevertheless, Mary replied carefully.

"Of course not. But I will accuse him of cruelty."

"That is thy right."

"Thou art a witness."

"To what?"

"To the way I was treated. To the things he said and the things he did."

Here Catherine stopped and looked down at the cobblestones. She sighed. "Yes, I heard him speak hard words on occasion, but most of the time it seemed to me he was reminding thee of thy station."

Mary considered chastising the girl for her own temerity. But Mary was more interested in understanding Catherine's mind this morning than she was in disciplining the servant for disobedience. "Dost thou believe I endeavor to transcend my station as helpmeet and wife?"

"I meant no offense. I only meant . . ."

"Go on."

"I only meant that on occasion thou hast spoken with the surety of a man. When my master chastised thee, I believe it was in the hope that thou might rein in thy mannish presumption. His guidance was always administered with concern for thy soul."

"He seems most concerned for my soul when he is drink-drunk."

"But did he ever raise a hand to thee? Not that I saw. It does not seem to me to be in his character, which I find righteous and kind."

"Was I not a good wife to him?" Mary pressed.

"He was a good husband to thee."

"Ah, he was a good provider. There I will not attempt to see thy mind changed. But that is not the only criterion. And thou chose not to answer my question. Why?"

Catherine sniffed. "Fine," she agreed. "From what I saw, thou were a good wife. But I know also what others have seen."

"What art thou suggesting?"

"I should not say more. It is just the talk of the gossips."

"I thank thee for understanding and admitting that."

"Thou owest me no thanks."

"And tell me: was I not always a good mistress to thee?"

"Yes. Thou were."

"Then let me ask thee plainly, Catherine: Dost thou believe I am possessed? Hast thou ever seen me behave in such a fashion that would suggest possession?"

"I have not."

"Dost thou believe in thy heart that thou saw me performing a Devil's rite or offering myself to Him as a handmaiden?"

"I do not want to speak of this on the Sabbath."

"Then when?"

The girl said nothing and much to Mary's astonishment started to walk away from her. With her one good hand she reached for Catherine and took hold of her arm beneath her cloak.

The girl was stunned and stood there speechless. She was pretty, so very pretty. How could she protect and possibly desire a man such as Thomas Deerfield, when the city had men such as Henry Simmons and Jonathan Cooke—oh, not those two specifically, but a servant of that sort—who were so much more suitable? And yet Catherine did feel something inappropriate for Thomas: Mary could see it clearly in the girl's face.

"Then when?" Mary asked again, her voice unashamedly urgent.

Instead of answering, Catherine gathered herself and said in a tone so dignified that Mary would have laughed if the speech had not been so dangerous to her, "I know this, ma'am, and this alone: Thou art barren but desire a child. Thou took the

Devil's tines and a pestle and were using them to perform a kind of dark magic that night. I know what I saw."

And with that, she shook herself free from Mary and walked briskly down the street and toward the house where once Mary had thought she herself was going to build a life and start a family.

❧ ❦

On Monday morning, Mary thought she might visit her scrivener for the simple reason that she was anxious and she had found the man's tidiness and evident attention to detail comforting. She had prayed, but she wanted this compulsive, expert man's reassurance, too. As she was passing the whipping post and scaffold near the Town House, however, she heard her name. There was Constance Winston emerging from the crowds bustling about the marketplace.

"Mary Deerfield," she said again, and Mary tried to squash her unease that the person calling out to her was an outcast not numbered among the saints. The fact that Mary had, in essence, shunned her when the woman's simples and tea had failed to result in a child made her feel even worse: guilty and spineless, too.

"Constance, hello," Mary replied. She wasn't sure that she had ever seen the woman here in the center of the city. Whenever she had met with

Constance, it had been in her modest house out along the Neck. She would go there surreptitiously, careful not to draw attention to her visits.

"It's been a long time."

"It has," Mary agreed. She heard the judgment in the other woman's voice. Constance knew that she had been avoiding her. "I have been most busy of late."

"Of late? Well then, thou hast had a busy year."

Constance was a head taller than Mary and carried herself with the same aristocratic bearing as Mary's own mother. She had green eyes and silver hair pulled neatly beneath her coif, and the lines on her face in no way diminished her beauty. Constance was in her fifties and wearing a scarlet cape lined with sarcenet the color of cinnamon. She had assets, not simply because she owned such clothing, but because she would be fined for trying to dress above her station if she did not.

"I have. I—"

"Thou owest me no explanation," said Constance. "Thou art under no obligation to me."

"No. It's just . . ."

"It's just the gossips," said Constance, and she pointed up at the scaffold. "A quiet day, it seems. No one is being shamed or hanged. How are we to pass our Monday?"

"I think it speaks well of our community that no one has transgressed."

"Nonsense. It means only that our transgressors

either are impenitent or haven't yet been caught—or, perhaps, the magistrates simply haven't met lately."

"Perhaps," Mary agreed. "They meet next week."

Constance digested this news. Then: "Yes, of course. They are in thy future, aren't they? I've heard. When we last met, thou were interested in conceiving a child with thy husband. Now thou cravest as much distance from him as the law will allow."

"As I said: I have been busy."

"Imagine if the nettle tea had worked its magic. Thou were fortunate."

Mary held up her left hand, still wrapped in cloth. "I am not sure I agree. If thou hast heard of my design to divorce Thomas Deerfield, then perhaps thou hast heard also of the violence that inspired it."

"Yes. I had been told there was such a catalyst: a rather vicious ingredient that opened wide thine eyes."

"May I ask how much thou heard?"

Constance shrugged. "Stories like thine are like geese. They travel far and fast."

"He is claiming that I fell on a teakettle."

"Which, I must admit, I presumed was a lie."

"Thou art astute."

"How much did thy servant girl see?"

"Nothing."

The other woman sighed. "Nothing?"

"Alas, not."

"Mary, I do not know and I do not need to know whether thou pulled me from thy life like a bad tooth because my simples failed thee or because there are those who view my interests as peculiar—because, to be blunt, thou feared an association with someone of my sensibilities."

"I told thee," Mary said quickly, "I have simply had much to tend to."

"I don't care. All I want thee to know is this: thou art a woman facing men who would be comfortable to see thee dangling there," she said, and she pointed up at the scaffold with the hanging platform. "I harbor no ill will and no grudge. I believe we are more alike than thou art willing to admit. If I can ever assist thee, do not hesitate to renew our acquaintance."

Mary glanced up at the dark wood and then at the imposing walls of the Town House. "I thank thee, Constance," she said finally. "I do."

The other woman smiled at her and squeezed her right arm affectionately. Over Constance's shoulder, she saw a group of women watching them, some of whom she recognized from the church.

"It seems we are walking in the same direction. Shall we?" Constance asked.

To continue toward the scrivener's would mean continuing to walk with Constance. Mary knew that when she faced the magistrates next week, no good could come from an association with this woman from the Neck. Here was one of those inescapable moments when pragmatism and cruelty were yoked. And so even though it pained her, deepening her contrition, she said, "No, I think I am going in the other direction. I've chosen to live with my parents and I am heading there now."

Constance saw through the ruse and smirked ever so slightly. "Very well. Good day, Mary," she said, and walked on.

❧ ❧

For the next three days, unnerved by her encounter with Constance Winston, Mary stayed home with her mother and her mother's servant girls. She and Hannah put the garden to bed and tended the animals, she and Abigail mended clothing for the winter and put up stores of root vegetables, and she and her mother wrote long letters to her brothers back in England. She was neither efficient nor fast, hobbled as she was by her left hand. But she did her best. The scrivener came twice to the house, and that was reassuring, even when on the second visit he told her that he was going to see Catherine Stileman that afternoon. She slept in the room that had been hers before she married Thomas, and it seemed largely unchanged: small and dark and far from the hearth, and she recalled how chilly it would become in the winter. One night when she was seventeen, she had taken the bed warmer and run hot coals beneath the counterpane—as she had most nights that winter—and suddenly the white fabric was starting to smolder. Quickly she poured water from a washing bucket onto the bed and extinguished the fire before it could start. But that night she slept in damp bedding, and for the rest of the winter she slept in a cold bed.

And now winter once more was starting its remorseless approach; the sun was setting earlier and rising later. The rains were frequent and they were cold.

Her parents insisted that it had rained more in England, but her memories told her otherwise. In her mind, her bedroom as a girl had always been sunny.

Twice her father had brought up the fact that next week the Court of Assistants convened and they would hear her petition for divorce. Both times he had said they must be sure that Benjamin Hull had lined up their witnesses to ensure the magistrates understood Thomas's violence and drunkenness. When Mary had reminded him that Catherine might testify to his harsh words but that was all, he had nodded gravely and said it was critical at the very least that she did that. He took the liberty of reaching out to the fellow who owned the tavern where Thomas drank most frequently and reassured her that the man had met with the scrivener and would speak ill of Thomas's habits. Mary was less confident: James Burden was an important figure in the city, but so was Thomas. And while Thomas might not be as esteemed or as wealthy as her father, he was respected enough, and he patronized that tavern often.

Meanwhile, her mother fretted that Catherine was going to deny having planted the forks, should it come up, and there was no one else they could reasonably accuse. There was no one else they could imagine who had done it.

One afternoon when Abigail was churning butter and Hannah was hauling logs into the firewood rack, Mary took the mysterious pestle from beneath her bed where she had been hiding it and stared at the Devil's tines that had been carved into its handle. She knew what was occurring that autumn in Hartford and why her mother was anxious. Mary Sanford already had been hanged as a witch. Ann Cole had admitted to her possession. Rebecca Greensmith had confessed that the Devil had carnal knowledge of her body. Mary ran her fingers over the mark on the pestle and thought of what she used to do to herself in her bed, her husband beside her, and questioned as she had dozens of times before whether this was an enticement from the Devil, a gift from God, or something that had as little to do with the Lord and Satan as the hours in her life she spent at the spinning wheel.

But she was certain of one thing: she had not planted those forks that first time in the earth, and never had she planted this pestle. She would make that clear if the divorce trial devolved into some appalling—and, yes, dangerous—litany of accusations into who was a witch and who wasn't. But if she had not planted the forks, the question quickly would become, who did? Catherine? Thomas? Someone or some **thing** else? She couldn't say.

She stripped and searched her body in the cold air of her room to be sure there was nowhere upon her a witch's teat or Devil's mark. There wasn't—which surprised her not at all. As her own husband had said to her that awful night when he had plunged the fork into the back of her hand: she was many things, but she was most certainly not a witch.

꿏 꿐

By Thursday, she could no longer endure being inside the ever-darkening house or in the back with the dying gardens and the animals, and so she dressed and managed to carefully slide a glove over her left hand. She walked past the Town House and toward the warehouses down by the harbor. The sky was gray and flat, and the water in the cove was choppy with whitecaps. It was likely going to rain before supper. The anchored ships bobbed as they waited their turn to approach the piers and unload their cargo, their sails wound tight against their masts, and the men on the wharves moved methodically up and down the planks with their crates and casks and the occasional large, elegant cupboard or table built by artisans back in England.

She avoided her father's warehouse and tried to convince herself that she was but getting some air and wandering aimlessly. Yes, to be aimless was to court the Devil, but after all she had been through and what loomed next week, she felt she had earned a little purposelessness.

For a moment she stood on the cobblestones across the street from the door to Valentine Hill's office, the warehouse stretching behind it along the wharf. She was, she realized, almost trying to will Henry Simmons to emerge—if he was even inside there, which was no guarantee. Was this reminiscent of a simple prayer or was she flirting with Satan? If Henry should see her through the window and come out, would that be a sign? If he should choose that moment to leave, unaware that she was standing there waiting, was that a coincidence, a temptation, or an indication of the good fortune that was nearing for her in this world and the sanctification that awaited her in the next?

But he didn't emerge, and she felt the first drops of rain. She should go home and cocoon by the fire; it was ludicrous to have come here.

As she started away from the water, however, she saw Eleanor Hill—Valentine's wife—emerge from the warehouse. The woman was bundled tightly inside her frock and her hood, her hands ensconced in a fur muff. "Good day, Eleanor," she began. "I see thou art bundled up nicely against the chill."

"And rain," said Eleanor. "I fear this rain is a harbinger of the snow to come. It's so cold. Art thou visiting thy father?"

"No. I just wanted to smell the salt air. I just wanted to walk."

"Then let's walk and try to beat the worst of the rain. I would enjoy the company home. How is thy hand? Healing?"

"Yes."

"Good," Eleanor murmured, but her tone seemed distracted, as if suddenly her mind were elsewhere. Then Mary understood why: "The **Amity** docked yesterday," the older woman said. "I can't tell thee how many pipes of Portuguese Madeira were unloaded, but it was a great deal. Valentine put aside some for us for tonight. He loves it—as do I. Already I am sick of this season's cider. I said I would bring some home and I completely forgot to retrieve a bottle or two. Come with me." She pulled her hand from the muff and took Mary's good hand in hers and led her back into the front of the warehouse, where her husband kept his offices, and there he was, Henry Simmons, and Mary felt a thrilling little rush in her chest. He was seated on one side of a large mahogany desk, more ornate than even the one her father used, with brass pulls and seating for chairs on both sides. He stood when he saw Eleanor and her, his quill in his hand and a thick ledger book open on the tabletop before him.

"Henry," said Eleanor, "I forgot the Madeira. I believe Valentine left it for me in the near storeroom." Then she said to Mary, "I shall be but a moment. I believe thou knowest Henry."

"Yes," she said, as Eleanor vanished through the door behind the great desk.

"Good day," he said to her. "Here is a blessing I had not anticipated this rainy afternoon."

She raised an eyebrow at his flirtation: he couldn't possibly view her as an actual blessing. This was the third time she had spied him, and on each occasion he had been more suitably dressed than the time before: his doublet today was crimson, the material a Flemish mockado wool. His cuffs and collar were pristine.

"Good day, Henry," she replied formally, though she pulled back her hood. She noticed a small tremor in her voice. Had it been apparent to him, too, in so short a sentence?

"My aunt and uncle have told me of thy troubles."

"My hand is much better. But I thank thee."

"I was referring to the much greater tribulation."

"Sometimes the Lord sees fit to test us."

"That He does. But I am sorry nonetheless. I have not met Thomas Deerfield, but it sounds to me that thou will be well once rid of him."

"It will be a life with improvements, yes,"

she said, and she pointed at her left hand with the fingers of her right. "But it will not be the life I expected. Nor will it be one that will be easy."

"God applauds toil. I think He rather expects it." There it was again: a sentiment that on the surface would be at home in one of Reverend Norton's sermons at the First Church but sounded peculiarly sacrilegious when it came from the mouth of this Henry Simmons.

"Did I see thee in church this Sunday past?" she asked him.

"If thou dost not recall, then clearly I am not making the impression I desire."

"And what sort of impression is that?"

"Here in this place? Oh, a man most godly and chosen. Of course."

"But one never can know that now, can one?"

"One cannot."

"Hast thou joined the church?" she asked him.

"I have not. But I would point out that thy husband is a respected member and his behavior toward thee hast been something less than a model of Christian charity."

"But thou wilt join?"

He nodded. "Yes. After all, someday I will be expected to manage this business."

"That is no reason to join."

He placed his quill down in its stand and thought long and hard before replying. "No," he agreed finally, "it is not."

"Wilt thou be there on Sunday next?"

"Most definitely."

"Good."

"May I ask thee something, Mary?"

"Certainly."

"For what dost thou pray when thou considers thy petition before the Court of Assistants?"

"I do not pray about that."

"No?"

"I prayed for years for a child and I have none. I prayed for months for William Stileman to get well and he died. Since my childhood I have prayed for the living and the dead, and—"

"And thou hast seen no prayers answered."

"It is not that," she corrected him. "It is my acceptance, finally, that our Lord has His plan for us and it is not for me to try and influence His vision. We cannot—and so it has come to me of late that there is no reason to appeal."

"I have heard it argued that prayer does not change God's mind; rather, it changes us."

"The act."

"Yes, the act."

"I will ponder that idea."

He nodded. "And thou wilt be an agent of thine own destiny by divorcing Thomas Deerfield."

"Just as I was my own agent when I married him. We are flawed; we make mistakes. We try our best to correct them."

And now when he smiled, she could see it was

only with approval, and though it was vain to feel this way, the rush of happiness it gave her was as real as the rain that was drumming now on the roof of the warehouse or the way her hood was bunched behind her neck. "My first sense of thee was accurate. It takes more than a brute with an oxcart to stop or slow thee," he said.

"Or," she replied, "a brute with a fork."

It was then that Eleanor returned with her Madeira. She looked back and forth between Mary and her nephew, and Mary wondered if the older woman could see the way her conversation with Henry—part frivolity, yes, but in equal measure something more substantive—had left her face joyful and flushed.

A husband who strikes his wife or is peevish with her puts to lie his profession of faith and has smashed soundly divine law and dishonored our Lord and Savior.

—The Testimony of Reverend John Norton, from the Records and Files of the Court of Assistants, Boston, Massachusetts, 1662, Volume III

Eleven

On Saturday, Mary's daughter-in-law, her husband, and their two small children surprised her when they came to her parents' house to visit. Mary was at the spinning wheel when Peregrine, Jonathan, and the girls appeared in the afternoon. Her father was at his office at the docks, and her mother had brought some broken pewter to the tinker for repair. Abigail was starting supper, and Hannah was outside milking the two cows. Through the curtains Mary saw the family walking beside Jonathan's horse, the children riding atop the pillion on the animal. She stopped work and went to greet them, opening the front door and welcoming them into the warmth of the parlor. The girls were three and four, and Jonathan lifted them off the horse and handed them to Peregrine, who plopped them onto the walkway. They raced like puppies past Mary into the house.

Peregrine rubbed her hands together and commented on how quickly the weather was changing. Jonathan—and Mary was struck, as she was always, by what a handsome man he was when he pulled off his Monmouth cap—was telling Abigail how wonderful the turkey smelled as it turned on the roasting jack.

"'Tis good to see thee, Mary," Jonathan then said, as he took Peregrine's cloak and hung it on a peg on the wall opposite the chimney.

Mary motioned at the chairs around the table and suggested they sit.

"Peregrine believes that she is again with child," Jonathan continued. "'Tis a blessing, yes, but neither of us had anticipated how tired she would be so early on."

The news was a small blow to Mary. She had expected that Peregrine would be pregnant again soon; it had been three years since Amity was born. She paused momentarily at the reminder of all she would never have.

"That is lovely to hear," she said to her daughter-in-law, joining her at the table. She alternated her gaze between Peregrine and Jonathan, and told them, "I am very happy. Thou dost deserve such a gift."

"We are grateful," agreed Jonathan.

"May the months pass easily, Peregrine. And if thou art not blessed with a boy, may the young one be as beautiful as this pair," Mary said, motioning at the girls as the two of them and their father stared at the painting and the tapestry on the walls. This sort of largesse was rare, and Mary knew that

Jonathan Cooke could not provide such elegance for his family, but it had always been evident that he craved it.

"In my family, the babies come quick," Peregrine volunteered.

Abigail handed the three of them tankards of beer before Mary even had the chance to ask her to bring the guests drink. Then the girl, sensing that this was a private matter, offered to take the two children outside to see the animals. She said that she and Hannah would watch them.

"And how hast thou been?" Peregrine asked Mary when the three of them were alone, her tone grave.

"As well as can be expected."

"My father-in-law is deeply saddened by this separation," Jonathan told her. "It sounds as if thou art, too."

"Is that why thou hast come to see me?"

Jonathan took a long swallow of the beer. "Yes, but also to share with thee the new blessing that has begun to grow inside Peregrine. And, of course, Thomas sends his greetings, Mary."

"He is well, I trust."

"Other than lonely without thee? I suppose," Jonathan told her. Then: "A scrivener came to see him. Fellow named Hull."

"Yes, Benjamin Hull. My family asked for his assistance."

"He came to see us, too," Jonathan continued. "Not a likable fellow. Expects me to make much of my noticing a bruise or two on thy face."

"He was doing his job. Some sorts of toil are more agreeable than others."

"His questions offended me greatly. They offended thee, too, did they not?" he asked his wife.

She nodded, one hand resting protectively on her belly. Her eyes were moving along the walls, over the map of Boston and then the sideboard with the tankards and cutlery.

"I would ask thee to forgive Benjamin," Mary said, "but it is I who caused the offense. And I am not sorry that my scrivener takes his work seriously."

Jonathan looked at Peregrine and then at Mary. He was always so good-natured; Mary did not enjoy seeing him exasperated, his discomfort so apparent. "My father-in-law asked me to inquire plainly: now that thou hast had some time to ponder thy plan and the Court of Assistants is soon to convene, hast thy thinking changed?"

"No. It has not."

"Thou hast been living at thy childhood home," he said. Then he quoted scripture: "When I was a child, I spake as a child."

"But when I became a man, I put away childish things," Mary said, finishing the verse. "I was a child back in England. Not here. I put away my childish things when I boarded the ship with my parents and we sailed to Boston. Returning to my father's house has not meant that I have climbed once more into my childhood gown with its leading strings."

"I miss thee, Mary. We all do," said Peregrine, changing their tack.

"I miss thee, Peregrine. I miss thee, Jonathan," said Mary, and she felt a strange eddy in the room when she said her son-in-law's name. She saw Peregrine was watching her, her head tilted ever so slightly. Did the woman suspect that Mary had unclean thoughts about her husband? For a second, Mary feared that she had revealed something in her voice just now—or over time, over all the meals and moments they had shared—but that wasn't possible. It just . . . wasn't.

"But dost thou not miss Thomas? Dost thou not miss the natural order of living with a man?" Jonathan asked, and there was a peculiarly academic cadence to the inquiries. It was reminiscent of the voice of a pastor while preaching, asking questions with obvious answers.

And so Mary reached for her tankard with her good hand and took a sip, stalling. The truth was, she did not miss Thomas Deerfield in the slightest. But she couldn't say such a thing in the presence of the man's daughter. And yet the woman had to know how she felt. It didn't seem likely, but Mary considered the idea that Jonathan was setting a snare for her, encouraging her to say something blasphemous before him and Peregrine. But there was also the opposite possibility: given both a daughter's invariable love for her father and the protectiveness she might be feeling right now toward her own marriage, was Jonathan hoping that Mary would express remorse? It was ridiculous for Peregrine to experience even a waft of wariness: Mary posed no threat to her. Yes, she may have had inappropriate thoughts about Jonathan, but he was a man who was handsome and funny and kind. Any woman might. But she had no designs on him or interest in him in any fashion that was unnatural, depraved, or (yes) sinful.

The fact was, to admit before Thomas Deerfield's daughter that she missed her father not at all would be hurtful. And yet Mary knew that what loomed at the Court of Assistants was going to be far worse. Finally, she put her beer back on the table and settled upon a question of her own: "Peregrine, thou art his daughter and thou lived with him for most of thy life. Thou witnessed his marriage with thy mother. What was his attitude toward her?"

"Toward my mother?"

"Yes. Toward Anne."

Peregrine rested her second hand atop her belly and looked away. It was as if she feared Mary's gaze alone could curdle the child growing inside her. "She was his helpmeet," Peregrine murmured. "He was her husband."

Mary sat up straight. She had expected a more enthusiastic defense of Thomas and Anne's relationship. "Did he love her?"

"In his fashion."

"In his fashion?"

Jonathan looked back and forth between the women, and Mary could see that he was surprised, too. "Peregrine?" he asked.

"He loved her," she said, backtracking, "as he loves thee, Mary."

"Was he ever harsh with thy mother? Prithee, Peregrine, I beg for honesty."

Once again, Peregrine's stare wavered, and her eyes wandered around the room, resting this time on the Dobson painting of Mary's grandfather. Then she stared into the fire in the hearth and replied, "No."

"No?" Mary pressed. "Not once was he quick to anger?"

"Only in love."

Sometimes when Thomas disciplined Mary (his word, not hers), he suggested it was because he was saving her. She recalled his speech before he tried to impale her hand on the table with the Devil's tines: **Thou hast a soul that is much imperiled by pride. Thou believest too much in thine intellect as a woman.** Perhaps Thomas treated his first wife similarly. "He was quick to anger in love?" she asked. "Was Anne Drury but a child to him in need of scolding?"

"The book of Revelation does not specify children in the third chapter," Peregrine said.

"I know the verse: 'As many as I love, I rebuke and chasten.' But is that not the prerogative of parents and the Lord?"

"And of husbands," Jonathan corrected Mary.

"Yes, certainly. And how did he discipline thy mother, Peregrine? With words or the rod? With education or the back of his hand?"

Jonathan reached over and rested his fingers gently on Mary's shoulder. "Prithee, now. We did not come here to challenge thee. We did not come here to unleash hard feelings."

She looked at his long, slender fingers near her collarbone, and when she did, he removed them. But the weight lingered. Her mouth felt dry and she wanted another sip of beer, but she didn't dare move. Peregrine's eyes were unblinking as she watched her husband and Mary. The small room went quiet.

"No. I understand that," Mary said carefully, breaking the silence because she had to. She quite literally had to. She thought of the trial—a literal one, but also a cross—that awaited her next week, and it was paramount that she learn what she could while she had this chance. "But, Peregrine, thou hast avoided my question. Were thy father's words, even if spoken in love, ever too harsh for a man to speak to his wife?"

"I can tell thee, Mary, that never once did I see him strike her."

Surely at least once, Thomas's anger—unreasonable and fueled by too much hard cider or beer—had flared up when Peregrine had been a child. After all, how many times could Mary recall him striking her or hurling her into bricks or coat pegs? Thomas had lived with Anne Drury considerably longer. Still, it would not help to challenge Peregrine directly or accuse her of a falsehood. It was possible that just as Thomas shielded the worst of his temper from Catherine, he had managed to hide it from his daughter. And so Mary said simply, "But that does not mean it never happened."

"I never saw such a thing, and our servants never saw such a thing," she replied.

Jonathan shook his head. "Mary, he shot the horse that broke his wife's neck. He shot it. He loved Anne. He was devastated when she died."

"I understand," she said.

"And remember," he continued, "the house in which Peregrine grew up was no castle. She would have known." He seemed increasingly troubled with the direction the conversation was taking and began to fiddle with the fastener of his breeches along his right knee. The women said nothing. He looked up at them and asked, "Mary, dost thou realize what thou art risking? Thou art challenging all that we are trying to build here. Thou art defying God's natural order and risking the dis-approbation of the Lord."

"I have heard now twice what thou hast said about a natural order. But a woman is not a serpent to be crushed under her husband's foot," she answered. She hoped her tone had not gone shrill. "No, I cannot go back," she said more softly. "I cannot."

"Dost thou know what Catherine will say?" Peregrine asked, and Mary understood that her daughter-in-law had hoped not to bring this up. This was their last resort.

"I have my suspicions," she answered. "There is no truth to her wild and unschooled accusations."

"They may be wild," said Jonathan, "but the world is awash in wildness. It is why we have both Bibles and sentinels." He took a breath, wanting desperately to broker peace. "Prithee, Mary, heed our warning. Thomas wants thee back, as do we. We are a family."

Peregrine put her hand protectively on her husband's, and the meaning was not lost on Mary. **We want thee back,** that small gesture said, **but make no mistake: this man is mine.**

"And Jonathan?" Mary replied. "I hope with all my heart that the three of us and thy girls—and the babe in thy womb, Peregrine—can remain family. Or, at least, on friendly terms. But I will appear before the Court of Assistants, and when it is my turn to speak, I will tell my story."

"Thou art resolved," said Jonathan, wistful and resigned.

"I am."

For a moment they sat in silence, and Mary heard the great squawks of seagulls outside. Then the other woman stood, pressing her palms onto the table, and her husband rose with her. He said he would retrieve the children.

"Fare thee well," Peregrine said to Mary when they were alone, her tone unreadable.

"Pray, remember me," she said in response.

Peregrine met her eyes. "I will," she said. "I do." Then she followed her husband into the yard for their daughters.

⁂

The Reverend John Norton was fifty-six years old, exactly one year older than Mary's father and three years her mother's senior. But he seemed considerably older than that. He wasn't frail, not at all. But his presence was so august. He stood six feet tall, even now, and his beard was an immaculate dapple gray. He'd been in the colony since 1635, but he had traveled to and from England earlier that year with Governor Bradstreet to address King Charles II after the Restoration and confirm the king's commitment to the colony's charter. He was an unwavering disciplinarian, eager to see the Quakers punished for their madness and the sinners among his own congregation suitably chastised.

Monday, the day after the Sabbath, Mary's parents brought her to see him. It was neither her choice nor her parents'. The reverend had summoned them. James and Priscilla Burden were well acquainted with the leader of the First Church. James reassured his daughter that Thomas would not be present; the minister had made it clear that this might be a prequel to mediation, but at this point he wanted merely to understand the specifics of the marital crisis.

"I am tired of explaining to everyone why I am doing this," Mary had seethed when her father had told her that the reverend insisted on seeing them. "By the time I address the Court of Assistants, the tale will be but stale pottage, even to me." Nevertheless, she knew the power of the minister and so she had acquiesced.

Now, after she told the minister of the times that Thomas had struck her and the story of the fork, after she had told him that he often abused her cruelly with words, she sat back in the upholstered chair in the study in the man's house. It was among the most sumptuous and comfortable chairs she had ever seen here in Boston, the fabric a French paragon and the pattern blue irises. Her parents were seated in the cane-back chairs her father and the minister had brought into the study from the dining room. John Norton leaned across the desk and said, "I am sorry for all thou hast endured, Mary."

"I thank thee."

"No need. I do not begrudge thee for considering such an extreme step."

Mary watched her father's reaction. Was he relieved? Did it seem to him, too, that this most powerful reverend was going to support her petition for divorce? But then John Norton continued, "Thomas denies ever hitting thee."

"So, he adds a lie to his ledger," she said.

"Perhaps. But he speaks highly of thee. He speaks with appropriate reverence. He claims not to understand thy womanly venom."

"I have no venom, womanly or otherwise. I am no serpent and have not sought association with serpents—neither real ones nor ones clad in linsey-woolsey."

The reverend's gaze grew a little cold. She had not been impudent, but she wasn't acquiescing, either. "If we are to be role models, we must exhibit our justification," he said. "The Lord scowls at impertinence. Let us not forget the price of rebellion."

"I am not rebelling against the Lord. I am seeking only to divorce myself from my husband." From the corner of her eye she saw that her mother appeared anxious.

"The scrivener Benjamin Hull has come to me

and requested I appear at the hearing," said the reverend.

"What has he asked of thee?" her father inquired.

"He believes it would be beneficial to thy daughter if I shared the Church's opinion on whether a husband may strike his wife."

"I am grateful," James said.

"I have not yet decided whether I will appear in person. I may merely give testimony he can write down and present to the magistrates." Then the reverend turned his attention back upon Mary. "I have heard tell of this three-tined fork. There has been much discussion of thine opinions of its use."

" 'Tis just a utensil, John," her father said, before she could respond.

"It seems needless to use a three-tined utensil when a two-tined one has always been sufficient," the reverend observed.

"For carving, yes," James said.

Mary closed her eyes, frustrated at the turn this conversation was taking. But she opened them when she heard the reverend saying, "I've always found a knife and a spoon sufficient, but my sense is that if the Devil tries to seduce one, He will find better means than a fork."

"I agree," said her father. "If thou wouldst like to try one—"

"No. But I thank thee, James."

"For Thomas, it was but a weapon," Mary reminded them. She felt it was important to reiterate that the issue was how her husband had attacked her with the fork—how that had been the last and final blow she would endure. Could they not feel her longing, as palpable as the sun on one's face in July, to be free of him? "It was just a few minutes ago that I recounted for thee how he stabbed me with it."

"I understand, Mary. I do," insisted Norton. "Now, it is not common knowledge, but I am sure thy father knows this: I opposed the execution of Ann Hibbens six years ago."

"I do recall that," her father agreed. Her mother's face had grown ashen. Ann Hibbens had been hanged as a witch in Boston in 1656, and neither her wealth nor the fact that she was the sister-in-law of a former governor of the colony had spared her. John Endicott himself had handed down the sentence. The idea that Ann Hibbens was even a specter in their conversation was chilling: Mary's petition was about divorce, and yet somehow it kept blowing like a dead leaf back toward Satan.

"I would have preferred excommunication," he continued. "But I am sure thou hast heard the news from Hartford, of the handmaidens the Devil has mustered this year."

"Yes, we have heard," James told the minister.

"If thou dost insist on this appearance before

the Court of Assistants, Mary, there will be aspersions upon thy character. There may even be accusations," the reverend said.

"There will also be justice," she added.

"Perhaps. Perhaps not. We are mortals, and try as we might, we see through a glass darkly. Among the people I expect will be summoned to speak against thee are thine indentured girl, Catherine; Goody Howland; and Dr. Pickering. There may be others."

"But I have done nothing! Why would Goody—"

Her father put his hand on her arm, silencing her with his grip. "This is sage counsel, John. I thank thee for thy candor."

"Mary, I have urged thee to reconsider, and I understand thou wilt not. That is a choice. I understand thou hast no interest in mediation. That is a choice, too, and I will not enlist the elders. But if thou were to take but two small bits of advice from me, it would be these."

She waited, cross.

"First," said the reverend, "give Goody Howland and Catherine Stileman a wide berth between now and thine appearance before the court."

"And the second?" she asked.

"Trust thy father and me. I do not want another Ann Hibbens on my ledger—and I do not want to see the madness in Hartford affect us here, too."

And she knew. At least she thought she knew.

She knew because she witnessed the way her parents and the Reverend John Norton were glancing sidelong at each other, conspiratorial eddies drifting among them. She could see in their eyes how, if she weren't careful, there was a possible fate looming before her that was far worse than a life with Thomas Deerfield.

I was shocked deeply by what I saw. I speak as a witness, not a gossip.

—The Testimony of Abigail Gathers, from the Records and Files of the Court of Assistants, Boston, Massachusetts, 1662, Volume III

Twelve

Benjamin Hull stopped by the home of James Burden to inform Mary that her petition was going to be heard by the Court of Assistants later that week, most likely on Thursday. Based on the other items on the docket, he expected they would get to her soon after dinner. She did not ask who the other petitioners were, because she feared knowing would only make her more restless. But she was, Hull said, the only divorce. Of course.

After the scrivener had left, she went to her room and pulled the small chair to the window. There by the afternoon light she wrote in her diary, her ink on the sill and her ledger in her lap. She wrote not of the pending trial, nor of her fears about the accusations that would be leveled at her with the aim of a fowler's musket. She did not write about the handsome Indian she had seen trading in the marketplace, or the way the spark and flame at the blacksmith's had struck her as more beautiful that morning than a sunset. She wrote instead of a moment when she had been a little girl in England and she had rolled over and over down the hill on the estate where her brother Giles now kept his sheep. She had been seven that summer, and the air had been sticky but she hadn't minded. She'd been alone at first, but then the younger of her two older siblings, Charles, had joined her, and they had pretended they were logs rolling down a ravine, and when they'd stood at the bottom of the hill, the world spun and their legs wouldn't quite work and they'd pretended that they had imbibed too long at the tavern. They slurred their words. They fell down with great histrionics. But then they would claw their way to their feet, ascend the hill, and do it all again.

She read what she had written. She'd always assumed that someday she would come to the top of a hill and spy her daughter—and in her mind she had auburn hair beneath her bonnet, and eyes that were playful and round—and see the child rolling in precisely that fashion down the meadow. But no. No. It seemed that was not meant to be.

She recalled how back in England grown-ups played cards. Even her parents. She missed their laughter when they played.

She missed Christmas.

She closed her eyes because the reality that card playing and Christmas should come to her now could only bode ill. She obeyed the scriptures as best she could. But it seemed that her best was not good enough. Perhaps she was frivolous when viewed in the kindest light and wicked when viewed in the worst. She opened her eyes and turned toward the bed. She knew what she had done there just last night when she was alone in the dark, her mind fixated on a man named Henry Simmons who was not her husband.

At one point she looked up from the window and saw a tremendous flock of geese flying south, awed by the size of the V. Winter was coming. The cold and the ice and the snow.

She told herself that there would be justice when she shared her story with the Court of Assistants and that she should be grateful that she lived here in Boston, where divorce was even a possibility. But she remembered the look that had passed between her parents and Reverend Norton and feared that she was being naive.

She scraped a smudge off one of the diamond-shaped panes in the window. Hell was awash in flame. This Mary knew. And God would not justify the wicked. This she knew, too.

But this frigid world of New England? It was no Heaven, either.

       ≈ ⊱

As Mary and her parents and the servant girls were finishing supper that night, they heard the sound of a horse whinnying in their yard. Hannah went to the door, and there stood Thomas Deerfield, his hat in his hands, his horse roped to the post at the edge of the dooryard.

"Hannah," he said.

Mary and her mother did not rise, but her father stood.

"What brings thee here, Thomas?" James Burden asked.

"I hoped to speak to thy daughter one last time. I remain open to mediation, even if it means the intrusion of the elders into my life. I am still praying there is a way to stop this madness before it reaches the Town House."

"There is none," her father said, and Mary glanced awkwardly at her parents and at Abigail and Hannah. They were all looking at Thomas and at each other. It was as if she were invisible.

"Thomas, if thou wishest to speak to me, thou mayest," she said, standing. "What good it will achieve is beyond my ken, but I will hear thee out."

"I thank thee," he said.

"Mary, thou dost not have to see him," her father said.

"I do," she told him. "I do."

"May we speak alone?" Thomas asked, and he sounded shy, as if he were a suitor—more a boy than a man closer to her father's age than to hers.

"Yes," she said, and she took her cloak from the peg near the fire. "Let us speak outside," she told him, and she nodded to her parents, hoping to convey to them that she was fine and this conversation did not trouble her. Then she pulled the front door shut behind her, and so they were alone in a night that would have been wholly dark were it not for the light from the candles and the fire radiating out from the windows.

For a long moment, he just looked at her. She could see his breath, and she smelled the beer he had drunk at supper or afterward at a tavern. But his countenance did not suggest he was drink-drunk. Finally, he spoke: "I miss thee, Mary."

"That is gratifying," she said. "But our love is now but apples that fell and were never harvested."

"I disagree. There is no rot in my heart. The fruit there is still as fresh as when I first cast eyes on thee."

She held up the back of her left hand, which though healing still sent a message in her mind more powerful than words. Then with her finger she touched the spots on her face where he had hit her in the course of their marriage. "To thee? My face was but a fruit thou couldst bruise."

"I sinned, yes," he admitted, and she detected a trace of sorrow in his eyes. "But no more. I make thee a vow: if thou returnest, I will never again hurt thee. Never."

"Thou hast made that promise before."

"But never before had I been given a taste of the bitterness of actually losing thee."

She wondered what precisely he missed. His

access to her body when the spirit so moved him? Her work as a helpmeet and wife? The fact she kept the pillowbeers clean? Yes, he had Catherine, but surely he was having to work harder around the house and with the animals than ever before. He would have to acquire a second servant. Or, perhaps, this was but vanity and shame, and he feared the public ramifications of divorce: the idea of failure. "What dost thou miss the most?"

He looked up at the sky, the stars and the moon hidden tonight behind clouds. "Is this to be an interrogation?"

"I asked but one question."

"And I have come to thee humbled and chastened. Is that not enough?"

"I do not crave thy praise; once I craved thy love. But thou seemest to believe that to be humbled is sufficient foundation for a marriage."

"What dost thou want, Mary? I have made thee a vow."

"What dost thou want, Thomas?" Mary asked in response. "Thou seemest unable to offer me one thing that thou hast missed while I have retreated to my parents."

"I have not missed thy disobedience."

"I was an obedient wife."

"Fine. I miss thine obedience."

"And that is but sand. Build thy house on rock."

"Obedience is more than sand. If thou art going

to throw scripture at me, don't heave the words as if thou were . . ."

"As if I were what? As if I were but a woman with white meat for a brain?"

He folded his arms across his chest and gazed down at his boots. "There are moments when thy mind vexes me. It is not that thou art slow, but rather that thou dost not understand thy need to heel."

"My knees exist but to bend?"

"It pained me when I hurt thee. Thou mayest not believe that, but it is true. I know what our Lord God wants from us. I have no desire to cause thee discomfort, but some rebukes will sting more than others. I would rather thou felt pain that will pass in this world than agony that will be ceaseless in the next."

"I am not sure that either of us can be so presumptuous as to read the mind of God."

He exhaled loudly and long. Already he was growing frustrated. "That is precisely what I mean."

"So, my brain is cheese because I think," she said. "Is that thy logic?"

"Man is an imperfect vessel, Mary. I am but a man."

"And I am an imperfect woman, and—"

"Yes," he agreed, cutting her off, "thou art. And when I have disciplined thee, it has always been because I fear for thy soul. I have said it before and

I will say it again: I tremble mightily before our Lord, and I am not at all sure that thou sharest my fears."

Inside she was enraged by his hypocrisy, by the brazenness of either his lying or his monumental self-delusion, but she was able to restrain herself. She had heard from him before this justification for his cruelty. "Perhaps our imperfections together make but mist at best and anger and unhappiness at worst," she suggested.

"Well, they certainly did not make a child."

She nodded at the barb. He had spoken reflexively, without thinking. People did not change. "I will see thee at the Town House, Thomas."

He took her arm and his grip was tight. "If thou believest that one-third of my mill and my house will ever be thine, thou art encumbered by the falsest of hopes."

"My recompense will be a future free of thee: a future that does not hold for me fear and a life in which my husband views me as but an animal he can beat at will."

"I never beat thee at will. And I told thee: I never wanted to hurt thee. Thou wouldst give me no choice."

Did he believe that? She couldn't decide. But she also didn't care. She pulled free of him and rested her fingers on the handle to the door. He was as misguided as he was violent. She regretted snapping back at him because one could never win an argument with a person so fundamentally un-reasonable. She recalled what Jesus had taught the multitudes on the mountain. "Let us not speak thusly to each other," she said quietly. "I believe thou loved me once; once I loved thee. Thou hast smited me on the right cheek; I give thee my left."

He smiled, but it was mean and foreboding. "And if any man will sue thee at the law, and take away thy coat," he began, quoting the verse that fol-lowed that passage, "let him have thy cloak also." He pulled off his deep green cloak and threw it on the ground at her feet. "Take it, Mary. But I assure thee as the sun will rise: that is all thou wilt ever get from me." Then he walked to the post where he had hitched his horse, climbed into the saddle, and rode with uncharacteristic speed down the street.

᪣ ᪥

The next day there was a letter from her brother Charles. It had arrived the day before on a massive, one-hundred-ton brigantine called the **Hopeful Mary,** and Priscilla Burden thought it a lovely sign that there was a letter from home on a ship of that name. And the news indeed was all good: no sickness, another child born healthy—this one a daughter—and the right amount of rain and sun. James Burden expressed his thanks to the Lord in his prayer before dinner that afternoon. Then he left for the North End, not his warehouse in the harbor, and when Mary asked her mother where he was going, she said he had a brief errand, but then would be back in his office near the docks. Mary pressed her for details, but her mother said she didn't have any.

After lunch she considered walking to the wharf. Her father had said that the **Hopeful Mary** would soon return to London, and she wanted to see it before it departed, if only because of the vessel's name. Her father was also excited because any day now a sloop was due from Barbados that would be heavy with sugar and salt and dyes. But Mary was aware in her heart that if she went to the docks, it would also be, at least in part, to see Henry Simmons, and that was a temptation she was resolved to avoid. So instead she walked west toward Watch Hill, though just as she was planning to avoid Henry, she would be sure and steer clear of the North End and her husband's gristmill as well.

❧ ❧

At one point, Mary stood on the top of the prominence and gazed out beyond the city. In one direction there was still forest extending into the distance, a world of animals and Indians and the excommunicated. In others, there was the land they had cleared and the farms where the last of the corn had been harvested earlier that autumn, and she rather doubted that she had anywhere near the bravery of the women and men who lived and worked there. She knew of two widows who lived alone on their small plots, far from family and neighbors and help. Was it any wonder that women like them turned to the Devil for assistance?

She decided she should walk to this section of the city more often. It was different from the marketplace and the harbor: it was quieter. There were birds beyond seagulls. When she started back, she walked briskly past the street where Thomas had his mill.

⊰ ⊱

She was surprised when she got home to find that the Devil had brought His temptations here: there, chatting amiably with Abigail as she prepared supper, was Henry Simmons. His doublet was green today, his dark hair combed. He was standing beside the kitchen table. When she entered, he helped her with her cloak, a gesture that was chivalrous but still, it seemed to Mary, inappropriately intimate.

"Where is my mother?" she asked Abigail.

"The apothecary, ma'am."

"And what brings thee here, Henry Simmons?"

He pointed at a bottle on the table. "A gift of rum from my uncle for his friends, the Burdens—and, of course, for their daughter."

"I thank thee."

"All thanks are due only to my Uncle Valentine. I was merely the messenger."

"Thou dost much for him."

"And most of it no more demanding than breaking an egg."

At this Abigail looked up from the cheese and corn flour in the bowl on the table before her and smiled. "I have seen many a man break an egg rather badly," she said.

"I break them rather well."

"I have my doubts," said Abigail. "I suspect thy strength resides in a calling outside the kitchen."

"Oh, I am unsure precisely what my calling is meant to be."

"Not egg breaker," the servant girl said, and while a small part of Mary was jealous at the way Abigail was flirting with Henry, mostly she was interested. She appreciated the girl's audacity; she was titillated by the exchange.

"Perhaps that is precisely why I came to Boston. The colony is in dire need of men capable of making a most dire mess in the kitchen."

The girl rolled her eyes and then wiped her hands on her apron and said, "I need a great many eggs right now for these fritters. Rest thy hands and when I return thou canst show me thy talents." Then she left for the back of the house to retrieve the eggs from the family's chickens.

"Is she always so delightfully forward?" Henry asked Mary when she was gone.

"No. Thou dost bring out the worst in all of us, Henry," she told him, but her tone was playful, not scolding.

"Now that is a noble calling. That is a reason for me to have journeyed all the way here."

"Oh, the Devil may come with a handsome face, but it takes more encouragement than that to lead one astray."

"I have a handsome face? 'Tis good to know."

"Thou knowest it too well."

"There it is again: that particularly deadly sin of pride. I succumb to it often. It will be the death of me yet."

"Ah, but who among us will be the agent?"

"It won't be thee," he said, and he went to her. He stood so close that she could feel his breath on her face.

"And why is that?"

He looked at her intently. "Because, I think, we are much alike."

"In what fashion? We know each other but little."

"A falcon knows its kin at a very great distance."

"And its prey."

He smiled. "Exactly. I am in thy talons." Then he leaned in closer still, and she felt him taking her right hand in his. "And, Mary, never lose sight of this: thou art far more comely than I am handsome. 'Tis a fact as unassailable as the waves in the harbor and the way the leaves here grow red before falling." She realized that he was about to kiss her, and the idea stopped her short. But then without thinking, her body moving with a will of its own, all want and need, she stood on her toes and opened her lips to his.

And it was then, that moment, she heard the bowl fall and the eggs break, and there stood Abigail with her hand on her mouth.

We see the Devil's work in the temptations He dangles before us all, and most clearly in the inducements He offers the nulliparous—those persuasions He will offer the barren.

—The Testimony of Reverend John Norton, from the Records and Files of the Court of Assistants, Boston, Massachusetts, 1662, Volume III

Thirteen

On the day her divorce petition was to be heard, Mary ate little for breakfast. At dinnertime, just before noon, at her mother's insistence she nibbled a piece of sourdough bread, picked at a turnip, and tore some meat from a turkey leg. Abigail and Hannah said almost nothing to her, but they had said little since Abigail had seen her mistress on her toes leaning into Henry Simmons, her hand enmeshed in his. Mary now lived under the same roof with Abigail and she had known the girl since she had arrived in the colony, but it was as if rather suddenly they had become strangers. Mary understood Abigail's predicament: the girl's testimony could enrage her employers, but lying came with far greater consequences, because they were eternal. Mary had confessed to her parents precisely what she had done with Henry and what Abigail had seen, and Mary's father had pressed the girl on what she might say. "I hope, Abigail," he had said with Mary present, "thou wilt never forget the injuries that Thomas Deerfield has inflicted upon my daughter. Look at her hand. Recall what it looked like when she returned to us. There already will be allegations about her that may dog her forever. Weigh earnestly in thy mind the smallness of what thou might have seen with the greatness of the harm that will befall my daughter's reputation if this petition became a tale of something other than the basic facts of her husband's meanness."

"I will remember that, sir," she said, but Mary had felt more embarrassed than relieved. She knew what she had done. She knew how she had been tempted and how that moment of weakness might cost her. Her father had also gone to see Henry Simmons. He would not share with her specifically what he had said to the younger man, but he had reassured her that if this trial turned upon adultery, Henry was prepared to shoulder the blame and take the lashing. Her father had reminded her that Abigail had only seen them kiss and then demanded from his daughter confirmation that, indeed, they had never done more than kiss. Adultery, after all, was a capital offense.

Still, she knew what she felt toward Henry. This was allure. This was temptation. She felt a giddiness around Henry that she had never felt around Thomas. For weeks now she had thought of him during the day, and she had thought of him when she was alone in her bedstead at night.

Mary and her parents were aware that her husband had retained a lawyer and that the lawyer had spoken yesterday to both of the Burdens' servant girls. The attorney, among the few in the colony, was a pudgy fellow with black-and-white caterpillars for eyebrows named Philip Bristol. He was universally detested, principally because of his profession, though no one doubted his intellect. But it was one thing to retain a scrivener such as Benjamin Hull; it was quite another to ask a lawyer to plead one's case before the court. That was unseemly. Still, among the magistrates were men who had received legal training back in England, and so it was no longer unheard of to see a lawyer at the Town House.

The attorney told the servant girls that he wanted to understand Mary's actions the morning she had come to her parents' home; Abigail had assured Mary's father that he hadn't inquired about Henry Simmons—Why would he? she had asked James Burden—but of the two servants, so far only Abigail's presence had been requested at the Town House for the trial. This was ominous, it seemed, a bad augur of what might be part of her testimony.

Mary had thought often that week on her conversations with Thomas, trying to parse his motives for investing such effort in preserving their marriage. Was it pride? The risk of losing one-third of his estate? Or did he actually love her? She didn't know the answer, but she presumed the third of the possibilities was the least likely. After all, in his eyes, she was either a foolish wench or a prideful sinner; in either case, she was in dire need of tute-lage in the form of barbarism and beatings.

She had spent part of the day before the hearing with Benjamin Hull and her mother at this very table in her parents' house, reviewing the testimonies that Hull had meticulously written down, but Mary couldn't see how anything anyone had said would help all that much. At one point she had grown so ill—so appalled at Thomas Deerfield's untarnished reputation and Catherine Stileman's obsession with witchcraft and forks—that she had gone outside into the garden and there, behind the small coop with their chickens, vomited. When she went to wipe her mouth on her apron, she had looked at the wound that was going to forever mar her left hand. The gooseneck on a teakettle? Who could possibly believe that was the cause? One could almost see the mark of the three tines.

But only almost.

She presumed the bone was mending, but still it hurt and she did as many of her chores as she could with only her right hand.

When she went back inside, her mother asked her if she was feeling poorly because of anxiety or whether she was ill. She replied that she was fine. Had she not menstruated since leaving Thomas, the notion might have crossed her mind that she was pregnant. But she wasn't pregnant, this she knew.

Just as she knew she never would be.

The scrivener said that he had brought to the Town House some of the testimonies he had recorded, but there were others that he had not presented to the magistrates to read. They weren't useless, he had explained; they just weren't helpful. But Hull said he might spend that afternoon rounding up a few additional people to appear at the Town House the next day to provide oral accounts of their history with Thomas and Mary and what they may (or may not) have witnessed.

"Tell me something," Mary had said to the scrivener that Wednesday.

He had sat back in his chair and waited. Her mother had, too.

"When the aspersions upon my character are complete and I am perceived as a sinner unworthy of angels . . ."

"Go on," said Hull, but her mother's face was growing alarmed, more worried even than when Mary had risen to go outside a moment earlier.

"When it is clear to the magistrates that I am disobedient and prideful and drawn to the most sinful pleasures; that I am, perhaps, already a handmaiden of Satan—"

"Cease such talk," her mother commanded. "No one shall ever believe such a thing."

"Oh, Mother, they will. They will. Thou hast seen what Benjamin has written. We all know what Catherine will say and what Abigail saw."

The scrivener looked back and forth between the women. "Prithee, Mary, continue."

"What is likely to be my future? Thou hast spent many a day at the Town House. Thou hast watched the magistrates rule and seen the sinners fined and whipped and sent to the stocks. Have I any chance at all?"

"I cannot presume to foretell the future," he said, and he glanced at her mother. "But a man may not strike his wife. The law is clear. I most definitely do not see the stocks in thy future."

"The hanging platform, perhaps?" she asked, willfully ignoring his optimism.

Her mother took her hand and said, "Mary, thou art being silly. Thou hast no such blackness in thy soul that anyone tomorrow will actually believe Catherine Stileman's nonsense. Besides: it was thine own father who imported the forks."

"And people will say that it was I who buried them."

"But thou didst not," said Priscilla Burden.

"I did not the first time."

"Yes. The first time," the scrivener repeated, almost a murmur.

"We do not know whether it was man or woman or demon who first pressed the tines into the earth—or the pestle. I just know that it was not me," Mary continued.

Benjamin dipped his quill and wrote himself a

short note. Then he said, "Let us not stew upon these details, Mary. As thy mother said: thou hast nothing to fear in that regard."

And once again the eyes of the older adults met for the briefest of seconds, sharing the sort of conspiratorial secret that she had detected in the exchanges her parents had had with magistrate Richard Wilder and Reverend John Norton. She was unsure whether she found comfort or fear in whatever machinations were in the minds of these elder saints.

＊ ＊

There were the county courts in Cambridge, Boston, Salem, Springfield, Ipswich, and York. They were the inferior courts and weighed in on civil disputes when the stakes were smaller than ten pounds. But they also heard the petty criminal offenses: those in which a guilty verdict would not lead to banishment, the severing of a limb with an ax or a knife, or death by hanging. They were known for disciplining the idle, punishing those whose apparel was deemed too ornate, and fining anyone who bought and sold from the savages without proper license.

Above them was the colony's Court of Assistants. It was composed of the governor, the deputy governor, and twelve elected assistants, but rarely were all fourteen magistrates in attendance together for a full session. They were busy men, and only a quorum of seven was required to render a verdict on the civil petitions—such as Mary Deerfield's request to divorce her husband—or the criminal accusations brought before them. They listened, they asked questions, and sometimes they deliberated in private. Then they voted and the majority ruled.

Today there were eleven magistrates present, including the Burdens' friend Richard Wilder, when Mary and her parents and Benjamin Hull arrived on the second floor of the Town House. Governor John Endicott was in attendance on the bench, too. He was nearing seventy-five and struck Mary as frail as he limped toward the front of the great room. There was a large crowd of petitioners and witnesses milling about, easily thirty or thirty-five people, and she saw Thomas. He was standing against a wall with his hands clasped before him, his attorney beside him. She nodded at Thomas, bowing deferentially, and then cursed herself inside for her reflexive subservience. His eyes looked strangely soft, his countenance kind. She presumed this was a strategy.

The other magistrates were seated behind a long, polished oak bar, their benches imposing and high, and they were in their black judicial robes. Mary scanned the room to see who else she knew in the throng, but she saw no one she recognized. This caused her no relief, however, because she knew that her parents' servant girl Abigail had been summoned, and Goody Howland was planning to speak as well. They—all those who would be testifying—were likely milling about the marketplace or the Town House and would appear when requested.

"They have no more than three or four petitions to hear before thine, Mary," Hull told her. "None are especially complicated and I expect they will be disposed of quickly. But one never knows. Sometimes even the most obvious decisions can be rendered with a fastidiousness that borders on the pedantic." She nodded but said nothing. Soon she would speak on her behalf. She had not risked the wrath of the magistrates by employing a lawyer; Thomas had chosen the opposite tack, but she presumed he himself would still have to answer questions. She was nervous, but her anxiety was not debilitating. She had rehearsed carefully over the previous week, working in much the same way that she had as a girl back in England, when she had been given an assignment by her tutor. Her father had ensured that she had a proper education, bringing in teachers in language and music. Other girls were also given lessons in dance and grace, even some of the girls among those families who were planning eventually on emigrating to New England. After all, the Bible had no prohibitions on dancing. She remembered being jealous of those girls, but her father had stood fast in his decision: dancing could lead to lasciviousness. Mary had taken her preparation for today far more seriously, however, working with a ferocity of purpose that she had never felt as a child.

Her mind was focusing on what she would say and how she would respond to the questions of the magistrates when a constable who worked for the Court of Assistants rapped on the wooden floor with a pike and asked for quiet. The crowd went silent and turned as one toward the magistrates. The governor had just finished slipping his arms into the sleeves of his robe.

Then the constable announced that there were no petitions to be heard this afternoon that warranted the impaneling of a jury, but there would be tomorrow. He announced that the first petition involved the collision of two shallops in the harbor, and the broken leg incurred by a fellow named Knight. The fisherman lost his boat, too, the craft sinking unceremoniously to the bottom of the harbor. Witnesses said the defendant, Lewis Farrington, whose boat was damaged but did not sink, had been drunk and piloting the craft recklessly. For a time, Mary watched the back-and-forth with interest; neither Knight nor Farrington had retained a lawyer, but Knight had used a scrivener and, though hobbled by crutches, was bringing forth sheaths of paper: the testimonies the scrivener had taken, including the sailors who had fished the poor man from the water. But the outcome of the case seemed so clear that Mary grew bored. In the end, it was just as she had predicted: Farrington was guilty. He had to pay Knight the cost of building a replacement shallop, plus twenty pounds; in addition, he was fined five more pounds for drunkenness and had to spend the day after next in the stocks.

He was followed by an Indian who was sentenced to thirty lashes for breaking into a house and accidentally overturning a cider barrel while drink-drunk. In this case, the verdict—the whole process—left her strangely unmoored. The Indian was no more than sixteen or seventeen years old, and it was unclear to her how much English he spoke and how much he understood. He had been dressed in pants and a shirt much too big for his slender frame. His eyes were dark, and she could see the fear in them. No one spoke in his defense. The owner of the cider barrel, a handsome man with golden hair, expressed his indignation that he was not to be paid treble the cost of the barrel of cider, but Wilder sat back and asked the petitioner precisely how he expected the savage to pay him a single penny. When the Indian was led away, Mary's heart broke a little for the young man. He was all alone and soon to be whipped only because he was unschooled in the ways of the Lord.

Finally, there was an appeal from the county court in Ipswich, something about a fence obstructing a right of way. The matter was dull, and Mary whispered to Benjamin Hull, "Does the court often hear matters this mundane?" Hull smiled and corrected her in a quiet voice, "It is only mundane if the fence does not impede thine animals from grazing on land thou ownest." The magistrates reviewed what the lower court had decided and discussed the written testimonies they had received. They heard from the plaintiff and the defendant and from witnesses who could speak about the character of the men in question. It was all taking forever: the sun was descending in the sky and the room was beginning to grow dark. Someone lit the candles in the ceiling fixtures and along the sconces on the west wall. In the end, the magistrates overturned the county court and ordered that the fence be disassembled.

And then, almost the way a thundercloud can appear from nowhere on a summer day, it was her turn. She heard one of the magistrates, Daniel Winslow, summon her by name. For a moment she stood there, frozen, but then her father murmured into her ear, "It is time, Mary. Stand tall. The Lord is with thee."

I simply observed that if Thomas Deerfield had meant to murder thee, he would not have targeted thy hand.

—The Remarks of Magistrate Caleb Adams, from the Records and Files of the Court of Assistants, Boston, Massachusetts, 1662, Volume III

Fourteen

"Cruelty," said Richard Wilder, "may be defined as violence without provocation and discipline that is excessive. We have before us a wife who seeks separation from her husband because, her petition alleges, he has treated her with needless and consistent wickedness. He has struck her, and he has physically abused her, ignoring the fact that a woman is a weaker, more fragile vessel." Mary nodded, though it seemed as if the magistrate was speaking more to the other men than to her. "Mary Deerfield is asking for a divorce from Thomas Deerfield. Will the petitioner come forward?"

And Mary did. She stood before the bench, feeling naked and exposed. She had tied her lace collar and cuffs with blue ribbons, ones that she thought matched nicely with her bodice and skirt, which were made of green wool. Her hair was pulled tightly back beneath a pristine white coif. Her cloak was black.

"Good day," said the magistrate.

"Good day," she replied. She viewed him as an ally, but her father and Benjamin Hull had been clear that they had no idea how the others would rule. It would depend on the testimony, at least some of which was going to be—and this was the word Hull had used—perilous. She grew self-conscious as she was sworn in, wanting to smile to show that she was pretty and kind, but fearful that smiling would suggest she was frivolous: oblivious to the stakes before her.

"We have read thy petition. Thou sayest that Thomas Deerfield would call thee a whore and concoct wild stories about thee. Thou sayest that he would strike thee often, sometimes even on the face. Occasionally, he said it was discipline, but often it was because he had consumed too much cider or beer. Is this accurate?"

"Yes."

"How many years hast thou been married?" asked John Endicott.

"Five."

"And how many times dost thou claim that Thomas has hit thee?"

She knew not the precise answer, but she knew the proper response for this court. Hull had coached her. Nevertheless, the truth hurt: she stood tall against the humiliation of what she was about to say, but she could feel her face growing red. This was the sort of public spectacle she had never expected would center around her; and while she understood that this was not her fault, still she felt shame. "I cannot tell thee an exact number," she replied. "But he has hit me no fewer than a dozen times, often on the side of my head where the bruise would be hidden by my hair or my coif. He chose the spots with a deliberation that belied the violence: he knew the wrongness of the blows and wanted not for others to see the evidence of his barbarity. One time, he hurled me into the hearth. He poured the remains of our boiled supper on me. It was when he stabbed me with a fork that I knew I could abide this level of woefulness no longer and began to fear for my life. It was time to divorce him."

"Tell us precisely: why would he strike thee?" asked Richard Wilder.

She could feel Thomas watching her, but she dared not turn. This was hard enough as it was. "There was never a good reason. He was tipsy from too much cider or beer. He wanted his supper served on pewter, and I had used the wooden trencher. He was unhappy with the dinner I had prepared. Something had happened at the gristmill, and he was just cantankerous."

"Thou didst nothing to encourage the beatings?"

"Never."

Caleb Adams, the youngest of the magistrates—he was only thirty, but well known for his piety and intellect—sat up in his seat. He had a Flemish beard that was impeccably trimmed, and now he rubbed his jaw through it in a needlessly dramatic sort of way. "Did thy husband view his discipline as a form of guidance?"

She thought to herself, **A primer on how to be cruel? It certainly was that.** But she restrained herself because she knew no good could come from such impudence. And so instead she replied with a question to see if it might compel the magistrate to replace the vagueness of **discipline** with the specificity of **violence** or **beatings.** "By **discipline,** sir, dost thou mean his anger and his aggression?" she asked.

"Let me be more clear," continued Adams, and she felt a small flutter of pride at the possible success of her tactic. "If it seemed to thee that his discipline was excessive, is it nevertheless possible that he administered it rather as a husband might to a recalcitrant or unschooled wife?"

"No," she replied, though she recalled her exchange with Thomas in the dooryard of her parents' home, and how he might have convinced himself that his cruelty was in her best interests: he beat her for the sake of her soul. And this knowledge caused her to worry that her dissembling at least hinted at the possibility that she was as damned as her husband.

The magistrate Daniel Winslow was sitting with his hands together on the bench. "How violent was Thomas?" he asked. "Didst thou honestly fear for thy life?"

"Yes."

"For how long?"

"It was when he stabbed me with the fork that I grew much afraid."

"And that was this autumn?"

"Yes. The bones are still mending."

"Tell me something, Mary," said Caleb Adams, his voice calm.

"Ask me anything," she replied.

"I have been told these were three-tined forks. The Devil's tines. Thy petition merely says **fork.** Was the instrument that thou claimest thy husband stabbed thee with a two-tined carving fork or something more questionable?"

"It was a three-tined fork."

"And he stabbed thee with it?"

"Yes, which is why I know a fork can be a weapon most terrible."

"In that case, I have two questions," Adams continued. "The first is this. Thou sayest he stabbed thee in thy hand. No mortal wound can be struck there. Why didst thou fear for thy life?"

"It was getting worse. The cruelties. He would hit me and then he would hurl me and then he stabbed me."

"In the hand. He stabbed thee in the hand."

"How does that diminish the cruelty?" she asked in return, raising her voice, and she heard a whoosh of air behind her, an almost collective choral gasp from the people in the Town House in response to her tone. They hadn't expected her to challenge the magistrate. Usually inquiries—rather than mere requests for clarification—came only from the bench. When someone disputed a magistrate, it tended to be a lawyer, whose unpopular profession was known for its tendency to bark and bray.

"I simply observed that if Thomas Deerfield had meant to murder thee, he would not have targeted thy hand," said Adams. Then he shrugged. "My second question is this: why were there the Devil's tines in thy house in the first place?"

"My father had imported some. They are growing common in Europe."

The governor looked at Adams, and for a moment she was relieved that there would be no more nonsense about a piece of cutlery. But she knew she had misread that glance when John Endicott said, "There is much that is common in Europe, Mary. It is why we have come here." At this the men on the bench nodded as one, even Richard Wilder.

"There is also talk," continued Adams, "that thou were using the Devil's tines as more than a mere utensil."

She wanted to cry out in exasperation, **May we just call it a fork?** But she knew from her earlier question that she shouldn't. And so she held her tongue and waited, and started in her mind to carefully form her response. She knew the stakes. But she also knew two truths: someone or some thing had buried the forks in her dooryard—and then she had reburied them after initially removing them from the dirt. There was so much to say, so very much to explain. Just as she was about to respond, Adams continued, "We have written testimony that thou mayest have been using them in some evil manner—"

"More evil than plunging one into a person's hand and breaking the bone?" she snapped, interrupting Adams as she lost completely her line of thinking. But this was too much. Just too much. Still, she knew instantly that it had been a mistake. But she was appalled that the questioning seemed to be moving away from her reasonable request for a divorce and into this ridiculous and possibly disastrous discussion of a new kind of cutlery.

"Perhaps, yes," Adams said simply. "There is a witness who saw thee burying the Devil's tines in the ground as an offering."

She took a breath to compose herself. "A fork is not a seed," she replied. "What could possibly grow from a piece of silver planted into the earth?"

"I said it was an offering. Not a seed."

"An offering for what? A knife? A spoon?" Behind her a few people laughed, but she took no pride in their amusement. Before Adams or any of the magistrates could take offense, she continued, "Forgive me. I mean no impertinence. I just see not what can be the benefit of planting a fork into the earth."

The governor whispered something into Richard Wilder's ear, and Wilder nodded. "Mary," said Wilder, "prithee, stand aside for a moment. We see that Catherine Stileman has arrived, and we would like her testimony at this point. The moment seems relevant."

And there she was. The servant girl looked terrified and small, her coif pulled tightly around her face so she seemed but a pair of eyes and a petite, slightly upturned nose. She came up behind Mary and was standing no more than six or seven feet to her right, staring up at the magistrates. Mary knew the girl wouldn't dare look at her, at least not right away. Perhaps she would in a few minutes, when she had been emboldened by the likes of Caleb Adams.

But for now? It was only Thomas's lawyer, Philip Bristol, who nodded at her as Catherine was sworn in—and then, much to Mary's astonishment, smiled.

᪥ ᪥

"Goodman Bristol," began the governor, his annoyance evident at the attorney's presence beside the servant, "art thou planning to speak on behalf of Catherine Stileman?"

"I am here if she needs me," he said. "I can elaborate if necessary."

Endicott nodded wearily. "Catherine, prithee, tell the court what thou witnessed thy mistress doing in the night two weeks ago."

"May I begin earlier, sir?"

"How much earlier?" the governor asked.

Bristol jumped in and explained, "Only earlier that day. We will not be taking up the court's time with an exhaustive history."

"Fine. Begin earlier."

Catherine nodded deferentially. "During that day," she started nervously, "while I was carrying eggs into the house, my mistress approached me."

"Go on."

"She said she had found the Devil's tines planted in the dooryard—two of them—and she showed them to me. They still had dirt on them. She accused me of placing them there."

"In the ground?"

"Yes. I told her that I knew nothing of such a thing and had not planted them."

"Were thee offended?"

"I was frightened. I was frightened there was witchcraft about."

The room began to buzz. Bristol held up a single finger and said with gravity, "There is more, governor, there is more. Go on, Catherine."

The girl continued, "And I was frightened I might be wrongfully accused of such a terrible crime."

The governor smiled in an almost avuncular fashion. "This petition has nothing to do with thee, Catherine. Thou art here merely as a witness."

Catherine clasped her hands before her, entwining her fingers as if she were praying, and said, "Then, that night, I awoke when I heard someone outside the room where I sleep—"

"Outside in the yard," Bristol added.

"Yes, in the yard. And so I peered out the window, and when I saw Mary Deerfield there, I went to her. I was much perplexed as to why she would be out in the night in her shift."

"And what didst thou see?"

"I saw my mistress placing the Devil's tines into the earth, burying them."

"Re-burying them," added her lawyer helpfully. "Catherine saw her mistress returning them to the ground. But the tale does not end here."

"Speak then, Catherine," ordered Caleb Adams.

"She had a weapon of some sort."

"I had a pestle," Mary interjected. "I had just discovered it, too, in the yard. But it was a pestle, not a weapon."

The governor looked at her crossly. "Thou wilt have a chance to speak again, Mary. Now it is Catherine's turn." Then he said to the servant, "Thou art a smart girl. Why dost thou believe she was burying these implements?"

Catherine stood a little taller, emboldened by the

compliment. "I feared it was witchcraft," she said. "I did not know the spell or what deal my mistress might have struck with the Evil One, but I thought of all the time she had spent with my brother and all the simples she had brought him."

Richard Wilder leaned in. "But what has that to do with the forks? Thy brother by then had already gone to the Lord."

"May I?" asked the lawyer.

Wilder nodded.

Bristol looked down at one of the papers he was holding and explained, "We are not accusing Mary Deerfield of witchcraft. At least not formally. Catherine Stileman is merely testifying to what she saw that night and what she was thinking. When she saw her mistress with the Devil's tines, she feared that Mary Deerfield may not have been helping her brother all summer long with her simples, but was in fact exacerbating his illness. Mary is friends with Constance Winston, a strange old woman who lives out along the Neck, and who we know was friends with the hanged witch Ann Hibbens. Constance Winston is the one who taught Mary Deerfield whatever it is she knows about simples."

"Yes, I am aware of who Constance Winston is, and I understand her relationship with Ann," said the governor, and he sounded sad and tired. "Hibbens," he then added suddenly, the two syllables a strange exclamation, as if by referring to the hanged witch only as Ann he had suggested too much familiarity.

"It seemed possible to Catherine," Bristol went on, "that Mary Deerfield was trying to make her brother sicker. Mary was ensuring that Satan got Catherine's brother and—in return—Mary, hitherto barren, would get a child."

For a long second, the room went utterly silent at the enormity of the accusation, and Mary thought to herself, incredulous, **I was bringing but comfrey and dill.** But then the throng began to speak so animatedly that the constable pounded his pike on the floor over and over until they began to simmer down. Behind her, she heard among the burble, rising up like whitecaps on the sea, the words **witch** and **witchcraft.** She saw her mother was leaning into her father, hiding her face in his shoulder. Her father nodded at her, his gaze firm and comforting amidst the maelstrom.

When the crowd had grown sufficiently quiet for the testimonies to resume, Mary said, her voice filled with a quiver she didn't like but couldn't control, "I was only trying to help. I was only bringing William Stileman simples from my garden."

Richard Wilder heard her and said, "Let me remind everyone that this is a divorce petition, not a trial for witchcraft. We are hearing a civil petition, not weighing evidence in a criminal matter." Then he smiled ever so slightly and said, "We are gathered in Boston. Not Hartford."

But his small jibe at the city to the southwest and their recent battle with Satan fell flat. Mary saw both the governor and Caleb Adams glare at him.

"Catherine Stileman," asked the governor, "hast thou ever seen any sign of possession in Mary Deerfield?"

"No, sir," she said.

Then he spoke to the crowd: "Is there anyone present today who has ever seen any sign of possession in Mary Deerfield?"

Mary waited. Was there someone there willing to risk the wrath of the Lord with a lie? Was there someone who had indeed made a pact with the Devil and she, Mary Deerfield, was the offering? And the wait, though probably not long at all, seemed interminable, and she felt her knees growing wobbly beneath her petticoat. But no one said a word. No one was going to add to Catherine's allegation by suggesting they had seen any indication that she was possessed.

"Very well," said the governor. "Let us continue with the petition before us. If we need to turn our attention to witchcraft, we will." He looked at the magistrates lining the bench on either side of him and then at Catherine. "Tell us something," he continued.

"Yes, sir."

"Hast thou ever seen Thomas Deerfield strike his wife? Her petition alleges that he hit her often and without reason."

"No. Never," she replied. "He is not that type of man. He is a wonderful master, and my indenture to him has always been a blessing. He is God-fearing and God-loving. I never saw him hit Mary Deerfield. Not even once."

"Not even once?" Endicott asked. "Thou lived with them since arriving in Boston."

"No, sir," she said, and Mary wondered if Thomas was smirking but didn't dare venture a glance.

"So, thou saw Mary Deerfield with the Devil's tines," said Caleb Adams. "What happened next?"

"She denied that she was planting them. She denied she was in the midst of the Devil's work."

"And thee?"

"I fled, sir. I ran. I ran fast."

"Thou art indentured to Thomas Deerfield. By what right didst thou flee?" Wilder asked.

"I did not think. I was too afraid. I wanted to be far from whatever spell Mary Deerfield was casting. But though I live now with the Howlands—because it would be most improper to live alone with my master—I return to him daily to do my chores and the work that is my indenture. I hope that my master has no grievance with me; I certainly have no grievance with him. I am sure that he has forgiven me for leaving that night, because that is the sort of righteous man that he is. I am sure he understands that I was scared and I meant no dereliction."

"But thou didst leave."

"Yes."

"So, thou didst not see how Mary Deerfield broke her hand that night," Wilder said.

"She fell on a kettle," Catherine answered.

Wilder shook his head. "That may or may not be what happened, Catherine. I merely asked what thou saw, and it is clear thou saw nothing more that is relevant today." He looked at the governor, and the governor shrugged.

"We thank thee," said John Endicott.

Catherine stood there a moment more, and Mary thought the servant girl might have the spine to glance at her. She almost craved the confrontation. She waited. But while Catherine's head bobbed once in her direction, either out of fear or guilt the girl was unable to follow through and meet Mary's eyes. She turned instead toward Philip Bristol, and Mary thought the lawyer said to her that she had done well. She had done well indeed.

❧ ☙

The governor, after Catherine Stileman had been dismissed, turned his gaze upon Mary and motioned for her to come forward.

"We will be speaking with Reverend Norton in a moment," he said to her, "but I am curious. Thou hast been resistant to mediation. I know there are elders willing to buffer a Christian peace between Thomas and thee. Why wilt thou not consider it?"

"Because I do not feel safe in his house," she answered. "Because I do not believe that he will change his ways. Because he has broken the law and treated me with cruelty. I am sorry and I grieve the death of our marriage, but I cannot live with a person so rich with sin that he will stab me—his obedient helpmeet."

Endicott nodded, but Caleb Adams shook his head and reminded the governor, "Let us not forget, John, there are two shores to this sea. And no witnesses. We do not yet know whether the wound was caused by the Devil's tines or a teakettle; we do not yet know whether Thomas did what Mary claims. We may never know. It is worth noting that the girl—the indentured girl—has a very different view of the man than does his wife."

Wilder looked at both magistrates, his eyebrows peaking. Mary could see that she still had an ally in Wilder, but he seemed to believe no good would come from rebuking or disagreeing with his associates on the bench publicly.

"Hast thou pondered thy future if this divorce is granted?" Adams asked her.

"I have."

"And what wilt thou do? Keep bees?"

She was appalled by the condescension in his tone but was careful not to respond in kind and be pulled down by his meanness. "Before my family came here, Salem had its maid lots for unmarried women. There was even a season when they had to wear veils. Salem soon changed those laws. Boston has never had such strictures on its women. And while the reverend can speak to God's laws with far more knowledge and eloquence than I, I believe there is nothing in the Bible about it being a sin for a woman to live alone. The world is awash in widows and women who never wed."

"Such as thy friend, Constance Winston."

She almost denied her friendship with the woman. After all, they really weren't friends anymore. But she would not succumb to that sort of frailty. "I do not believe that Constance lives alone," she replied instead, her voice even. "I believe she has a servant girl."

"So, thou wilt live alone—unless thy circumstances allow for a servant girl?"

"No, I will not live alone. At least not at first. I will live with my mother and father."

"With one-third of Thomas's estate."

"That is the law. But I am not taking this step to sever our marriage because of my share."

"Thy share?" asked Adams. "It sounds as if thou believest thy petition has already been granted."

"Oh, no. I believe no such thing."

There was an awkward silence in the Town

House. Mary waited. Finally, the governor said, "We thank thee, Mary. As we hear from the other witnesses, I expect there will be additional moments when we will need thee to respond to accusations or to provide clarifying details. But I believe we should allow John Norton to speak, so the reverend can return to his work."

She looked to her scrivener, who nodded, and with that she took a step back and retreated into the crowd beside her mother and father and Benjamin Hull.

She was behaving abominably. It was as if we were back in London among the damned and she was but a wench awaiting the sailors.

—The Testimony of Beth Howland, from the Records and Files of the Court of Assistants, Boston, Massachusetts, 1662, Volume III

Fifteen

The Reverend John Norton's beard was as groomed as it was on Sundays when he stood in the pulpit of the First Church, and he smiled at the governor. His doublet was black and lush. Here were two of the most powerful men in the colony, friends, and Mary felt a pang of guilt that she was taking up any of their time. It was audacious. And while audacity was not a sin, it seemed eerily close to pride.

"Good day, John," said the governor. "We thank thee for joining us."

"Oh, I thank thee for thy service."

"What canst thou say of Mary Deerfield?"

"She has always seemed to me to be a righteous and devout soul: a young woman who seems mostly to keep good company. I believe that she loves our Savior and desires to manifest good work. She has never struck me as more sinful than any of the other faces I see before me on Sunday, and perhaps she is even less so."

"What of these Constance Winston allegations?" asked Caleb Adams.

"I know little of the woman or Mary's friendship with her."

Adams nodded, and for a moment Mary feared he was going to say more, to press this connection and make much of her acquaintanceship with Constance. Before he could, however, the governor spoke, and Mary was relieved.

"And Thomas Deerfield?" the governor asked. "What are thy thoughts on him?"

"He seems an able miller. He attends to the Sabbath. He tipples excessively."

There was a ripple of laughter in the Town House and even two of the magistrates smiled involuntarily. Quickly Philip Bristol chimed in, "But, of course, the gentleman has never been fined or shamed for tippling. He has done nothing to suggest that he is in fact some sort of savage unfamiliar with the dangers of excess."

"No," replied the pastor. "I agree. He is not breaking into houses and overturning barrels of hard cider." Again, a few people snickered, but Mary recalled the Indian and the lashing that loomed for him.

The magistrate Daniel Winslow leaned in and asked, "Thou knowest the basics of Mary Deerfield's petition, correct?"

"I do. She wants to divorce her husband."

"Hast thou heard any rumors or stories of his beating his wife?"

He shook his head. "Only when she told me herself that he was abusive and cruel, and she wished to see their marriage covenant severed."

"So, prior to this autumn, Mary never approached thee about the behaviors she has contended that her husband manifested regularly?"

"No."

"Should she have?"

He pondered the question. Finally, he answered, "I summoned Mary and her parents last week and offered to enlist the elders in mediation. We expect a man's government of his wife to be easy and gentle, and, when it is not, something is amiss. Something needs to be remedied. A husband should rule in such a fashion that his wife submits joyfully. Certainly, the Lord wants a marriage to succeed, and to succeed in a fashion that is pleasurable here on earth and celebrates in all ways His work. But we are but imperfect vessels. Sometimes mediation is a sound alternative to divorce. But not always."

The governor raised an eyebrow. "Sometimes? Not always?"

Now there was no hesitation. "A husband who strikes his wife or is peevish with her puts to lie his profession of faith and has smashed soundly divine law and dishonored our Lord and Savior," he said firmly, as if speaking from the pulpit. "It is a civil crime, yes. But 'tis more as well."

Mary found herself nodding. She allowed herself

a small glimpse at Benjamin Hull, and her scrivener seemed well pleased.

"But we do not know that Thomas ever struck his wife," her husband's lawyer reminded everyone. "Prithee, let us not forget that."

"Mr. Bristol is quite right," said Caleb Adams. "Reverend, may I ask thee about Catherine Stileman's other accusation?"

"Of course."

"Let me begin with the most basic of womanly roles and womanly desires. What does it mean that Mary Deerfield is barren?"

"Do we know that she is?"

"My observation is that she is twenty-four years in this world and has been wed to Thomas for five. She is otherwise healthy and strong. And she has yet to produce boy or girl, while Anne Drury, Thomas Deerfield's first wife, produced three children, one of whom lives still."

Again, the reverend paused to consider his response. "I see the reality that Mary Deerfield has not been blessed with children as no indictment of her behavior. I see no indication this is divine retribution. She has shown great faithfulness. The Lord may yet reward her with offspring," he said.

"Faithfulness to the Lord or faithfulness to her husband? The Apostle Paul—"

"Yes, the Apostle Paul was clear about what is exemplary in relations between a man and his wife: Their duties. Their obligations. Their compassion.

Mary Deerfield has behaved in no way I am aware of that suggests a faithlessness."

"Except that she has asked for a divorce."

"And, as thou knowest well, Caleb, that might matter to others, with their mistakes and misunderstandings of God's word. It has no bearing on us here in Boston."

The magistrate looked chastened. "Yes," he said. "True. But I am not questioning Mary Deerfield's right to divorce. I am trying to get at something else. Forgive me for meandering off the path."

"Thou dost not need forgiveness."

Adams looked intensely at Mary and then back at John Norton. "Mary Deerfield, dost thou want a child?"

The question caught her off guard since this time belonged to the reverend, one of the most important men in the colony. "Yes, sir," she answered. "I do want children. I have yet to serve our Lord as a mother: the fashion to which He would desire and for which I have been made."

Adams nodded and said to Reverend Norton, "Let us return to Catherine Stileman. She said she believes that her mistress was hoping seed would take root in her womb if she conspired with the Devil. What dost thou make of such an accusation?"

"There is no question that we see the Devil's work in the temptations He dangles before us all, and most clearly in the inducements He offers the nulliparous—those persuasions He will offer the barren," he answered. "But we have no reason to believe that Mary Deerfield has made such a pact. As we heard earlier, no one has seen any signs of possession in the woman."

"No," agreed the magistrate. "We have not. At least not yet."

⊰ ⊱

The governor looked at Richard Wilder, who, in turn, looked at Daniel Winslow. They leaned in together, murmuring, and then John Endicott said to Mary, "Thy scrivener presented us with the written testimony of Dr. Roger Pickering. Is the physician present to address the court's questions?"

From the back of the room a gentleman called out, "Here. Present." And a moment later the doctor had pushed himself to the front of the crowd and was standing beside her. "Good day, Mary," he said.

She nodded. According to her scrivener, he had said nothing damaging about her, which was why Hull had entered the testimony into evidence. But when he had examined her hand, she also had the sense that he was not especially fond of her as a person, either because he occasionally kept company with Thomas and her husband had said disparaging things about her, or simply because she came from privilege and it rankled him.

"Good day, Roger," the governor said.

"Is it now?" he asked. "It's cold and damp. And look out the windows at how dark it already is. The sun fell fast today behind the hills."

"Thou art not enamored of autumn?"

"I am not enamored of cold and damp," said Pickering. "My bones feel too well what's coming next."

The physician was known for his cantankerousness, but he was also respected for his kindness and humor with the dying and the sick. People jested about his ill temper, because he did himself. He was roughly fifty years old, his hair white, his skin as leathered as a sailor's. His wife had died twenty years ago, and he had never remarried. His children lived now in New Haven.

"We have but a few questions for thee," said the governor. "This should take but little time."

"It's warmer in here than out there," he said, and he pointed at the gabled window nearest him. "There is no need to rush me back outside into the dusk."

The governor smiled. "We have thy remarks to Benjamin Hull in regard to Mary Deerfield. We thank thee. Thou hast been brought here also because of the testimony of Catherine Stileman and how it relates to Mary Deerfield's request for a divorce. Thou knowest Mary. Had thou ever treated her prior to whatever incident led to the wound on her hand?"

"Yes. Never for anything serious. Her body seems ruled by blood: her humour sanguine. She can be fiery. She has survived both smallpox and measles admirably."

Daniel Winslow sat forward and asked, "Might that explain why she is barren?"

"No. Women who've had smallpox and measles bear children all the time."

"Then why?" asked Caleb Adams. "We have been given no reason to believe from the testimonies provided thus far that Thomas Deerfield and Mary do not have normal conjugal relations, as did Thomas with his first wife, Anne Drury."

"Well, Mary has petitioned for divorce. It seems to me that suggests their conjugal relations are anything but normal," the physician said, and the men in the room chuckled, but Mary could only blush and stare down at her shoes. The idea they were discussing Thomas's and her conduct in their bedchamber was devastating: Benjamin had warned her, but still she was unprepared for the idea that their coupling—or not coupling—was being debated in court. She felt queasy and ashamed, and she was tired of the attention.

"I think, Dr. Pickering, thou knowest what I am suggesting," said Adams. "But let me be clear: is there a moral putrescence that may be the cause of her barrenness?"

The physician waved one of his hands as if the notion were a fly and he was brushing it aside. "Mary Deerfield may be barren, yes, but is she unclean? I will not dissemble and suggest that I know. Only our Lord and Savior can say why she has never been with child."

"I see," said Adams.

"I hope so," said Pickering.

"So, thou didst examine Mary's hand, yes?"

"I did."

"And?"

"It was broken. It's healing. Had she called me sooner, perhaps it would be further along. But she and her mother, like many presumptuous women, felt themselves sufficiently trained to manage it. In all fairness, there is little to be done for a broken bone in the hand other than leave it be. It's not as if I could have set it back in place. The bones there are all so small."

"What caused it?"

"I know only what has been presented to the court. Thomas Deerfield says she fell on the spout of a teakettle. Mary insists he stabbed her with a fork."

"The Devil's tines," corrected Caleb Adams.

"Cutlery," said the physician.

"Thou couldst not tell from the wound whether it was a tine or a spout that broke the skin?"

"I could not."

"Dost thou have an opinion?" asked the governor.

"Only that it was a grievous injury. But, at least, it was not made worse by womanly care."

"Thou treated Catherine's brother, William, true?" asked Adams.

"I did, yes."

"How?"

"He was bled and cupped. We purged him. We gave him eggs. Fennel. Rum. I thrust boiled and dried toad dust into him. Into his nose. We tried spiders. But it was his time, and nothing changed the trajectory of his disease."

"Art thou aware that Mary Deerfield was bringing him her simples?" pressed Adams.

"Yes," he said, drawing the word out, and Mary heard the great dollop of derision he had managed to wedge into that single syllable.

"Prithee, thy thoughts?"

"She is neither healer nor midwife. Her simples may not be of the Devil, but neither are they healing. Her teacher was that old woman who lives out by the Neck. And I believe no midwife would ever allow so barren a womb to be present at a birth."

This was factually wrong, and Mary could abide his contempt no more. "Four times I have assisted midwives at births! Four times I have been present!" she said to him and to the row of magistrates behind the bench. "Why is this even an issue? Aren't we here because Thomas Deerfield broke my hand with a fork? Because Thomas Deerfield would—"

"That is enough, Mary, we have heard from thee," said the governor sternly, raising his voice to cut her off. Then he glanced at the other magistrates before turning back to her, his tone softer and almost mischievous, "and I am confident we will hear from thee again. Now, this time belongs to the doctor."

"Oh, I have nothing more to add," said Roger Pickering, and he rolled his eyes. "May I go and have my supper?"

"Thou mayest."

As he left, he nodded toward Mary in a manner that seemed deferential, but she knew was meant to be condescending. She took a breath to gather herself after the governor's chastisement.

"Is Jonathan Cooke present?" asked Winslow.

"I am," Mary heard her son-in-law call out, and he stepped forward. He looked more somber than she had ever seen him. There was no twinkle in his eyes as he was sworn in. Hull had told Mary that Jonathan's testimony implied that he thought it possible on at least two occasions her bruises had been inflicted by his father-in-law. Consequently, no good could come for him from speaking here today: either he savaged his father-in-law or he added a lie to his ledger.

"We have but a few questions for thee," said

Richard Wilder. "Apparently thou noticed bruises on Mary Deerfield's face."

"Yes. I did."

"How often?"

"Twice that I can recall."

"There may have been more than two times?"

"Yes, sir."

Caleb Adams leaned in toward Jonathan. "What did Mary say was the cause of her injuries?"

Jonathan pulled nervously at his cuffs. "She said one time it was a coat peg. Another time, the spider."

"Mary did not accuse her husband of hurting her?"

"No."

"But thou had doubts?" asked Wilder.

"**Doubts** is too strong a feeling. I wondered at the frequency with which she seemed to hurt herself. But she never said that Thomas hit her."

So, that was that, Mary thought. Jonathan had chosen his path. It really could not have been otherwise.

"We thank thee," said Caleb Adams.

"Caleb," observed Wilder, "I think it's clear that Mary may have been hoping to protect her husband from the community's disapprobation. She may have been wanting to spare Thomas a measure of humiliation."

"Tell me then, Richard," said Adams, "art thou

suggesting that Mary Deerfield was lying then and telling the truth now?"

Wilder looked exasperated. "Yes, she may have been lying when she did not reveal right away to her son-in-law—in the presence of her daughter-in-law—that the man's father-in-law had struck her. And, if we are to cast aspersions on the likely truthfulness of our witnesses, let us not forget the rumors about Jonathan Cooke. Arguably, we shouldn't believe a soul in this sordid story."

Jonathan looked as if he himself had just been sent to the stocks: crestfallen and embarrassed and scared.

Mary turned to her scrivener and whispered, "Jonathan? What do the gossips say about Jonathan?"

"He gambles with the sailors who come and go. He plays cards with them," Hull murmured.

Mary had had no idea. Jonathan's boyishness and cheer seemed different to her now, a signpost that suggested his irresponsibility.

"Jonathan, hast thou more to add?" Adams was asking.

"I do not," he mumbled, humiliated.

"Very well. Thou canst leave," said the governor, and Jonathan disappeared into the crowd, resisting eye contact with everyone. Mary wondered who would be next. Thomas? Abigail? Goody Howland?

Instead, however, she watched John Endicott speaking softly with Richard Wilder and Caleb

Adams. Daniel Winslow was motioning toward the eastern windows of the Town House. It was black outside. Night had arrived.

"We are going to recess this petition until tomorrow. We will not finish tonight," Endicott said. "We will resume first thing in the morning. We will expect all parties to be back here then."

Thomas stepped forward and said, "Governor, I was away from my mill all afternoon. Dost thou expect me to be away from it tomorrow as well?"

"Only if thou hast the desire to preserve thy marriage, Thomas," Endicott said.

"And the entirety of his estate," Benjamin Hull whispered into Mary's ear so that only she heard.

Then the constable banged his pike hard on the floorboards, and Mary realized they were indeed done for the afternoon. Her petition was going to drag into a second day. Now she had to return to her parents' home—sharing the night once more with the disapproving eyes of Abigail Gathers—and try to rest so she could be a town spectacle again in the morning.

I saw her showing sympathy for a
Quaker, and I was disappointed and
appalled.

**—The Testimony of Isaac Willard,
from the Records and Files of
the Court of Assistants, Boston,
Massachusetts, 1662, Volume III**

Sixteen

As they arrived home that night, Mary and her parents were stopped short when they ran into Peregrine Cooke leaving the Burdens' dooryard.

"Peregrine, I am sorry we missed thee," Mary said, "but thou must have known we were at the Town House."

"Yes. I heard it will take a second day to resolve."

"Has something happened?"

The woman had dark bags under her eyes. "No. I was feeling bad about how we parted when I visited thee last."

With her right hand, Mary touched Peregrine's arm and said, "Shhhhhhh. Say nothing more. I was too curt, as well." She turned to her mother and father and said, "I will join thee inside presently."

Her parents looked at the two young women, so close in age despite the fact that one was married to the other's father, and then Priscilla Burden smiled warily and said, "Very well. Peregrine, it is lovely to see thee. Have a good night."

"I brought some boiled apples and raisins," said Peregrine, as the older couple went inside.

"Rebeckah Cooper and I made batches. I just dropped some off with Hannah. A peace offering. I am sure thy parents smelled it the moment they opened the door."

"Oh, I love boiled apples!"

"I know. Rebeckah told me."

"How art thou feeling?"

Peregrine tilted her head and shrugged. She patted her stomach. "I am sorely tried by this one. But the Lord will give me nothing I cannot bear."

"Is there anything I can do?"

"No, there isn't. I just want thee to know . . ."

"Know what? Thou canst speak plainly to me."

"I will not try again to change thy mind. My father might. But I understand the path thou hast chosen. I respect it."

Mary was so moved that she wanted to embrace the other woman and felt her eyes welling up. "I'm sorry," she said simply.

"May I ask thee one thing, Mary?"

"Yes, ask me anything."

"I fear little in this world."

"I have always suspected that."

Peregrine wasn't wearing gloves and blew on her fingers, and Mary could see the other woman's breath in the night air.

"I know thou art formidable. I know the things people say about thee and that thou hast consorted with Constance Winston."

"What art thou implying?"

"Be more scared, Mary."

"I hope thou dost not believe that nonsense that I am in league with the Dark One."

"Prithee," Peregrine said. "I have seen the way that my husband looks at thee. I know thy body has been unchanged by childbirth. Do what thou must in regard to my father. But be wary of my husband. He, too, has frailties."

"I have no designs on thy husband! Why wouldst thou think such a thing?"

"He speaks most highly of thee."

"Bury that fear. It is ridiculous," Mary said. She recalled what Benjamin Hull had said about the fellow at the Town House.

"The world is awash in sin."

"But, Peregrine—"

"Fine, I will speak no more of this. We were friends once, as well as family. And so what I am about to say, I say with reverence for the person I once knew well."

"Thou knowest me still. I have not changed."

Her voice was keen and low, the agitation clear. "Be careful. The worst is yet to come. Thou knowest those men; but so do I. I may know them better than thee. There are dangers I doubt thou hast ever contemplated."

Was Peregrine about to say more? Mary thought so. But they heard Hannah outside now, and it sounded as if she were by the coop with the chickens.

"I just . . . I just hope thou dost enjoy the apples." She shook her head, smiled sadly, and turned to go. Mary considered calling after her, but knew in her heart that Peregrine had already said more than she had planned. A part of her was grateful.

But another part? She wasn't sure whether she should be more offended by the idea that the woman considered her an adulteress or frightened by the possibility she might be hanged as a witch.

❧ ❦

They ate supper that night later than usual because Hannah had been alone at the house. She had worked with characteristic efficiency, but she was accustomed to having Abigail and Mary's mother—and lately Mary herself—to share the labor. But Mary and Priscilla had been upstairs at the Town House all afternoon, and Abigail had been pacing nervously there on the first floor, waiting to be summoned. The five of them—Mary and her parents and their two servants—ate their beans in molasses and pork largely in silence after James's prayer, dining off their most casual trenchers. They spoke not at all while eating the dessert that Peregrine had brought. Mary thought the boiled apples, though a well-intended gift, were more tart than she liked and ate but one bite. Only Hannah seemed to enjoy them and finished her serving. There wasn't a fork to be seen among the utensils, but there hadn't been since Mary had returned home to her parents.

Her left hand was aching tonight more than it had the day before, and so she had a second and then a third mug of beer. She was confident it was healing and attributed the pain entirely to the cold that was settling in for the gray season: the days when the leaves are gone but the snow has not yet arrived, and the skies are endless and ashen and flat.

⁂

As Abigail was rinsing the cutlery and the bowls in a water bucket and Hannah was bringing the remnants from the trenchers to the animals, Mary heard a horse's hooves and feared it was Thomas. She had been about to go upstairs to her bedchamber, and when she heard the sound she looked anxiously at her mother and father. Clearly, they suspected the same thing. Her father went to the door and opened it, and there indeed, tying his horse to the post, was her husband. When the animal was hitched, he came to the doorway.

"Hello, Thomas," her father said, his tone flat.

Thomas saw Priscilla and Mary standing behind him and took off his cap. "James," he began. "Ladies."

"Why hast thou come?" her father asked.

Mary noted the way that Thomas had planted his boots hard in the dooryard and locked his knees. She knew that posture. He was trying to hide how much he had drunk. It was, perhaps, a greater miracle that he hadn't ever fallen off Sugar in this state and broken his neck than that he had managed to avoid the stocks all these years.

"Nothing has happened, other, of course, than the continued diminishment of my reputation this afternoon at the Town House," he said, his voice gravelly, speaking slowly and with the precision he used when he was in this condition. "And so, given what looms tomorrow, I have come to discuss thy daughter's petition."

Her father started to speak, and Mary rested her hand on his arm, cutting him off, and said, "'Tis my petition, Father." Then to Thomas she continued, "Peregrine suggested thou might visit."

"Did she? She knows her father, that one does," he said, and he sounded rather proud. "She brought me some boiled apples and raisins tonight. Delicious, they were."

Mary waited for him to continue, saying nothing.

"I was just at the tavern," he went on, "and I learned that thy scrivener took up much time with Ward Hollingsworth."

"Good," Mary said. Hollingsworth owned an ordinary that her husband patronized often.

"I can assure thee, it was a waste of effort. Ward told me that he said nothing of consequence to the flea thou retained to assail my character."

"We shall see tomorrow," said Mary. She had read the testimony that Hollingsworth had provided Benjamin Hull. And while it wasn't damning, the man had acknowledged that there had been nights when he had ceased refilling Thomas's tankard.

"And there is this," he went on, his voice grave. "I heard also that Rebecca Greensmith of Hartford told the magistrates there that the Devil has had much carnal knowledge of her body. She's in prison."

"That has nothing to do with me," she said. "Besides, that is but tavern talk."

"They're going to hang her, Mary."

"I repeat: that has no relevance to my petition."

"I disagree. It will weigh heavy on the minds of the magistrates tomorrow. They know of the outbreak in Hartford and how the Devil has encroached upon their sanctuary. Even some good woman named Cole—Ann Cole—a woman of real piety they say, has taken to fits."

"I lose no sleep over gossip," she said, though she felt another of those sickening pangs of fear and doubt.

"Mary Sanford has already been hanged," he reminded her, almost as if he could sense her dismay. "That is not gossip."

"Catherine Stileman has done her worst. She made her accusations, and the magistrates took none of it seriously. Do I seem possessed to thee?"

"Oh, I know thou art not possessed. But I know also that the Devil likes to see the innocent chastened and the godly hanged. Likewise, it seems not to vex the Lord in the slightest to see the prideful dangle from the end of a rope or burn like so much cut brush. And Mary? Thou might be godly. But I know, too, the presumption that lurks within thy soul."

"And thou knowest all this how? What special insights into the mind of the Devil and our Lord dost thou have?"

"Mary, that is enough," her father rebuked her, and she turned to him in surprise. Her mother, beside him, looked frightened and ill.

"Tomorrow," Priscilla said, "the magistrates will hear from Goody Howland and Abigail. There are others. They will hear from thee, Thomas."

Abigail looked up from the bucket at the sound of her name, but said nothing.

"They will," he agreed.

"Dost thy lawyer know thou hast come to see us?" her father asked.

"No."

James nodded, and once more Mary had the sense that although her husband was drunk and her father was irritated, they were yet in league. They were adversaries, this was clear; but she felt again the prickle she had experienced periodically over the past two weeks that there was plotting beyond her ken.

"Thomas, Father?" she began, looking back and forth between them. "Is there something I need to know? If there is, thou must tell me. 'Tis my life we are discussing, and it will be my life that the magistrates will be weighing."

"Not thy life, little dove," said her mother. "This is only a petition for divorce."

"Only a petition for divorce?" Thomas barked, emphasizing that first word sarcastically. "Thou makest it sound but a dispute over the price of a bag of cornmeal! It is thy daughter's life—and mine! It is our reputations. And, yes, Priscilla, thou knowest well it could be about thy daughter's very survival if she doesn't tread carefully through the swamp of the Town House and the vipers in their black robes."

"Thomas," her father said, but her husband cut him off.

"I will take my leave, James, fear not. And I will testify tomorrow and—I swear to thee—do what I can to end this madness." He turned and started back down the walkway, stumbling once on a stone but catching his balance. He looked back to see if they had noticed, and then with extreme care climbed atop his horse.

※ ※

When the three of them joined Abigail inside the house, Hannah was returning from the back with the animals. Suddenly the girl closed her eyes and pressed her palms flat on the tabletop, and allowed her chin to collapse against the base of her neck.

"Hannah," Mary asked, "art thou in pain?"

The girl nodded and then turned toward the hearth. "I felt a most awful cramping, but 'tis not my time," she whispered, grimacing. "I . . ."

"Go on," said Abigail.

But Hannah fell to her knees and said, her voice doleful, "I'm going to be sick." Mary and Abigail knelt beside her, Abigail rubbing her back, and Hannah brought her hand to her mouth. But then she gave in to the nausea and vomited into the hearth, amidst the hot coals but feet from the flames.

"I have been feeling a little seasick, too," Abigail said to her, rubbing her back. "Not so bad as thee, but poorly."

Mary brought Hannah a tankard of beer, but the girl shook her head. She sat back against the warm bricks and said, "I just need to rest a bit."

Mary looked up at her parents, who seemed more alarmed than she might have expected.

"I wonder if it is the pork that doesn't agree with thee," her mother said.

"I felt a twinge of something, too," added James Burden. "Little dove, how dost thou feel?"

"I feel fine," she told her father. "And I ate the meat."

Priscilla looked at her servant girls and her daughter on the floor, and she focused on Hannah. An idea had come to her. "Thou ate much of the boiled apples," she observed.

"Yes," Hannah said, as she brought her knees up to her chest and squeezed her eyes shut against another cramp.

"Abigail?" Priscilla asked.

"I ate just a bite. I didn't enjoy one of the spices."

"And what spice was that? Thou art most knowledgeable in the kitchen."

"I did not know it," Abigail answered. "I just thought something tasted off."

"I felt the same way," Mary agreed. "Usually I love boiled apples."

Her mother nodded. "Hannah was the only one of us who ate her share. The rest of us nibbled and gnawed—"

"Even me," agreed James. "Barely a mouthful."

"Mother, art thou suggesting that Peregrine was trying to poison us?" Mary asked.

"I think that's unlikely, Mary," her father said. "But perhaps the apples were rotten. Or one of her ingredients was rotten."

"James, thou art being kind. This was no accident. I can see well why she would want to poison us," said Priscilla.

"So we are too sick to return to the Town House tomorrow," Mary chimed in. "Or at least that I am too sick. If I were not there to defend myself—to speak on my behalf when it is necessary—it would be more likely that my petition would be denied."

"Yes," her mother agreed.

"But . . ."

"Go on," said Priscilla.

"Peregrine made them with my friend Rebeckah. And she also brought some to Thomas."

"Well, if Peregrine was hoping to make us ill, she most likely was not in consultation with Thomas," her father said, and Mary realized that he was reminding her mother of . . . of something.

"Why do I feel that thou both have secrets?" Mary asked her parents.

"We have none," James said, and his tone was categorical.

"None?"

"None," he said again, but still she didn't believe him.

With her sister's help, Hannah stood. "May I lie down?"

"Of course," Priscilla said. Then she took the pot with the boiled apples and started out back. "James?" she said, pausing at the door.

"Yes?"

"The ground is not yet a brick, correct?"

"The surface is hard, yes. But I doubt it is frozen much beneath the skin."

"Come with me, prithee. I am going to bury this, and I may need thy help digging. I don't want even the pigs to eat whatever venom Peregrine spooned into this abomination."

Her father nodded and joined his wife, while Mary helped Abigail settle Hannah into bed.

∽ ∾

Hours later, unable to sleep, Mary stood at the small window in her bedchamber and gazed out into the moonlit night. The rest of the house was silent, the homes along the street dark.

She tried to follow the bats that were darting playfully like swallows, and on the walkway below her she noticed a honey-and-white cat in search of prey. The animal was pressed flat into the dirt, half hidden by the rosebush that had grown quiescent for the winter. Was it a rat it was stalking? A chipmunk?

She knew what some people said of cats, but she saw nothing demonic in the animal. It was a mouser. That was its purpose. But what really did she know? She rapped on the pane of glass with the knuckles of her right hand, and the cat looked up at the sound. At her. She felt their eyes meet. But still: it was just a cat. Of this she was sure. It was no one's familiar. It had not been sent by a witch to spy on her.

When her parents had been speculating on why Peregrine might want to sicken them (to sicken her; the others were mere ancillary damage), she had suspected another motive: to warn her away from Jonathan by demonstrating that she, too, was a formidable opponent and was prepared to do whatever was necessary to protect her marriage. She had considered sharing this possibility with her parents but decided this must be one more secret she needed to keep to herself. What good could possibly come from her parents knowing that Peregrine believed their daughter had designs on Jonathan Cooke—her husband's son-in-law? It was squalid. It was reprehensible. And, most certainly, it was sinful. Wasn't Mary's reputation sufficiently tarnished already? Her parents were well aware of what Abigail had seen. Imagine if Abigail or Hannah were present for a discussion of the possibility that Mary wanted to steal Jonathan Cooke from Peregrine? It could destroy any hope she had of her petition being granted and her reputation surviving this nightmare intact.

But, then, how could she be sure that Peregrine had wanted to poison her? Thomas had eaten the boiled apples, too, no doubt a helping that would have dwarfed even what Hannah had consumed. And then there was this: Peregrine had not made the boiled apples alone. Rebeckah Cooper had been with her, the two of them cooking in concert. That further suggested her daughter-in-law's innocence.

Or . . .

The idea was too depressing to contemplate, but consider it she did.

Perhaps her friend Rebeckah had poisoned the dessert. She chastised herself for suspecting for even a moment the other woman of evil, and could conceive of no reason why Rebeckah might wish ill upon her or her family. But the possibility had lodged there, one more pebble in her boot.

More than anything tonight, she was disappointed that the trial had oozed into a second day. She wanted it done. In every way she could imagine, this was a more humiliating spectacle than the stocks or the pillory—and perhaps more painful than a lashing. She gazed down at her left hand. Could the whip hurt more than what Thomas had done to her with the fork? It seemed unlikely. How was it that so much of the testimony that afternoon had been about her and not about him? How had it centered so much on her behavior and so little on his?

Tomorrow, she knew, he was going to speak at the Town House and he was going to lie. He was going to tell the magistrates that he had not plunged a fork into her hand. He had not hurled her into the hearth. He had not beaten her about the face. She was just a clumsy wench with white meat for a brain—though, of course, he would not say that precisely—who walked into clothes pegs and fell upon teakettles. He would add that he feared for her soul and did his best as her husband to school her. The worst he had done? He had accidentally banged her with the cooking spider while

Catherine was gone and he was trying to assist with their supper.

He was despicable.

Yes, she, too, was a sinner. Perhaps she was not among the elect. But neither did she believe that she was capable of that kind of cruelty. Lust was a terrible and terrifying affliction, and it might lead to her damnation; but her worst crime was kissing Henry Simmons. And while she may have defiled her own body, she had neither debased anyone else's nor degraded in any way the magic of the Lord's myriad works.

She sighed. She wondered what Henry Simmons was doing tonight. She thought of him often, her mind taking comfort in fantasies of him when she was alone in this room. Surely tales of what had occurred today at the courthouse had reached him. No doubt, he had heard what people had said about her. The discussions of her barrenness. The debate about the forks. How could he possibly be attracted to her? Good Lord, for that matter, how could Jonathan? She should have said that to Peregrine: no one could ever want her who wanted children.

And yet Henry Simmons had desired her, hadn't he? He had. He had pulled her into him to kiss her. That was a fact, as undeniable as the way the leaves turned crimson in this new world before dying or the marvels of those magnificent lobsters. Their size and their sea-monster-like claws. He had been drawn to her as she had been drawn to him, a magnetism as real as that which spun compass points to the north and as indisputable as the presence of Satan. Even here. A person could traverse an ocean so wide it took six or seven weeks to navigate, invariably storm-tossed and sickened, and here the Devil would be waiting. Yes, He had taken a knee before the Lord, but He hadn't bowed.

Henry Simmons wanted her, just as she wanted him. She could speculate her entire life on whether this was a temptation from the Devil—a lure to coax her to Him. She would never know until her life was done and her soul gone to Heaven or Hell.

Now she allowed herself a daydream: her petition for divorce was granted, and with one-third of Thomas's estate, she and Henry married and set off for Hadley to the west or Providence to the south. Somehow, she proved not to be barren and they had children, and the boys and girls lived.

They lived.

It was then that she saw the cat spring, pouncing upon a massive rat. The feline rolled onto its back, holding the animal with its forepaws and using its back legs to tear out the rodent's intestines. Then it sat up and gazed down at the corpse almost curiously. Another bat raced past her window. The cat looked up toward the bat and saw her still behind the glass. The animal bobbed its head between her and the dead rat as if to say, I have thee in my sights, too, Mary Deerfield. I do.

There were nights when I chose not to refill his mug.

—The Testimony of Ward Hollingsworth, from the Records and Files of the Court of Assistants, Boston, Massachusetts, 1662, Volume III

Seventeen

Neither Mary nor her parents summoned the physician in the morning because Hannah insisted that she felt somewhat improved. But she had been sick again in the night, and she did not stir from her bed. Before Mary and her parents and Abigail left for the trial, Hannah rolled over and faced them, giving them a small, weak smile. She said she would be up and about by the time they returned and offered to have dinner waiting. Priscilla commanded her to do no such thing.

Meanwhile, James looked at the rest of his family and concluded that there had been nothing insidious about the apples; whatever was afflicting Hannah was most likely attributable to the change in the season.

᚛ ᚜

At the base of the stairs on the first floor of the Town House, Mary and her parents and Benjamin Hull ran into Beth Howland. The weather had grown icy in the night and Beth's eyes were running from the cold, and she was wiping at them with the edge of her coif. For a moment she was so focused on her eyes that she was oblivious to Mary. When she saw her, she blinked and started to say something. Then, just as quickly, the awkwardness of the encounter led her to stop.

"Goody Howland, hello," said Priscilla Burden, smiling. Even now—the morning when Beth was going to suggest that Mary was an unregenerate sinner—Priscilla was civil, either because her heart really was that filled with Christ's love or because she believed that Beth's testimony might be swayed at the last moment with a small act of courtesy. "I pray thy family is well."

Goody Howland's face grew flushed. She looked at Mary's parents and at Hull and must have felt cornered. Ambushed. In the end, she nodded, and continued ahead of the Burdens up the steps to the second floor. Mary wished she understood, if only an inkling, why the woman despised her so.

⁂

It was colder in the Town House in the morning than in the afternoon, both because the sun hadn't had a chance to warm the building after the first truly frigid night of the season, and because the fires in the great hearths weren't lit until breakfast. Mary was aware of the way that her whole body wanted to curl up inside her cloak, her shoulders hunching, but she stood tall, hoping to project a confidence that she did not in fact feel.

Once more she stared up at the magistrates behind their high bench and waited with her parents and her scrivener, who stood like a phalanx around her. The constable rapped his iron pike on the wooden floor, the crowd—smaller than yesterday because the other petitioners had been alerted that the day would begin with the continuation of the divorce proceedings—grew quiet, and John Endicott swiveled his head and gazed at the men on either side of him.

"No jury again today?" he asked Richard Wilder.

"Not this morning. We have impaneled one for the petitions we will hear this afternoon."

The governor nodded. He seemed even older than yesterday.

Across the room, she saw Thomas and their eyes met. He smiled at her and she looked away. He seemed to be suffering no ill effects from the apples. Abigail was beside her mother, and still Mary was unsure precisely what the girl would say. It crossed her mind that the idea Peregrine may have tried to poison them might make a difference. The notion gave her hope.

Philip Bristol, Thomas's lawyer, took a step forward and said, "If it pleases the court, might Thomas Deerfield speak next? I know thou were planning on hearing Goody Howland and Abigail Gathers first, but Thomas has a farmer traveling here from Salem this morning. Thomas expected we would have finished yesterday afternoon, and so, one can suppose, the gentleman will arrive as planned with his very last delivery."

"And why must the miller be present?"

"There is still some negotiation to be done."

"Does he propose to speak and to leave? To not remain for our decision on the petition?" asked the governor.

"He plans to return. He hopes to meet with the good fellow from Salem and then immediately ride back here," Bristol said, pointing a finger toward the floorboards as if planting a stake in the ground.

The governor didn't seem to mind when he understood the plan, but Mary thought her principal ally among the magistrates, Richard Wilder, looked exasperated. "Then we shall begin with the husband," said Endicott. "Prithee, step forward, Thomas."

She watched Thomas stand before the bench, rising a little in his boots as he was sworn in. "What hast thou to say in response to Mary Deerfield's request to divorce thee?" asked the governor. She studied her husband's profile and was struck by the veiny redness of his nose, and how from this angle it looked too big for his face. She had assumed when they married that she would come to love the man. A thought crossed her mind, and it frightened her: Did he know on some level that she had never loved him and that was why he mistreated her so cruelly? Was this all her fault? She shook her head and banished the idea. She had done nothing to be hurled into a hearth or beaten about the face or have her hand speared by a silver fork. Still, the reality gave her pause. The truth that she did not love the man did not justify his cruelty, but it could possibly explain it.

"I view Mary as a good helpmeet," Thomas replied. "I love her as a man should love his wife."

"Thou dost not wish to be divorced from her," said Caleb Adams. It was a statement, not a question.

"I do not."

Adams looked down at a paper before him and then said, "She has accused thee of beating her. Dost thou deny it?"

"Yes." The magistrate waited for him to elaborate, but he didn't. The room was silent but for the sound of the wood crackling as it burned in the two great fireplaces.

Finally, Adams continued, "Thou hast never hit her?"

"Never," said Thomas, and Mary had to take a deep, slow breath to contain her frustration at his lies. If he lied a third time, would she hear a cock crow? Then she felt guilty at the very idea that she—so meek and lowly—would liken her plight to her Lord's. Still, the lies galled her. Moreover, it seemed as if Thomas had understood the cue from Caleb Adams: the magistrates were desirous that he offer a more embellished response. And so he went on, "As I said: I love her. I am a sinner, yes, but I understand my role as a husband."

"How dost thou correct her failings?"

"As our Lord would wish to correct us: with love and with kindness."

"Mary wrote in her petition and testified here yesterday that a few weeks ago thou plunged the Devil's tines into her left hand, breaking the bone. Dost thou deny it?"

"Thou heard the physician yesterday afternoon. She fell on the spout of a teapot."

"No! Dr. Pickering never said that!" Mary cried out, a reflex. "He said only—"

"That's quite enough!" snapped Adams. "Thou wilt hold thy tongue. We are hearing now the testimony of Thomas Deerfield."

Daniel Winslow gently touched the other magistrate's forearm through his robe. "The woman is correct, Caleb. Dr. Pickering said he could not say how Mary broke her hand."

"Or, perhaps, how it was broken by someone else," added Richard Wilder.

Adams sighed. "To clarify: Thomas, thou sayest that thou never struck Mary with the Devil's tines. Is that correct?"

"Yes. That's right. I have never struck her with anything. She broke her hand when she fell on the teapot in the night."

Mary shook her head at his audacity, but remained silent.

Wilder steepled his fingers and then said, "And thou didst what?"

Thomas seemed confused. "I told thee: I did not hurt her. She hurt herself."

Wilder shook his head. "No. Prithee: let us suppose, as thou hast said, that she fell on the teapot. It's nighttime. What happened next?"

He had to think about this. He cleared his throat. Eventually he answered. "I helped stop the bleeding," Thomas said. "I expected in the morning we would summon the physician."

"In the morning, according to testimonies presented by Mary's scrivener, thou went to thy mill. Thou didst not summon Dr. Pickering. Didst thou have a change of heart?"

"The bleeding had ceased. The wound seemed much improved."

"So, thou went to work?" pressed Wilder.

"Yes. We prayed and had breakfast and I went to the mill."

"Thy servant girl was gone. What did thee think of that? Where didst thou suppose she was?"

He shrugged. "Catherine had run off the night before. I know she is a fine girl. I supposed she had gone to the Howlands' and she would come to her senses and be back to assist Mary with dinner. I fretted only for Mary and her wounded hand."

"But instead, Mary left, too. That very morning. To what dost thou attribute her leaving?"

"I can think of no reason."

"Didst thou squabble? Men and their wives do squabble, Thomas," Wilder said. "That is not a crime."

"Nor is it a reason for divorce," Philip Bristol chimed in, but the magistrates as one looked askance at the lawyer. Even Thomas seemed surprised that his attorney had felt the need to say something. It was precisely the sort of behavior that gave lawyers such ignoble reputations.

"Thomas seems fully capable of answering for himself," said Wilder.

The lawyer nodded but did not appear chastened.

"No," said Thomas, "we did not squabble. I was worried about her. She was in pain. It would not have been a moment to argue. Besides, there was nothing about which we might have disagreed."

"Forgive me, prithee, but had thou been tippling the previous evening to the point of drunkenness?" Wilder asked.

Again, his lawyer chimed in: "Sir, were Thomas to confess to that, it would be confessing to a crime for which he has not been accused. This is not a hearing about whether he drinks to excess."

Wilder looked at the lawyer, his irritation apparent. He seemed about to say something, but then Thomas began to speak.

"I know the taverns and ordinaries," he began. "That is no secret and nothing for which I need either this court's or the Lord's forgiveness. But have I ever been fined for too much drink? No. Hast thou ever lashed me publicly for such offense? Of course not. This court knows me, it knows my mill. And, yes, though there is evil within me and my heart is inclined to sin; though I have reason often to be ashamed before God; the truth is that I have tried always to glorify God in all things. Though I will have many failures to answer for in the end, my comportment toward my wife, Mary Deerfield, will not be among them."

There was a pause as most of the magistrates and the small crowd seemed genuinely moved by his speech. Unlike them, Mary was outraged. She wondered if he had rehearsed it or been taught the remarks by his lawyer, and had been waiting for the right moment to share his faux confession and well-acted prostration. In the end, it was Richard Wilder who responded. His response was short but focused, and Mary could see that perhaps he alone on the bench had seen through the facade.

"So, thou canst offer absolutely no motivation for Mary's decision to return to her parents that morning?"

"None. Have I not told thee that? Have I not made that clear? My attorney says that the remedy for slander is a public retraction. Perhaps I should be filing a petition of my own demanding that Mary retract her charges that even once I have behaved with such low regard that would I strike her. Perhaps—"

"Thomas has no plans to do any such thing and take up the valuable time of the Court of Assistants," said the lawyer, cutting off his own client. But it was clear, instantly, that much of the goodwill that Thomas had planted had been washed away like seeds in a storm. Mary shook her head. She told herself that if it came down to her word against his, they very well might take her word, even though she was a woman, because there was so much he could not account for and because his behavior—and his lawyer's—was so distasteful.

Caleb Adams sat up straight and tried to focus the discussion once more on the case before them. To the other magistrates, he said, "Here is but a part of the puzzle I cannot parse. Thomas Deerfield is adamant that he never struck his wife. Yet the First Church—as we all know—recently excommunicated Mary Wharton for her abominable curses against her husband and for hitting him most violently. Likewise, the church excommunicated Marcy Verin for similar offenses. It cast out James Mattock for denying his wife a conjugal relationship, and William Franklin for the cruelty he evidenced toward his servants and his helpmeet. But the First Church has contemplated no such

action against Thomas Deerfield—nor has there even been a mediation."

"Go on, Caleb," said the governor. Mary glanced at her scrivener, curious where this was leading, but Hull discreetly shook his head. He had no idea.

Adams stared gravely at Thomas. "So, we have before us no logical reason for her to leave thee— unless . . ."

"Unless what?" asked Thomas, and Mary finished the magistrate's thought in her mind and grew relieved: **Unless thou art lying and in fact plunged the Devil's tines into thy poor help-meet's hand.**

But that wasn't what Adams was thinking. Not at all. "Unless," said Adams, his voice stern, "she is behaving erratically because Mary Deerfield has indeed been possessed by the Devil."

It took the crowd on the second floor of the Town House a moment to absorb the reality that Adams once more had brought the petition back to witchcraft. Mary felt a rush of nausea and dizziness and took her father's elbow for support, aware of the way that everyone around her suddenly was murmuring. He gazed down at her, his face reassuring, and brought one finger to his lips, but her mother looked frightfully scared. The constable struck the floor twice and then a third time with his pike, and the crowd went quiet.

Wilder looked at Adams and then at the governor and said, "I would like to remind everyone on the bench beside me that this is a petition for divorce. We are not adjudicating on witchcraft."

"She is barren," said Adams. "Do I need to remind thee that a witness saw her planting the Devil's tines in the dooryard? Is that not **maleficium**?"

"Mary Deerfield is most certainly not possessed," said Thomas loudly, forcefully, and with a protectiveness she would not have expected of him. "Mary Deerfield is not a witch. I can assure the Court of Assistants that she loves our Lord and Savior with all her heart. I pray that deep inside she loves me, too, with a love second only to her love of Jesus Christ. And I pray that whatever melancholy led her to leave me will pass and we will resume our lives together as man and wife."

"I thank thee, Thomas," said the governor. He looked at the magistrates. "Dost any of thee have any further questions?"

When there was silence from the bench, even from Caleb Adams, he said to Thomas, "Hast thou anything more to add?"

"I do not."

"Then go meet thy farmer from Salem. But be back quick. There are only a few more witnesses from whom we will hear. I hope we can render our verdict by dinner or just after dinner."

Mary watched Thomas bow to the magistrates. Then he nodded at her and her parents, but he gave them a wide berth as he approached the stairs. It sounded to her as if he took them quickly, with the speed and agility of a much younger man.

A man—and she thought of him with a guilt that unnerved her, because how could she possibly think of him now?—such as Henry Simmons.

I never saw my father strike my mother.

—The Testimony of Peregrine Deerfield Cooke, from the Records and Files of the Court of Assistants, Boston, Massachusetts, 1662, Volume III

Eighteen

A small parade of witnesses spoke briefly after Thomas had left. Mary's friend Rebeckah Cooper informed the magistrates that she had noticed bruises on the side of Mary's face three times that she could recall, reiterating what she had told the scrivener.

"And did Mary tell thee that Thomas had hit her?" asked Caleb Adams.

"No."

"Did thee ask?"

"No. But I—"

"But clearly thou were not alarmed," observed the magistrate.

It was painfully reminiscent of Jonathan's testimony, and when Rebeckah was leaving the Town House, Mary tried to imagine what she and Peregrine discussed when they were together. Was it their children? Their chores? Recipes for boiled apples and raisins? Or was there more to their friendship than Mary had ever conceived?

The tavern keeper, Ward Hollingsworth, followed, and said there were nights when Thomas

Deerfield drank more alcohol than was needed to quench his thirst, but he never behaved badly. His voice might grow loud and boisterous, but Hollingsworth insisted that he had worse customers.

"And so thou managed him," said Wilder, and Mary viewed it as an innocuous statement from the magistrate until she heard Hollingsworth's response. Only then did she understand Wilder's cleverness.

"Oh, there were nights when I chose not to refill his mug," said Hollingsworth, and he said it proudly, and the damage he had inadvertently inflicted on Thomas Deerfield was evident on the faces of some of the men on the bench.

Next came her neighbor Isaac Willard, and Mary had no idea why he had been summoned. Her scrivener had not approached him. But when Caleb Adams initiated the questioning, she understood: this was yet more character assassination. Adams wanted details about that afternoon when she had stopped Goody Howland's children from adding to the misery of an old man as he was lashed behind a wagon.

"And so thou made a decision to intervene?" asked Adams.

"I did. I saw Mary Deerfield showing sympathy for a Quaker, and I was disappointed and appalled," Willard answered.

"Hast thou ever seen her behave in such a strange fashion?"

"Women who are barren often act strangely. It would be like an owl that couldn't fly: it would be antithetical to our Lord's purpose, and the animal would, by necessity, go mad," he pontificated, and Mary wanted to throw up her arms in aggravation that the old man was allowed to make such pronouncements. The magistrates seemed to be absorbing the statement as if it were gospel wisdom, when Wilder finally spoke.

"Thou art speaking opinion only," he said. "Thou art not speaking as a reverend."

"I read the Bible faithfully."

"I am sure thou dost," Wilder said, and the governor thanked Willard and told him he could leave.

"May it be possible, governor, for Thomas to add another witness?" asked Philip Bristol as Willard was exiting the Town House.

John Endicott waved the back of his hand dismissively, but said, "Fine, Philip. Fine. But, prithee, let us proceed with haste."

"Yes. Of course," said the lawyer. He looked over his shoulder and motioned for a woman to come forward, and Mary saw that it was Peregrine Cooke. She had seemed tired to Mary the night before, but she looked beautiful this morning, and Mary attributed her loveliness both to daylight and to the grace that came with carrying a child.

It was as if even her face had grown rounder in the last few days, as her body had started to accommodate the baby inside her. The sight of the woman caused Mary a pang of envy, and she lamented the state of her soul that she could begrudge Peregrine this happiness.

But the woman's presence also caused her mother to whisper something into her father's ear, and when Mary raised an eyebrow inquiringly, her father just shook his head. "Tell me," she whispered.

"How dare Caleb Adams—or anyone—suggest that my daughter would ever consort with the Devil, while that one knowingly tried to poison us," Priscilla replied softly.

"We don't know that," her father said. "And, by the light of day and with the evidence that only Hannah was sickened, I tend to think she tried to poison no one."

"I disagree," Priscilla muttered.

"Thou art Thomas's daughter, correct?" Daniel Winslow was asking.

"I am. My name is Peregrine Cooke," she said, tucking a loose strand of her almost apple-red hair back beneath her coif.

"And what dost thou wish to say?"

"I don't wish to say anything, sir. I am here because my father's lawyer urged me to be present."

"Well, then, prithee, tell us why thy father's"—

and here Winslow sighed before saying the word with unhidden scorn—"**lawyer** has prodded thee onto this stage."

"He asked me to answer thy questions."

Winslow looked at the magistrates. "Do we have any?"

There was an awkward pause before Caleb Adams took the initiative. "Didst thy father ever strike thy mother?" he asked.

She looked out the eastern window before replying, "I never saw my father strike my mother."

"And thy father raised thee well?"

"He read the Psalter every morning to my mother, my brother, and me, and then to my mother and me after my brother passed."

Mary noted that these were not likely the categorical responses that either Bristol or the magistrate had expected.

"Peregrine," Adams pressed, "thou sayest that thou never saw thy father hit thy mother."

She nodded.

"Didst thou ever see him diminish her with words that were cruel or in a fashion that was profane?"

"Not in a fashion that was profane."

"But cruel?" asked Wilder.

"Cruel is a relative term, Richard," Adams said. "We might have different interpretations of the word. But profanity is an absolute, and Peregrine has made clear that Thomas never diminished his first wife in a manner that was profane."

"Fair," observed the governor, and Peregrine did not dispute this. Her gaze was blank.

"When thou were fourteen years old, thy father shot his horse because it kicked and killed thy mother. That seems to me an indication of the breadth of his affection for Anne," said Adams.

"Dost thou have a question hiding in that recollection, Caleb?" Wilder asked, his tone almost good-natured.

"No," Adams admitted. "I was young then. I still remember how moved I was."

By a man shooting his horse, Mary thought.

Wilder leaned forward. "Peregrine, since thy father married a second time, hast thou ever seen bruises about Mary Deerfield's face?"

Peregrine's hands were clasped before her, almost as if in prayer. Mary waited. The court waited. Finally, she replied, "Yes."

"Go on."

"On the side of her face."

"Dost thou know the cause?"

"My father or Mary explained them as thou hast heard. One time in the night she walked into a clothes peg. Another time there was a bruise from the spider."

Wilder said, "And then there was the time when—supposedly—she hurt her shoulder when she fell."

Peregrine said nothing.

"And most recently she—again, supposedly—fell upon a teapot."

When Peregrine once more remained silent, Wilder asked, "To what dost thou attribute her string of . . . accidents?"

"We all have accidents," she answered. "One time I stumbled on cobblestones and most severely twisted my ankle."

But Wilder had made his point.

The governor looked at the men on either side of him and asked if they had any more questions. When they did not, he thanked Peregrine and asked that the next witness be brought to the front of the room.

As Peregrine started toward the stairs, Mary noted the way her father had a secure hold on her mother's elbow, and how her mother glared at the pregnant woman with undisguised venom.

∾

Mary listened as Goody Howland smeared her character, calling her "naught but a sinner whose heart is all lust and who has no acquaintance with shame or remorse," and thought darkly to herself, **Well, at least she is not accusing me of murdering her indentured servant. At least she is not accusing me of witchcraft.**

"And so," Caleb Adams was confirming, "thou

saw her with Henry Simmons—Valentine Hill's nephew—near the wharf."

"Yes."

Mary wanted to tell everyone that Henry had been helping her when she had nearly been run over by an oxcart, but she had learned her lesson: interrupting a witness curried no favor with the magistrates.

"She was behaving abominably," said Beth. "It was as if we were back in London among the damned and she was but a wench awaiting the sailors."

"Didst thou see her debase herself with other men?" Adams asked.

"When William Stileman first grew sickly and bedridden—before he was mostly sleeping and incapable of speech—Mary would visit, and the two of them would chat and chat. It was most unseemly. I grew much alarmed."

"Alarmed?" asked Richard Wilder. "I can understand experiencing a great many emotions if what thou sayest is true. But, prithee: why in the world wouldst thou have been alarmed?"

And here Goody Howland began to shake her head energetically and said, pointing her finger at Mary, "She is a shameless, impious, and lustful woman. By her sins, she will not only pull down judgment from the Lord upon herself, but also upon the place where she lives."

Some of the crowd nodded, as did Caleb Adams.

And so Mary turned away and watched a servant throw two great logs onto the fire in the nearby hearth, and the sparks rise up into the chimney like fireflies. Her mind began to wander from the Town House and the testimony. She knew she should be listening; she should focus because this was her future, but she couldn't. Not anymore. This was madness. Catherine had suggested that she had been trying to kill her brother; Goody Howland was suggesting that she wanted to seduce him. It couldn't be both; the fact was, it was neither. Still, her mind roamed to the mysteries of the Devil's tines and her barrenness. She thought of her needs in the night. She knew who she was; she knew what she was. Yes, Goody Howland was exaggerating either by delusion or by design. But did it matter? The woman had seen clearly into her soul.

Maybe she would have been better off if she had finished her portion of Peregrine's or Rebeckah's poisoned apples and died—or, like Hannah, been too sick to come here this morning. After all, she wouldn't have had to listen to her character so roundly diminished. The truth was, she wanted nothing more right now than to leave. To turn from the magistrates, descend the stairs, and go . . .

Go where? There was nowhere to go. Here was her destiny.

She felt her father's hand on her shoulder, and he was scrutinizing her with a look that was rich with love, but also with intensity. He was trying to draw her back. She stared up at him, unsure whether she was smiling or frowning or her mouth was a cipher.

Her left hand, cosseted by her glove, began to throb, and she massaged it with two of the fingers on her right hand. She told herself it was just the cold, but in her heart she feared it was something more: it was a sign.

Because, if one looked around carefully, wasn't everything?

ॐ ॐ

Caleb Adams asked Abigail Gathers whether she had ever seen Thomas Deerfield strike Mary, and no one was surprised in the slightest when she said no. After all, she was indentured to Mary's mother and father and lived with them. She didn't live with Thomas and Mary; she was never going to be present in the night when he did his worst. Adams asked the question for no other reason than that it would result in the magistrates hearing yet again that Thomas had never hit his second wife.

Was this really why Philip Bristol had taken her testimony the other day and, as Thomas's lawyer, summoned her here this morning? Neither Mary nor her parents knew precisely what the girl had said to the attorney, and whether she might have revealed anything that was incriminating.

"What sort of person is Mary Deerfield?" Adams was asking her now.

Before Abigail could respond, Wilder turned to his colleague and said, "Caleb, that question has no relevance. Even if she is a sinner of the most reprehensible sort, a man has no right to strike his wife. Punishment is meted out here."

Adams stabbed a finger at him, smirking. "And vengeance? We know to whom that belongs."

"I would not be so glib," said Wilder.

"The question is relevant because of the potency of Mary's allegations and the magnitude of her petition. Do we not have a right to know more about the woman's character?"

The governor looked back and forth between Adams and Wilder and weighed in. "The question is allowed. Abigail, thou mayest answer the magistrate's question."

Abigail seemed to think about this. Then: "I like her much. She is very kind."

"I thank thee," said Wilder, but Adams again raised his index finger.

"Is she a sinner?" Adams asked.

"Aren't we all?"

"Hast thou ever seen her sin?" he asked, and Mary feared that somehow, some way, he knew something.

"I do not know what dwells in her heart," she replied.

"But thou knowest the meaning of adultery, yes, Abigail?"

The girl nodded.

"And thou knowest an unclean thought when one is brought forth in body and action?"

"I hope so. I listen attentively to the Psalter readings of my master, James Burden, and to the sermons of Reverend Norton."

"Very good, Abigail. So, prithee, hast thou ever seen Mary Deerfield behave in a manner that is unclean?"

"He is but fishing," Hull whispered into Mary's ear. "He is merely trying to build upon what Goody Howland said."

But Mary could see that Abigail was stalling, when she asked, "Unclean?"

"A fashion that suggests her willingness to allow her defiled soul to roam free."

"I am but a small bird and my sight is clouded by youth. Besides . . ."

"Yes?"

Abigail glanced at James and Priscilla Burden. Mary realized how meticulously her scrivener or her parents had coached the girl. "Besides," she continued, turning back to the bench, though her eyes were lowered, "who am I to cast a stone?"

Adams folded his arms across his chest. He cleared his throat and asked, his exasperation evident, "Hast thou ever seen her sin, Abigail? And answer knowing that thy Lord and Savior are watching thee as intently as I."

She nodded her head ever so slightly, and her voice cracked when she responded. "Once. Perhaps."

"Tell us, child."

"Once—just the one time—I saw her and Henry Simmons holding hands and kissing. No, perhaps, they were only about to kiss. It all happened so quickly."

"About to kiss?" asked Adams, wanting more. He sounded lustful himself.

"I am not sure I saw them, in fact, kiss."

"Art thou suggesting they stopped because they saw thee?"

"Or they stopped because they came to themselves. They knew it was wrong what they were contemplating. Mary Deerfield is kind, sir. She is good." Still, the girl looked forlorn.

"Why do I have a feeling there may be more to it than that?" Adams pressed.

"I know not what else there could be," she said, her voice timorous. Mary thought the girl might cry at what she had to view as her betrayal of her master and his family.

"Speak, child!" roared Adams, his voice all frustration and pique.

And so the girl did, though her voice was halting and broken: "Perhaps they stopped because I dropped my bowl of eggs."

"Elaborate."

"I surprised them and I was surprised, in turn, by what I saw: Mary's hand in his and their faces so close. I dropped my eggs."

"And they heard thee?"

Abigail nodded.

"This is a grave accusation," Wilder told the girl. "Art thou convinced of the rightness of thy memory?"

When she responded now, she was in tears, her shoulders heaving with every syllable. "I was shocked deeply by what I saw. I speak as a witness, not a gossip," she mewled. And she was saying more, but her words were garbled by her crying, and Mary felt her skin tightening and thought: **This is the price of my sin. I have earned this because I am craven and low, and I have brought this danger upon myself. I earned every bruise and broken bone, and I merited the wrath of my husband and having him dump a boiled salad upon me as if I, too, were but rubbish and ruin. I am . . . damned. I am a wastrel and a whore, and I have taken my Lord God's love and treated it like sewage.** She wanted to disappear, to vanish, to shrink into nothingness.

She might have gone on that way until, like Abigail, she, too, was wrecked before the magistrates, but then the crowd was parting and there— and she saw his shadow first, the darkness on the floor cast by the sun pouring in through the eastern windows—was Henry Simmons, striding up toward the magistrates. Confused, she looked toward her scrivener and her parents. Were they as shocked as she? She couldn't decide. The constable, roused either by Abigail's bleating sobs or the outrage of the crowd that this seeming interloper had appeared out of nowhere, rushed with his pike and stood between Simmons and the magistrates as if he expected the young man to attack one of the important men behind the great wooden balustrade. He held his wrought-iron spike as if it were a piece of horizontal field fencing, a barricade of sorts.

"I would like to speak, governor, if I may," Henry said, his voice firm.

Endicott looked at the magistrates on either side of him, fixating first on Richard Wilder and then on Caleb Adams. Adams ruffled his hair and told the governor, "This is Valentine Hill's nephew. Henry Simmons."

Endicott said, "The one Mary Deerfield is accused of—"

"Yes," said Wilder, and Mary had the sense that he was interrupting the magistrate so Endicott would not give voice to the crime. "Good day to thee, Henry," he continued. Then he said to the constable, "Valentine Hill's nephew poses no threat. We are not under attack. Thou canst stand down." The constable rocked back and forth on his heels and toes, glowering at Henry, but retreated.

"Sir," Henry continued, "I am grateful for thy time. I have come here to give account of my behavior and atone for my sins." He looked at Abigail, who was wiping at her eyes with her sleeve, trying to gather herself.

The governor nodded. "Abigail"—and the girl visibly flinched at the sound of her name—"we thank thee for thy candor. Thou art finished and can return home."

The girl bowed and then withdrew, choosing a path to the stairs that kept her as far from Mary and the Burdens as possible. If Mary were not fixated on Henry, she thought she might have gone to the girl and told her that she had said nothing untrue and to think well of herself. But there wasn't time and, besides, Henry was about to speak.

"Henry, what hast thou to add?" asked Wilder.

Henry spoke without hesitation. "I am but a crumb of dust and unworthy of thy attention. I cast myself on the mercy of the court though I deserve none. Yes, I tried to kiss Mary Deerfield, just as that honest and fine young servant told thee. But we did not kiss, and the reason is that Mary resisted my advances. She said, and she said so without hesitation, that she was married and would not be seduced into an adulterous moment that would shame her before this community and before her Lord and Savior."

Wilder crinkled his eyes almost good-naturedly. "So, thou art saying that we do not need to add adultery to her ledger?"

"That is correct."

"But only to thine?"

"Yes."

Wilder whispered something Mary couldn't

hear to the governor and then spoke softly to Caleb Adams. She felt a roaring inside her ears, a black-smith's flame, and thought she should rise up and admit that she, too, was a sinner, every bit as culpable and as rich with blame as Henry Simmons. She should tell them that Henry was lying, and though he was lying to protect her, it was still an outrage to the Lord. She started forward but felt her father's grip on her upper arm, his fingers long and firm, the tentacles of the sea monsters sometimes drawn to great effect on the maps. He was squeezing her arm hard: she understood that she was to remain where she was. And so she did, hating herself even more for what she defined in her mind as a stomach-churning concoction of cowardice and obedience.

"Was this the only time that thou tempted Mary?" the governor asked.

"Yes. The only time."

"And she resisted?"

"She did. Most capably and most determinedly."

Adams turned to the other men: "Should we ask the servant girl to return? See if she will corroborate what this man is saying?"

"No, Caleb," said the governor. "We needn't do that. This is Valentine Hill's nephew. I believe we can view his narrative without skepticism." Endicott then leaned over the balustrade and said, "There was clearly no fornication. I think a lashing will suffice. Tomorrow at ten a.m., Henry

Simmons, thou art ordered to appear in the square where thou wilt be whipped"—and he paused ever so briefly—"fifteen times on thy bare back."

He nodded, and Mary thought of the Quaker she'd seen flogged, though his lashing was far more severe and he was paraded down the streets. But she'd seen other men and women whipped, their backs reddened and ravaged and scored until they looked more like butchered meat than a human's torso. Mary glanced one last time at her father, and he shook his head slightly. She was quite sure that she alone had seen the gesture and knew what it meant. And though she was awash in grief and self-loathing, and though she knew that if she hadn't been damned before she probably was now, she stood silent and still and waited to see what would happen next.

※ ※

But there wasn't anything next; there wasn't anything more. There were no more witnesses to hear, no more testimonies to examine.

The governor said, referencing the small room where Mary and her parents had first met with Richard Wilder, "We will retire to the quills and discuss the petition. Has Thomas Deerfield returned?"

The constable reported that he hadn't.

"Retrieve him, prithee." Then he said to Mary, "This deliberation shouldn't take long."

"Wouldst thou suggest we retire for dinner?" her father asked.

Endicott rubbed at his fingers, which Mary could see were badly swollen at the joints. "No," he said. "My hope is that we can render a decision quickly." She glanced at her scrivener, worried that a decision that seemed obvious to the governor boded ill for her, but hoping in her heart she was mistaken. The scrivener, however, did not return her gaze, and his countenance was inscrutable.

Whenever we ponder a petition of
this magnitude, I am obliged to ask
myself this question. If now I were
dying, how would I wish I had behaved
during my life? For what would I crave
remembrance, and for what will I have
to answer to our Lord God and Savior?

**—The Remarks of Magistrate Richard
Wilder, from the Records and Files
of the Court of Assistants, Boston,
Massachusetts, 1662, Volume III**

Nineteen

Mary needed desperately to sit and she could see that her mother did, too, and so Benjamin Hull suggested that they return to his office, where he had the chair behind his desk and the bench before it. It wasn't a long walk, but Mary noticed how unsteady her mother was on her feet and the tenacity with which she clung to her husband's elbow. Meanwhile, Mary kept her eyes peeled for Henry. She knew she didn't dare speak with him if she spotted him, but her desire to see him after what he had done was almost unbearable. He was taking a lashing for her. He had preserved whatever remained of her reputation. She wondered what her sullen and big-shouldered husband would have said had he been present at the Town House when Henry had appeared and spoken with such cavalier self-disregard. Thomas was physically bigger than Henry Simmons, but was he a match for the younger man? Yes, Mary decided, he was. He was also a mean drunk and had the spine of a brawler. Regardless of how the magistrates ruled on her petition, regardless of whether tonight she was a free woman or imprisoned once more as the wife of Thomas Deerfield, Henry Simmons would need to be wary and alert, as attentive as the city's sentinels.

When they arrived at the scrivener's office, Hull insisted that Priscilla take his chair and Mary sit on the bench. He hadn't any beer for them to drink, but he opened a bottle of Madeira because they all were desperately thirsty. He had but one tankard, and so the Burdens and Mary shared it and Hull drank from the bottle. He leaned against an inside wall, and her father stood beside the window, his gaze moving back and forth between the street and the rather ornate lantern clock—its bronze face had tulips—Hull kept on a side table across from his desk.

"I think we have a little time," he said to the family. "The Court of Assistants renders their verdicts quickly, but the men on that bench today have many opinions and they will all want to be heard."

Mary considered asking him what he thought they would decide but was too afraid. She had the distinct sense that her mother felt the same way. And so she tried to push aside the anxiety that was gathering inside her like thunderclouds the color of burnt wood by half listening to her father and Hull's small talk, but mostly by creating in her mind a ledger of the witnesses who had helped her cause and those who had hurt it. Some, she understood, belonged on both sides. She thought it revealing of the meanness of her spirit that she felt more anger at the moment toward Goody Howland than she did toward Thomas. Her father offered her mother another sip from the tankard, but her arms were wrapped tightly around her chest and she was sitting perfectly still. She shook her head, her eyes riveted on the clock.

"Peregrine Cooke may have tried to poison us last night," Priscilla said when the two men grew quiet.

"Priscilla," her father began, but her mother cut him off.

"Our scrivener needs to know this," she said.

Hull waited, and so James Burden explained, "Peregrine brought us an apple dessert last night, and one of our servant girls got sick. It may have had nothing to do with the apples, and if it did, it may have been an accident. She made some for Thomas, too, and he felt no ill effect."

"It most assuredly had to do with the apples. All of us tasted something rancid and foul and ate but a bite or two—except the girl, who, apparently, rather likes tart apples. And she is the one who collapsed."

"Why would Peregrine do such a thing?" Hull asked.

"To prevent Mary from speaking today," Priscilla replied.

"Did she?"

"Did she speak? Thou knowest the answer to that. No, but Peregrine could not have foreseen that. And certainly Mary's presence made it more difficult and unpleasant for Abigail to share what she saw."

"Priscilla," James said, "Abigail was going to do all that she could to protect our daughter, regardless of whether Mary was present."

"It could have been Goody Cooper," Mary murmured.

"Rebeckah?" her mother asked. "She is thy friend."

"I only mention her name because Peregrine and Rebeckah were cooking the boiled dessert together. If we are going to pursue all possibilities—"

"Mary, that is enough," her father said.

She looked at him and then at her mother, but Priscilla was glaring out the window. Her father was correct. She needed to stop worrying that thread. And the scrivener was right, too: Peregrine probably hadn't been thinking about the trial when—if—she had mixed something fetid and evil in with the apples. Mary recalled her suspicions when she had been alone in her bedroom last night: perhaps her daughter-in-law wanted to sicken her—or, perhaps, murder her. She wanted to keep her away from Jonathan. Hadn't the other woman made that clear when she brought the dessert to the Burdens' house? But even this seemed absurd when she thought it through: how could Peregrine expect to sicken only Mary?

Oh, but maybe she didn't care. Let the others grow ill, too.

She sighed. Why couldn't people just desire the people with whom God had blessed them? Catherine may (or may not) have craved Thomas; Peregrine feared that Mary was desirous of Jonathan and, conceivably, that Jonathan thought too highly of her; and she herself was lusting after Henry Simmons. It was all so complicated.

"Mary?"

She looked up. It was Hull. "More Madeira?" he asked, leaning across the desk.

"Maybe in a few minutes," she said. She watched her father pat her mother's right hand good-naturedly, which made Mary think of the bones so recently broken in her left.

⊰ ⊱

For the next half hour, Mary and her mother said little. Occasionally Hull and her father conjectured about what may have been transpiring at the Town House, but it was all speculation. By now the messenger had reached her husband's mill, and he was on his way back to the center of the city. Carefully she pulled off her left glove and gazed at her hand. The swelling was down considerably and the wound healing well, but still there were moments when her store of valerian was little match for its ache. She watched a spider scuttle across the desk near the bottle and then disappear down the side of the wood. She asked the scrivener to refill the tankard and took a long swallow, finishing the wine and hoping both to quench her parched tongue and to silence the rhythmic throbbing in her hand. She hoped to calm her nerves. It was unsettling that where she would sleep tonight remained a mystery even now.

"Does it hurt much?" her mother was asking.

"No," she replied. "I'm fine."

"Mary," her father said, his tone grave, "whatever happens, rest in the knowledge that the Lord knows what is best and holds thee in His hands. Take comfort in the fact that thou hast a fine scrivener." He smiled in a paternal fashion at the other man, and Hull shrugged modestly.

Mary tried not to give greater meaning to her father's words than probably he had meant. But she could not help but hear foreboding in them. She recalled the moments during the last few weeks when she had seen or felt signs of conspiracy—the lengths they would go to . . .

To what? To protect her?

And yet returning to Thomas Deerfield was no protection, unless there were dangers out there far worse than his base cruelties. She put the tankard on the scrivener's desk beside his inkpot. Once again, she ran the tips of the fingers on her right hand over the wound on the back of her left and thought of the forks, including the one that Thomas had wielded as a weapon. She thought as well of the pestle.

"Mary, art thou with us?" her father was asking.

She watched the wind off the harbor cyclone the scarlet leaves in the streets up and off the cobblestones, and was struck by their beauty. Even dry and dead they were lovely. God's work. God's world.

"Yes," she said. "I am."

The men chatted for a few more minutes and her mother watched her, worried, but said nothing. And then, almost abruptly, they all saw through the window a boy of perhaps fourteen, an apprentice to one of the magistrates, running toward the office. Even before the lad rapped on the scrivener's door, Hull clapped his hands together and said, " 'Tis time. They have rendered their decision. Let us return."

❧ ❧

Their faces were inscrutable. The men behind the bench. Did Caleb Adams look satisfied and self-righteous, was he feeling contentment that justice had been done and a marriage preserved? Mary couldn't decide. Was Richard Wilder frustrated that his friend James Burden's daughter was being sent back to the beast, or was he relieved that her petition had been granted and she was going to begin her life anew? His eyes were impenetrable. Daniel Winslow seemed intent largely on whatever paper was before him on the bench. Governor Endicott looked only exhausted. When no one would make eye contact with her, she felt a quiver of anxiety.

And there was Thomas standing across the floor from her. He smiled at her, but it was derisive and mean. She feared that he knew something. Beside him was Philip Bristol, his hands clasped behind him as he rocked ever so slightly back and forth on his heels and toes. She had been aware that the lawyer was shorter than her husband, but only now was she struck by how much: Thomas was a head taller than the man.

She heard the governor saying to the constable, "I see that everyone has returned. Let us proceed."

The constable rapped his pike on the wooden floor, and the murmuring in the Town House grew silent.

"Richard, it is for thee to render the verdict," Endicott said, and for a moment Mary was engulfed by a wave of confidence. The idea that it was Wilder who was going to announce her fate might be a sign that God was smiling upon her and offering deliverance.

"Whenever we ponder a petition of this magnitude, I am obliged to ask myself this question," Wilder said. "If now I were dying, how would I wish I had behaved during my life? For what would I crave remembrance, and for what will I have to answer to our Lord God and Savior? A court such as this is a most imperfect vessel, and our judgment is dyed badly by our frailties and by sin. We have neither the wisdom nor the glory of our Maker. We all know in our hearts the myriad ways that daily—daily!—we offend Him."

She felt an ache in the small of her back from standing and thought of her mother and father, so much older than she, who had been standing all this time yesterday and today beside her.

"We are but rats skulking in corners. And yet we do our best, because that is what we must. A few thoughts." He directed his gaze firmly on her father. "James, thy daughter's petition has nothing to do with thy business. There is no law against importing three-tined forks. But, as might be expected, no good has come from thy presumption. Our hope is that we hear no more about them ever again in this Town House." He raised a single eyebrow and, despite his words, looked more bemused than angry. Her father nodded sheepishly.

"We have discussed the petitioner's request for a divorce and weighed carefully what everyone had to say. We thank everyone for their candor," he continued, and then the register of his tone once more grew somber. "Here is what we know. A saint is wedded to God in a marriage that is divine. Our covenant with God is spiritual. When a man weds a wife, there is a parallel. In this case, of course, it is a civil covenant. But consider the similarities. God loves a mortal, despite his foolishness and sin, just as a man should love his wife—despite her foolishness and sin. God loves a mortal, despite his weaknesses and craven impulses, just as a man should love his wife—despite her weaknesses and craven impulses. Though a woman may be willful and passionate and show behavior that is rife with pride, that does not demand the forfeiture of the marriage. She is a helpmeet, yes, but she is the weaker of the two vessels and must be cared for."

Mary looked to her father, angered by this lecture, because she was beginning to fear where it might be going. But her father didn't seem alarmed; he was actually nodding as if in agreement during a sermon.

"Was a man's wife unfaithful? That may be a reason for him to divorce her; likewise, if a man was unfaithful, that certainly is grounds for her to divorce him. But it seems there was no adultery in this marriage. There may have been a temptation, but that was all—and Henry Simmons will be appropriately punished. So, let us gathered here focus on the petition and only on the petition, and not lose sight of the wisdom of God's carefully wrought hierarchy: He rules over man and man rules over animals. Likewise, parents rule over children—and a man rules over his wife."

Was Thomas smirking? He was, and Mary felt acutely the pain in her back and in her hand. She thought she might cry right there in the Town House.

"We in this court will never know the truth of what transpired the night when Mary Deerfield's hand was broken and Thomas Deerfield's servant ran off. There has been much hearsay and many accusations. Only Thomas and Mary and our God know all that occurred and all that was in their hearts. Was there cruelty?" He paused and stared intently at Thomas. "There may have been. There may even have been a pattern of misbehavior. I have my opinion. Others on this bench have theirs. As many a great pastor has observed, we see in this world with a vision obscured by transgression."

Then he turned back to the crowd, continuing, "Just as man comes to God awash in whorishness and shame, so do a man and his wife come to marriage. Which brings us all to the Apostle Paul and his admonition: we must strive to cleanse ourselves from the filthiness of the flesh and the spirit. We must. We will fail, but there are degrees of failure. Now, this petition for divorce is founded neither on criminal uncleanliness nor fornication. There has been no desertion: I see both man and wife present in this room. And despite the lack of a child, there is no reason to suppose a conjugal insufficiency." He shook his head. "This petition has been requested on one cause and one cause only: severe cruelty. But, alas, we have no witnesses to that cruelty and

we have no proof of that cruelty. We have compet-
ing stories, that is all. And so we are denying Mary
Deerfield's petition for divorce. She is being ordered
by this court to return today—this afternoon—to
her husband, Thomas Deerfield. That is all."

And that was it. It was done. Mary was aware
that Thomas was vigorously shaking his lawyer's
hand and of how smug the two men seemed.
Caleb Adams looked pleased in a way that caused
her contempt for him to solidify into something
solid and hard: dough into bread. Slaked lime
and sand into brick. His condescension toward
her—toward all women—rankled her. She felt her
mother rubbing her back, and then Priscilla whispered into her ear that this was good, all would be
well, and she was safe. But the word **safe** galled
her. Safe? How did returning to a man who would
try to skewer her hand to a table with a fork keep
her safe? And then Thomas was approaching,
and she saw the constable leading a jury into the
room to weigh in on the afternoon's petitions,
but she stood there mute. She was forlorn, yes,
she knew this was her outward visage; but she felt
something inside her moving from a simmer to
a boil. There was within her a great magazine of
emotions, a warehouse her father's size, and among
them was her knowledge that the rot of her marriage was not worthy food for pigs, and the verdict
of the court was an injustice that would not stand.
Thomas's violence would only escalate with this

vindication, of this she was sure. And as he reached her side and took her right hand gently in his, she looked into his eyes—he was so very pleased with himself—and saw in the lines of his deep brown irises a pair of three-tined forks. Whether this was a vision or her imagination she couldn't say. But she didn't care. Yes, vengeance belonged to the Lord. But this decree was wrong. Perhaps those forks were a sign, after all: a sign for her. An idea, inchoate as the wisps of clouds that precede a great storm, began to form. Thomas was saying something to her. Her father was, too. But the words were lost in the burble of the Town House and the pelf of her memory, because one thought was lodging itself as firmly in her mind as yew roots in the ground. Yes, she thought, revenge belongs to God. But justice? That will be mine.

THE BOOK of the WITCH

Mary Deerfield, thou hast been accused of witchcraft. There is much evidence to corroborate such a charge. Tell us plainly so we know where we stand: Dost thou wish to confess to falling prey to the Devil's enticements and signing a covenant with the Dark One?

—The Charges, as read by Governor John Endicott, from the Records and Files of the Court of Assistants, Boston, Massachusetts, 1663, Volume I

Twenty

Catherine prepared a dinner for the three of them of well-seasoned squash and mussels that Thomas had instructed her to buy that morning at the market. There was also cornbread and cheese.

At one point, Thomas rested his fist on the table beside Catherine's trencher and said to the girl, "Dost thou still believe thy mistress is possessed?" Mary tried to decipher the tone: on the surface it was paternal, but there was something about the way he stressed the inherent sibilance of the last word that gave it a more threatening cast.

Catherine shook her head grimly, and then brought one of the mussels to her mouth, sucking the cooked animal from the shell. The girl was cornered. What could she say? They agreed that she would retrieve her clothes that afternoon from Goody Howland's and then resume her life with the Deerfields. That night she would sleep once again in the kitchen, as she had every night she had lived in Boston, with the exception of her time at the Howlands'. Mary had a feeling that the servant would not sleep deeply but felt no sorrow at her plight. If she lusted after Thomas, it seemed he did not return her ardor; if she truly believed that Mary was a witch, now she was trapped with her inside this house. Yes, Mary had lost; but so, it seemed, had Catherine.

"Good," Thomas said. "Thou wilt be happy here again." He took a swallow of beer and smiled benignly. He reported that he had asked the physician to visit that afternoon and examine Mary's hand to see how it was healing.

"That's not necessary," she told him.

"Certainly, it is," he said, and then parodied what she'd said at the Town House. "After all, Mary, a teakettle can be a weapon most terrible."

Mary did not reply. She turned to Catherine and told her, "I still miss thy brother. I am sorry that he passed so young."

"He is with the Lord. He is well now," she murmured.

"Yes," Mary agreed. "He is."

When they had finished dinner, Thomas returned to his mill. She and Catherine cleaned up the remnants of the meal. Then Catherine left for the Howlands', and Mary sat alone at the kitchen table. The room was utterly silent. She thought back on their meal. Thomas's prayer had been short, but he had thanked the Lord for returning to him his wife. It was altogether nonjudgmental and suggested no atonement was necessary on his part: it was as if she had been thought lost at sea and suddenly, much to everyone's surprise, been found. His conversation had vacillated between ominous and ordinary. At one point, he had tried to be pleasant and told a story of the farmer from Salem he had dealt with that morning. Another time, he had glowered at the squash and ruminated aloud, "What do the two of thee think? Do I need a cupbearer? Shall I search out and retain my own personal Nehemiah to be sure that my food has not been poisoned?" Mary recalled the man's daughter's apples, but neither she nor Catherine had responded.

Now, Mary realized as she sat in solitude, she was stunned. Once, early that summer when she had been walking at the edge of the city, she had seen a hawk plunge into a farmer's field and then arise with a chipmunk in its talons. The chipmunk was alive, but it wasn't struggling. It was dazed. Stupefied. Mary understood that her situation was not that dire: her death was not imminent. She wasn't about to be eaten. But she found it almost unfathomable that but two hours ago she was standing in the Town House hoping to hear that her petition had been granted and she'd been set free. Instead she was a—and the word came to her and she thought it not melodramatic—prisoner.

She was a prisoner of a man who had within him a monster. It lived among his four humours, and he was pliant to its whims. When he was drink-drunk he was especially susceptible to its brutality and fancies, but it would be a mistake to attribute his violence to his penchant for too much cider or beer. She knew what he was capable of even when he was sober. Moreover, there was a deliberation to his evil: he attacked her only (and always) when there were no witnesses present.

Finally, she stirred. She went to the bucket where Catherine was soaking their knives and spoons, and pulled from the water a knife. She held it in her right hand and thought again of that chipmunk in the hawk's claws. She felt gutted, the emotions spontaneous and almost overwhelming, the sorrow deep inside her, and she started to cry. She collapsed onto the floor, her back against the wall, and stared through her tears at the blade. She pressed it against her left wrist, curious if she could or should slice through the skin and watch her blood puddle onto the wooden boards.

She turned her left hand over and looked at the mark where he had stabbed her and recalled the pain. She thought of Corinthians:

O death, where is thy sting?

The answer? **The sting of death is sin.**

But she knew the sting of the Devil's tines.

No, she knew the sting of a fork.

It was cutlery, no more devilish than this knife in her hand or the ones soaking with the spoons in the bucket, and henceforth she would call it that and only that. It was a . . . fork. And would the sting of the knife be an agony any worse than what Thomas

had accomplished with a fork? Someday she would know God's eternal plan for her, whether she was among the damned or the elect. Did it really matter if she discovered that in ten years or ten minutes? It did not. God was inscrutable. She could die here and be but sweat and tears and the macerating remains of her fiery humours when Catherine or Thomas returned, her soul already gone to Heaven or Hell.

She turned the knife so the tip was against the back of her wrist and pricked the skin until it bled. It was a small cut, but deep enough that she watched the blood pool. She imagined slicing through her flesh as if butchering a hog. She had that sort of strength in her right arm. She could end this lying down and then meet her Savior or Satan. She could. She stared up at the heavy table and the window beyond it, at the afternoon light. She loved the light this time of the year. She loved it in the trees when the leaves turned their kaleidoscopic reds and yellows, she loved it when the leaves were gone and the slim black branches of the oak but black lines against a sapphire sky. At the right time of day, it was like seeing the world through gauze, and the sun gave the world a calming, tawny cast.

Two words came to her now, each syllable distinct and clear: get up. Was it her Lord? It most definitely was a command. Get up. Get up now. She looked into the hearth, which almost was out,

and saw there, too, a beauty in the fire. The voice, if that's what it was, was neither Maker nor Devil. It was . . . her. It was her soul reminding her that her hap in the end was in God's hands and had been in God's hands since the beginning of time, but her moment on this earth was hers. It. Was. Hers. The self-pity had been accreting inside her like January snow on the sill—blinding her—since the moment she had stepped back inside this house. She began to fear that if she didn't move, she would take the knife and sculpt a cup of flesh from her wrist and never get up again. And that wasn't really what she wanted. Not at all. She wanted more, she wanted life. Where was the woman who had stood in the Town House and vowed that she would have justice when the unjust verdict had been rendered? Where had that woman gone? She recalled her resolve there and leaned over, dropping the knife back into the bucket and using both hands—her left, too, despite the pain that shot from the back of the mending bone up her arm and caused her to wince—to push herself to her feet. She would not wallow here on the floor. She would fight. What was the naval term? Line of battle. She would turn her broadside cannons upon her husband, while standing tall against the Catherine Stilemans and the Goody Howlands and the Peregrine Cookes and perhaps even the Rebeckah Coopers of Boston. She would learn who had buried the forks and the pestle in the yard—and why. And most of all?

She would be free. She could not and would not live like this: a creature contemplating its own demise at its own hands. A mistress haunted by her own servant girl and scared of her husband.

She went to the window to gaze out at the world and the light that God had made, a gift to be relished—and for a moment she did. But she was not meant to enjoy it long. She saw the physician Roger Pickering, astride his majestic gray-and-white horse, coming to a stop at the end of the dooryard. As he climbed off it, their eyes met. He tipped his cap and then hitched his horse to the post. She took the hem of her sleeve and pressed it against the back of her wrist where she had pricked the skin with the tip of the knife, wiping away the blood that was hardening there. She wondered if the doctor would even notice it.

ح ع

Thomas took her over the bedstead that night, violently, and her fingers clenched at the comforter against the pain. He grabbed a rope of her hair, yanking back her head toward him, and hissed into her ear that she was a sinner and a whore and she was disobedient. Her feet were bare against the floorboards, and she tried to focus only on the patch of rough wood beneath her right heel, but her mind kept returning to the pain between her legs and the pain along her scalp where it felt like he would pull out whole clumps of her hair. He had wrenched her head back so far that when she opened her eyes, she was looking upon the peak of the house and the beams that ran like bridges between the two slants of the roof. She wondered: Was there only hatred for him in the act now? Was he even attempting to curb the loneliness or the animal lust within him or was this just another way of punishing her? He wasn't drink-drunk, this she knew. After all the allegations and suggestions at the trial, he had been careful to take smaller sips of his beer tonight at supper.

When he was through, he let go of her hair and pushed her down onto the comforter by her shoulders. She thought he was done and started to reach for her shift. But he grabbed her right arm and whirled her around, pulling her toward him. Then, as she felt his seed dripping down her thighs, he took her left hand in his and whispered menacingly, "The physician says thy hand is healing. Thou must be more careful, Mary. I know thou believest I hurt thee for no reason, but that is not true. Thou needest breaking like a horse. Humbling like a fallen angel. Art thou merely dull or something worse? Something prideful? Something that will get thee damned?"

She wanted to remind him that whether she was damned or saved was long foreordained. But she knew it would be a mistake to utter a word.

"I know for sure only this," he continued. "Thou

canst not afford another accident like that incident with"—and here he paused briefly—"the teakettle. I feel thine agony, Mary. I do."

Then he held her left fingers in his for a long moment, surveying in the dim light from the room's lone candle the part of her hand that he had broken.

"Yes, it is healing," he added, his tone pensive now, as if he honestly could tell. But she could see also that an idea was curdling inside him, and it was a dark one. "And these don't look like the claws of a witch."

She waited, silent and wary.

"Tell me something," he commanded.

"Yes," she said carefully, alert for whatever physical or verbal brutality was looming.

"Dost thou know why I lied in the Town House?"

She was taken aback by his candor. She knew there were a dozen answers she could offer, ranging from the vacuous and false to the most damning and true. She could say that he loved her or she could say that he was prideful and hoped to salvage a semblance of his reputation. She could suggest that he couldn't bear to lose one-third of his estate. She could even say that he had risked his immortal soul with lies because he wasn't in fact gambling at all: he knew already that he was most assuredly not among the elect, so what did one more falsehood, even one this brazen, matter?

Perhaps if she had begun to understand how she would have the last word—the absolute last word, justice, not merely the last word tonight—she would have known what to say. But unsure, she replied simply, "I do not know. But . . ."

"But what?"

"I am pleased that—at least with me, here beside our bedstead—thou dost acknowledge the truth."

He released her hand. He raised an eyebrow and told her, "I had to lie. Oh, it was in my best interests, too. That is obvious to angels and demons alike. It was the only way to get thee back under my roof where, as my wife, thou dost belong. But listen carefully to what I am about to say because it is true: I did it for thee, too."

"For me?"

He nodded. "We did it for thee," he said, emphasizing that first pronoun. "Thy father and his friend at the Town House. The magistrate."

She was surprised, but more by the idea he was telling her this than by the notion that there were conspiratorial tides washing about her. She had been feeling them since that day when she and her parents had first met with Richard Wilder.

He continued: "It was—and, yes, thy father and that magistrate and I discussed this two times—the only sure way to protect thee from the charges of witchcraft. Recall the accusations of our girl downstairs. Recall the innuendo lodged as fact by Goody Howland. Think hard on the death of

William Stileman. I am an imperfect husband and an imperfect man. This, too, is fact. But I care for thee enough to school thee, even if sometimes that knowledge is administered in a fashion that causes us both pain. And Mary? Think hard on this, too: I am a far better alternative than the noose."

She started to stay something but he put a finger on her lips. "All along, from the very beginning, thy petition had but the chance of a small bark in a hurricane. No, not even that. Of a butterfly through a blizzard. Thy scrivener did his work, but thou art but a woman—and a woman whose behavior has been more suspect than her husband's has been unkind. Yes, thou hast a powerful father. But, as we have seen here and in Hartford, even the most powerful man is powerless against a mob—especially a mob of magistrates—that sees a witch in its midst."

He put his hand on her neck, but he didn't squeeze. The grip was as gentle as it was threatening. "I know my hands, in thine opinion, have been unkind to thee. But they are not a rope. And I know this, too: We can move forward as man and wife. We can. I can be better. But thou must meet me halfway if thy father and I are going to be able to protect thee."

She swallowed hard, aware that he could feel the muscles moving in her neck. Her mouth had gone dry. "Meet thee halfway? What dost that mean precisely?" she asked, her voice unexpectedly hoarse.

"I've no idea what designs thou hast and what thou were thinking with the Devil's tines; I've no idea how far thy dalliance with Henry Simmons progressed. I don't even know if thou hast continued to visit that strange woman out on the Neck. Constance Winston." He dropped his hand from her throat. "But understand that thou must be careful. Do not court the Devil. He is a far crueler master than I."

He pulled on his sleep shift. Then he turned from her and lifted the chamber pot from the floor and went to the corner of the room. She sat at the edge of the bed and wrapped the quilt around her, unmoored by what he had said, but not wholly surprised. It was only what she had suspected. She thought back on her days at the Town House.

But she recognized this also: she had done nothing wrong and—somehow, some way—she would yet be free of this man. Moreover, her liberation would not come because the magistrates who had sentenced her to a life with him had added to their iniquity and turpitude by sending her from this world to the next via the hanging platform.

"Mary?"

He was back now and sitting beside her on the bedstead.

"Yes?"

"Thou needest rest after what thou hast endured. Close thine eyes and calm thy mind."

She nodded, outwardly obedient. But it would

be hours before her mind would be calm enough to sleep.

⛥

And in the night she dreamt, and the dream was so real that when she awoke she stared at the wall from the bedstead and pondered in her heart whether it was a sign—and if it was a sign, what it meant. She wrote it down in her ledger because she wanted to preserve forever what she had seen.

The dream (if that's what it was) was of a little girl who was no more than six years old and was dressed in a sky-colored shift and eating raspberries from a sky-colored bowl. The child's hair was yellow and fell down her back in a ponytail held tight with a pink silk ribbon, and her eyes were so green that Mary thought of a cat. She was wearing the sort of elegant slippers that Mary herself had worn as a little girl, the pair that one of her father's friends had imported from Bombay. The child did not speak like a child, however, she spoke like an adult who was sensible and wise, and who had lived a long and sensible life.

In the dream, Thomas was asleep beside Mary and didn't stir when she saw the child with the raspberries. The room was lit well by the moon, and the girl was radiant. Mary was not afraid of her. Nor was she worried about why this young thing was out in the night and wearing clothing so helpless against the New England cold. She was merely surprised. She sat up and swung her legs over the bedstead and asked her who she was and whether Catherine had seen her enter the house and come up the stairs.

"Catherine doesn't know I've come," the girl replied.

"And the berries? We haven't had fresh raspberries in months."

The child took one of the berries and extended it to Mary as if this were part of Communion, and Mary ate the berry as if it were bread. She held it on her tongue a long moment before biting into it. It was delicious, the perfect combination of sour and sweet.

"But who art thou?" Mary asked again. "What art thou? An angel? Tell me, prithee, that thou art an angel."

"I was given the name Desiree, but all who know me will call me Desire."

"All?"

The child smiled as if the single-word question was absurd—as if it had been asked by a child herself. "All who know me," she repeated.

"Art thou mine?"

The girl was quiet and her calmness unreadable. And so Mary persisted: "By thy silence, am I to suppose that I am not barren and will yet have a baby?"

And now Desiree held up her index finger, and

the tip was stained red from the berry. She took the pad and pressed it against Mary's forehead and then took a step back to survey her work. The finger had been warm, and the touch had been firm.

"There," the child said. "I have marked thee."

"Tell me, prithee," Mary begged. "Art thou my child? Art thou the daughter I would pray for until . . ."

"Until what? Until thou gave up hope? Until thou lost faith?"

She sat up straight in her defense. "Until I understood that rearing a child was not God's plan for me."

But this time the girl did not respond, because she was gone. Vanished.

In the morning when Mary wrote down all that she could remember, she wished she could recall how the girl had disappeared. Had she walked from the room and back down the stairs? Or had she ascended into the sky to sit before—not beside, no, not that—their heavenly Father? It was only when she had finished writing and Thomas was beginning to stir on his side of the bedstead that it crossed her mind to go to the looking glass and see if there was a mark on her forehead.

There was not, and it was only then that her eyes welled up and, despite Thomas's confusion, she began to weep.

Expect no leniency from this court if thou art convicted.

—The Remarks of Governor John Endicott, from the Records and Files of the Court of Assistants, Boston, Massachusetts, 1663, Volume I

Twenty-One

After Thomas had left for the mill, Catherine cleaned their clothes in water she had boiled in a great pot over the fire and then hung lines in front of the hearth because it was too cold now to dry them outside. It was spitting snow, and Mary thought that the flat, gray sky to the west suggested that soon snow would be falling in earnest. Perhaps the first blizzard of the season was nearing. Again this morning, she and her servant had found a heavy frost on the ground when they went to gather eggs from the chickens and feed the animals. They'd planned to make soap in the hopper out back, but it was too cold.

"I am glad Goody Howland treated thee well," Mary said to Catherine as she sewed a tear in one of Thomas's sleeves.

"Yes, she did," the girl replied.

"Dost thou miss living with them? Were thou happier there?" Mary hadn't planned to bring this up. But her mind had roamed to the questions, and she spoke before thinking.

"My needs are few and mean. I was content."

"And here?"

The girl was hanging a pair of Mary's woolen stockings beside one of her petticoats. "May I speak honestly?"

"Of course."

"Thy husband is a better man than thou art willing to acknowledge. Better and kinder. I accept where God has placed me."

Mary did not look up from her needle and thread when she said, "Thou left because thou feared me. Thou supposed I was a witch. And now?"

"I am alone with thee."

"So, thou dost not believe I have become a hand-maiden to the Devil."

"Or that I have no choice."

Or that thou art too happy by far to be in the presence of my husband, Mary thought, but said nothing. She knew that if she were her mother, she would have chastised the girl for her impertinence. But she wasn't her mother. After a quiet moment, the only sound the crackling of the wood as it burned in the hearth and the occasional gust that rattled the windows, Catherine said, "May I ask thee something?"

"Yes, certainly."

"If thou didst not bury the pestle and the Devil's tines, then who did?"

Mary sighed. "They were forks, Catherine. They were forks. They were no more the Devil's tines than hey were my father's tines or Governor

Endicott's tines or the tines of the hordes of men and women in the Netherlands or France who use them now. I will not debase the majesty of our Sovereign in Heaven ever again by attributing to them any sort of power beyond their ability to skewer a piece of meat or a scallop from the sea."

"Yet when thou accused me of placing them into the ground, thou were much afraid. I have not forgotten. Thou accused me of evil designs or an intrigue with the Dark One. Thou were scared."

Mary put down the sleeve and noted how sharp the tip of the needle was. She recalled her moment yesterday on the floor with the knife. "Then why in the world wouldst thou suppose I was a witch? If I were frightened, wouldst that not suggest—"

"It was that night when I spied thee at work. Thou seemed so secretive."

"That is fair," she admitted. "And thou art correct: when I first discovered the forks, I was scared."

"So, if I may, I will repeat my inquiry: if thou didst not bury the pestle and the Devil's tines, then who did?"

"I do not know."

Catherine looked upon the washing board and then nodded as if an idea had just come to her. "And perhaps it is that, more than anything, that frightens me most when I contemplate where, once more, I am living."

⇥ ⇤

Mary tried not to parse too deeply what she was doing, but she sensed it was a longing to share the pain that Henry Simmons had volunteered to endure on her behalf. She knew it would be excruciating for her to see him lashed: it would aggravate her own festering corruption and guilt. But Thomas never told her that she couldn't watch Henry Simmons be whipped. She guessed that it hadn't even crossed her husband's mind that she would go. And so, after she had finished her sewing, she reminded Catherine that Thomas would want meat for dinner and then asked a question to which she knew the answer: "Have we enough bread?"

"No, ma'am. Shall I bake some? Or shall I visit Obadiah Wood?"

Mary shook her head. "I'll go. Thou hast much to do, and I rather enjoy the baker." Wood was old and glib and, though a saint, prone to chatter. Then she bundled up against the snow, climbing into her heaviest, hooded cape and pulling one glove carefully onto her left hand and one with more ease onto her right. She doubted the storm would cause the constable to rethink the timing of the court-ordered lashing, and even wondered if the cold and snow on the poor man's back might in fact be a good thing: perhaps it would numb the skin and mitigate the pain.

❧ ❧

The snow picked up, and the cobblestones grew slippery. She nearly fell twice on her way to the center of the city, her feet sliding out from under her as if bedeviled because of the glaze on the embedded rocks, but she was able to recover each time and vowed she would walk more slowly. For all she knew, there was no reason to hurry: the whipping was finished or had been postponed. She passed the bakery and saw through the window that Obadiah still had plenty of bread. She could purchase a loaf on the way home. The world had grown muffled by the snow in a way that was beautiful and calming, despite the nature of her errand.

As she neared the square, through the swirling snow she spotted a small crowd of two dozen people assembled before the raised platform where the deviant were punished by the devout. No one was heckling yet, which Mary attributed more to the cold and the snow than to the gravitas of the punishment. She had seen criminals decried often as they were whipped or stood in the sun imprisoned in the stocks. Hadn't she watched the Howland children that autumn add what torment they could to that old Quaker as he was whipped while being paraded through town? But she also heard neither the crack of the whip on flesh nor Henry's cries against the pain. Either they hadn't begun or they had finished, because not even snow could stifle the sound of the scourge at a distance this small. She rather doubted that Henry's aunt and uncle would be present—she wouldn't have come if she had thought there was a chance—because most assuredly they did not approve of what he had done. Attempting to kiss a married woman? The sin was profound. Still, she pulled her dark hood tightly around her head in the event there was someone else watching who knew her and her alleged history with the man.

When she reached the crowd, she understood that, for better or worse, she had timed her arrival to coincide with the commencement of the punishment and felt both anxiety and regret at what she was about to see. But she knew also that she hadn't a choice: she had to be here. The constable had just finished reading the charge, adultery, and then a captain of the guard whom Mary did not recognize—he was tall with handsomely chiseled cheekbones above a blond beard—took the lash and uncoiled it. The punishment was fifteen strokes and confinement in the pillory until sunset.

And there he was, his shirt off, his head and his arms imprisoned in the stocks, the black padlock that held tight the wooden slats with a flour-like coating of snow. His fingers were balled into fists, and there were icicles in his hair. Her chest went tight, and she said a prayer of penitence for what she had wrought and asked forgiveness for what she had done. Most of the spectators were standing behind Henry so they would have a view of his back. She paused before him. His head was bowed, though she couldn't decipher whether it was due to exhaustion or resignation. It most assuredly was not humiliation. Henry Simmons was as mortal as any man and as capable of embarrassment, but not over this. He had volunteered for this. His sins were sins of defiance; his sins were born of hubris and pride. Nor did she believe he was scared. She was more frightened than he was. He was going to be lashed, and it would hurt—it would hurt mightily—but then it would be done. She guessed he wasn't the sort who couldn't handle a good whipping. No, his head was bowed most likely because he was tired and just wanted this over with, or he was vexed by the way the punishment had robbed him of his day. Of time.

The captain raised the whip and landed the first blow, the sound cutting through the falling snow like a rare, wintry clap of thunder, and as it did Henry's head reflexively popped up, his eyes wide, and though his mouth was open he barely grunted against the pain. She herself flinched. And it was then that the crowd finally spoke, hollering dismissively at Henry as one, a cacophonic stew of hoots and cackles, the group calling him a sinner and a scamp and a snipe, and when the second lash cut into his flesh, Mary took her thumbs and pulled back her hood so it fell against her shoulders. If he was going to endure this on her account, then she would be a presence that did not skulk in the shadows. And their eyes met. Each time the whip tore into him, his body jerked like a badly managed puppet and he'd blink, but then he'd stare back at her—squinting now as if reading small print at his desk at his Uncle Valentine's warehouse—and she told herself that in his gaze she saw gratitude. He was glad she had come.

Meanwhile, the crowd found a strange sense of order around the sixth or seventh lash, and began to count with the captain, as if this were one of those appalling drinking games she had heard about that they sometimes played at the taverns and the ordinaries.

When the captain had finished, he reached into a bucket and took what Mary thought for a split second was snow but then understood was salt and tossed it onto Henry's back. Then he coiled his rope, stepped down from the pillory, and pushed his way through the men and women who had gathered to watch. When Mary turned her gaze back toward Henry, she saw that he was shaking his head ever so slightly, his face awash in sweat despite the cold and the snow and the ice in his hair, and she realized that while his initial reaction to her presence may have been one of thanksgiving, now he was only alarmed and he wanted her gone.

For a moment she hovered, aware of the flakes that coated her face and coif, too. She felt them on her eyelashes and her nose. She was torn. He jerked his head toward the left—her right—and she turned, half expecting to see Goody Howland or, God forbid, her husband. But there was no one there that she knew. He was motioning only toward the street and urging her to move on.

And so she pulled her cape back over her head and brushed the snow off her face. The people who had come to gawk had seen what they craved and were leaving now, and so she looped around the pillory to see where the flesh had been ripped from Henry's back: the striping was bleeding and raw, from the top of his breeches to his shoulder blades, and she felt a wave of nausea because it looked more like a slab of badly butchered meat than human skin. There was blood streaming down his spine and puddling at the fabric at his waist, and the snow by his boots looked stained by Madeira. In addition to the long black lines crisscrossing his back, there were blotches, one almost the shape of a star, that she realized were open wounds.

She rubbed at her eyes, which had grown wet, but not from the cold. She was tearing up with sadness and regret. She had done this to Henry Simmons: she had draped him in this excruciating livery, she had clad him in this pulpy abomination.

But he was right: she needed to gather herself and walk on. And so she did. She left the pillory, recalling her pretext for coming to the center of the city. Bread. Obadiah. She rubbed gently at the setting bone in her hand and wondered at her wretchedness. At man's wretchedness. At the way her anger, once more, was bubbling inside her.

This would not stand. It would not.

Yes, she would buy her bread and return home. She recalled something from a play—an ungodly play, true, but a drama she was aware of nonetheless. The line of dialogue existed like a bird high in the sky, distant and hazy but real. It was something about a pound of flesh. It came to her now because of Henry's ruined back and because of the injustice that was her world.

Before winter was done—if not sooner—she would have her pound of flesh.

❧ ❧

As she was leaving the baker's, she and Rebeckah Cooper spied each other simultaneously, the goodwife's two children at her side. Mary felt her guard rising because of the boiled apples and raisins, and the fact that Rebeckah had been cooking them with Peregrine. But her friend—at least a woman she had supposed was her friend—was all smiles and rushed over to her, pulling her daughter by a leading string and urging her son to be quick.

"Mary!" she exclaimed, "I heard the news that thou art reconciled with Thomas."

"And that seems to thee a cause for joy, knowing now my history with the man and the way that he treated me?"

"No. I am just happy to see thee. I have missed thee, that's all."

Mary nodded. "I am sorry. I sounded peevish."

Rebeckah took Mary's right hand in both of hers and said, "That is understandable. I did not mean to diminish thy disappointment in the judgment from the Town House. I'm sorry for thee, too. Tell me: how is thy hand mending?"

"Well. It is." The woman's daughter was looking up at her curiously, and Mary thought of the girl who had come to her in her dream.

"I'm glad. Relieved. I will come visit thee. May I?"

"I'd like that," she said.

"Did thy parents and thee enjoy the treat that Peregrine and I baked?" She motioned at her children. "'Tis a favorite of this pair."

"Didst thou make some for thine own family?"

"We did. And for Peregrine's too. We just had so many apples this year. Such a blessing."

"Yes," Mary agreed. "A blessing." She told herself that any distrust she had been feeling toward the woman was unfounded. It had to be. Goody Cooper might just be her only real friend left in the world.

⊰ ⊱

She made one last stop on the way home. She visited her parents' house to see how Hannah was feeling. The servant girl still felt weak and her color was poor, but she was up and about and assisting Abigail with the chores.

"I checked to see if someone had planted the Devil's tines in the dooryard," she told Mary, "but the ground was too hard. I don't think that was it."

"No," Mary said. "I rather doubt it was, too."

⊰ ⊱

In the night, the storm continued, but it did not grow worse. This was not the sort of blizzard with icy blasts that shook the windows and blew snow into the house, and made the fire rise and fall in the hearth, the flames at the beck and call of the drafts. But the snow fell silently and relentlessly, an early-season storm that by morning had left six or seven inches of heavy powder in the city by the sea. Mary stood in the bedroom before the glass, a blanket wrapped around her like a shawl, and gazed at the quiet of Boston. It was still overcast, but the snow had ceased. The trees, which thankfully had lost their leaves weeks earlier, still had branches bowing down to the earth beneath great blankets of white, and one slim evergreen near the street looked as if it might snap in two.

But there was not so much snow that the city would grow paralyzed. Soon the sleds would be out, and men would emerge with their shovels. A horse could traverse six or seven inches of snow, and Thomas would go to the mill and expect his men to be there.

Her husband was still asleep in the bedstead, his breathing more a wheeze than a snore. She looked at him and sighed. There was no part of him that she did not detest. Even his beard, scruffy from a night against the pillowbeer, repulsed her. His left hand sat beside his face, the fingers splayed and reminiscent of a spider, and she wondered what it would be like for him to be awakened by a fork being plunged into the back of it. Or by having a pot of boiled salad dumped upon him.

Somewhere in another part of the city, Henry Simmons was waking, too. In her mind, she saw him swinging his legs over the side of the mattress, grimacing at the pain along the broad swath of his back. Had the Hills tended to him? Had they brought in a physician? Perhaps in the opinion of his aunt and uncle, a part of his punishment was to live with the discomfort until the skin began to heal on its own.

Downstairs she heard Catherine stirring and knew she should join her to warm the house, tend to the animals, and prepare breakfast. But she had thought of the forks, which led her naturally to the pestle, and then once more to Henry Simmons's back. It was all connected. The world was connected. She thought of the two days she had spent at the Town House and the things that people had said about her. This was connected, too. And it was then that an idea began to form in her mind. It was vague, the details beyond definition. But she was starting to see its contours, like the shore when a ship first spies land on the horizon.

She needed to venture out to the Neck and the street near Gallows Hill to visit with Constance Winston. The woman had no reason to forgive her, but it was clear from when they had met the other day that neither did Constance harbor so much ill will that she would shun her. She understood why Mary had kept her distance. Though Constance had never been formally accused of witchcraft, not even during Ann Hibbens's trial, there were murmurs in the city that she had a great and particular knowledge of the dark arts.

The truth was, Constance had been kind when their paths had recently crossed.

Well, Mary decided, once more she needed to speak with her, despite the rumors of witchcraft that swirled about her like dead leaves in a September windstorm. After all, if anyone could tell her why someone had planted two forks and a pestle in her dooryard, it was Constance. If anyone could assist her—carefully and with great stealth—with her emancipation, it was likely to be an independent woman with a subversive streak in her soul.

Today, as soon as she and Catherine had tended to their responsibilities and sent Thomas off to the mill, she would journey to the Neck.

I felt something in the pocket, and when I put my fingers there, I discovered the Devil's tines.

—The Testimony of Catherine Stileman, from the Records and Files of the Court of Assistants, Boston, Massachusetts, 1663, Volume I

Twenty-Two

Mary had hoped that Constance would be alone, but when she answered the door that morning her young servant was helping to prepare dinner: there was a chicken descending on the roasting jack and a kettle with boiled squash on the fire. As Mary recalled, the house was suitably modest for a home this far out on the Neck: the walls were unadorned, and the second floor was accessible only by a ladder that looked rather rickety.

Constance had donned that regal scarlet cape and was about to leave, and so Mary offered to return another day. Instead Constance shook her head and said, "I know where thou livest, Mary. I am walking in that direction, too. So, we can walk together—that is, if thou art comfortable walking with me. In public."

"Of course."

The woman smiled cryptically. "Not all are. I am flattered by thy change of heart. And I understand when people would rather converse with me in the privacy of my"—and here she swept her hand over the small, smoky room—"estate."

"I sought thee. I am not ashamed."

"Well. What a brave goodwife thou art. Today."

"Constance, I—"

"Or mad. Or desperate," she said, cutting her off. Then she told her girl that she would be back from the cabinet maker before too long and they could resume their spinning after eating. Mary was wearing snowshoes and expected Constance to put on a pair, too. Instead, however, she pulled on fur-lined boots of the sort that Mary had seen on trappers, but they were feminine and lithe—and quite clearly a costly import from London.

"The treadle is broken," Constance continued offhandedly as they started off.

"I am grateful once more to be in thy company. Thou must know . . ." And here Mary's voice trailed off. This time, Constance waited. "I did not mean to expunge thee from my life."

The woman narrowed her eyes and smiled in a fashion that was indecipherable to Mary, but she felt as if Constance were reading her mind. "I would, if I am going to speak plainly, have preferred that thou had plucked me from thy world like a weed because my simples failed thee than because thou trembled before the gossips. There are many things in this world we should fear, but to bend one's knees to the smallest of minds? That is beneath a mind as sharp as the one that the Lord God has given thee. It suggests a cowardice incompatible with a woman sufficiently courageous to attempt to divorce a monster who wants to claim title over the very air that she breathes. I am sorry thine effort to escape that beast of a man failed."

Mary nodded. There was nothing she could say in her defense. She was surprised, but not greatly, that Constance already knew about the ruling at the Town House.

"Yes," the other woman continued, "thy tale? It travels like a schooner with a good wind. But I applaud thine initiative; I wish the men in their black robes had risen to the majesty of their clothing. Timid little creatures they are."

Constance was walking quickly now, but she slowed when she saw that Mary was having trouble keeping up.

"How much hast thou heard?"

"Which aspersions upon thy character art thou pondering? The idea thou art an adulterer or thou art a witch? I am going to speculate it is the latter. People don't come to me with questions of the heart. No one suspects an old woman has wisdom of that sort."

"Thou art not old."

"I know what I am."

They passed a potter, his kiln in a shack with a door so decrepit they could see him inside at his wheel. "I am not an adulterer," Mary said, but she knew that she spoke without conviction.

"I am neither beadle nor magistrate. I couldn't care less."

"But I can assure thee: that is not why I have ventured to the Neck."

"As I said: no one seeks a crone's wisdom if they need counsel of that sort."

"Thou knew Ann Hibbens?" Mary asked.

"Yes. But much of Boston did."

"I do not believe she was a witch."

"Why?"

"She was gentlewoman—a woman of standing."

"I don't think the Devil makes that distinction when He searches for disciples and acolytes."

Mary had expected Constance to defend Hibbens. Certainly no one in Mary's own circle believed she was a witch. "Were thou Ann's friend? Truly?"

"Truly I was."

"Was she possessed?"

"No."

"But she was excommunicated from the church."

"That was years ago. Thou were still a child. Thy family had not even arrived here. She lived sixteen years separate from the church."

"Why was she excommunicated?"

"People are excommunicated for many reasons. Think of Edmund and Esther Hawke. They simply prefer the wilds of the woods to the alleged civility of the First Church."

"And Ann Hibbens?"

"She was difficult and opinionated, and she fought with the joiners who overcharged her for work that was shoddy. She might have been hanged then, but her husband was still breathing."

"So, she was hanged unfairly?"

"She was sent to the scaffold because she had a sharper tongue and a shrewder mind than her accusers. It is always the case when men hang women. Look at Magistrate Caleb Adams: there is nothing that frightens that man more than a woman who does not live happily under a man's thumb."

"God has His plan," Mary replied, but her heart was not in her response.

"He does. And in it a woman is a man's helpmeet, not his slave. There is a difference. A woman has a mind, too, and that scares the likes of our esteemed magistrates."

"Sometimes, my husband insists that my brain is but white meat. If that is the case, then perhaps I should take comfort that whatever indignities loom before me, they will not involve a rope," she told Constance.

"Men call bright women dim whenever they are threatened. So, take no relief in the names that any man calls thee. There is no safe harbor there."

Mary nodded. She suspected this was true, because while Thomas frequently maligned her for being dull, he was also likely to contend she was too smart for her own good.

"And . . ." Here Mary paused, unsure how to frame her next question. She watched a pair of squirrels ascend an oak tree that hadn't been girdled in a dooryard.

"Speak plainly. Ask me whatever thou likest. No one can hear us but those squirrels. Clearly there is a matter of importance to thee."

"There is. Prithee, tell me: dost thou eat with a fork?"

The other woman stopped and smiled, and though her teeth were crooked and yellow, the grin was nonetheless charming. "So, this is about the Devil's tines."

"Yes."

"I do not," she said, and resumed walking. "I have always found a knife and a spoon sufficient."

"Dost thou fear them?"

"No."

"Someone buried a pair of them in the dooryard to my house. Why would someone do that? Hast thou heard of such a spell?"

"A spell involving a fork?"

"Yes."

She was silent as she thought. Finally, she replied, "Not precisely a fork. But something **forked**."

"Go on."

"Shakespeare referred to such a potion."

"I have not read Shakespeare since we left England," said Mary carefully, "though I recalled one of his plays just the other day."

"In **Macbeth,** there are witches, and they use the forked tongue of an adder in their brew."

"There is a difference between a forked tongue and a fork."

"I agree. But suppose the witch could not obtain a snake—and, thus, a snake's tongue? Perhaps the fork was all she had handy."

"There was also a pestle," said Mary, and she pulled it from her pocket. "Note what has been carved into the handle. A trident."

"That makes sense. From what I have heard—and what I am about to share with thee is hearsay, because I am most obviously not a witch," Constance said, studying the object.

"No," Mary agreed, because she understood that she was supposed to say this.

"This pestle is more of a metaphor than an ingredient. The Devil's tines, too. Whoever was casting a spell was using this and the forks in lieu of a serpent's forked tongue, properly dried and mashed in a mortar."

"Would such a thing work? Would the Devil listen? This is not an actual concoction."

"Of course, it's not," said Constance patiently. "It is, however, an offering. The Devil is less interested in the specifics of a potion than in the conversion of a saint. Again, this is just what some people—including the good men in our pulpits—say."

Despite the snow, the streets were growing

crowded now that they had left the Neck and were approaching the more settled sections of the city. Mary lowered her voice as they walked, asking, "What did the person who buried the forks and the pestle crave? What was she asking of Satan?"

"With her offering?"

"Yes."

Constance pointed at a low-slung house with slits for windows and a stone chimney that was belching black smoke. "Here we are," she said, and she returned the pestle to Mary.

"The cabinet maker?"

She nodded. "My hope is that he will have finished his work, and my girl and I can resume our spinning."

"Thou didst not answer," Mary said. "What would be the purpose of a spell that involved a properly mashed or ground adder's tongue? I need to know so I can try to learn who might have planted the forks. It has become imperative."

"Thy husband stabbed thee with a fork. True?"

"Yes. He stabbed me with one of the very same forks that I pulled from the dooryard."

"Shakespeare may not be in thy library, but good saint thou art, I suppose thou knowest well thy Bible."

"I try to."

"Hast thou consulted it?"

She felt a pang of guilt as she shook her head.

"Shame on thee," the other woman said, and she made a tsk-tsk sound with her tongue.

"Should I read it for the word **fork**?"

"Thou could read every word in the Old Testament and the New and find it but once. Maybe twice. And in no fashion that is helpful to thy study."

"Thou knowest the book well."

"I have had many more years than thee to read."

"But if not **fork,** then what?" she asked, but even as she was forming the question, the answer came to her. Before Constance could respond, she continued, "**Serpent.**"

"Good girl. Thy husband is mistaken: thy mind is nimble and quick."

"I am grateful thou believest that."

"Yes, I think **serpent** would serve thee better than **fork.** My point is simple: thou art pursuing game that will leave thee hungry if thou viewest the ingredient as but the Devil's tines."

"'Tis but a fork," said Mary firmly, recalling her vow that she would view the device as nothing but a kind of cutlery.

"Correct. But when the ingredient is a substitute for a serpent's tongue? Well, that may be a food that is more satisfying. Also? That might be an ingredient one who verily is possessed would plant like a seed into the ground of thy dooryard."

"May I see thee again, Constance?"

The woman looked into her eyes and said, "Thou

mayest. I am grateful that thou hast chosen to re-kindle our fellowship, even if the embers were bil-lowed by questions and need. I like thee and respect thee, Mary: I am always pleased to see thee. But thou were wary before. Thou should be wary now."

"Because?"

"Because the hatefulness in Hartford may soon travel here, and I may yet become a particularly dangerous person with whom to socialize—unless one wants to leave Boston via the hanging plat-form. Already there are aspersions upon thy char-acter that should give thee pause."

"I used to have more fears than I have now. After what I have endured this autumn? Now I have but few. And the principal one, at least while I am breathing still? It is the prospect of a life lived only with a man thou dost rightly call a beast. And Constance?"

"Go on."

"There comes a time when resistance is not zeal-otry, but sanity."

"Even if it leads to a noose?"

"I shall move with caution."

"Thou hast become a brave girl. Less tamed than thy facade, thy countenance a cloak. I approve."

"I thank thee."

There Constance patted her shoulder, smiled, and went inside to see the cabinet maker.

⊰ ⊱

If thou believest in Me, Mary thought, walking back toward the center of the city.

If thou believest in Me . . .

John, chapter 11, verse 26: "Whosoever liveth and believeth in Me shall never die." Such were Jesus's words to Martha.

Those who doubted were among the damned. As they should be. As were those who believed and yet still sided with Lucifer.

She wasn't sure what and how much her husband believed. How could he treat her the way that he did if he wanted to follow his Lord and Savior with all his heart and with all his soul? Did he honestly suppose that his violence toward her was remediation? Nevertheless, he went to church and read the Psalter and prayed before they ate. How many others in the church lived with such hypocrisy? Feigning a future among the elect when in fact they were damned?

Perhaps Thomas really did believe, as he'd suggested that night after her divorce petition had been decided, that she had planted the forks and pestle in their dooryard. Maybe it was his opinion—and the opinion of her parents—that he was protecting her.

Equally as likely, however, it was mere justification for his calumny and lies.

Either way, it didn't matter. Someday he might kill her.

Mary removed her snowshoes when she got home. Catherine asked her where she had been, the question no more than a pleasantry. Mary responded that she had walked to the brazier, but he hadn't any ladles today and so they would need to make do with the one they had.

"But the one we have is fine," said Catherine.

"Good," said Mary. "I thought it was starting to show its age. I am relieved I was mistaken."

∾•

In the night, she read her Bible until the candle was small and the words had become hazy blurs. She ran her finger down page after page, her mind searching for one word and that one word in a context that might make sense to someone who has given his soul to the Devil: **serpent.** At some moments, she was utterly oblivious to the sentences and stories as she scanned the chapters, and would find herself flipping back the pages to read the passages again.

In the morning, both Catherine and Thomas noticed her commitment the night before and expressed their approval over breakfast.

The Old Testament was so big, she thought, and the New Testament so rich with parable and revelation. It seemed that the task was beyond her ken. To find one word in one context that might solve the riddle? It would demand the finest minds in the colony.

But still, she vowed, she would soldier on.

❧ ❧

Even now, sometimes, Thomas could confound her.

They were in bed, the candle was extinguished, and the room was dark. It had been out for a while, and she presumed he was asleep, a little surprised that he wasn't snoring. But then he spoke.

"Mary," he said, rolling over onto his back. "I am troubled by something."

His tone was pensive, not angry. This wasn't about something she had done or failed to do.

"Prithee," she murmured. "Tell me."

"Jonathan Cooke," he said, and instantly she grew alarmed. Perhaps she was mistaken and somehow he had sensed—or even witnessed—the way she had looked at the man, her eyes wanton.

"Go on."

"He has asked me for money. 'Tis not the first time, but this time he asked with desperation. He came to the mill, his hat in his hand, but his attitude fierce."

"Fierce?" She had known neither that Jonathan and Peregrine were in need, nor that the man previously had approached her husband. She thought of what her scrivener had whispered to her during Jonathan's testimony: he gambles and plays cards.

"Entitled. Angry that so far I have not opened my purse."

"The dowry thou gave to Peregrine was munificent."

"And long gone."

"Did Jonathan put it into the construction of the house?" she asked. She didn't tell Thomas what Benjamin Hull had alleged, because she did not want to bring up the trial now or suggest that she knew the things he was keeping from her.

"It would seem that Jonathan put it into games of chance with sailors."

She heard an animal skittering in the wall, a mouse most likely. "Really?" She hoped that she sounded surprised.

"He is in waters that he thinks will drown him. Two children, a third on the way. His own family has no means to help him."

"How much did he ask for?" she asked. Now she was taken aback. She had never imagined it was this bad.

"He had no precise figure. But he suggested my daughter and grandchildren could anticipate a miserable winter without my help. A miserable future."

"Is he now going to avoid the temptations at the docks?"

"Wilt thou?"

"What?" she asked. The revelation of the depth of Jonathan's gaming problem combined with the idea that Thomas suspected that she herself had sometimes looked at the sailors had her aghast.

"Mary, I know thou hast great affection for the abundance that arrives here daily. I see no sin in gaping at the fabrics and furniture thy father imports," he said, and she was relieved. He wasn't referring to the sailors, but to the plenty they brought.

"What wilt thou do?" she asked. She presumed that Jonathan made a good living as a carpenter. But, then, she knew little of economy.

"I will help some. I will provide him with ground corn and flour."

"I can't imagine the family ever needing the almshouse or becoming the responsibility of the selectmen."

"Or giving up on Boston and settling elsewhere. I agree. I think the problem is not that they will ever be flirting with destitution or hunger, but that the fellow has ambitions beyond the Lord's plan for him. He wants . . ."

She waited. And when he continued, he was almost chuckling, "He wants the world that comes and goes through thy father's warehouse. It's not so much that he and my daughter will ever be among the town poor; it's that neither will they be among the town rich."

"Thou art generous to help fill their store for the winter."

"No. I just don't want my daughter or grand-children hungry," he said. "That wouldn't reflect well on me." Then he rolled onto his side and grumbled—his small attempt at humor more ominous and disconcerting than funny—"It seems that Jonathan should have married thee, Mary, instead of my daughter. He wants thy family, not mine."

It was about the size of a coin. A shilling. But it was not a shilling. It was made of wood, and it had carved into it a five-pointed star in a circle: the sign of the Dark One.

—The Testimony of Catherine Stileman, from the Records and Files of the Court of Assistants, Boston, Massachusetts, 1663, Volume I

Twenty-Three

On Sunday morning before dinner, Mary Deerfield
sat in her pew beside her mother at the First Church
and prayed to her Benefactor and listened to all
that the Reverend Norton said from the high pulpit
in the corner. She was aware of both Thomas and
Henry Simmons across the church but honestly
wasn't sure if her husband knew the proximity of
the other man. Henry was seated in the second-to-
last row, while her husband was, as always, among
the wealthier men of the city. If Henry was still
in pain from the lashing, he wasn't revealing it.
But Mary, though tempted, had been careful not
to look back with any frequency. When her mind
wandered, she wondered if he was watching her.

She also found herself contemplating the presence of Jonathan Cooke and thinking less of him.
What a duplicitous couple he and Peregrine made:
one was gaming himself into poverty and needed
now to access his father-in-law's plenty, and the
other may have sprinkled venom onto apples to
sicken (or kill) her mother-in-law, even if it meant
afflicting others.

Today John Norton was preaching from Deuteronomy, and she tried to concentrate on all that Moses had shouldered. When the pastor reached the thirty-third verse of the thirty-second chapter, she gasped ever so slightly, but with such anguish that both her mother and Catherine turned to her.

"Their wine **is**"—and the minister emphasized the verb, just as it was emphasized when she looked down at her own well-read copy of the Bible in her lap—"the poison of dragons, and the cruel venom of asps." She had gasped reflexively, in awe, because this was a sign, as clear as any that the Lord God had ever shown her. And it had to be her risen Savior speaking to her, it had to be; it could not be Satan. Not here. Not now. Not in this place, this church, this pew. She nodded at her mother and Catherine, reassuring them that she was fine, they needn't fear that she was either frightened or possessed, and stared down at the word: **asps.** There it was. Snake. Serpent. Adder. Asp.

The poison of dragons, the venom of asps.

Not a fork. A forked tongue.

She recalled her walk with Constance. Was it possible that whoever had planted the pestle and forks was hoping to poison her with a spell more toxic than Peregrine's polluted dessert? A spell that demanded the hand of Lucifer Himself? Or had Peregrine done this, too, and only resorted to the apples when Mary had discovered the forks?

"I will make mine arrows drunk with blood," Norton continued, raising his voice as he quoted the Lord in the chapter, speaking with a passion so heated that everyone in the sanctuary could feel it as if it were July and they were outside and this was the sun beaming down upon them, and then he pounded the sides of his pulpit with both hands and abruptly went silent. Somewhere in the back of the church a woman was weeping. Mary understood that anguish: the pain of knowing the grievous sin that was in one's heart and the way that it disappointed the Lord, and what it meant when one contemplated the fires of Hell that awaited. To be among the damned and not the chosen? There was and there could be nothing worse.

And yet people daily made pacts with the Dark One. His seductions were smooth, a vortex from which, once enticed, there was no escape.

"Remember," Norton said when he resumed, "this is thy God. There are those of us present— our sisters, our brothers, our children—who already are condemned. And rightly condemned. Justly condemned. Oh, they flatter themselves. I shall not face those flames. I am here in church. I know the Commandments and I read my Psalter. But God is mindful of their wickedness. Men who crave darkness are the objects of a wrath that no mortal mind can imagine. They will see their skin seared from their arms and their bones blackened, they will watch the flames turn their legs to charred logs and their feet to ash. And they will see it and feel it every single day for eternity. Every single day. Every minute and every hour, their eyelids burned away so they cannot close them to their deformity and torture and shame. Yes, shame. The shame of the sinner, the worst shame there can be. They will live always with the smell of burnt hair and burnt flesh, with flames on their skin that cannot be smothered by their sweat or their humours or even an ocean as wide as the one that separates our world from the one we left. But their eyes will never melt—not first, not last, not ever—so they can see always what Satan can and what Satan will do. Their screams will be shrieks that will make thunder quail.

"But their condemnation is not merely theirs and theirs alone. It will be our condemnation, too, if we do not strive with greater zeal to live the life that God wants for us. His anger is justified, and it is that very justification that so vexes Him, since all He desires from us is to hear His words and love Him as we should: to not reject the remarkable gift that He has offered us. Life. And, yes, a life here. He has given us a new world, a chance for a new England. But we must not be deluded: His patience with us will be short. After all, He did not give us this new earth to serve Satan; He will not tolerate our poisoning it the way we did Eden and Israel and France and England and everyplace else where man has walked and everyplace else where man has disappointed him," Norton said, and Mary's mind coiled itself like a snake around the word **poisoning.** Here was yet another sign.

She could reread the Bible as meticulously as John Norton and not find a more apt biblical verse to explain what had occurred in her very dooryard.

She would never dabble with spells like a witch; but was she capable of replicating the fine art of an apothecary and creating a potion? A poison?

If Peregrine could, she could.

She would.

She tried to push the idea from her mind for now because she was in the Lord's house, but it was a boulder lodged well in a river; the currents would be parted by it for centuries before they might be capable of moving it even an inch.

She glanced across the church at her husband and his head was bowed, though she could see it was not because he was in prayer or he was heeding the words of the pastor. His head was bowed because he was unmoved and he was sleepy. He was bored.

If, in the end, anyone was going to feel the pain of Hell, it was him.

Unless, of course, she made sure that he felt it here first.

⁂

Much of the snow had melted, but there were still piles along fences and beside dooryards, some of it still pristine but most of it black with ash or brown with animal excrement. The streets were clear and the walking easy. Mary stared up into the sun as she and Thomas and Catherine were leaving church for the dinner break, and she enjoyed the feel of it on her face. But her mind was occupied by what the minister had said—and, thus, what the Lord had said. So often she felt that the Sunday message was directed at her, and given her notoriety of late, it would have been reasonable to suppose that the minister was thinking of her. She wasn't pondering this idea because of her usually avid desire to understand the meaning of the sermon as a Christian, however, but because of the sudden and profound confluence of forks and adders and poison: yes, it seemed as if John Norton was speaking to her, but not because of what she had done, but rather because of what she might do. Was it possible today that the reverend had been a conduit to inspire her? And if the minister was but an instrument, was the musician God or the Devil? Inside the First Church, she had been quite sure it was God. Outside, she was less sure.

They hadn't walked far when she felt Thomas taking her elbow and pulling her close. It might have been construed as a chivalrous gesture—or one of affection—by someone who did not know

how his mind worked, but Mary did, and she understood that something was about to happen and it would not be pleasant. When she turned from the sun to the street she saw that Henry Simmons was walking beside them.

"Good Sabbath," he said, his tone absolutely without guile. He was like a cheerful puppy, though she knew that in truth he was not. She knew how dark his thoughts could run from the exchanges they had shared.

Thomas was walking briskly now, pulling her along with him, and he glared at Henry, seething. He said nothing, and so she remained silent, too.

"Thomas, I owe thee an apology," Henry continued, and it was then that Thomas stopped. This was unexpected, and Mary was unsure what she thought of Henry expressing contrition to her husband. She would have preferred that he had kept his distance and said nothing, both because she saw no possible good emerging from their confrontation, and because she didn't like to imagine Henry bowing before a cad like her husband.

"Catherine," Thomas commanded their servant, "go home and start dinner. We shan't be far behind."

The girl looked nervously between the two men and scurried ahead.

Her husband turned back toward Henry and said brusquely, "I know thee from the allegations of James Burden's servant."

"Yes. As I confessed to the Court of Assistants, I had a lapse in judgment and tried to take advantage of thy wife. I have expressed my regret to our God and to the magistrates, and, after that particularly fine sermon, I want to share with thee as well that I made a mistake and I am sorry."

An idea came to Mary: **Henry is doing this for me because he is worried that Thomas may be treating me worse than usual because he believes I was unfaithful—or, perhaps, had thoughts that suggested an illicit desire.** Either way, Henry believed that an apology was going to help. She knew that he couldn't have been more wrong.

"It seems thou hast worries for thy soul. I am not sure that is genuine regret. I would categorize it merely as fear," Thomas told him.

"I heard the word of the Lord," said Henry, smiling. "But after the lashing, I don't fear much."

"The lashing was but a small taste of what awaits."

"Perhaps."

"If we were still in England, I might demand satisfaction," Thomas told him, and Mary felt his grip on her arm tightening. He may have spotted the derision behind Henry's grin. "I think thou showest a cavalier lack of self-regard."

"Let the aristocrats duel over there," Henry said. "Over here? Let the humble apologize and the godly accept a concession in the lowly and sincere spirit in which it is offered."

"I am not sure, despite thy claims, that thou were sufficiently humbled at the whipping post. Now, my dinner awaits. I urge thee to stay away," her husband said, and Mary felt him pulling her forward. But Henry reached for her husband's shoulder and spun him back.

"Thomas," he began, but he didn't get another word out, because with a speed and an agility that shocked Mary—even though she knew that her husband's temper could crack with the suddenness of lightning—he released her, turned, and smacked Henry hard on his spine. Mary watched as the younger man flinched and started to rear up, but Thomas hit him again, this time joining his hands and using his arms as a club to pound one of the spots on Henry's back where undoubtedly the flesh was raw from the whip. Even through his doublet and cloak, the pain had to have been excruciating, and Henry staggered. For a moment, she thought he was going to fall to the ground. But he righted himself, and Mary grabbed Thomas before he could strike the man again.

Thomas looked at her, his eyes wild, and then regained his composure. He prepared himself for any counterattack that Henry might offer, but Henry seemed to believe that he had earned this and had no plans to retaliate. He stood there, a little shocked, and when he said nothing, Thomas spoke: "I dare thee to tell either beadle or constable that I struck thee. See how they will respond to a cur the likes of thee."

And with that Thomas took her arm, roughly this time, and started to pull her home.

~ ~

Mary knew that Thomas would do nothing to hurt her with Catherine present over dinner. He was too crafty. The three of them ate in absolute silence.

And then they returned to church for the afternoon portion of the service. Mary saw no sign of Henry in the sanctuary.

~ ~

The cold came again in the night, and the windows in the bedroom grew a glaze that resembled hoarfrost. They ate lobster chowder for supper, and Thomas spoke little, other than to observe that it was good to eat something warm when the ground was locking in for the season. Upstairs, he stripped off his clothes except for his stockings and pulled on his sleep shift, and then he extinguished the candle and climbed into bed. He had done nothing since attacking Henry, but she remained guarded. She undressed quickly because the room was cold and put on her own shift. She glanced once at her left hand and flexed her fingers. It mostly hurt now when she stretched them.

Then she got into bed and pulled up the coverlet. The moment she did, he was upon her. He rolled her onto her back, grabbed her by her wrists, and pressed her arms down onto the mattress. He leaned into her, his mouth beside her left ear, and whispered, "If ever again I see thee with Henry Simmons . . . if ever again I hear of thee with Henry Simmons . . . if ever again thou speakest the dog's name . . . I will destroy him in just the same way that the girl beneath us plucked the claws from the lobsters and ripped the meat from their chests. That boy's skin and ribs are but paper compared to the shell of those beasts, and I will treat him with savagery and without mercy. And thee? Thou wilt die a witch at the hanging platform. I will see to it: thy wrists bound behind thy back and with a rope carving slowly but surely into thy neck like a dagger in need of sharpening. Mark me, Mary Deerfield: the Hell that awaits most sinners is but sunshine and spring compared to the Hell I will rain down upon thee and that pathetic runt of the litter that darest to kiss thee. Dost thou hear my words?"

She nodded.

"Speak, woman," he hissed, his breath beery, his voice cool. "Dost thou hear my words?"

"Yes."

"Yes?"

"Yes, I hear thee and I understand thee."

He released one of her wrists and brought his hand to her mouth, and then he bit her hard on the lobe of her ear, the teeth gouging the flesh. But he was pressing his fingers so firmly against her lips that her cry was lost before it had any chance to fly free.

If thou hast a mark, it would suggest thou art a witch; but just because thy body is clean, it does not mean thou art not one.

—The Remarks of Magistrate Caleb Adams, from the Records and Files of the Court of Assistants, Boston, Massachusetts, 1663, Volume I

Twenty-Four

Rebeckah Cooper asked the question the following afternoon, and it was a non sequitur that caught Mary off guard. Her friend was keeping her company while they did needlework together before the fire, and though Mary had her guard up, it had been a pleasant hour. Catherine was out back with the animals when Rebeckah inquired, "What dost thou think of Peregrine these days?"

"I accept that she is Thomas's daughter, not mine, and my petition has altered her view of me." Mary answered carefully. "She took her father's side at the Town House, as one would expect. Once, her family was likely to join us for dinner on Sunday. No more. Perhaps someday our relations will resume an appropriate amicability. We'll see. Why dost thou ask?"

Rebeckah focused upon her needle and the design on her linen. It was a fir tree. "When we were leaving church yesterday, at the end of the afternoon, she was ahead of me. She was walking with one of her friends and with their children."

"And soon Peregrine will have a third child. She is much blessed."

"Yes. Her friend is with child, too. The woman told Peregrine that she would be frightened to have thee at a birth and recommended to Peregrine that thou were not present when it was her time."

Mary put down her own embroidery, a trio of falling maple leaves, and rolled her eyes. "Fine. I'm not a midwife."

"But thou were present at Peregrine's other births?"

"I was there for one of the girls. The other was born so quickly that I only heard the next day. But my presence at the birth of her first daughter did not elicit from Peregrine a monster or deformity. Both of my granddaughters are beautiful and healthy."

"When wilt thou see her next?"

"Peregrine? I don't know."

"Prithee, Mary. Be careful."

"She seemed most pleasant when she brought us the apples and raisins the two of thee boiled together."

"She brought thee some?" said Rebeckah. She sounded surprised.

"She did."

"And they were agreeable?"

Mary nodded, hoping her face revealed nothing.

"I am glad. But be wary of some of the other

women. The likes of Goody Howland are liable to say most anything these days."

"I know," she said. "And I know that my petition cost me greatly, and it looks to the world as if I have nothing to show for my efforts but tribulation."

"I'm sorry."

"Thou hast nothing to apologize for," Mary reassured her, keeping her voice cordial. "And thou needest not worry on my account. I will be fine."

"Why art thou so confident?"

Mary sighed. She thought of a verse from the second chapter of Luke when the Virgin Mother vowed to ponder only in her heart the reactions of the angels and shepherds to the birth of the Lord, and so Mary said nothing right away. Then she answered in a fashion that was as cryptic as it was honest. "I am not confident. I understand how little I know of God's plan for me."

"Hast thou found any more indications of Satan's presence here?"

"Art thou referring to what was buried in my dooryard?"

"Yes."

"I have not."

"Hast thou any idea who was possessed?"

"Or who is possessed?"

Her friend nodded.

"I have no idea," she said, and she studied

Rebeckah's face—which was as masked, it seemed to Mary, as her own.

They heard the door to the backyard opening and Catherine returning. The two women both looked up at the servant and smiled as she hung her cloak on a peg. Mary thought her own behavior toward Catherine had become oddly deferential, but she understood why. What surprised her was that Rebeckah seemed a little afraid of the girl, too.

&

Later that day, there was a knock on the door while Mary and Catherine were preparing supper, and Mary left Catherine at the table chopping the root vegetables. It was her mother, and initially Mary was worried that something must have happened to her father, but then she saw that her mother was smiling. She handed Mary a basket and said, "The **Falcon** docked this morning, and Valentine and Eleanor asked me to bring thee some treasures. It came north from Jamaica and the Antilles. After what thou endured at the Town House, Eleanor thought a bit of the bounty might cheer thee."

"How lovely. How kind of them to think of me," she said. "Dost thou know what's in it?"

"I don't. It's a surprise that Eleanor put together."

Mary pulled aside the canvas and peered inside.

There were oranges, almonds, figs, and tea, and she wrinkled her nose and savored the aromas. It was then that she noticed there was an envelope sealed shut with wax at the bottom. She started to reach for it, but stopped herself. If the note were from her parents' friends, it would have been at the top. And this was buried—almost hidden—beneath the imported treasures.

"It's wonderful. Such a thoughtful and unexpected gift. I will thank the Hills. But when thou seest them, prithee, share my deep gratitude."

"I will. Didst thou have a pleasant afternoon?"

"I did. I saw Goody Cooper."

"Rebeckah? I like her rather much."

"I do, too."

Her mother paused to appraise her more carefully. Then: "I am happy thou art not stewing on the verdict, Mary. Thy father and I are pleased to see that thou art finding other ways to occupy thyself."

She nodded. Ways other than what? she wondered. Witchcraft? Inside she felt freighted with her plans, that slow, heavy solidifying of her resolve she had experienced ever since she had first heard that appalling verdict.

"What art thou cooking?" her mother asked Catherine.

The servant girl looked up from her chopping and answered Priscilla, and Mary took the note from the basket and hid it inside her sleeve. Then, with great histrionics, she unpacked the wicker so the other two could see all—almost all—that was in it.

❧ ❦

She knew before opening the note that it would be from Henry Simmons. She read it while Catherine was mucking the horse stable and after Thomas had left for the ordinary. Her husband had claimed that he was going to meet there with a farmer. And maybe he was. Maybe they would discuss a delivery of grain, even one this late in the season. But mostly they would get drink-drunk.

She read the note carefully, the paper on the table by the candle, standing with her back to the door in the event Catherine surprised her.

It was short, but as she read it, she experienced a shuddering in her chest that left her giddy.

Mary,
Thou art an exquisite thing, a sun that warms my soul. Thy tenderness is so ardent that even while I was being lashed in the cold, when thou appeared from nowhere—Diana draped in a winter frock—I felt ensconced by a fireside in-glenook. I was no longer chilled or in pain.

Or, at least, in great pain.

But be circumspect, Mary, a fox that knows the safety of the shadows. Things could be

different had the magistrates seen fit to set thee free. I do not fear thy husband any more than I fear the pigeons and gulls that pick at the wharf. But the magistrates ruled as they did, and so there looms only heartache and sorrow if we pursue a dream that is gossamer.

This city is not built upon the precious stones of Revelation: we are not so pure. The scar on thy wounded hand is but one small testament to the evil of which we are capable.

And so whether I am blessed to see thee to-morrow or tomorrow's tomorrow, whether it is here or that other, blessed City to which we all aspire, I will not risk thy reputation or thy soul again while thou art wed to Thomas Deerfield. Thou meanest too much to me—far too much.

Sincerely,
Thy Distant Admirer,
Henry Simmons

She wanted to keep the note, to cherish it like a totem, but didn't dare. She understood the danger it represented. And so she placed it deep into the fire in the hearth, and watched it burn until the scraps blended in with the rest of the ash.

෫ ෫

Later, while Catherine prepared her bedstead and donned her sleep shift, Mary poured herself a cup of tea at the table in the main room of the house. She rarely intruded like this upon Catherine's privacy, but she wasn't yet ready for bed. She was too excited by Henry's note. She appreciated his chivalry, but her reputation was not his to soil. It was still her reputation, and she could do with it as she pleased so long as she did not indict him.

And she would yet be free. She was sure of this. Resolved.

She stared for a moment at the spout of the teakettle. It was bent ever so slightly. She hadn't noticed. Apparently, Thomas had been a step ahead of her: if the magistrates had shown more inclination to believe her side of the story than his, he or his lawyer probably planned to present the teakettle with its now crooked spout as proof that she had fallen upon it. But rather than incense her, his machinations only inspired her further.

She was rereading Deuteronomy. Thomas had not yet returned from the tavern, but Catherine had finished raking the fire and even her nearby presence did not disquiet Mary's soul. Inside she was smiling, aware of the insidiousness that had steeped inside her like the tea in the pot on the table. She was careful to shield from the girl the passages she was reading. Constance Winston's counsel had been invaluable.

So far, Mary had found many Bible verses with serpents and snakes in Genesis, Exodus, and Numbers, and written them in her ledger. Yes, the Bible was vast, but since returning from her walk with Constance, she had pinpointed the passages that might matter to a witch.

It was the Psalms, however, that mattered to her, because these were the verses that seemed most to mirror the sections that Reverend Norton had chosen for his sermon that Sunday, and the sign her Lord God had given her. The fifty-eighth Psalm and the 140th Psalm in particular seemed relevant.

The first reminded her, "Their poison is like the poison of a serpent: they are like the deaf adder that stoppeth her ear."

The second suggested even more of a connection, because it used the word **tongue:** "They have sharpened their tongues like a serpent; adders' poison is under their lips."

How interesting it was to her now that Thomas had joked that he was the one who might need his own personal cupbearer or Nehemiah to be sure that he wasn't poisoned. He really was very smart, she had to give him that. But he didn't know what she was thinking. Not now. No one did. At least no man. She looked up from the Bible and into the hot coals in the fire. They were red like a demon's eyes. They were beautiful.

Questions came back to her that had been hovering, rather like a raptor on an updraft, ever since she had met with Constance: Was she possessed? What did it mean that she saw conspiracies everywhere, even in the otherwise benign gaze of

Rebeckah Cooper? What should she make of the idea that Jonathan Cooke gambled with sailors and was in need of assistance from his father-in-law? Did a woman who was possessed not know it until it was too late—until the Devil had His claws so deeply inside her that extraction could only come via the noose? She imagined crouching inside her, rather like an infant in her womb, a monstrous imp—a shrunken gargoyle at the beck and call of the Devil—its talons ready to gouge out her flesh. This would be the beast she would birth, and the only one ever.

But she didn't believe that. Not really. She believed only that she was married to a brute who was going to Hell, and it was not she who was possessed and dabbling with cutlery to cast spells. She slipped her quill on the page with the 140th Psalm, closed her Bible, and resolved that tomorrow she would see Constance Winston once again.

❧ ❧

Most of the snow had melted, and Mary found the walk to the Neck more pleasant now that she was not encumbered by snowshoes. Constance and her girl were home, and the older woman invited Mary inside. Before Mary entered, however, she said, "I want to speak with thee about things best kept in confidence. I worry how our conversation could be misconstrued by someone who—"

"Thou canst speak plainly before my girl," said Constance, cutting her off. "Joy and I have no secrets."

"Art thou sure?"

The girl was drying porringers and placing them on the lowboy in the corner. She looked up at Mary and her mistress.

"Yes. But if it will make thou feel more at ease, she can finish with the soap out back," Constance said, glancing at Joy. The servant took her cloak and disappeared out the door by the hearth. "Wouldst thou like a cup of tea?" she asked, motioning for Mary to take one of the seats at the table by the fire.

"That is kind, but not necessary," Mary said, sitting down and pulling back her hood.

The other woman sat, too, folding her hands in her lap. "Why hast thou returned to the beauty of the Neck?" she asked.

"Thou art so cynical about this part of the city. It is as lovely as any section."

"Thou art sweet, but a lie like that is an insult to us both," Constance said. "Tell me: why dost thou risk thy reputation once more?"

"Very well," said Mary. "Aqua tofana."

"What would I know about poison?" she asked, her tone outwardly innocent, but the tilt of her head belying the fact that she almost anticipated such a question.

"Thou set me on the proper path."

"In what way?"

"Someone planted the forks to poison Thomas or Catherine or me. That was the spell and the pact they had made with Satan."

"And who might that someone be?"

"I do not know."

"But thou desirest now to concoct an actual poison?"

"I do. Aqua tofana is made of arsenic and lead and belladonna. That's how the Italians prepare it," said Mary.

"And it is undetectable. At least that's what people say."

"People say lots of things. Recall what they say about thee, Constance. In thy opinion, and given all that thou knowest, is it true that it is odorless and without taste? That even a physician cannot recognize its presence?"

"All true. It **is** undetectable. Rest well in that knowledge. A person just grows weak and sick and then dies."

"Always?"

Constance smiled. "Always. Aqua tofana is steeped by wives who hope to become widows. Would that be thee? Dost thou plan to poison the ogre to whom thou art married?"

"Prithee—"

"Thy servant who suggested at the Town House that thou might be possessed? Is she thy prey?"

"Catherine Stileman? I don't anticipate that she will become sickened," she replied evasively.

"Well, if thou wishest to take thine own life, there are far easier and less painful methods. It is also far slower than either musket or blade."

Mary recalled her moment on the floor with a knife, the first time she was alone in her house after the court had demanded that she return home to Thomas. It had felt like a criminal sentence, and she really had contemplated killing herself. But she was beyond that now. She had other plans. "I have no intention of meeting either God or Lucifer anytime soon," she replied.

"Good. Because I cannot imagine where one might find arsenic here. And I have never found belladonna in my walks in the woods."

She was disappointed, but not daunted. She thought this likely the case. "It need not be aqua tofana specifically," she continued.

"Thou simply want a poison that is efficacious."

"Yes. One that is merciless."

"And undetectable, I presume."

"That would be my preference. But I can work with one that is not. In some ways, one that boasts its presence might even be preferable."

The woman stared at her and said, "Thou art a mystery, Mary. Let no man underestimate thee, ever."

"Or cross me."

"In that case, I think something involving monkshood would be worth considering."

Had Peregrine—or Rebeckah—used monks-hood in the boiled apples and raisins? Would that have accounted for the taste they noticed? "Thou couldst give me the recipe?" Mary asked.

"I could make it for thee."

"No. Thou must not risk incriminating thyself in this world or damning thyself in the next."

"Oh, simply providing thee with the knowledge is likely to ensure my time with the Devil—that is, if He actually wants to waste His time with the likes of me. I am honestly not sure that He does. But thy point about this world? I thank thee. 'Tis kind counsel. But thou canst trust me to protect myself and to protect thee. I am nothing if not dis-creet."

"So, thou wilt guide me to a poison that is ef-ficacious?"

"I will. But only if thou wilt assure me the vic-tim is the fiend who tried to spike thee to a table. I do not countenance murder—only furthering the speed with which those already deserving of Hell make their way there."

"Fine. Yes, 'tis Thomas."

She nodded. "If the winter were not so far along, I would bring thee to my garden to harvest the in-gredients. But, alas, we have already had snow."

"I need to wait for the spring? Or, worse, the summer?" Mary asked, and she feared her dis-appointment had made her voice grow shrill.

"Calm thyself. I know where thou canst still find what thou cravest. I know where there is some harvested and well-preserved monkshood."

"And that is where?"

"The woods."

"The same snow that fell in the city fell in the forest," said Mary.

"Art thou willing to go into the woods?" Constance asked, her tone more adamant, ignoring the point that Mary had made.

"Yes. I am."

"Which means thou wilt need an excuse."

"I will find one."

"Very well. Just as I do, they begin with monkshood. Wolfsbane."

"They?"

"Edmund and Esther Hawke. They make the tincture for his arrows."

"That excommunicated family?"

Constance nodded. "Precisely. 'Obdurate disobedience.' It's in her humours: her mother, I believe, was an antinomian. Recanted. But still . . ."

"They have a small brood and a large farm."

"Quite right. They live near a village of praying Indians. In a rebellion of sorts, they have taken on some of their ways."

"How will I find them?"

"They live a little east of Natick. John Eliot sometimes visits them on his way to the praying Indians."

"And they make poison arrows?"

"I presume Edmund uses them only on deer. He has certainly not killed one of us. At least not yet."

"Will they sell me this tincture or the plant itself?"

"Thou wilt tell Esther that I am thy friend. She knows me. She will give thee the plants and thou wilt bring them to me."

"But—"

"I shall prepare the tincture. Or we can mix it together. Or I can teach thee. It makes no difference."

But Mary still worried that Constance was taking too great a risk. "Thy hands and soul will be much sullied," she said. "Thou wouldst have insufficient distance from the crime, both in the eyes of the Court of Assistants here and in Heaven above."

"Let me worry about the magistrates in Boston and the angels in the firmament. I have always been rather self-sufficient and unencumbered by the idiosyncrasies of man."

"I cannot change thy mind?"

"No, because thou canst not do it alone. Now, may I give thee one additional suggestion?"

"Prithee."

"Outwardly thou must not merely be in church. Outwardly thou must be more than merely obedient. Outwardly thou must be more saintly than thou hast ever been in thy life."

"My good works must be a beacon."

"Do something that practically invites martyrdom and that gives thee allies in the church who are staunch."

"Who can protect me against charges of witchcraft."

"That is correct."

"Well, I am not interested in witchcraft. I am interested in what might be more appropriately viewed as apothecary."

Constance leaned into her and said, her tone almost whimsical: "No. Thou art interested in murder. That, my young friend, is what has its hooks in thee."

I have a righteous fear of Lucifer.

**—The Testimony of Catherine
Stileman, from the Records and Files
of the Court of Assistants, Boston,
Massachusetts, 1663, Volume I**

Twenty-Five

Mary stared up at the steeple of the First Church against the midday sun, and thought of the comfort she had once found inside it. She rehearsed in her mind her story—her plan—and felt a deep pang of fear. But she had resolved that she hadn't a choice, none at all, and asked God to have mercy on her soul.

When she went inside, she saw that Zebulon Bartram was sweeping an aisle between the pews. The elder saw her and came to the front of the church. He was in his sixties, Mary guessed, stoop-shouldered, his hands so gnarled that they resembled apple-tree branches. He had been a cooper before the labor had grown too much for him. But he still needed to work—he craved it, a sign, one could suppose, that he was among the elect—and he was an excellent elder. He leaned the broom against the wall and bowed slightly.

"What dost thou need, Mary?" he asked.

"Is the reverend here?"

"He's writing in the back."

"Prithee, may I see him?"

"Certainly. Art thou well? Has something happened to Thomas?"

She smiled to reassure him. "I am fine and so is Thomas."

"Then is this"—and here he hesitated briefly before continuing—"is this about thy marriage and the verdict of the Court of Assistants?"

"No. I am not here about my marriage." And now it was her turn to pause, in this case because she was about to lie, and she knew it was the first of many that she was going to speak in the coming days. If this was a sign she was damned, so be it. But her Lord God was a mystery and had placed monsters before her. And so it was just as possible that she was merely a pilgrim doing her best to navigate the evils in a path that would eventually lead to paradise. She screwed up her courage and said, "I accept fully the verdict of the magistrates and have prayed that the Lord will be with Thomas and me, and help us to feel His love in our love," she told the elder.

"The reverend will be well pleased."

"I have an idea for something I can do for the Lord, if Reverend Norton thinks it is fitting. It is what I have come to discuss."

"Let me fetch him," said Zebulon, and he gestured toward the apse, behind which was a small room where the pastor worked. "I'll be but a moment."

Mary smiled and looked into the sanctuary, her

eyes moving beyond the elder to the pew where she had sat for years beside her mother. Was it a worse sin to lie inside these walls than outside them? Was it especially damning that she was planning to lie to John Norton, a minister? She understood how sinful were the adornments of the churches back in England and the cathedrals across France, the hanging images of Christ on the walls and in the stained-glass windows, but she wondered if she would be able to proceed if she were speaking such appalling untruths beneath the gaze of her risen Savior. It was going to be easier to lie amidst walls this spare.

When she heard the sound of men's boots echoing on the wood in the empty church, she turned her focus upon the altar, where she saw the reverend starting down one of the aisles, his elder trailing behind him.

"Good day, Reverend," she said. Zebulon took his broom and said he would sweep the light dusting of snow from the front steps, his intent to give the parishioner and her pastor their privacy.

"How art thou recovering from thine ordeal at the Town House?" the reverend asked, smiling as he rubbed at the tip of his beard. "It could not have been easy, especially given that the ruling was not in thy favor."

"I just told Zebulon: I respect the wisdom of the magistrates. I will respect the covenant that I have made with my husband."

"Thou art a wise woman."

She said nothing, and she could tell that he was unsure whether to see docility or defiance in her silence. "Tell me," he said. "What hast thou come to discuss?"

"I would like to be a missionary of sorts—to some children. I know there are men who work with the savages. I have heard much of the efforts of John Eliot."

"John is a rare breed. Hast thou read his books?"

"I have not. But I know of them."

"He has learned their language. He is so fluent that he is translating the Bible into Algonquian. Dost thou plan to learn it, too?" he asked, his tone skeptical.

"I was thinking of the Hawkes. Not the savages—at least not yet. The parents were excommunicated, but they have five children on a farm."

"The Hawkes are difficult people. Stubborn. There is good reason for their excommunication."

"I do not doubt that. It is the souls of the children I care about."

"And thou art asking my permission? If so, that is a decision for Thomas, not me."

"Not thy permission," she said, lowering her eyes deferentially.

"Then what?"

"I would like an introduction to Reverend Eliot. He passes the Hawke farm on the way to the praying Indians east of Natick. I would like to ask him to escort me there and back on the days he is with the savages. I may never know precisely why God chose not to bless me with children of my own. But I accept that, and I pray that what I am suggesting does not mask an ill-advised pride. I want to help the Hawke young ones grow into adults who love their Savior as I do—as we do—and to behave appropriately."

Norton gestured vaguely with the back of his hand at the world beyond the doors to the church. "Thou wouldst prefer that the children do not grow into heretics."

She was unable to read his tone. She heard a tinge of good-natured sarcasm, but he may also have revealed he was taking her seriously. "That is a level of specificity beyond what I was imagining," she replied.

"John Eliot is doing work that is as dangerous as it is important with savages. Thou hopest to do the same with a small English tribe barely more civil. Why dost thou suppose they would want thee in their life?"

"I may not succeed. But is a missionary worse for failing or failing to try?"

"I appreciate thy courage."

"And the Reverend Eliot knows them, true?"

"He does. And Thomas? What are his feelings?"

"Thomas has no objections," she lied. She wasn't sure that her husband and John Norton had spoken a dozen words together.

"Well, then. I have but one more question."

"Prithee, ask."

"What were Henry Simmons's designs upon thee?"

She hadn't expected this, and reflexively stalled by asking in return, "Art thou asking why he tried to kiss me?"

"Yes."

"I gave him no sign I was interested in a liaison of that sort."

"I expected the magistrates to pursue that possibility with more curiosity than they did, Mary."

She arched her back. "Speak plainly, Reverend. I will answer with neither prevarication nor falsehood."

"Thou petitioned for a divorce because thou claimed that Thomas treated thee with needless cruelty."

"Cruelty by definition is needless."

He nodded. "Fair. But the magistrates determined that Thomas did not treat thee cruelly. So, if thou didst seek to break thy covenant with thy husband because he was . . . cruel"—and he emphasized the word as if it left a bad taste in his mouth—"but Thomas was in fact fair in his dealings with thee, then perhaps there was another reason why thou tried to sever thy marriage."

"And my claim of cruelty was what? A pretext? A ruse?"

"It is a question a reasonable man might ask, yes. Caleb Adams thought it a possibility."

"No, Reverend," she replied, struggling mightily to hide her exasperation, "I did not petition for divorce on false grounds. There has been no adultery between Henry Simmons and me."

"Except for his attempt to kiss thee."

"Yes. Which I resisted."

"Thou hatched no conspiracy to malign Thomas Deerfield for thine own ends?"

"Most assuredly we did not."

He clasped his hands behind his back. "Very well. I had to ask."

She wanted to tell him that he had no such obligation, but held her tongue. When she said nothing more, Norton continued, "I will speak with John Eliot about thee and vouch for thine intellect and resourcefulness. He is a good man."

"I am most grateful."

"I know thou art, Mary," he said. Then he added, his voice an eerie combination of menace and jest, "And when thou place the trenchers and cutlery on the table today, perhaps do not set before thy husband a fork."

❧ ❧

The reality that John Norton had brought up Henry Simmons, even suggesting that she had falsely accused Thomas of cruelty to try to achieve her divorce, led Mary to change her plans that afternoon. She had been hoping to walk to Valentine Hill's warehouse by the harbor. It would have been brazen to ask the merchant how his nephew was mending—or, perhaps, even Henry himself if he had returned to work—but she had planned to present her inquiry as mere Christian charity. Henry had made a mistake attempting to kiss her, and she was going to extend to him her forgiveness. At least that was how she would have presented her visit to anyone who was paying attention. She would know the truth. So would Henry. He knew that she hadn't resisted his advance.

Today, however, she didn't dare venture to the waterfront. Perhaps next week.

But the sun was starting to break through the clouds when she left the First Church, and she could feel the temperature rising. A ship had arrived recently with tortoiseshell combs. Her mother had brought her one, and Mary had seen the way Catherine had coveted it. Some of those combs were likely for sale now at the apothecary. And so instead she went there to buy the girl a comb as a gift. On some level she was hoping to curry the girl's favor, an endeavor that was pathetic if viewed solely in this manner. But it, too, was an act of Christian charity. It would make Catherine happy.

And given the wolves she was about to unleash, that was a good thing.

The Devil is nefarious and can make evil
a child's plaything if he wants.

**—The Testimony of Valentine
Hill, from the Records and Files
of the Court of Assistants, Boston,
Massachusetts, 1663, Volume I**

Twenty-Six

Catherine did like the comb.

Over supper, Mary asked Thomas, with the girl present, if she might have his permission to tutor the children of the excommunicated Hawke family. John Eliot could escort her to and from their farm on his way to the praying Indians. Thomas had put his knife down on the table and stared at her, his eyes narrowed, his gaze suspicious. He asked why she had grown interested in the Hawke brood, and she told him that she had been inspired by the Reverend Norton's most recent sermon. She added that the minister thought it was a fine idea for her to explore whether she had an affinity to assist with the children, and her next step would be to visit Eliot. Thomas questioned whether she thought it was reasonable for a woman to make so rash a decision without consulting her husband first, and she had responded—and she had rehearsed this sentence—that before she burdened him with the idea, she wanted to see if it was even a possibility. She added that Norton agreed it was a fine way for her to use the gifts God had given her to glorify Him, and this was, perhaps, why He had made her barren.

"My supper will be ready when I get home?" he had asked.

"If Reverend Eliot should allow me to accompany him?"

"Yes."

"I will be sure it is," she had assured him, and then she looked at Catherine, who was staring down into her trencher as if the chicken bones there had regrown their flesh.

And that was that.

⊰ ⊱

John Eliot was not tall, but he was massive: he was round like a pumpkin, and his face was a plump almond with a mustache that he waxed into curlicue tips. He was fifty-eight years old, but his hair—though streaked with white—was lush and thick and hadn't begun to recede. He parted it perfectly in the middle, and it fell in two waves down the sides of his face to his shoulders. His eyes were feminine and kind, and he rose from behind his desk when Mary entered his study, guided there by an indentured servant no more than fifteen who was, like her master, portly and attractive. After Eliot dismissed the girl, he threw another log on the fire. His house was as impressive as her parents' home.

"I do not know thy father and mother well, but James does great service to the colony," he said. He had a shelf of books on the wall, most about Indians, including two he had written. On the tabletop was a well-thumbed Bible, ink, a quill, and a thick stack of paper. Though the sun was still high and the desk was near the window, he had two candles burning. The study had but the one ladder-back chair, and Eliot insisted that she sit in it while he stood by the window.

"My father's work is of little concern compared to the efforts thou art making on behalf of the savages," she said.

"Do not underestimate the value of importing civilization. In the woods, I see the need for enrichment all the time. Sometimes that enrichment comes in the word of the Lord; sometimes it comes from a chair," he said, smiling, and he motioned at the fact she was seated. "Thy father brings us ships rich with such civilizing amenities."

"I will share with him thy gratitude."

He nodded. "I spoke to John Norton yesterday," he said.

She knew that the reverend was going to mention her to Eliot, but felt the need to suggest her humility that these two great men were discussing her. "I am flattered. Thou both did me an honor I do not deserve."

"Nonsense. He told me thou dost wish to work with the Hawke children."

"I do."

"Is it because thou hast not yet been blessed with children of thine own?"

"The fact I am barren—"

"That word is needlessly harsh. Thou art young. Thou may yet have a child."

She started to stroke the back of her left hand where Thomas had broken the bone, worrying it through her glove, but stopped herself. It was becoming a habit. "The fact I have not yet had a child," she said, correcting herself, "gives me time to do the Lord's work in ways I might not have contemplated had I been already blessed with girls or boys of my own. But there are other motivations."

"And they are?" His tone was benevolent.

"When the magistrates were weighing my petition to divorce Thomas, there was much discussion of Lucifer. It reminded me how present He is even here—in our world on this side of the ocean."

"Thou dost not fear the woods?"

"I have far greater fears."

"Thou wouldst be surprised by what grows there."

"I rather hope so."

The reverend chuckled. "That's the spirit."

"And if the Devil wants me, He will as easily come for me here in the city as He will in the forest," she replied, and she thought of the forks and the pestle in the dooryard of her home.

"Perhaps. But the woods are a labyrinthine world in which the Indians see paths we never shall. And people like the Hawkes? They are as savage and un-schooled as the Indians."

"I will not lose myself," she promised. "I under-stand there is a community of praying Indians east of Natick."

"And thou wouldst like me to bring thee to the Hawkes on my way there?"

"I would."

"Those savages are becoming accustomed to the light of the Lord. It is a small community, but one with promise."

"Perhaps someday, I can be an asset with them, too."

"In time. Feel no weight on thy shoulders." He went to the books on his shelf and handed one to Mary. "Hast thou read it?"

She looked at the title: **The New England Primer.** "I have not. But my grandchildren have a copy. The books arrived from England this summer."

"One of thy father's imports, perhaps."

"I believe that is true."

"Bible stories. A catechism. Absolutely beauti-ful woodcuts of John Rogers and his family being burned at the stake."

"Peregrine and Jonathan's older girl finds them gruesome, and so she turns always to those pages first."

"I am not surprised."

"I own a copy of **Spiritual Milk for Boston Babies.** Shall I bring it?"

Eliot handed her his copy of the primer. "That would be a good idea, yes. Read this and bring it, too."

She thumbed through it, pausing on her granddaughter's favorite woodcut: the burning of the Rogers family. "**Spiritual Milk** has no pictures," she murmured.

"That won't be a problem."

"Good. I look forward to the journey."

"It seems that thou dost not fear the Hawkes," Eliot observed. "I rather wish thou didst."

"Why?"

"They barely tolerate me. I doubt they would tolerate my ministrations."

"I understand."

"I expect I will find thee sitting alone on a stump outside their farm when I return. Exiled from their house."

"If they choose to be inhospitable, I will at least know that I tried."

He looked at her left hand. "How is thy hand healing, Mary?"

"It is feeling better."

Eliot turned his attention from her to the window, gazing at a pair of crows that were picking at the remains of a dead raccoon in the dooryard.

"Well, as dangerous as the woods can be, at least thou wilt not confront a teakettle."

"No," she agreed. She could tell that he did not accept Thomas's story. Most of the men of the city were of one mind: believe one thing and speak another. But Eliot, it seemed, wanted her to know that he knew Thomas had lied.

"Art thou able to join me tomorrow?" he asked.

"Yes. Before dinner or after?"

"All day. I will leave at sunrise and return just before sunset. Is that a problem?"

"No."

"Good. The praying town I will visit is neither far nor deep into the woods. But it will take us two or three hours to reach the Hawkes. So, expect at least five hours atop a horse. I will spend perhaps three with the Indians with the days already this short. View thy time with the family as but the first page of a catechism."

"I am grateful."

"And, prithee, do not suppose thou wilt accompany me always or often. Let us take this one day at a time. One journey at a time."

"So long as I am glorifying God, I am at thy service."

He studied her a long moment. "I may be rather large, but thou art rather small. I've a pillion: thou canst ride with me. But the path will be muddy with melted snow. Dost thou own splatterdashes?"

"I have stirrup stockings."

"Fine. Be here at sunrise."

She stood and thanked him. Thomas might say something cutting about how quickly the events were proceeding when she told him her plan, but he was unlikely to stop her. She now had the blessing of both Reverend Norton and Reverend Eliot. For all she knew, Thomas would, in fact, appreciate the idea that he needn't return home for dinner, but could instead have an extra tankard or two at the tavern near the mill.

❧ ❧

On her way home, Mary stopped at her parents' house. She gazed up the stairs and thought of how much she had enjoyed living back here, despite the stress of her petition or the unease she had felt around Abigail after the girl had seen her and Henry kiss. She told her mother of her plans to meet the Hawke family the next day, and how two of the most esteemed men in the colony championed her decision. She knew her mother would tell people, and the more people who knew of the faith that John Norton and John Eliot had in her, the safer she would be against rumors—or even actual charges—of witchcraft.

Her mother paused after Mary described her plans in detail. Mary could see that she was both

proud and worried, which was essentially what Mary had anticipated.

"And thou art going tomorrow?" her mother asked, her eyes wary.

"Yes. I couldn't be happier at the prospect."

"Into the woods?"

"Not terribly far. Thou needest not fret. We will leave in the morning and be back by sunset. We will not be in the forest after dark. I view it as a small test to see if my aptitude matches my desire. I believe he views it much the same way."

"I trust the reverend."

"I do, too."

"Still, Mary. Be careful."

"My soul is in the Lord's hands. I trust Him, too," she said, aware after the words had left her lips that while what she was saying was not technically a lie, she was misleading her mother and using the Lord as a tool in her machinations.

"I will want to hear all about it. It is noble that thou want to help the Hawkes: keep thine eye on Heaven, but temper thine expectations."

"I have no expectations," she said, and she laughed. She almost said that she felt a calling from God, but a lie like that was too much. It was one thing to stand beside the fire: it was quite another to walk right into it. Instead she continued, "I will do what John recommends and heed his counsel. I expect to be useless tomorrow, but to learn much."

"About the Hawkes."

"Yes, about the Hawkes," she agreed, though in her mind she saw monkshood. She hoped she would learn about that, too.

⊰ ⊱

At home, soon after sunset, Jonathan Cooke stopped by the house while Mary and Catherine were preparing supper. He said he was hoping to see Thomas. His jacket was buttoned against the cold, and he had pulled his hat down far on his forehead.

"He is due any moment if thou wouldst like to wait," Mary told him. She tried to view him with charity, but she thought considerably less of him after what Thomas had told her. The idea that he had come to her husband for money did not trouble her, but the idea that he squandered a dowry gaming did. She was disappointed in him, so much so that a face that once had seemed handsome now struck her as rakish.

"Yes, I would," he said, smiling agreeably, and Catherine poured him some cider.

"How is thy family? How is Peregrine feeling?" Mary asked.

He stood by the fire, sipping his drink. "She has had some bad mornings. Either the baby or something she ate. Maybe the change in the weather."

Mary pondered this. "Is it like when she was carrying thy other daughters?" she pressed.

He shrugged. "A bit. But I heard one of thy parents' girls—Hannah—had the same thing."

"As Peregrine?"

"I'm not a physician, but yes," he said. She considered asking him more, but he continued, "Thou must be relieved thy petition is behind thee—though, I suppose, it did not end the way thou hoped."

"I am here," she said. She was surprised he had brought it up.

"Indeed, thou art. Thomas is much blessed. Thou art, too, Catherine.".

The girl looked slightly alarmed that she had been brought into this conversation.

"After all," he continued, "thy mistress has returned. All is well with the world, right?"

"All is well," she repeated demurely, but Mary could tell she didn't believe that.

"No more of this devilishness about forks?" he said, after taking a long swallow of the cider. Mary wasn't sure to whom he was speaking. His comportment seemed to suggest that he had stopped at an ordinary on the way here.

"Jonathan, there is nothing devilish about forks that Catherine or I deem worthy of conversation," she said carefully.

"Thou savest it for public display at the Town House?"

"I never brought it up there," Mary reminded him.

"No," he said, and he wagged a finger suggestively at the servant. "She did. Well, today this must be a house that is rich in love and trust and the peace that passeth all understanding."

"Art thou mocking scripture?"

"No. I am only quoting it, Mary. Only quoting it."

Outside, she heard her husband's horse. "That would be Thomas," she said. She was surprised by how quickly the visit had grown uncomfortable.

He put down his tankard. "I thank thee, Catherine," he said. "I thank thee both. I need thy husband but a moment, and so I will say good night here." Then he left them and went into the dooryard to greet Thomas.

When he was gone, neither woman said a word about Jonathan's behavior. Mary didn't want to, and Catherine didn't dare.

·❧ ❧·

Catherine went out back with the animals after supper, and so Mary had Thomas alone. She asked him whether Jonathan had pressed him again about money.

"He did," Thomas said, as he pulled on his coat.

"Thou art returning to the tavern?" she asked.

"I am."

"What didst thou decide?"

"About Jonathan? I told thee: I am going to give him some ground corn and flour."

"Will that suffice? He seemed much in need when he was here."

He looked at her, and his face grew dark. "Why art thou harping on this?"

"Thou brought it up to me in bed the other night. I am trying to be a faithful helpmeet."

His eyes went to the door to be sure that Catherine was not yet returning. "Sometimes, I think he wishes me dead so Peregrine would get her share."

"Jonathan?"

He closed his eyes and rubbed at the bridge of his nose. "'Tis not thy concern."

"I'm sorry."

"They will be fine. All of them."

"Peregrine is feeling poorly," she said.

"She is with child."

"Unless it was something she ate."

He shook his head in abhorrence. "Thy mind, Mary, thy mind. One day it's dull as an infant's, and the next it is attempting to unravel the mysteries of the humours. I am tired. I am vexed by thee, and I am vexed by the godless peacock that married my daughter. Don't make me . . ."

She waited in silence. She knew not to finish the sentence for him or urge him to finish it himself.

"It doesn't matter what ailed her," he said finally. "She is mending." And then he was gone.

For a long moment, until Catherine came back into the house, she was lost in the thought that she had misjudged Jonathan and Peregrine—and, perhaps, Rebeckah—and was seeing plots that were but phantasms and missing the poisons that were real. Once more, the idea came to her that she was, in fact, possessed.

I believe she may have learned things—
dark things, evil things—from a woman
such as Constance Winston.

**—The Testimony of Catherine
Stileman, from the Records and Files
of the Court of Assistants, Boston,
Massachusetts, 1663, Volume I**

Twenty-Seven

Mary sat on the pillion behind John Eliot as they passed the last of the fields on the outskirts of the city—quiescent, the ground locking in hard for the winter—and watched geese against the flat gray sky as they flew south. She hadn't seen a great V of geese in weeks and wondered what it meant to see so large a flock today. From how far north had they come that they were only now flying over Boston? Eliot hadn't spoken since they had ridden through the Neck, and there he had only observed how far the city's reach was extending. She found their silence companionable.

It had been years since she had sat on a horse. She couldn't recall the last time she had ridden with Thomas. Had her family remained in England, she might have learned to ride alone there. She might have had her own horse, one very much like Sugar.

Eliot's animal was a massive black gelding that the minister called Jupiter, and the creature moved at a clip that compelled Mary to hold on tight to the grips of her seat. Only when they reached the woods did the animal slow. There it picked its way carefully along the path, clomping through the fallen leaves that coated the ground like a carpet. It was wide enough in some spots that two horses could have ridden side by side, and even a wagon could have passed. But then the path would narrow, and both Mary and the pastor would have to duck beneath a branch.

"Remember, Mary: the Hawkes were excommunicated for a reason," Eliot said, breaking the quiet. "They still live largely in darkness. They may not be slaves of Satan, but they are unschooled."

"And the children?"

"They are more like their mother than their father. Quiet. Intense. I've no idea what lurks behind their eyes."

And then, suddenly, she saw light beyond a great copse of pine and understood it was a cornfield, the crop long harvested and the stalks cut. She heard the sound of a river and knew they had arrived at the farm.

⊰ ⊱

They paused before a thatched cottage with a massive chimney at the rear, a plume of smoke curling into the sky. Behind it they saw a small barn and beside it the square where Esther kept a kitchen and herb garden. There was neither a stone wall nor wooden fencing, because no one lived near the Hawkes.

"Is it what thou expected?" Eliot asked.

"I had no expectations," she said.

A woman emerged with a baby in her arms, and two girls running about her legs: a toddler and a girl Mary supposed was four or five years old. They disappeared quickly behind the cottage, but Mary could hear them giggling.

"Edmund has two sons from his first marriage. They're older. The three of them are likely hunting," Eliot murmured. "But this is Esther."

The woman's dress was frayed and her apron badly stained. Great tentacles of unkempt red hair fell from beneath her bonnet. She was slender but not to the point of gaunt.

Eliot urged the horse forward, dismounted, and then took Mary's hands—pausing briefly when he reached for her left hand, but she nodded that she was fine and he should proceed—and helped her climb to the ground. She had a satchel with the two books over her shoulder, and it bounced against her hip when she landed.

"I have brought a new friend with me today," he began. "This is Mary Deerfield. Mary, meet Esther Hawke."

"Art thou risking thy soul, too, visiting the likes of us on the way to the praying Indians?" Esther asking, appraising Mary as she spoke.

"My soul is at peace," Mary said.

"And she's not joining me," Eliot added. "She's not coming to the village."

"I was hoping to visit with thee and thy children while the reverend is with the Indians," Mary told her.

"Well. Aren't we blessed," said Esther.

The two little girls reappeared and started trying to tag each other, treating their mother as if she were a tree they could use as a shield. Eliot was looking at Esther, and Mary couldn't decide if he was frustrated by the children's lack of discipline or fearful that they would behave immodestly. And so Mary knelt and smiled at them. "Is this not why I have come?" she said to Eliot over her shoulder.

He nodded vaguely. The older child ran her hands over Mary's cowl and her flannel gloves, still swanskin white, a little awed.

"Ah, thou art a governess," Esther said. "The First Church has decided I need assistance and generously sent me a servant. Art thou my indenture, Mary Deerfield?"

"Oh, Mary is married to one of Boston's most successful millers and the daughter of one of our most important merchants: James Burden," Eliot explained. He couldn't have missed the derision in Esther's tone; it seemed he had chosen to ignore it in the interest of harmony.

"But I am here to be of help, if thou wouldst like that," she said.

"With the washing or the cooking?"

She pulled **Spiritual Milk for Boston Babies** from her bag and showed it to Esther. "I know thy history, and I know thou art alone."

"Alone? Verily, I crave solitude some moments!"

"Thy family is alone. Forgive me. But thy point buttresses why I have come. I meant it when I said I can help thee."

Esther looked at Eliot. "Since when does the church want anything to do with us?"

He chuckled. "The church doesn't. But Mary feels a calling rather like mine."

"We are thine heathen, Mary Deerfield?"

"Oh, I have a feeling, Esther, thou art going to teach me far more than I could ever teach thee."

⋘ ⋙

After Eliot had left, Esther brought Mary inside the cottage, where there was a long, sturdy table, a spinning wheel, and but one rickety chair. The floor was dirt. But the fire was strong, and it was comfortable inside. There was a second room where Mary supposed everyone slept, but Esther wasn't offering a tour, and so she sat with the girls on blankets while Esther began to nurse the infant, who had started to fuss.

The older girl looked into Mary's eyes and said something in Algonquian. Momentarily Mary was taken aback. "She speaks the Indians' tongue?" she said, and in her incredulity, it came out as a question.

"Honour wants to know if gloves so delicate keep thy fingers warm," said her mother, translating. "We all speak two tongues. Look at where we live."

"Yes," Mary answered the child. "My gloves do their work well. So, thou art Honour. And thy sisters' names?"

"Dorcas and Serenity," the girl said. "Serenity is the baby."

"Hast thou children?" Esther inquired.

"No. The Lord God has not favored me in that fashion."

"How hast He favored thee?" Esther asked, and Mary could not miss the edge in the question. This woman would have done well as a magistrate on the Court of Assistants.

"He has given me life and the bounties of His world," she answered.

The other woman rolled her eyes. "Tell me, prithee: why hast thou really come?" Dorcas was staring up at her. "Dost thou honestly believe we want thy help?"

Honour was on her knees, her hands on her thighs, leaning over the book in Mary's hands. Mary looked at the opening page of **Spiritual Milk:**

Q. What hath **GOD** done for thee?
A. **GOD** hath made me, He keepeth me, and He can save me.

The books were but a ruse; they weren't why she had come. But she needed them to work her way there. This first tract was a scholarly way to initiate Christian tutelage, but she recalled the woodcuts in **The New England Primer.** She should begin there instead. She flipped to the pages with the images of John Rogers being burned alive at the stake and the one of his children, their gazes beatific, as they were herded to their deaths. Those were the pictures that held the most allure for her older granddaughter. She recalled the fairy tale book she had owned back in England. Those stories, of course, were inappropriate fare for any Christian, and she understood that now. But she had loved them, and she felt a pang of guilt recalling the pleasure they had given her.

"Perhaps I've come but to read," she answered, and she began to read aloud: "Mr. John Rogers, minister of the gospel in London, was the first martyr in Queen Mary's reign, and was burned at Smithfield, February fourteenth, 1554. His wife with nine small children and one at her breast followed him to the stake; with which sorrowful sight he was not in the least daunted, but with wonderful patience died courageously for the gospel of Jesus Christ."

Honour pointed at the image. "Why are this man and his children being cooked?" she asked.

"Thou knowest the answer to that," Mary scolded the child gently. But when neither Esther nor her girls said anything, she continued, "This man loves our God so much that he is willing to die for Him."

The girl took the book from Mary's lap and started to thumb through the pages. Esther finished nursing her baby and stood. "I have work to do. If thou desirest to care for my children, Mary Deerfield, they are thine. But don't suppose that because we live near the Indians, we are so pathetically unschooled as to need thy tutelage. Honour will, with cause, challenge thee."

Mary rose with her. If Esther was going to be so forthright, then, so be it, she would be, too. "Esther," she began, "it is I who needs thy tutelage."

The woman waited. "I need thy help," Mary continued.

"I rather doubt an excommunicated soul like mine can offer thee anything."

"Thou art mistaken," she said, and she took Esther's elbow and guided her gently away from her older girls. "We share a friend: Constance Winston."

"Art thou like Constance?" Esther asked.

Mary couldn't decide what that question meant: **Art thou like Constance?** "In addition to being self-sufficient and handling thy excommunication with courage, I believe thy husband and thou art wise," Mary said, evading Esther's question.

"Wise? Because we choose living here rather than under the thumb of the likes of John Norton?"

"John Eliot has not cut all ties with thy family."

"He views us the way he views his praying Indians. Misguided and unschooled."

"Fine. But here is one point on which I am confident we agree," Mary said. "The Devil is real, and He is here in Massachusetts."

"Yes. So?"

"He is using someone in Boston to attack me."

Esther said nothing. She watched her girls with the book.

"Dost thou understand?" Mary asked again, not trying to stifle the urgency she was feeling.

"How?"

"He is trying to poison me with a spell. He is using a witch to try to poison me and"—and here she exaggerated to enlist Esther's support—"my husband and our servant girl."

"And thou knowest who this person is?"

"I do," Mary said, now speaking an outright lie.

Esther placed her baby on the blanket and went to a deerskin satchel on the floor in the corner of the cottage. She pulled out a small bottle with a cork. "This will heal some poisons," she said, handing it to her. The tincture inside was watery and brown; it reminded Mary of the water that puddled in her muddy dooryard in the spring. She had seen bottles just like it when she had visited Constance.

"Esther, what dost thou want most for thy children? What . . . things?"

"Thou hast brought us books with woodcuts of people being cooked," she replied. "What more could we possibly desire?"

"Perhaps we could begin with better boots for thy girls. Dost thou want very warm boots? Better cloaks?" Mary looked toward the doorway to the room in which the family slept. "Pillowbeers?" she continued. "New comforters?"

"Thou needest trade me nothing for medicine," said Esther. "I was not censured because I was cruel. We were censured because we called out the crooks among the elders and the fiends who hanged Ann Hibbens."

"I appreciate that," Mary said, and she understood she would have to reveal more. "Wilt thou keep a secret as a mother? Wilt thou tell no one of our words?"

Esther waved at the air around them. "There are throngs who hang on all that I say."

Mary nodded. "I thank thee. I want to trade for something else, and I will give thee much, if it can be a secret."

"Boots and cloaks," said this mother definitively.

"Yes! I will return with boots and cloaks, plenty of each. I promise."

"If I tell no one."

Mary knew she would deny these girls nothing, regardless of how Esther answered. She would return with better clothing against the cold, no matter what. That was the charitable thing to do and thus would not be part of the negotiations. But she could sense that she had hooked Esther as surely as if she caught her in a grapnel, and so it was easy to respond, "My father has been much blessed and he brings many things to Boston from England, as well as Jamaica. I will bring thy family gifts because thou needest them. And because I can."

"But I have something thou cravest that is not in this bottle?"

"Yes."

Esther checked the swaddling on her baby, who had started to doze. "Thou cravest something dark. Is that thy secret?"

"Justice and retribution are not dark," Mary replied.

"Thou art panting after something no Boston apothecary will concoct. I understand now. I will have to speak to my husband. Edmund and I will decide together."

"I respect that. I can return." She gazed at the girls. "I **want** to return."

"And if Edmund wants to know thy target, art thou willing to share that, too?"

"No. I would not wish to implicate thee."

Esther smiled knowingly, almost conspiratorially, and Mary was at once agitated and exhilarated when she imagined the forces she was about to unleash.

I answered thy question: we had tea.

—The Testimony of Constance Winston, from the Records and Files of the Court of Assistants, Boston, Massachusetts, 1663, Volume I

Twenty-Eight

"Esther Hawke mostly was occupied, and so I was blessed to spend time with two of her girls," Mary told Thomas and Catherine that night over supper. "The children were sweet."

"Except likely they're damned," Thomas said. His tankard of beer was nearly full. In her mind, Mary saw herself emptying the entirety of a small bottle of monkshood into the pewter. She wondered if a nearly full tankard would be sufficient to mask the taste of the poison.

She shook her head, trying to will the vision away; though determining the specifics was critical, they distressed her. It was still but the abstract notion that prodded her forward.

"And the boys and their father were hunting?" Catherine was asking.

"Yes," Mary said, and she told them about her plan to return with gifts of boots and cloaks, though Thomas did not seem especially interested. As she spoke, she realized just how exhausted she was: almost five hours atop a pillion on a horse, more than two more with the Hawkes, the air always chilly. Then there was the stress of her negotiation with Esther—and the reality that now both this other woman and Constance Winston knew she was interested in a recipe for poison. As soon as she had returned home, she had thanked Catherine copiously for preparing Thomas's dinner and their supper on her own, and managing the daily chores and the animals without any help. And yet now it was she herself who almost lacked the energy to tell the two of them of her day. But she owed it to them.

And, of course, sharing what she had seen and how she might help bring the Hawkes back to church was self-preservation. One never knew if someday she might need this dislikable young woman with whom she was eating to testify on her behalf.

❧ ❧

In the morning, Thomas read from the Psalter before breakfast, and when he was done, he ripped off a piece of bread and sliced himself a piece of cheese. As he chewed, he asked Mary, "And today: the Hawkes again?"

"No. John Eliot is not returning to the praying Indians until next week."

"That is probably well. Thy leaving? 'Tis a burden on Catherine."

Mary turned to the girl and said, "I thank thee, as do the Hawke girls."

"It is good the work thou art doing," Catherine said. She might have said more, but a log collapsed in the hearth. Quickly Catherine went out back to retrieve an armful of wood.

When she was gone, Thomas lifted the block of cheese from the board and stared at it. Then he said, his tone strangely ruminative, "White meat. Thy brain, Mary. 'Tis not like eating the bread and body of our Savior. But still indicative. When my teeth mash the white meat, I think of thee and of thy brain."

She sighed. "Why this anger, Thomas? Tell me: what have I done to merit such a statement?"

He swallowed. "I do not know what thou art planning," he said. "I do not know what thou hast in mind. But thou art contemplating something sinister. I know not what, but—"

"Either I have white meat for a brain or I am plotting evil," she snapped at him. "Cheese is not known for its perniciousness. Which is it: am I a dullard or a witch?"

"Be careful with thy tone," he said, lashing back. "I would hate to see thee have another accident."

They both turned when they heard the back door opening and Catherine returning with an armful of wood. "I think thou bringest much to the Hawkes, Mary," he said. "So long as

Catherine doesn't feel an onus because of thine efforts—"

"My calling," she corrected him, and though this was yet another challenge, she was careful to smile when she spoke.

"So long as Catherine doesn't feel a disagreeable increase in her work while thou art away, thou mayest continue thy . . . calling."

"I thank thee," Mary said. She watched Catherine place two logs on the hot coals and the bark start to catch. It was beautiful, and she was reminded of the woodcuts of John Rogers and his family as their skin was peeled off by the flames and their bones turned to ash.

❧ ❦

She had to see Henry Simmons. It wasn't a physical craving the way food and warmth were; it was, she told herself, a matter of practicalities. Yes, she knew that she—and when the word came to her, it gave her an unexpected ripple of happiness—**desired** him. But this wasn't that. He simply needed to know that things were about to happen and they might happen with a rapidity she could not control, but she was determined that the two of them, eventually, would be together. (He could never know her plan, and she would deny it if he ever suspected. If she were damned, she was resolved not to damn him, too.) She considered writing him her intentions, but she couldn't risk the existence of a note. It would be too easy for it to be discovered. She knew after her failed divorce petition that she couldn't trust even her parents; they loved her, yes, but they were more fearful of the magistrates than they were, it seemed, even of their Lord God. To protect her from the noose they had consigned her to this prison of a marriage. And they would be aghast at her intentions. They would be ashamed. She could never tell them such things.

And so she was going to have to risk a walk to the wharves where her father and Valentine Hill had their warehouses. But to minimize the chance that any of the gossips might note her presence, she walked the long way: she detoured around the market and the Town House. Boston had grown so fast that now even the side streets were alive with commerce. She passed a cobbler's shop, an apothecary, another bakery—not Obadiah's, a new one she had never used—a brazier, a tailor, a cooper, a cabinet maker. She did not doubt that her people were doing good work here, the work of the Lord, civilizing this corner of the earth. And yet it all felt increasingly like . . . London. At least what she remembered of London. Boston was smaller, yes, and cleaner. At the same time, it also lacked much of the refinement and the accoutrements of great wealth. But that would come. It came daily on the ships. Increasingly when she was out and about, she felt the bustle and she felt the crowds and she felt purposeless. Had they separated from the church and all that they knew merely to create a smaller, less refined version of the metropolis they had left behind? She thought of the university across the river. Just this year they'd finished the Great Bridge, linking the city with Cambridge.

She watched a hawk circling overhead and wondered what prey he spied. Quickly, she lowered her gaze back to the street, alert for anyone she might know, prepared to choose another day to go to the harbor if she saw someone she recognized.

What she could not decide as she neared the warehouses, however, was whether she felt a distance from her Lord because of what she was planning—whether this was the Devil working His way inside her—or because the speed of Boston's growth was blinding them all to His vision. Her doubts about what they were striving to build in this new world felt woeful and lurid, but what, in fact, had they accomplished if she looked rather specifically at her own home? She had a husband who was vile, a servant girl who was either evil or deluded, and parents who had relegated her to the dungeon of Thomas Deerfield. Yes, John Rogers had willingly walked into the fire for God, and yes, he had willingly consigned his wife and children to those very flames. God wasn't asking that of her. She wasn't sure that God was asking anything of her. Certainly, her good works for the Hawke children were but an inadvertent result of her plotting and scheming. But God knew all: Had He not set all of this in motion so that she would bring to those girls the sorts of things they desperately needed? Boots and cloaks?

She paused before the warehouses. There they were: her father's and Valentine Hill's imposing monoliths. There were the sailors and the men working in their leathers against the cold and wet spray, hauling the crates and casks from the two ships that had docked at the far end of the wharves. She pulled her hood tight and walked faster. Her heart was thumping hard, but she took comfort in the fact that she had spoken to no one on the way here and no one had spoken to her.

❧ ❧

There he was in the doorway to the office at the front of the warehouse, the storeroom before him. Henry Simmons was standing with a ledger in his hands, surveying the empire of goods as if it were his. He was motioning for a pair of burly young men to deposit an ornate highboy against a wall with equally well-crafted lowboys and dressers and desks. All of the furniture was exquisite, well beyond what they produced here in New England. But, she knew, it was only a matter of time before they had cabinet makers here who were sawing and sanding and joining work this grand.

Henry turned when he saw her, a wave of alarm passing over his face. But he put the ledger under his arm, glancing back once to be sure that the highboy was being placed where he wanted, and went to her.

"Mary, why hast thou come?" he asked in lieu of a greeting. There was no anger in his tone, but his apprehension was evident. "I asked my aunt to bring thee my letter."

"Thine aunt is kind, but she never mentioned the letter. She—"

"Dear God, did it fall into the wrong hands? Is that why thou hast ventured here?"

"No, worry not. I read it. It was beautiful," she told him.

He exhaled, a great sigh of relief. The two men passed them on their way back to the end of the wharf, where others were unloading the ship and stacking its inventory on the pier. Henry motioned toward the vessel. "'Tis the brig **Jamaica Wind.** She's a beauty. Carries eighty tons. This shipment? Furnishings and furniture of a sort seldom seen here."

"Seldom seen here in the past. But seen now with increasing frequency."

He smiled and raised a single eyebrow. "Art thou judging, Mary?"

"Not at all."

"Tell me, then: why hast thou come? Thou knowest the dangers."

"I would say I know the impropriety of it. But, Henry, there is an ocean between an impropriety and a danger."

"Not here."

"Perhaps," she agreed. "But I view it as a good deed: I am giving the gossips something new to discuss. They must be in dire need since I am no longer a figure at the Town House."

"Is that really thy desire? To be the subject of ghastly stories?"

"No," she answered honestly. "Rest assured: I took the long way here. I avoided the market and the Town House completely."

"I am glad," he said.

"I have come because I have an idea."

"Oh?"

"Thy letter gave me hope. And that is a great gift."

"That is comforting, so long as it has not emboldened thee to recklessness."

"Oh, but it has," she said, and now it was her turn to smile. Two more sailors approached, together hauling a crate that was almost the size of a chicken coop, and Henry turned away from her to show them where to deposit it.

"So," he said, returning his attention to her. "What recklessness art thou contemplating?"

And she told him nothing but that she saw a way out, a way to escape her marriage. But before she proceeded, she wanted to be sure of his commitment. She watched as his face transformed in stages from curiosity to surprise and then alarm: not because he was not committed, but because, he said, he did not want her taking undue risks. But she could see that he was taking her seriously and that he was supportive.

"Tell me what thou art planning, so I can help," he said.

"No. I must be a hawk gliding solo above my prey."

"But—"

"'Tis the only way we can have a future together," she said, cutting him off. "Dost thou trust me?"

"The psalms suggest we trust God."

She felt a spike of fear that she had lost him— that he doubted her. But then he arched an eyebrow and smiled. "But, in this case," he continued, "I am comfortable putting my trust in a goddess."

❧ ❧

On her way home, she stopped at the cobbler in the market that everyone in her circle used, and bought the warmest boots the fellow had for the two Hawke girls. She noticed that his apprentice was hammering a pair of wooden heels into a rather nice pair of women's shoes, and considered briefly how impractical they were here and now.

"And for whom might these be?" the shoemaker asked, referring to the boots. "I believe one pair might be for thy granddaughter. Peregrine's older girl. Am I right?"

She shook her head. "They might fit her well, but they are for another child. The smaller pair is for her younger sister."

"Oh?"

"I was out by Natick with Reverend Eliot the other day. He took me to meet a poor family on his way to the praying Indians. These are for their girls."

He was about to place the pounds she had given him into his money box. But when he heard the boots were charity, he paused. He started to return the money to her, but she held up her hand to stop him. "No," she told him. "That is a most Christian gesture. But thou paid good money for the leather and fur, and then worked hard to fashion them into these shoes. 'Tis a gift."

"Thou art a good woman, Mary," he said.

She smiled and said, her tone oozing a modesty that she didn't feel, "We know well that a gospel of good works is but the path to Hell. I am a sinner like the rest of us."

But she appreciated his gesture, and inside she felt better about Boston than she had on the way to the harbor. And she also took pleasure in the fact that the cobbler was sure to tell others that Mary Deerfield was friends with the Reverend John Eliot and raining charity down upon the poor.

⊰ ⊱

It was starting to snow when she arrived home. She stared at the patch of dooryard where she had unearthed the two forks and the pestle. The whole ground was locked in hard and deep now. For all she knew, whoever was in league with the Devil and wished ill upon her had made sure that the spell had been once more cast before the ground was solid as iron and nothing more could be buried there—and so something resided in that earth now.

Rebeckah Cooper presumed the witch who was after her was Catherine, but Mary was not convinced. Mary was no longer sure she trusted even her friend. Besides, was Catherine smart enough to portray an innocent victim with such absolute and righteous sincerity? Maybe. But it was a most convincing performance, so Mary was dubious. Moreover, Catherine's brother was dying when the forks were planted, and Mary supposed the girl was too preoccupied with tending to him and to her grief to be dabbling with the Devil. Besides, she showed no outward signs of possession. If Catherine was responsible, she had help. A teacher. She was not working alone.

And while Mary understood there were people who disapproved of her, what could she possibly have done to lead someone to choose Lucifer over the Lord? Nothing in the behavior of anyone she knew suggested they were now in league with Satan.

It was a puzzle.

But Mary's inability to make sense of it only deepened her resolve. She hugged the girls' boots close to her cloak and thought of the magic of wolfsbane and the potential of her intrigue, and felt an unexpected but deep eddy of contentment. Her future, at least while she breathed, yet held promise.

I have no desire to meet [the Devil].
Not ever. I have seen too much of His
likeness here in Boston, even among the
saints.

**—The Testimony of Constance
Winston, from the Records and Files
of the Court of Assistants, Boston,
Massachusetts, 1663, Volume I**

Twenty-Nine

Two nights later, she and Thomas had supper at her parents' home, and while the girls were clearing the plates—no trenchers here, not with her parents having her and her husband over—she asked her father which ships were expected in the next few weeks.

"For what art thou hoping?" he asked good-naturedly. "What goods wouldst thou like to see unloaded by the boys?"

Before she could respond, Thomas placed his left hand on her right and said, an attempt at charm, "Thy daughter enjoyed her weeks with thee this fall. Thy home is very comfortable. It seems I will have to spend more time greeting the next vessel from England and assessing its contents."

"Or Jamaica," said Priscilla. "With winter arriving, we see more ships from the south than the east. The passage from Europe is neither pleasant nor easy this time of year."

Thomas smiled. "Jamaica then. The bounty that

Eleanor Hill brought us in that one basket? Marvelous. Absolutely marvelous."

"I was merely curious," Mary said. "There is nothing in particular I desire."

"When dost thou visit the Hawkes next?" her mother asked.

"Monday. After the Sabbath. John said he could bring me with him then."

"Mary has bought boots for the beasts," Thomas said, still grinning. He rather enjoyed his alliteration.

"And thou callest the reverend **John**?" her father asked. "The Reverend Eliot is a notable man. Thy familiarity with him is impressive, Mary."

"We shared five hours atop a horse. We will share five hours more. It is a long, hard day and two cannot help but become . . . familiar."

Mary knew when she spoke that she was poking a stick at the animal to whom she was married, but she knew also he would say or do nothing in front of her parents. He might when they got home: there might be deeply unpleasant and even painful ramifications there. But the chance to jab him here before her parents was irresistible, and she savored the glee that it gave her.

❧ ❦

And, indeed, he took her that night with anger in his eyes and in his hips, at one point grasping her neck in his hand and choking her for so long that she thought, **This is it, this is the end, I am about to meet either the Devil or Jesus Christ.** When he was done, he whispered into her ear, "That is familiarity, Mary Deerfield. Become familiar with another man, whether it is that pathetic pup Henry Simmons or that fat pigeon John Eliot, and I will finish thee. Or, better still, I will be sure that the men of the Town House, those bloody magistrates, do it, by slipping a rope around thy neck. Did my fingers there hurt thee? 'Tis nothing compared to the agony of a noose."

When he went to the chamber pot in the corner, she rolled away from him. There was a floorboard in the bedroom on her side of the bedstead that gave ever so slightly when she stepped upon it. It creaked. It had begun to warp. When she had had a moment alone earlier that night, she had examined it. One of the iron nails protruded perhaps a quarter of an inch and she was able to pull it free with her forefinger and thumb. Then she lifted the board and saw there was room there to hide a tincture bottle. Now, by the light of the candle on the table, she stared at the tip of that iron nail. Someday soon, when she had her wolfsbane, she would conceal it there. She took comfort in that nail, and wondered if this was what Catholics or Anglicans felt when they hung a cross on a wall in their homes.

❧ ❧

"We don't preach from Malachi often enough," the Reverend Eliot mused on the Monday after the Sabbath, as Jupiter walked briskly beside a field where Indians had grown corn.

"What passages specifically?" Mary asked. Her fingers were cold, despite her gloves, especially on her left hand where Thomas had stabbed her. She tried to recall the biblical text to take her mind off the discomfort. She also had less room on the pillion than the last time, because she had with her a sack with the clothing and boots for the Hawke children and a cloak—a surprise—for Esther.

"Chapter one, verse eleven. I used it on the title page of one of my first mission tracts." She could tell that he hoped she would quote it back to him, because that might mean she had read his book. But she hadn't, and though she knew the Bible well, she was weak on Malachi. When she said nothing, he continued, " 'My name **shall be** great among the heathen, saith the Lord of hosts.' We are making the pure offering God demands of us."

"A pure offering," she repeated.

"Our intentions. Doing His work because of our love for Him and our desire to see the souls of the heathen brought home to Him."

"Yes," she agreed. " 'Tis why we do this. There is no other reason."

◅ ▻

The children looked adorable in their cloaks. Mary was well pleased. They were made of a thick, shaggy wool, but they were deep red, the hoods with drawstrings to pull them tight. Esther's was a dark burgundy, too. The girls put theirs on right away and clearly felt rather fashionable. But the clothing was also functional; that was what Mary cared about.

John Eliot had sermonized rather dramatically when she had presented the garments and boots. When he brought clothes to Indians, they were castoffs and rags, the dregs that not even the poorest of the British would wear. But these were new: cloaks and boots and stockings and mittens for the girls, as well as that cape for their mother. Mary had fretted when Eliot had used the word **gift** repeatedly, because this was a trade. Certainly Esther viewed it that way. But the other woman said nothing to correct the pastor, and Mary's anxiety passed.

Now Esther was holding the boot for Honour, kneeling in front of the child, and the older girl slid her right foot into it. It looked a little big, which was what Mary had hoped. She handed the child a stocking and then said to Esther, "The stocking will take up a little room and make the boot more comfortable. And, perhaps, the boot will still fit next winter."

"Or it will fit Dorcas."

"Quite so."

"When thou art on thy knees, Esther, tending to the feet of another, it is reminiscent of when our Lord Jesus Christ washed the feet of his disciples," Eliot pontificated.

The woman gazed at the reverend, and Mary could see that she thought what he'd said was absolute idiocy. Esther was just being a mother. And even Mary Deerfield, childless and barren, understood that.

❧ ❧

After Eliot had left and Mary was alone with the Hawkes, she opened **The New England Primer** and started thumbing through it for the next lesson. But Esther spoke before they could begin.

"Thou dost seem more interested in that book than in our barter," she said. Apparently, Esther had expected her to bring up the wolfsbane right away. "Men—Indians and English alike—would not tarry so after they had struck a bargain," she continued.

"I trust thee," said Mary.

"Thou hast not changed thy mind?"

"No."

The woman brushed a lock of hair off her

younger girl's forehead. "I am not sure where thy plans fit into the teachings of men like thy John Eliot," she said.

Mary considered quoting Exodus 21:24—"eye for eye, tooth for tooth"—but did not see what good could come from sharing any more than was necessary. And so she answered, "Thou knowest not what my plans are."

"No. But I know wolfsbane. So does Edmund. My husband had many questions when I told him what thou wanted."

"Such as?"

"He is not sure I should trust thee. He is not sure whether we should trust anyone from Boston with such things."

"Thou may rest assured, Esther, that my intentions will never implicate either of thee."

"Edmund's wolfsbane is powerful."

"I hope so."

"It has slain many deer and many wolves."

"Dost thou have any regrets with our bargain, Esther? I will not hold thee accountable. I understand if thou wouldst prefer not to proceed."

"Thou canst not hold me accountable because thine own intentions are suspect," Esther said, and Mary felt the ground shift at the woman's acknowledgment of how she had compromised herself. Suddenly, she was a little bit scared of this exile. But then Esther continued, "I only want to make sure thou knowest that wolfsbane is a river and, once crossed, there is no returning."

"Thine husband seems to cross back and forth across that water."

"He has never used it on a man."

When Mary said nothing in reply, Esther continued, "Very well. Edmund will leave a bottle with thy friend and his occasional trading partner: Constance."

"A bottle? A finished tincture?"

"Yes."

"But why? Why would he do such a thing for me?"

"Thou hast brought our family many gifts. And, yes, because thou art a friend of Constance."

"I am overwhelmed with gratitude. I know not what to say."

Esther pointed at the book in Mary's hands. "All of thee dost speak much of lambs and love, but thy actions . . ." She stopped and shook her head, the repugnance unmistakable.

"Prithee, continue."

She sighed. "Thy actions? Thou art wolves, Mary. All of thee who shunned us: thou art wolves."

Mary didn't defend herself. She didn't defend her people. If Esther was mistaken, it was only in that she was comparing them to wolves instead of snakes.

❧ ❦

The next day, when Mary passed Rebeckah Cooper's dooryard, there was Peregrine weeping in her friend's arms. Mary asked what had happened, the idea crossing her mind that this had something to do with Jonathan. His gaming or card playing had landed him in the stocks, or some sailors had beaten him over his debts and left him bloodied.

The two women parted, and Peregrine wiped at her eyes with a handkerchief with delicate blue flowers on one corner.

"It's the child," said Goody Cooper. "The baby inside her has, according to the midwife, died."

"Oh, no, Peregrine, I am so sorry," Mary told her, and she forgot her supposition this had to do with the woman's husband or that Peregrine had expressed her fear that Mary would try and seduce Jonathan. She even put aside her belief that the woman might have tried to poison her. All she felt was sorrow. She hugged Peregrine, a reflex, and though the woman did not resume her crying, she melted into the embrace.

" 'Tis God's will," said Peregrine, her words stoic but her tone despondent.

"I know. And there is comfort in that knowledge. But, still, thy ache is real." And then Peregrine described the physical pain and the bleeding she had experienced yesterday, and how only this afternoon she had left the house. She still felt weak.

"There will be other children," Rebeckah said to her.

"There will," she agreed, and Mary knew she believed this—and should. Then Peregrine said she had work to do before supper and had to return home. Goody Weybridge was with the girls, and, apparently, that older woman's patience was a short candle that burned fast.

After Peregrine had started down the street, Rebeckah shook her head and said, "It is good that thy divorce was not allowed."

Mary was baffled by the remark, which seemed an utter non sequitur. And she said so, asking the woman to explain what she meant.

"Isn't it obvious? If thou were alone—a woman unmarried, no longer wed to Peregrine's father—it would be just one more reason to suppose thou were possessed."

"Because Peregrine's baby died?"

"Yes! First William Stileman and now this baby! Mary, 'tis obvious: some people would say for sure thou were a witch!"

❧ ❧

Constance Winston sat back in her chair and pulled from her apron the small tincture bottle. Her girl was outside, and so it was just the two of them.

"And that's it?" Mary asked, her heart beating fast in her chest.

The older woman held the bottle of poison in

her hands as if it were a jewel. "What thou hast accomplished is not insubstantial," she said.

"I did nothing. I merely followed thine instructions and went to meet the Hawkes."

"I was hoping at best that Edmund would provide thee the plants and I would make the potion. The idea that thou convinced Esther—"

"I traded with Esther," corrected Mary. "It was a trade. Remember, I returned with boots and cloaks for her children." They were drinking tea, and the mug was hot and warmed her fingers. It had snowed last night, and she wondered if it would snow more on her walk home from the Neck. "I want to be forthright in my negotiations and relations: art thou sure that Edmund wants nothing more from me?"

"The Hawkes think little of most of the men who live here in Boston. If there is one less? He would not weep."

"I have the sense thou wilt not shed any tears, either."

She smiled. "Now, people—the right people—know of thy friendship with John Eliot?"

"They do. I speak of it often."

"Excellent. They hanged another witch in Hartford."

"I heard," Mary said. "Goody Cooper believes it is well that my divorce was not granted. She suggested it would cast a deeper shadow upon me as a woman untethered."

"Rather like me."

"No! I only meant—"

"Goody Cooper is right. I am not offended," Constance said. "View thyself as a hawk soon to be free of its jesses." Then she uncorked the bottle and sniffed the poison, adding, " 'Tis monkshood. And something more."

"More?"

"Edmund told me that he wants there to be no doubt when a wolf's at the door. 'Tis wolfsbane and another most efficacious poison. He suggested it works quickly."

"And what does that mean? What shall I see?" Mary asked.

"Frothing from the mouth. Vomiting. Confusion."

"Then death?"

"Yes. Then death," said Constance, recorking the bottle. "Thou art verily prepared to use it?"

"I am," said Mary.

"When?"

"I am not sure. But I will allow Boston to hear more of my journeys into the forest with Reverend Eliot, and how the Lord is manifest in my behavior. There can be no aspersions upon my character: that is especially clear to me after the death of the child inside my daughter-in-law."

"Thou hast thought through thy plan well."

"Tell me something, prithee?" asked Mary.

"Yes?"

"What would mask the taste most effectively? Beer?"

The woman thought about this and sipped her tea. "Yes. I think so."

"Should I use the whole bottle?"

"Oh, take no chances," she said. "Use the whole bottle. Use every last drop."

I saw melancholy. I saw sadness.

—The Testimony of Catherine Stileman, from the Records and Files of the Court of Assistants, Boston, Massachusetts, 1663, Volume I

Thirty

When she got home, immediately she climbed the stairs to her and Thomas's chamber and went to the floorboard that bowed ever so slightly. She plucked the nail and pulled up the wood, and slipped the bottle of poison into the small, secret chamber. Then she pushed the floorboard flat and the nail back into its hole. No one would notice what she had done. No one. No one but she would know the bottle was there.

§

The next day, after Thomas had ridden to the mill on Sugar and Catherine had gone out back to muck the animals' stall, Mary went to the pegs by the front door where they hung their cloaks. She thought she might visit the utterly detestable Goody Howland and share stories of her missionary visits to the Hawkes and her work with John Eliot. The woman might not wish to see her, but that was irrelevant: it was all about spreading her story. Goody Howland was a veritable town crier.

She dropped her cloak by accident, however, and when she bent over to pick it up off the floor, she noticed a mark on the wood. It was small, barely the size of a shilling. She fell to her knees to study it carefully. She couldn't believe it was real, but it was. There on the bottom of the front-door frame, just above the wooden floorboard, someone had carved a circle with a five-sided star. The mark of the Devil. A welcome of sorts to Satan: a sign of conversion and allegiance, a signal that this was a safe house.

She thought of the forks and the pestle that had been buried in the dooryard and wondered once more if there were more out there beneath the stone-solid earth. Was it possible that her husband was in league with the Devil and wanted her poisoned by this spell? It didn't seem likely. He was evil, but his guile was limited to the reality that he would not strike her when there was a witness. Did that mean that it was Catherine, after all? Or was it someone else who wished her ill?

Or, far worse, was it an attempt by someone to have she herself, Mary Deerfield, hanged as a witch?

Quickly she stood and backed away so that Catherine would not know she had seen the mark if the girl returned that moment from the horse stall.

She resolved to go to the harbor and visit Henry

Simmons instead of seeing Goody Howland. Things may not in fact be moving more quickly than she had expected, but he needed to know of this new wrinkle. Her friendship with John Eliot would buy her time, but it was impossible to know how much.

❧ ❦

Henry pushed aside a stack of ledgers and sat on the edge of the broad desk in his uncle's office. He motioned for Mary to sit in the chair behind it. After she had told him what she had discovered at the base of the door frame, he mulled it over and said, his tone even, "I do not believe thou art in any more danger from the Devil's sign than thou were from His tines."

"From forks," she said. "And not from **His** forks. From my father's forks."

"My point is this: Dost thou feel poisoned? Hast thou felt sick?"

"Other than my hand where Thomas tried to impale me to the table? Not especially."

" 'Tis my point."

"But I would like to know who is possessed. See that corrupted and obscene person rightfully hanged."

He shook his head. "No, that is not thee, Mary. Thou dost not actually want that."

"Perhaps not. But I would like to know. And if the point is not to sicken me, then I especially want to know the witch, since in that case, the plan is more heinous still. Because then it is an attempt to have me accused of witchcraft and sent to the gallows."

He looked down at his boots. "We do not know that there is a connection between the forks and the mark that someone carved into the wood. They could be separate talismans."

"Thou canst not believe that!" she told him, exasperated by his attempts to be reasonable. "Thou knowest as well as I that these machinations are linked!"

"Yes. I believe that. But do I know it with certainty? No. We have no proof."

"Someone is conspiring against me, and if someone is carving the Devil's sign into my house, we both know: my efforts with the Hawkes will not be sufficient to protect me."

"Then tell me, prithee, what art thou planning? I know there is more."

"There is. But thou needest not know. 'Tis best."

"Dost thou want to confront this witch alone? She—"

"Listen to thy self. **She!** The witch could just as easily be a man!"

"Forgive me."

She closed her eyes and composed herself. "No. Forgive me. For my anger. We both know the truth. We both suspect my own servant girl. That is whom thou hast in mind, true?"

"Most likely."

"Sometimes when thou dost fix thine eyes on me, I wonder: dost thou see anything but a barren and venomous wretch?"

He hopped off the desk and stood before her. He took her hands in his and held them, rubbing gently the spot on her right hand between her forefinger and thumb. "I rather applaud thine anger. I do not care that thou might be barren. And if thou art a wretch, thou art one that is rather comely in my eyes." For a moment, neither of them said anything, and she heard only the seagulls outside the warehouse. "Mary?"

She waited.

"I see but an angel who is much abused by this world." And when he leaned in to kiss her, she opened her lips, and this time there was no one there to see them or stop them.

＊＊＊

It rained the next two days, chilling showers that fell intermittently, but it wasn't freezing and even in the night the dooryard didn't turn to ice and the trees didn't bow beneath the weight. And so while the rain did not inhibit the work of the city the way snow could, it was ugly and depressing and it affected Thomas's mood. It caused Catherine to grow sullen. Mary took comfort in the reality that soon, for good or ill, she would have acted.

And at church on the Sabbath she prayed, but no matter how deeply she tried to reach into her soul, she did not feel God's spirit. Instead she felt the presence of the mortals she detested with a hatred she knew she should reserve only for Lucifer.

But she was also aware of Henry Simmons, and knew that he was profoundly aware of her. He was her future and she was his. At least while she breathed. At least until, as her recompense, she was flung into the fires of Hell.

❧ ❧

She was asleep when Thomas returned from the tavern on Monday night. She awoke when he crawled into bed and started to pull up her shift. The clouds had parted—finally—and the room was flooded with moonlight. He was drink-drunk and rough, and for a moment she was prepared to acquiesce though he had plucked her from a dream, but then she recalled that her time of the month had begun soon after he had left after supper, and she had padding between her legs that would offend him.

"Thomas," she began, her voice sleepy, "'tis my course. 'Tis my time."

He wasn't listening, however, and already he was reaching there. He felt the rag and pulled away in revulsion. His anger followed quickly, the frustration exacerbated by the ale and the rain.

"Thy barren wife—thy stinking, filthy, dullard of a wife—has a body designed once more to repulse me," he said, his voice a malevolent whisper. "A dunghill. A walking, bleeding dunghill. Thy course is always and forever, a curse upon thee and a curse upon me." He sat back on his knees and put his hand across her mouth, and then took her left hand, the one that he had stabbed that autumn, and banged the back of it hard onto the corner of the night table. She started to cry out against the pain that shot up her arm in blistering waves, but he smothered her scream. Catherine likely heard nothing.

"Thou art loathsome, and I am not moved by thy tears. Drown in them, for all I care," he hissed into her ear. "It would be no loss. No one would mourn thy death."

Then he released her and swung his feet over the side of the bed. Her side of the bed. His feet were bare and his balance was wobbly. She felt a pang of fear as if she knew what was going to happen next, but there was nothing she could do to stop it. To stop him. It was happening too quickly and, besides, her hand hurt so much there was a ringing in her ears and she felt a little stunned:

a bird that has accidentally flown into a window. He stumbled against the wall, against the corner where the floorboard was warped and the nail protruded, and he was stepping upon it with one of his bare feet, and then he was cursing. One long, loud curse, a wounded lion, his shoulders jerking back as he fell into the wall. Catherine certainly had heard that. He bent over to pry the nail from the wood, and she had to stop him. She knew this, she knew this as well as she had ever known anything. And so she fought against the agony in her hand and rolled over, sitting up and climbing from the bed, too. "Thomas," she said, "my love, it can wait until the morning. Whatever it is—"

"It is a bloody nail!" he snapped, and already he had pulled it from the wood. "That's what it is!"

He was enraged, and she saw that he was about to rip the board from the floor, and even though it was night, there was sufficient moonlight in the room that he would see something was hidden there. He would see the bottle of poison. She took his shoulders in her hands, even though her left one was throbbing, and said, "Prithee, come to bed. Whatever has so angered thee, it will still be there when the sun has risen and thou hast had a chance to sleep."

He looked at her and seemed to calm. He sat beside her on the bed and studied the nail between his forefinger and thumb. In the morning, he would fix the board. She thought how she would have to stay awake until he was snoring and then remove the monkshood.

"Yes, whatever has angered me," he murmured, "will still be here when the sun has risen. Alas, thou art going nowhere. And if thou dost want to bleed to keep me at bay, well, let there be blood." Then, before she knew what he was doing, he took the nail and poked it so hard into the palm of her left hand—dragging it like a dagger—that she screamed.

"Catherine," Thomas called out, "thy mistress stepped on a nail on a warped board! It was the same one I stepped on a moment ago. No need to worry about either of us."

As he crawled into bed, he said to her, "Thou must be more careful. One of these days thou might wound thyself all too seriously. One of these days, I just might find thee dead."

She watched the blood pool in the palm of her hand, occasionally glancing at the brute beside her. As his breathing slowed, any hesitation dissipated, and her resolve grew profound. By the time he was asleep and she had retrieved the poison, she could see it all in her mind. Every act and every moment, the agonized eyes and the stringing spittle.

✥

She placed the poison at the very bottom of the chest with her clothing. Thomas neither rustled nor stirred. The rhythms of his breathing changed not at all.

❧ ☙

In the morning, after Thomas had nailed the floorboard back in place and left for the mill, Mary handed Catherine a pouch with coins and asked her to please visit the tinker and purchase three new spoons for them.

"Wouldst thou not prefer to choose them thyself?" the girl asked.

"Not at all," Mary reassured her. "I trust thee as a sister."

"Thy hand is swollen again," Catherine observed, and Mary couldn't tell from her voice what she was thinking. If this girl really did see goodness and wisdom in Thomas, perhaps now was the moment to disabuse her of the notion that he was anything but a vicious gargoyle with a man's face, and share the precise details of what he had done to her last night. But she recalled the chess set the family had owned in England—left behind like so much else—and thought how one always had to think many moves ahead to win. She had to think that way now.

"I banged it on the bricks in the hearth when we were making breakfast this morning," she said.

Catherine nodded and left.

When the girl was gone, Mary began her search.

She was not sure what she was looking for, but she began by thinking about where she would hide something if she were Catherine. And those would be the places where Catherine had the most independence—where her master and mistress were least likely to supervise or assist her. That meant the henhouse, the horse stall, and the wood-pile were out, because Mary was often retrieving eggs, Thomas was frequently saddling and unsad-dling Sugar, and everyone carried in wood. Mary stood with her hands on her hips. Then she pulled down Catherine's bedstead and ran her hand along the wall, wondering if she might find a compart-ment there. She did not. She ran her fingers around the bedding and shook out the comforter, discover-ing nothing.

And so she replaced the bed and stared at the girl's trunk. It seemed too obvious to hide some-thing there—the trunk had a latch but no lock—and yet Mary had to search it. Yes, it was a violation, but she had to know. And so, like a common crimi-nal, she pawed through the girl's shifts and frocks and stockings and sleeves, and then opened her Bible and flipped through the pages. But there was nothing incriminating. If anything, Mary felt a tremor of guilt at what she was doing in light of how little the girl had.

When she had repacked the trunk, she warmed her swollen hand near the hearth. She surveyed the kitchen, running her eyes over the spider and roasting jack and the hooks with their pots and spoons. It seemed mad, but she thought of the lie she had told Catherine and pushed upon the bricks a row at a time, half-expecting one to give and reveal a hiding place. But they were solidly in place.

She sat down at the table. Their home was not small, but neither was it palatial. Nevertheless, it was alive with nooks where one might conceal the tools of conspiracy or possession. She knew how, for a time, she had hidden poison beneath a floorboard.

But was it not possible there was nothing here to find? Perhaps Catherine was in league with the Dark One, but whatever she knew or whatever she had done, she had left neither totem nor trace of her iniquity where she lived.

An idea came to Mary. She put fresh shag between her legs, climbed into her cloak and boots, and started off. By now Catherine was well over halfway to the tinker near the marketplace. It was too late to see if the girl made any detours on the way there. But if Mary hurried, she could see—surreptitiously, as a spy—if her indentured servant made any stops on the way home.

☙ ❧

The girl was emerging from the tinker just as Mary reached the corner perhaps forty yards distant. Behind Mary was the open expanse that surrounded the Town House, but before her the street was narrow. She retreated into a doorway so Catherine wouldn't see her peering out and she could watch her pass. But the servant didn't appear, and when Mary leaned farther out, she saw the girl turning the corner in the opposite direction: she wasn't going home.

Mary followed her, keeping her eyes firmly on the girl's hood, prepared to crouch down and pretend to fix the laces of her boots—hiding her face—if Catherine looked back. But she didn't. She walked and walked, and as they left the marketplace behind, it dawned on Mary where the girl was going. Of course. It made all the sense in the world. Her destination was clear, and Mary watched as her servant knocked on the door and Goody Howland answered, looking around conspiratorially before beckoning the girl inside.

❧ ❧

Mary was sewing when Catherine returned. It was possible that the girl had just gone to the Howlands' for a visit: she had lived there while Mary's petition was being heard and it was where her late brother had been indentured. Perhaps the pair merely gossiped about what a foul and barren woman she was, and how sad it was that Catherine had to live with the likes of her. It was also possible that they chatted about a great many things, and Mary Deerfield's name never even came up.

But Mary didn't believe that.

She said that her left hand was throbbing and asked the girl to tend to the chickens and bring in some wood. The girl put down her satchel and obliged. Instantly Mary bolted from the chair and examined the contents of the bag. There were three new spoons and there was the remaining change from the money that Mary had given her to buy the silverware, and there was a handkerchief and her gloves. But that was it, there was nothing more.

Had she expected to find forks? Three-tined forks? A pestle? A wooden mark with a five-pointed star that might fit into one's palm? Maybe. But there was nothing incriminating. The tinker didn't sell three-tined forks, but in her mind, Mary had seen Goody Howland surreptitiously handing Catherine a pair.

Clearly, she was mistaken—though not about the girl. Mary remained confident of her convictions.

She returned all of the items to the bag and resumed her sewing. Fine, she thought. Fine. It would have been too easy to have found proof of the girl's duplicity—of her collaboration with Goody Howland and Satan—in the bag. That didn't mean that Mary was not surrounded by a swamp of snakes. She still believed that Catherine was behind the forks in the dooryard and that Catherine had carved the Devil's mark into the wood in this very house. She still thought it likely that the girl wished her ill, either because she saw in her mistress the cause of her brother's death or she saw in Thomas something that Mary herself did not—if only as a way up from her station.

So be it. Let that pestiferous child try and destroy her with fiendish spells and pretend poisons. Mary had a real one. And soon enough she was going to use it.

Tell us, prithee, what thou knowest
of Mary Deerfield and her penchant
for evil.

**—The Remarks of Magistrate Caleb
Adams, from the Records and Files
of the Court of Assistants, Boston,
Massachusetts, 1663, Volume I**

Thirty-One

It was unpleasant to walk during her course, and Mary had walked much the day before when she had trailed Catherine from the tinker's to Goody Howland's. But still that afternoon Mary walked to her parents' house. Her father was at the warehouse, but she had a lovely visit with her mother.

And when she left, she had with her two of the three-tined forks that her father had imported but her parents never again were likely to use. She had taken them from the highboy when Abigail and her mother were preparing tea and Hannah was outside emptying chamber pots. No one saw her slip them into her satchel.

Then she went home and waited. She waited with a peace and contentment that she supposed was felt usually by the elect.

❧ ❧

The timing was going to matter. She feared that Henry might fret when he did not hear from her, and so she asked Catherine to bring Eleanor Hill a linen apron she had made to thank the older woman for the basket of treasures—the oranges and figs and tea. She encouraged Catherine to please mention that she would be up and about by the end of the week, which was all that was necessary to convey to another woman that it was her time. Eleanor would likely say something about the gift of the apron to her nephew, and he would know that Mary was well.

Now she stood before the looking glass and, as strange as it seemed to her, tried out different presentations of sickness. She recalled what Constance had told her were the manifestations of wolfsbane poisoning, and opened her mouth into a rictus of pain. It looked fake. There was a reason why acting was shameful to God. It was childish. But she recalled what it had felt like to have a fork breaking the bones of her hand and then those very bones slammed into the corner of her nightstand; she remembered what it felt like to have boiled salad dumped upon her. And she grimaced. She practiced gagging. She put spittle upon her lips. She brought her hands to her neck.

She could do this.

She found it ironic that a widow received the same portion of a husband's estate as a woman who divorced him: one-third. She wiped the saliva from her lips and from the waistcoat where, in a most unseemly fashion, some had dripped. She shook her head and wondered at the time and the effort she had wasted with the men of the Town House. One-third of Thomas's estate. It would all come out the same in the end.

At least in this world.

And in the next? It seemed likely, based on her thoughts, that she was already destined for Hell, so a crime on her ledger mattered little. In fact, at this point, it mattered not at all.

❧ ❦

That afternoon, Reverend John Norton stopped by. He was in the neighborhood, and Mary was embarrassed that her hands were unclean from having just been out back with the animals. But, as if he could read her mind, he reassured her that the Lord had not likely ever chastised a shepherd for dirt under his fingernails. He apologized for interrupting her.

"What is the reason for thy visit?" she asked. She felt a pang of trepidation. She knew what she was plotting, and sometimes, it seemed, all of Boston had its eyes on her.

"I was speaking with John Eliot this morning," he said.

"Oh?"

"He thinks highly of thee, Mary. He is grateful to have a woman willing to work with the Hawke children. Next? The squaws and their young ones."

"I would like that, too."

" 'Tis not easy what he does. As I was passing by thine home, I thought it worth sharing his enthusiasm. We cannot hope to understand fully the workings of God. But I believe thou hast found a calling."

She bowed her head. "Wouldst thou like a cup of tea?" she asked.

"No. I can't stay. I just wanted to offer my gratitude. Thou hast clearly transcended whatever disappointment thou felt with the proceedings at the Town House."

"I accept the wisdom of those men," she lied, her eyes wide and a smile upon her lips.

"Thou art wise," the pastor said, and then he was gone.

After he had left, Mary turned and saw Catherine staring at the base of the front door, where the Devil's mark had been carved into the wood. Quickly the girl averted her eyes.

❧ ☙

She and Thomas and Catherine had dinner that Sabbath with her parents, and though Priscilla remained anxious about the time that Mary was spending in the woods with the Hawkes, it was clear that her daughter's good works—and the conversation about them in her circle—pleased her. Pride was a sin, but Mary could see that her mother was proud of her. Even the gossips were well pleased with her.

And when everyone returned to church that afternoon for the second half of the service, Mary wondered at how easy it had been to so thoroughly rehabilitate her reputation. When this was over, she would have to wander once more to the Neck to thank Constance Winston.

＊＊

The next day when Mary was alone, she poured the poison into a blue glass apothecary bottle the length of her middle finger. Then she took the empty bottle that Edmund had given to Constance, and Constance, in turn, had given her, and recorked it. She planned to hide it inside the coverlet of Catherine's bed with the forks she had taken from her parents' highboy.

But she stopped.

This was the first of the critical steps in her plan, and now, about to begin, she was having doubts.

She disliked Catherine and knew the girl viewed her with an animus as cold and sharp as an icicle. If only she had found proof in the girl's bag that she was involved in a coven or conspiracy. But there had been none. And by the light of day, it was impossible not to see why she had run when she had caught her mistress in the night with the forks, or the subsequent logic of her testimony at the Town House.

Mary gazed out the window at the dreary skies of winter, the bleak season just dawning. The bruise on the back of her hand was yellowing now. Her hand would never again be quite the same. It was always going to ache, and she felt twinges of pain when she stretched the middle and index fingers. She was most comfortable when she kept them curled. She gazed at them, unsure whether the look was reminiscent of predator or prey, of a hawk or its wounded game.

In the end, she did place the empty bottle in Catherine's bed. Maybe, Mary decided, she herself was possessed. But, at this point, it was easier to go forward than back.

❧ ☙

That night it was four of them for supper, as Mary had meticulously planned: Thomas, Catherine, and Mary, of course, but Mary had also invited their neighbor, Squire Willard. The old widower did not like her—his remarks to the magistrates during her divorce petition had been hurtful and mean—but he was lonely and old, and she knew that he would say yes. He probably viewed it as an entitlement, an invitation that should have been extended long ago. And on that count, perhaps he was not wrong.

But he would never know her true motive. He was the perfect witness to watch what was about to unfold: the murder of Thomas Deerfield. The attempted murder of Mary Deerfield. When the trial began, he would testify (and he would testify brilliantly) to the way that someone had tried to poison both Thomas and his wife, and that individual was most certainly Catherine. After all, the empty bottle was in her bedding. So were the forks. So was the pestle Mary had found months ago buried in the dooryard.

Mary helped Catherine serve the root vegetables, of which they still had plenty, and the pigeons which Thomas had shot that day. This time of year, Thomas was likely to spend more time in the woods and meadows just outside the city than at the mill. Catherine poured their beer, four pewter steins, and when the girl had gone to the roasting jack and Isaac Willard was regaling Thomas with his own tales of his day in the woods with a musket, she surreptitiously emptied the apothecary bottle of poison into Thomas's pewter tankard and set the mug before his place at the table.

◈ ❧

"I am pleased that so much of the snow has melted," Mary said, focusing on the small flames at the tip of the tapers in the center of the table and hoping that the quaver she heard in her voice was not really evident. "But we know this is but the beginning of winter."

"It is," said Squire Willard. "But I've never minded the cold. I rather like the snow. It gives me more time to read the Bible and to hunt. I like hunting in the snow: better tracks."

"Winter here is too long," Thomas disagreed, grumbling. "Eden? I think not." He took a first sip, and so Mary did, too. She felt her heart in her chest. He didn't seem to taste the monkshood.

"It's a wonder to me that the savages here survived so long amidst such cold. I see their furs and skins, but I am still surprised," she continued. She ripped off a piece of meat from the bird and saw that her fingers were shaking.

"When wilt thou return to the Hawkes next?" the old man asked her.

"I am not sure. Perhaps the end of this week. It depends entirely on"—and she almost said "John," but stopped herself—"Reverend Eliot and his schedule."

Thomas spooned some boiled carrots and turnips from the trencher. Then he washed them down with more beer, and so Mary did, as well.

"The boots thou brought the Hawkes? That won't make that family repent," her husband told her.

"Perhaps. But two little girls—"

"Little beasts," interrupted Thomas.

"Two children will be warmer this winter than

last. And it is not just the warmth that interests me: it is trying to bring them back to the Lord."

Isaac looked at her, and Mary saw approval in his eyes.

For a moment, Thomas stared at his tankard. She began to wonder if the poison might not work: perhaps wolfsbane was but a myth. Or the potion that Edmund had given to Constance was a fake. For the next few minutes, the four of them ate and drank in affable silence. Catherine and their guest had finished their beer, but Thomas had barely touched his. Two sips. And so she had barely touched hers. She had to be careful not to get ahead of him if the play she planned to enact was that Catherine had attempted to poison them. As soon as Thomas began to grow sick from the poison, she would feign his exact symptoms. She would gag and froth exactly as he did. The only difference? When he fell from the table or collapsed, she would be sure and overturn her beer as she toppled to the floor. Isaac Willard would see it all, noting—because he seemed to observe everything—that unlike Thomas, she had not finished her drink. She had only consumed a third of her tankard, which was why she had only been sickened. Most assuredly it was why she had survived.

Well, apparently two sips was not nearly enough to kill a man. Thomas was showing no signs of the monkshood at all.

"At least," her husband said, "'tis not the sort of December weather to slow the commerce that docks in and sets forth from the harbor. Mary, thy father's warehouse is probably busier than Decembers past."

"Thy parents are true saints," said Isaac Willard.

Mary nodded. Was it a sign that for one of the only times in his life Thomas wasn't guzzling his beer? Was the Lord giving her one last chance to turn away from murder? And it was not just the murder of her husband. No, not at all. She knew that Catherine would swing from a rope when this was done.

"They are," Thomas agreed, and he chuckled. "They endure the likes of me in their family." He smiled at her. She thought of her parents in Heaven without her. Because, surely, she would never see them there if she murdered Thomas and made sure that Catherine was convicted of the crime. She thought she had grown accustomed to this revelation, but clearly she hadn't. Oh, to kill him might be justice in this world, but it would offer only woe for eternity. And the same might be true for murdering Catherine. She just didn't know for certain: she might be killing a Devil's handmaiden, but it was also conceivable that she was slaughtering merely an unschooled and scared girl who had inappropriate feelings for her husband.

Yes, she decided, Thomas's uncharacteristic

restraint was a sign. God was offering her one final opportunity to turn back from this path.

And so she took it.

She did not know in her heart whether this was cowardice or righteousness, but it was tumultuous and uncontainable. In a flash, before she could change her mind, she reached across the table to take her husband's hand in hers, careful to knock his tankard to the floor, where the beer and the poison stained the wood and seeped through the cracks. Catherine leapt to her feet to clean it up, and Mary was standing, apologizing, and quick to bring her husband a fresh stein and a fresh pour. Thomas did not seem angered by her clumsiness. It was as if he expected this sort of thing from her. And none of the beer had spilled on him.

It surprised her how relieved she felt. She had expected only regret, and wasn't sure whether this was because her Lord and Savior had walked her away from the precipice to Hell, or whether it was because He had given her a much better idea.

Because He had. It was only beginning to form, but she liked everything about her new plan so much more than her original one.

And that was a gift, too.

❧ ❧

That night, while Catherine was outside feeding the animals, Mary took the empty bottle and the two forks she had hidden inside the girl's bedstead and placed them back in her trunk. She would need the bottle in the coming days.

Then, after Catherine had gone to sleep but while Thomas was still at the ordinary, she took her quill and a bottle of ink and wrote a letter. She wrote sitting on the edge of the bedstead, with the paper atop her ledger, leaning in close to the candle on the nightstand.

Thomas,

By the time thou hast found this, I will be gone.

Whether it is to Heaven or Hell, I know not.

But I drank a poison and it is finished.

My body? Thou needn't trouble thyself. Thou wilt never find it because I have no desire to see my remains excoriated by the men who wield such awful power in the pulpit and at the Town House. Someday it may be discovered deep in the forest, but by then—if God is willing to show me mercy—it will be but the unrecognizable bones the wolves did not devour.

If thou should marry once more, I urge thee: be decent and be kind. Our time on Earth is but brief and we sail with but little knowledge of how our Creator marks the winds.

Sincerely,

Mary

She did not accuse Thomas of any crime so that he would share the note wide and far. But she could not resist the dig at the men who had refused to pay her heed, and she knew her remarks about the city leaders would not stop him from taking the letter first to the reverend and then, with John Norton, to the constable. She imagined them searching for her. In her mind, she saw the men on horseback, riding across the snow and dodging the low branches in the woods. But they wouldn't find her.

Before blowing out the candle, she hid the note at the bottom of her chest with the two small forks and the bottle that once held wolfsbane. She would date the letter when she was ready. When it was time.

Am I a harlot or a witch?

**—The Testimony of Mary Deerfield,
from the Records and Files of
the Court of Assistants, Boston,
Massachusetts, 1663, Volume I**

Thirty-Two

As she walked toward the harbor, again taking the long way to avoid the Town House, she thought of the map of the New World that hung in her parents' home. There had always been options, and now she and Henry would discuss them. Imagine throwing a pebble into a pond and watching the ripples fan out in ever-widening circles. There was Rhode Island. There was New Amsterdam. But the world was vast, and Mary knew that she needed distance from Boston if she wanted to begin again. She craved separation from this city that so nearly had led her into the embrace of the Devil and the deaths of two people, only one of whom she knew for certain was a monster. But she also wanted to start again far from that bench full of small-minded and petty magistrates, and from the ogre to whom she was married.

And she wanted to start anew with Henry Simmons.

She had told him nothing of her plan to murder Thomas and see that Catherine was blamed for the crime. She had simply determined his support was unwavering and warned him not to worry about her when the likes of Goody Howland started their crow-like cawing.

She recalled something her father had said about a ship that was due before Christmas—a holiday that meant nothing at all here in Boston—but it was a date on the calendar that her father happened to have used as a reference when he mentioned the shipping schedules. The vessel was arriving from the West Indies and then going to return there. Her father knew the captain.

Mary wasn't sure of Henry's assets, but she knew that he had some. Still, he had not yet come into his inheritance. She was unsure what he had saved.

But he was resourceful and smart. They would figure it out.

Her new plan was that the two of them would disappear to Jamaica when that ship her father mentioned returned there. The island had been under British rule seven years now. Once the weather grew safe enough to travel back to England, probably by March, she and Henry would journey there on a different vessel.

Her parents would know she was alive, but no one else. They would not approve of her decision to leave Boston, and they would fear mightily for her soul. But they would be relieved that she no longer needed to fear Thomas Deerfield or the innuendo that trailed women who stood up to the men who ran the colony and led, invariably, either to exile or the hanging platform.

⇜ ⇝

Valentine Hill was seated behind his desk when Mary arrived at the warehouse. She saw no sign of Henry. The old man stood when he saw her.

"Good day, Mary. To what do I owe the pleasure? Hast thou also been to thy father's?"

"I am going there, too," she said. She hadn't planned on visiting her father, but she might now for the sake of appearances. "I have come to see Henry."

For a long second neither of them said a word. Then Hill placed his hands flat on his wide desk and looked down at the ledger there. Without meeting her eyes, he said, "Is that wise?"

"Art thou worried about the gossips?"

He looked up. "No. I am worried about thee. Why dost thou want to see him? May I ask?"

"Yes, thou hast every right. I have been praying much, and I want him to know that Thomas and I both forgive him."

"I can tell him that, Mary. And I would be happy to. 'Tis a gracious sentiment."

"Prithee, may I tell him myself?"

He smiled sadly, an avuncular kindness in his eyes. "Of course. Thou art a smart girl. But, I must confess, I fret that I am enabling the Devil—or, worse, my nephew."

She nodded at his small joke, but she replied, "If the Devil wants me, He will not come in the guise of thy nephew."

"I wish I were as confident as thee."

"Thou art my father's friend," she said, and she pulled off her glove and pointed at the back of her left hand. "See this bruise and this scar? No witch's teat. 'Tis the mark left by a fork, bruised once more after Thomas banged my hand the other night against the corner of a nightstand."

He looked at it and then rubbed his temples. "I know not if I have any hope of seeing Heaven—"

"Or I."

"But the **Pelican** docked late yesterday. Henry is on the second wharf. He is with the boys there."

"I thank thee," she said.

"I am not sure I deserve thanks. Thou dost not actually carry a message of forgiveness from Thomas and thee. Am I correct?"

"No," she told him, wanting to be sure that his soul was as much at peace as she could leave it. "All I plan to do is reassure him that neither Thomas nor I harbor him any ill will. We want him to look up to the firmament, confident in his complete and utter exculpation—in our eyes, at least."

She hoped he believed her. But after leaving, when she looked back at the warehouse entrance from the edge of the dock, she saw he was standing there, his countenance one of wistfulness and worry.

⊰ ⊱

Mary reached the end of the dock and stared at the anchored ships and smaller shallops amidst the whitecaps, and inhaled the aroma of the cold, salty ocean. The boards here were covered in spray, and she envied the way that the men in their leathers were warm and dry—at least warmer and drier than she was.

"Who art thou looking for?" asked a sailor who could not have been more than sixteen or seventeen. He paused with her at the bottom of the angled plank that climbed up onto the **Pelican**'s hold. His face was pockmarked with pimples and he had wisps of hair above his lip, but his eyes were round and kind and the color of coffee.

"I thank thee for inquiring," she said. "I am here for Henry Simmons."

He raced up the plank like a squirrel, using his hands to claw at the footholds.

While she waited, she watched the seagulls, one in particular with a great bull chest who stood like a sentry at the end of the handrail. But she didn't have to wait long. When she turned back to the **Pelican,** there was Henry, walking carefully down the plank in a leather doublet.

"Ah, 'tis my—and if I were a cavalier, I would

have a far better and more appropriate word for it—friend," he said, smiling.

"Mistress?"

"One kiss does not a mistress make."

"Muse?"

"That would suggest I am a poet, not a"—and here he waved his hand dismissively at the boat behind him—"dockworker."

"Thou hast responsibilities beyond that."

"Someday, perhaps." He looked toward the city. "What brings thee here? What has led thee to tempt the mobs?"

"And thine uncle. Do not forget him. He is most uncomfortable with my presence here."

"Thou saw him?"

"I did. I asked where I might find his nephew. He was kind and told me."

"I am sure he was sorely discomfited by the idea that thou were looking for me. If thou were inquiring about the arrival of a little rum or lime juice or salt? He would have approved. Nothing scandalous about importing luxury in my uncle's eyes. But clearly that is not why thou hast come."

"My father tells me a ship is due any day from the Indies. It will return there once it has finished its business in Boston."

"The **Amity,** yes."

"How big is it?"

He shrugged. "Not small, but not massive. One

hundred and thirty tons, I believe. A crew of fourteen or fifteen."

"And by the Indies, dost thou mean Jamaica?"

He nodded. "Art thou wondering if it takes on passengers?"

"Only two," she answered.

"They would, though the accommodations would not be as comfortable as a bedstead in Boston."

"That's fine. I tend to doubt, given the ship's origin and its destination, that among the manifest will be any forks."

"No. Though I can't imagine the sailors would know what to do with one if there were."

"Well, they would know not to stab a lady's hand."

"They would know that," he agreed.

"I think it would be fitting if I took one-third of the money Thomas keeps at the house."

"I think it would be wrong. And it won't be necessary."

"No?"

"No. I need not a dowry from thee."

For a long moment they stood in silence, staring out at the ocean. Then, almost as if dancing, they turned toward each other at the same moment and formalized their pact.

Mary Deerfield has been present at births with me and has always been most helpful. And the babies are breathing still.

—The Testimony of Midwife Susanna Downing, from the Records and Files of the Court of Assistants, Boston, Massachusetts, 1663, Volume I

Thirty-Three

Christmas came, unacknowledged in Boston, and went. Ships docked, unloaded their cargos, and took aboard pine timber, furs, and salted fish, but the **Amity** was not among them. Mary had a satchel packed with a little clothing—very little, because she did not want to billow the flames of rumor that she was in fact alive and had run off until it was too late—and a hairbrush that Thomas probably wouldn't notice was missing. She would be ready to leave at a moment's notice.

※ ❧

On the following Sabbath, she asked her father as they left church for dinner at her parents' whether port traffic had slowed or the captains were reporting stormy weather.

"Nothing in particular," he answered vaguely.

"So, thou hast not heard of any vessels that have been lost?"

"I have not," he replied, and he coughed against the chill in the air.

Thomas, who was walking beside her, glanced at her, his eyes narrow and curious. But he said nothing.

And no one noticed but her when, over dinner, Catherine helped Hannah and Abigail serve, and Catherine seemed to linger over Thomas and his trencher when she brought him more venison. It was as if he were a rose and she wanted to inhale its aroma.

❧ ❧

That night, when the two of them were upstairs in their bedstead, Thomas asked Mary, "Since when didst thou become so interested in the shipping news?"

"I have always been interested in my father's calling."

"I grant thee, it is more interesting than mine. I will try not to take offense." Then he blew out the lone candle, and Mary thought that would end the matter. But in the dark of the room he murmured, his tone ominous, "And while I believe there is mostly white meat behind thine eyes, I have told thee before that I know there is a sliver of something more. Something dark and serpentine. Something prideful. I have tried to break thee, the way one must a wild horse. But Mary?"

She stared up at the dark, blank ceiling.

"That is the part of thee that may lead thee to the gallows," he said.

She took this in and remained silent.

"I know thou art awake," he growled.

"I am."

"And?"

"Art thou accusing thine own wife of possession? If so, what have I done to earn such disparagement?"

"I know only thou art scheming. But when I know more? When I unearth the wickedness in thy heart? A teakettle will be the least of thy worries."

She considered asking him why he didn't just kill her tonight so Catherine could have him to herself, but she restrained herself. First of all, she didn't know if there was even a twinge of reciprocity, whether he cared for the servant in the slightest; second, she rather hoped that he did like her.

The two of them deserved each other.

⇛ ⇚

Finally, just before the New Year, the **Amity** docked. It was a Thursday. The ship arrived in the late afternoon, the sun already descending behind Beacon Hill. No one brought Mary word. She learned because every day after dinner she had walked to the harbor, except for when she and Thomas had supper with her parents and she could ask her father directly what vessels were coming and going, questions she hoped suggested no agenda but avarice.

But that Thursday she saw a large brigantine tied up at the edge of the wharf, the sails on its two great masts furled, and she asked a sailor its name. He told her, and not caring that she might further worry Valentine Hill if he saw her, she went directly to the older man's warehouse and tracked down Henry. Valentine had already gone home, but Henry was still there. He told her that it was too late in the day to unload the ship, and so the work would commence in the morning. (This assumed, he added, that the sailors did not become drink-drunk that night to the point where they were incapable of working at sunrise.) The ship would be reloaded with New England exports during the afternoon and set sail on Saturday.

"Art thou having second thoughts?" he asked her, his hands on her arms.

"I have none."

"I have none, either," he assured her, smiling broadly and with a confidence that was contagious. "By the time anyone knows thou art alive, we will be living in England, and Thomas will divorce thee for desertion. It won't matter who is in league with Lucifer. We will have an ocean between us and thy servant girl and the likes of Goody Howland."

"And, once I am divorced, we will wed."

"Yes," he agreed. "We will wed."

On Friday morning, she bundled up against the cold and went visiting. She left after breakfast, not caring that she was leaving Catherine with more than her share of the daily chores, and savored the blue sky as she walked. There were no clouds, only plumes of smoke from the chimneys that rose like plumb lines through the still air. She saw her mother, and though her mother was surprised, she did not deduce Mary's real reason for dropping by: a daughter's desire to see her mother for what might not be the last time, but with certainty would be the last time for a long time. Then she went to say hello to Rebeckah Cooper. She still wondered about her involvement with the boiled apples and the raisins, and her friendship with Peregrine, but the woman remained the closest thing she had to a real friend. Again, Mary strove not to signal her departure. But when she left the goodwife's, she found her eyes welling up.

Finally, she ventured to the Neck to bid farewell to Constance Winston. She did not go inside the home the way she had at her mother's and Goody Cooper's, because she needed to be back midday for dinner. But she stood before the front door of the house, and when it was clear to Constance that she was not coming inside, the other woman pulled on a hooded cape and joined her outside.

"Thou art leaving Boston," she said.

"Why wouldst thou think that?" Mary asked, a little shocked by Constance's intuition.

"If I am mistaken, I am sorry."

"Oh, thou hast done nothing that demands an apology."

Constance grinned, but her face was cryptic. "I have heard nothing of any illness in thy household or among thy friends. Thou must feel much blessed."

"Thou knowest the truth."

"I do not. Thou hast other plans for Edmund Hawke's tincture?"

"I chose not to use it."

"Ah, the spirit moved thee," she said sarcastically.

"I had a change of heart."

"One that I pray does not lead to thy death."

"I thank thee."

"Tell me . . ."

"Yes?"

"Art thou that fearful of being a woman alone?" Constance asked.

"That was not the reason for my decision to set a new course."

"What was the reason?"

" 'Tis not in my nature to use wolfsbane. I learned that when I had the chance."

"He's vile, Mary. And he's dangerous. I was serious when I said I will pray thou dost nothing that leads thee to an early grave."

"I won't. I am sure."

"But how?" the woman implored her, and Mary was moved by her urgency.

"Do not fear for me; my hap and fortune are assured. Let's leave it at that."

Constance saw that she could press Mary no further. "Very well. So, why hast thou come? Why wilt thou not come inside?"

"I wanted to wish thee well and thank thee. Thou art a remarkable person, and I am pleased to know thee."

The woman folded her arms across her chest. "Thou art leaving. Now I can see it for certain: I can see the red in thine eyes. This is goodbye."

Mary sighed. It may have been the sympathy in Constance's voice, but she felt a tremor inside her that was comprised of heartache and relief. She replied, a confirmation of sorts because the other woman deserved that, "Let me say, if our paths do not cross again, that I wish thee health and contentment, and I am grateful for all that thou hast done for me."

Constance embraced her, and Mary was surprised. She hadn't viewed her as the sort who would hug. But Mary leaned into her and was enfolded in her arms. She rested her eyes on the woman's wool cloak, allowing the fabric to soak up her tears.

⁂

As she walked home, her mood vacillated wildly. The idea that she was leaving tomorrow left her at once giddy and melancholy. She tried to focus only on how wonderful her life would be with Henry Simmons. This was the man she should have married. Once wed, she would devote herself to a life that glorified God. Yes, she might be damned. But until she knew, she would labor to exalt her Lord and Savior, and to love her second husband.

It was when she was two blocks from her house that she began to grow uneasy. She told herself that it was only because it was time for dinner and Thomas would be angry that she hadn't been home when he had returned. But she feared there was something more going on. She began to suspect that she had been followed, and tried to convince herself that this was nonsense.

But intuition was a remarkable thing; she had seen it from Constance that very morning.

And so as terrified as she was when she opened the door to her house and saw who was present, a part of her—a small part of her certainly—was awed that she had almost expected what she was seeing. It was as if she had known. It was as if she had foretold in her mind that this was how it would end.

There, crowded into their large room around the table, were Thomas and Catherine, the constable, the very same captain of the guard she had seen whip Henry Simmons, and the magistrate Caleb

Adams. And there on the table was her apron and two forks with three tines. Ones that her father had imported. Adams held up something else without saying a word, and she looked at it closely: it was a pine coin a little bigger than a shilling, and there carved into it was the Devil's five-pointed star. It matched exactly the mark that had been carved into the doorframe and, she supposed, they had already discovered.

She might have hoped they were about to arrest the servant girl, but she knew that wasn't the case. They were going to arrest her. There in the magistrate's arms was the small satchel she had packed and the note she had hidden in her chest.

Thou saw the Devil's mark in the doorframe of the house?

—The Remarks of Magistrate Caleb Adams, from the Records and Files of the Court of Assistants, Boston, Massachusetts, 1663, Volume I

Thirty-Four

Her cell was half the size of her bedroom at home, and the outer walls of the building had stone as thick as three feet in some sections. The room lacked a hearth, and so she huddled most of that day and then that night inside the blankets her parents—her mother weeping inconsolably—had been allowed to bring her.

The jailer was a tall, slender fellow named Spencer Pitts who was a little older than Thomas, with receding hair that was a mixture of faded red and bright white. He was courteous, if firm, when she had guests, and inscrutable when she was alone. He was Rebeckah Cooper's uncle, and he neither comforted her nor tormented her. But she sensed he was kind. She gathered he read his Bible during the day and made sure a boy brought her supper and emptied her slop pot before he left for the evening. One night she stared out into the dark through her wrought-iron bars, down the black corridor where he sat during the day, and realized she was the only prisoner at the moment. But for the rats, she was utterly, completely alone.

ॐ ॐ

On the second day of her imprisonment, despite the blistering cold, she was forced to undress for a panel of three women, including the midwife Susanna Downing, so they could search her body for the mark of the Devil. Susanna was a saint in good standing in her midforties, with silver hair and an aquiline nose. Mary had helped her bring into the world one of Peregrine's two children. She was efficient, hardworking, and much respected, which was why the court had enlisted her to inspect Mary's body. They studied her left leg and then her right, her back and her buttocks, her breasts, lifting them without ceremony, and then went to her arms and her hands.

One of the women with the midwife gasped when she saw the scar on the back of Mary's left hand. "This may be a mark," she said. Mary did not know her name, and Susanna had not introduced them. The midwife looked at the newer bruise and the older cicatrix and remarked, "No. This is but the work of the teakettle."

Mary considered correcting her, but saw no point. She was shivering in her nakedness and didn't want to prolong the humiliation. The other women accepted Susanna's explanation.

When the examination was complete, the midwife offered the slightest of encouragements.

"There's nothing here," she said, both to Mary and to her attendants. "I see no sign of the mark."

Mary thanked her and got dressed. Her clothing, it seemed to her, stunk of stone and mildew already.

⊰ ⊱

After four days, including the Sabbath, spent inside the jail on Prison Lane, Mary ached to see the world through more than the unglazed, barred window in her cell. In addition to the midwives sent to canvass her body for a sign of Satan, her visitors had included her parents every day and her scrivener, Benjamin Hull, every day but Sunday.

Thomas, it seemed, had had enough. The court had said that he, too, was allowed to see her but he had chosen not to. Mary was not in the least saddened by his absence. Nor was she surprised.

She prayed every day. Sometimes she prayed for forgiveness, other moments for guidance. Sometimes she prayed simply for help.

Her mother brought food and news, and would try to present her tales of the city with the same equanimity as if they were sewing together at one of their homes, but eventually she would break down and Mary would reassure her that all, in the end, would be well. The news was never about

Henry Simmons, but Priscilla shared stories of the ships that were coming, new construction she had noticed, and people they had in common. Goody Cooper. The Hills. Peregrine and her children, whom Priscilla had seen in the marketplace, and how Jonathan had been spotted consorting in the night with sailors, and one of these days was sure to wind up in the stocks.

"They are an awful pair," Priscilla said. "I know I demean myself when I discuss them, but thou needest to see that the apple fell not far from the tree: Peregrine is as vile as her father, and she married a man whose face, handsome as it is, hides a soul that is weak."

"Why, Mother," Mary said, unable to resist teasing her, "thou findest Jonathan Cooke fetching? I never knew."

Priscilla scoffed. "Serpents shed their skins. Apparently, some replace them with masks that are comely. Jonathan. Peregrine. Thomas. I wish I had seen they were a nest of vipers before thou were wed into that family of snakes."

"Peregrine and Jonathan's children are sweet."

"And the Lord God saw to it that the brood did not expand further."

"Mother!"

She shook her head. "I feel no remorse. The world will be better off without another demon from that woman's womb."

And so, as Mary did often when her mother

visited, she changed the subject. "What dost thou think of my jailer?" she asked.

"Spencer?" repeated Priscilla. "He is a quiet man. He is known for being fair with the prisoners who have to spend time here."

She nodded. She considered pressing further, but the man was such an absolute cipher that she couldn't even decide what to ask.

⁂

When Benjamin Hull would come to the prison, they would discuss her defense and how to save her life when she was brought, once again, before the Court of Assistants. But it seemed to Mary that she had been outplayed brilliantly by the servant girl. Mary supposed it was Catherine who had planted the forks and the coin in the pocket of her apron. Catherine was unaware that she had gone to Constance Winston's on the morning she was arrested, but the servant girl had followed her one of the other times she had gone there, and told this, too, to the constable when she rushed to see him upon her supposed discovery of the forks and the coin. She had pointed out to them the matching Devil's mark on the house's doorframe. It was inevitable the constable would then search the house and find the note and her satchel.

This was a lot of evidence to overcome; Hull had been clear.

And, alas, Mary knew things she would never tell anyone, secrets that Constance and Esther Hawke knew, but nobody else. She had planned to murder her husband. She had planned that Catherine be tried for the crime. The fact that she had come to her senses and changed her mind in no way diminished the possibility that the Devil had His claws inside her and she was possessed— that she deserved to be hanged and hope, for reasons that were inscrutable, that God would spare her the flames that most likely loomed.

On the other hand, here were the realities, and they were as absolute as the tides. She had not planted the forks or the pestle in her dooryard that autumn. She had not carved the Devil's mark into the doorframe of her house. Someone else had done those things.

Likewise, she had put no spell on William Stileman or the baby that had died inside Peregrine Cooke. She had no idea whether those souls had been taken from the earth because of deviltry or disease, but she knew, too, that she had had nothing to do with either's passing.

"It would be good if we could ferret out who had planted the Devil's tines," Hull said. "It mattered not in thy first trial. It will matter much in thy second."

"Catherine is the one who has the most conceivable motive and expresses toward me the greatest antipathy."

"Greater than Goody Howland?"

"Perhaps not," she admitted.

"And thou hast some suspicion that Goody Cooper may not be the friend that she claims to be."

"'Tis true."

"And Isaac Willard, of course."

"Yes."

"So, there are others who may have a grudge with thee."

She gazed down at the mouse droppings on the floor. There was so much. There were just so many creatures with whom she shared this small, dark box. She thought about what the scrivener had said. How had she become such a reprehensible creature that she could have so many enemies? But then she heard once more in her head Benjamin Hull's last four words and repeated them back to him.

"A grudge with thee," she murmured. "A grudge with me."

"What art thou thinking?"

"All this time we have supposed that I was the target of the spell: that someone was attempting to sicken or kill me."

"Go on."

"That suggests a self-importance that may be unfounded, Benjamin. What if the prey were, in fact, Thomas?"

"Well, that is an interesting possibility. But, alas, thou wouldst be the suspect most likely to wish ill upon him. I am not sure—"

"Or Catherine," she went on, cutting him off.

"Why would someone want to hex a servant girl?"

"Why would someone want to hex me?" she snapped.

"I see thy point."

"But Thomas? There is a creature worthy of whatever misfortune befalls him."

"Nevertheless, Mary, who other than thee would endeavor to foul Thomas's future and risk his own by conspiring with the Dark One?"

She didn't answer because she hadn't an answer. But she looked at the walls and the small window and knew she would give the matter all her attention that afternoon. It had triggered inside her another thought, another connection, but she was unprepared to speak it aloud.

❧ ❧

The next day, her parents joined her scrivener and her as they continued to plot her defense. Hull laid out her options, none of which seemed likely to result in her vindication. She could defend herself by claiming that she had been under the Devil's spell, but now the Lord had cast Him out and she was no longer possessed. She could, in essence, throw herself on the mercy of the magistrates. But one of those men, upon hearing of her arrest, had called her a nasty and sharp-tongued woman.

Neither Mary nor Hull thought that group would have mercy on a goodwife who already had petitioned the court for a divorce and who, during that first trial, had spoken with such blunt honesty and candor.

Or she could deny the charges of witchcraft, insisting that someone else had chosen Satan over their Savior. It might be Catherine, but it might be someone else. She didn't know whom—only that she was innocent. And her excuse for not coming forward right away with her knowledge? That was the problem, her scrivener said. She lacked a rationale that he thought presented her in a positive light.

And then there was the adultery. The magistrates were clearly going to hear of her jaunts to the wharf and Valentine Hill's warehouse, and piece together her note with her affection for Henry Simmons—and his for her. He, too, was going to have to appear before the Court of Assistants, but by then her corpse would likely be hanging from the platform by the Town House. She took comfort in the fact that they had not jailed Henry. According to Hull, he wanted to confess his involvement in the conspiracy to desert Thomas Deerfield and stand by her side but had been dissuaded because the scrivener had decided they would deny the charge of adultery. There was no proof. Yes, there were magistrates who viewed the letter for what it was—a ruse to cover her disappearance with Henry Simmons—but she could claim that she had written it while despondent, and the Lord had come to her and brought her back to her senses.

"Perhaps," Hull had murmured, thinking aloud, "thou couldst no longer bear Thomas's cruelty and mistreatment. The logic would be that thou wrote that note while terrified of him and were choosing death—and hopefully Heaven—over a continued life on earth with him."

"Yes," she agreed, "maybe something like that might work." Her teeth were chattering a bit against the cold in her cell, and her mother pulled the blanket around her shoulders.

"Unfortunately," her father chimed in, "the risk is that self-murder always suggests an egregious sickness of the mind and a direct challenge to our Lord's wisdom. It has been argued that such derangement is itself a sign of possession."

Mary looked back and forth between the two men. She couldn't bear her mother's despondent face. "Then what of this," she suggested. "Perhaps I wrote the note precisely because I was bewitched by someone. Someone planted the forks in the autumn as part of a plot to poison me. Perhaps we argue at the Town House that this person succeeded: this person poisoned my mind and my judgment."

"And this person is that wicked child, Catherine Stileman?" her mother asked.

"Most likely, it was her," the scrivener said. "But

Mary and I have come up with other names with other grudges and other grievances."

"All unfounded," said Mary, as if this mattered. But she wanted her parents to know that the likes of Goody Howland and Isaac Willard had no justifiable complaint with her.

"Dost thou harbor doubts that Catherine has earned such an accusation?" asked Priscilla.

"I do."

"Why? She is a vile creature!"

Mary took a breath and answered, "She may be. But that does not make her a handmaiden of Satan. But a few ideas dawned on me yesterday. Obviously, I have little to do here but pray and think."

"Go on," said her father.

"First of all, we do not know that the spell with the forks and the pestle was meant for me."

"Of course we do!" her mother insisted.

"No, we don't. The target could have been the girl herself. It could have been Thomas. It could have been Thomas and me—as man and wife. Tell me something, Benjamin."

"Prithee, ask."

"Just as Thomas could be a target, could he not also be the hunter? Why have none of us considered that it is Thomas who has conspired with the Devil? Why is not he a most willing acolyte?"

Everyone in the cell looked at her, and the room went quiet.

"I'm serious," said Mary. "Couldn't he have buried the forks? Couldn't he have carved the mark of the Devil into the doorframe? Is it not his house?"

"He's"—and Hull stammered—"he's a man."

"Does the Devil discriminate? I had no idea."

"No, of course, He doesn't," Hull said. "I just meant . . ."

"I know what thou meant. But the four of us know this, too: that man is a terror. If anyone has shown signs of possession, it's one who will plunge a fork into another's hand. Thou knowest but a small dollop of his cruelties."

"Dost thou wish to accuse him—and not Catherine?" her father asked.

"I don't wish to accuse anyone!"

"But thou must," said Priscilla.

"We shall see. But Mother? I have thought on this much. Prithee, know that I am prepared to fight. I am. Not because I expect still to be breathing come spring, but because, for better or worse, it is how the Lord hath made me."

"Continue," her father said.

"If I fail, which we all know is what we must expect, I will take comfort in the knowledge that our Lord knows my sorrow and feels my grief. He felt the sting of every thorn in His son's final crown. He felt the bite from every Roman lash. He felt the agony of each and every Roman nail. That is where love and lamentation chance upon one another, and that is where we find God."

Priscilla sank to the floor, crying, and James and Mary knelt beside her. Mary kissed her mother's wet cheeks. She whispered into her ear, "I have been tempted by the Devil. But in the end, I resisted. I have faith that God knows what is in my heart and—if it comes to this—will feel the noose and be saddened."

She lost her baby, the infant taken,
in my opinion, due to the spite that
exudes like sweat from the skin of Mary
Deerfield.

**—The Testimony of Beth Howland,
from the Records and Files of
the Court of Assistants, Boston,
Massachusetts, 1663, Volume I**

Thirty-Five

Mary walked with Benjamin Hull down the dark passageway that led to the front door with its imposing iron spikes, allowed outside in public for the first time in days. She was wearing clothes her mother's girls had cleaned for her, and they didn't stink of her or the rocks of her prison.

Hull reassured Mary that he had rounded up witnesses who were going to speak well of her goodness and faith, including the Reverend John Eliot, who would speak of her work with the Hawkes. Much of it was going to come down to her word against Catherine Stileman's, but that supposed, in the end, that Mary was willing to fling charges at the girl that could result in the servant's death. And Mary was not sure that she was capable of testifying, without proof, that Catherine was possessed and deserved to be executed. She loathed the girl, but she had learned when she had overturned Thomas's tankard with its poison that she was not capable of murder.

At least Catherine knew nothing about the wolfsbane. No one allied against her did. Not even her scrivener, because she had seen no reason to tell him. The only people who knew were an excommunicant couple in Natick and Constance Winston. And neither, for different reasons, was the sort to share their secrets with a Boston magistrate.

ঌ ঙ

Despite the fresh clothes, Mary knew how poorly she looked the moment she met her mother at the base of the stairs at the Town House. She could see it in Priscilla's eyes. Mary tried to calm her with a joke, remarking, "Once I am acquitted, Thomas will want no part of me. He'll divorce me and I'll get my wish yet. It simply will have taken a bit longer than we expected." But her mother didn't smile, and the captain of the guard did not allow Mary to dawdle with her parents. He pushed her up the steps and her parents followed.

She was first on the docket, but already the room was crowded. After all, this was the trial of a witch, and it was a snowless winter day. No one wanted to be idle, but neither did people want to miss the drama. Still, Thomas was absent. Mary's scrivener had told her that he might be asked to speak, but most likely not: he had nothing to add to the court's charges, no details that could corroborate what Catherine was going to tell the magistrates.

"And what if I were to accuse him?" she asked

Hull as they waited. "Suppose I were to say, 'I saw Thomas carving the Devil's mark into the doorframe the night before I was arrested, and he threatened to kill me if I said a word.' Would the men who claim to want justice demand that he appear? Or would even that not be sufficient to convince the magistrates that perhaps they should open their eyes to the evil that flourished in what once was my home?"

"Dost thou plan on making such an accusation?" the scrivener asked, and Mary couldn't decide whether the prospect alarmed or excited him. She had caught him off guard. They had discussed this possibility while plotting her defense, but not seriously.

"No," she said. "No one would believe it. No one would even bother to summon him: that was my point."

Her father looked at her. "But dost thou believe it is possible that thy husband has been bewitched?" he asked. "I know thou didst not actually see him make the mark. But might he be possessed?"

"I don't believe that. I believe only that he is a monster and utterly deserving of whatever flames our Lord has awaiting him."

Across the room, she spied Catherine. The indentured servant was standing against the opposite wall, careful to look everywhere but in the direction where her former mistress was waiting. The girl seemed uncomfortable, and maybe she was. But maybe it was only an act. She was a deceptively formidable foe, Mary knew.

The magistrates shambled in, and, once more, the constable pounded his pike onto a floorboard. But this trial was different: this time she was not a citizen with a petition asking to be heard; rather, she was a woman accused of a heinous crime. She tried to make eye contact with Richard Wilder, her father's friend on the bench, but he averted his gaze. This was worrisome, but his lack of responsiveness made her more angry than frightened. The fact was, she was furious, and five days in the jail had not broken her spirit; it only had kindled it.

And so she stood with her coif well tied and listened as Governor John Endicott read the charge against her: "Mary Deerfield, thou hast been accused of witchcraft. There is much evidence to corroborate such a charge. Tell us plainly so we know where we stand: dost thou wish to confess to falling prey to the Devil's enticements and signing a covenant with the Dark One?"

In other words, she thought, will I ask for the mercy of this court, a mercy that is unlikely to be granted? Of course, she wouldn't.

"No," she replied, her voice firm, "I do not wish to say that because it would be a lie. I am not in league with the Devil. Rather, it would seem, I have been the victim of a witch most conniving and possessed."

"Very well. Expect no leniency from this court if thou art convicted."

She nodded and stepped back.

Endicott looked to Caleb Adams. Apparently, Adams was going to be in charge of the proceedings. The man had gotten his wish, after all: the prosecution of a witch.

"Catherine Stileman, thou wilt speak first," he said, raising his voice into what Mary supposed he thought was appropriate magisterial grandeur. The servant walked to the center of the room and was sworn in. "Tell us, prithee, what thou knowest of thy mistress as it relates to the charges."

"It goes back to the autumn, sir. Before her divorce petition. Thou wilt recall, prithee, that Mary Deerfield claimed to have found the Devil's tines buried in the dooryard and accused me of witchcraft. But then I saw her burying them in the dooryard myself with my own eyes."

"Yes, we recall that," said Adams.

"Then, last Friday morning, when I was about to start preparing dinner, I fetched my apron. My master was at his mill. By mistake, I reached for my mistress's. I felt something in the pocket, and when I put my fingers there, I discovered the Devil's tines. Two of them. I dropped the apron right there on the floor. That's when I realized I had my mistress's apron, not my own."

"And where was Mary?" asked Adams.

"I do not know."

"So, thou had been left alone to prepare dinner?"

"And to do all of the morning chores," she added with a trace of indignation.

"Go on."

"When I picked up the apron, I felt another item in the pocket. I reached for it—"

"Even though thou had now determined it was not thine apron?" Wilder asked, interrupting her, a question that gave Mary a glimmer of hope that he had not turned on her, at least not completely, after all.

"Forgive me," Catherine corrected herself. "I did not put my hand into the pocket. Something fell out when I went to hang it back on a peg. I reached for it as it was falling. It was about the size of a coin. A shilling. But it was not a shilling. It was made of wood, and it had carved into it a five-pointed star in a circle: the sign of the Dark One."

There was a murmur in the court. The gossips and the idle were thrilled with this development, and Mary felt her heart beating faster. Yes, she was angry, but she was also scared. The proceedings had just begun, and already they were expecting that soon their winter tedium would be broken by a most satisfying diversion: watching her life being choked from her by a rope.

"And thou didst what?" asked Adams.

"I put on my cloak to find the constable. But as I went for the door, in my haste I stumbled. I fell and saw that Mary had carved the Devil's sign into the doorframe."

The governor leaned forward and said, "I appreciate thy candor, but we have not established that Mary Deerfield was responsible for the mark on the doorframe."

"I am sorry," said Catherine, and Mary was left to wonder: might this very man, John Endicott, who had sentenced Ann Hibbens to death, be feeling sufficient remorse that he would spare her—that he did not want the execution of two women on his hands?

"Thou needest not my forgiveness," said the governor. "Continue."

"Prithee, I have a question," Wilder interrupted. "Why didst thou race straightaway to the constable? Why didst thou not wait for thy master or mistress to return?"

"It was not disobedience, sir. I promise thee. I recalled the way I had seen Mary burying the Devil's tines and a pestle in the dooryard in the autumn, and I was much afraid."

"Very well."

"And so I went to the constable, and he suggested we get Master Deerfield. Given the horror of what I had found, we also brought with us a captain of the guard."

"Because," said Richard Wilder sarcastically, motioning at Mary, "thy mistress is so very frightening?"

"Because I have a righteous fear of Lucifer," said Catherine.

"Tell us, Catherine," asked the governor, "hast thou seen any signs of possession in Mary Deerfield?"

"I am not sure," the girl answered.

"Thou art not sure? Possession has rather evident manifestations. Didst thou ever find her shrieking most piteously or pulling at her hair?"

"No, sir."

"Didst thou ever witness a fit?"

Catherine shook her head, and Mary thought how easy it would be here for Catherine to lie. The girl could claim that she had seen any of these things. She and her scrivener had thought it possible, and their response would be to ask why she was only reporting possession now. But she wasn't lying, which both perplexed and relieved Mary. Either way, it seemed to suggest that while Catherine was the principal force driving her to the gallows, the girl might honestly believe that her mistress was in league with the Devil. This wasn't an attempt to accuse her of crimes that she herself was committing; she was actually convinced that Mary had been taken by Satan.

"Thou never saw a fit of any kind?" pressed Adams, and he, too, seemed surprised.

"I saw . . ."

"Go on."

"I saw melancholy. I saw sadness, which, given the station on which our Lord God has placed her and the blessings He has bestowed upon her, seemed odd to me."

Adams nodded, but Wilder jumped in. "That sadness, Catherine: could it not be attributable to the fact she has not been blessed with a child?"

"I am not schooled enough to know the answer to that," Catherine replied, and she almost curtsied in her response.

"And, Richard," said Adams, "let us not forget that it was suggested in the midst of her civil presentation in the fall that Mary may have made her pact with Satan and buried the Devil's tines precisely because she was barren and wanted Him to rectify that situation."

"I have not forgotten," Wilder said with a trace of exasperation.

"But I didn't bury the forks," Mary said, and for a moment she hadn't realized that she had spoken the words aloud. She had been focused on the absurdity of the exchange between the magistrates, and her response had been a reflex. But enough people heard her remark that a small babble enveloped the room, and the governor rapped his knuckles on the bench and commanded Mary to quiet down.

She felt her scrivener's hand on her sleeve and took a step back, hoping to be less obtrusive. She recalled his advice: be obedient and be calm. It took a moment for the rest of the crowd to adhere to the governor's admonishments, however: there were some who were muttering with indignation at the idea that Mary would dare dispute the charges that she was a witch.

"Didst thou ever ask Mary about her melancholy?" Wilder inquired.

"I never knew what to do when I saw my mistress in such a state," the girl said. "But I knew my place. Sometimes I would pray for her."

"Didst thou tell thy master?"

"I did not and I am woefully sorry. I hoped I was mistaken and that my mistress was not in the midst of a battle with Satan."

"What else canst thou tell us?" Adams asked next.

"She—my mistress—is friends with a woman who lives out by the Neck. A woman most—"

"Prithee," said Wilder. "Just tell us the woman's name."

"Constance Winston."

Again, there was a buzz in the room, either because people knew Winston or had heard of her. Mary felt bad that the woman had been drawn into her affair, but she had expected it. She had learned the hard way that this was a world in which a woman such as Constance hadn't a chance at having a reputation unsullied by slander and meanness.

"What dost thou believe was Mary's plan?" Adams asked, raising his voice so the room would settle down. "Why was she meeting secretly with Constance Winston?"

Mary whispered to her scrivener, "Secretly? Why does he assume my visits were clandestine?"

"Were they not?" he asked rhetorically.

She sighed. They were; but why would Adams cavalierly jump to that conclusion? And the answer, of course, was because Adams was a man, and Constance was a woman of independence.

"Again, sir, it should not be for the likes of me to conjecture about such things," Catherine was saying.

"The magistrate asked," said Daniel Winslow. "Prithee, feel free to . . . conjecture."

"Well," she said, "my mistress does not like her husband. That seems clear since she attempted to sever her marriage covenant with him."

"And what has this to do with Constance Winston?" asked the governor. "The woman does not mediate schisms between men and their wives."

"No, sir," said Catherine obediently, and that might have been the end of it, but Adams was not about to let a connection between Mary and the woman from the Neck remain unexamined.

"Is Mary Deerfield unnaturally cold to her husband?" he asked.

"She is colder to him than I presume is natural," the servant girl said.

"Has she been icier since her divorce petition was denied?"

"She has been gone more. This I know."

"Because I have been with Reverend Eliot. Because I have been trying to return the Hawkes to the Lord," Mary interjected.

Adams rolled his eyes, but the governor nodded. "Yes, Mary. 'Tis kindness thou hast bestowed upon that family. But, prithee, it is not thy time to speak."

She nodded respectfully.

"Catherine," said Adams. "Thou sayest Mary Deerfield was gone more. What didst thou make of this?"

"I believe she may have learned things—dark things, evil things—from Constance Winston. Goody Howland has told me what kind of person Constance is."

Adams raised his hand to pause Catherine, and whispered something to Daniel Winslow. Then they both spoke in hushed tones to Governor Endicott. He nodded and motioned for the captain of the guard to step forward, and though Mary could not hear every word, she heard enough to know that both Constance Winston and Goody Howland were being summoned to the Town House to testify. After the captain had been dispatched, Endicott said, "Catherine, thou mayest continue. Thou were telling us about Mary Deerfield's visits to the Neck."

Catherine took a breath. "I did not understand the point of the Devil's tines during her divorce petition. I was only scared. But as I have watched her unnatural coldness toward her husband every day and every night, I have come to believe this: in the autumn, she made a covenant with Lucifer to murder him. She wanted to cast a spell on him with the Devil's tines and the pestle. They were not an offering that had to do with her barrenness, but for something far worse."

Mary was utterly shocked: the girl had cracked the code and parsed the meaning of the spell. Maybe this girl was a witch, one with more guile than any person she had ever known, one who could feign obsequiousness with verisimilitude. But there was something else, too, and she watched with the same horror one watches a house burn, because she had a dreadful confidence in what Catherine would reveal next.

"And what was the spell? An attempt to poison him?" asked Adams.

"Yes, sir."

"Why the Devil's tines? Was it but a symbol?"

"I am neither a preacher nor a scholar and do not wish to overstep my place," she answered, bowing her head.

"No, I asked thee," said Adams. "We are all interested in thine opinion."

"I thank thee," she replied. "Yes, it is a symbol. A symbol for the tongue of that most wretched creature: the snake. The form the Devil took when he first seduced Eve. The pestle was there as a symbol for the grinding of its poison into use."

"Thou art wise beyond thy station, Catherine," Adams said, praising the girl. "Prithee, continue."

"When I caught my mistress that night in the autumn, she must have feared that she could not proceed with her plan, because now I knew. At least she thought I knew. At the time? No. But she resolved instead to divorce Thomas Deerfield, making up odious stories of his cruelty. And when all of thou saw through her fabrications and did not grant her petition, she once more went to the Devil, enlisting His help now with her husband's murder."

Mary looked at her scrivener, terrified, but he simply shook his head. She must remain docile and steadfast, even as Catherine uncoiled the rope that would hang her.

"How didst thou come to understand the point of the Devil's tines—of thy mistress's intent?" Adams inquired.

"From my reading of the Lord's word. And from what I found in my mistress's Bible."

This was it: this was that something else. The evidence, a proof as damning as if the girl had held up before the court the bottle of wolfsbane. Mary knew what the girl was going to say next, and she felt dizzy and sick. She had not seen this coming, this was a surprise, and she bent over and put her hands on her knees as the world grew dark. But she heard. Still, she heard.

"It didn't make sense to me at the time," Catherine was saying. "It only did later when I found the Devil's tines and His coin in her apron. She had left her quill in her Bible one night, and it was on the page with the 140th Psalm: 'They have sharpened their tongues like a serpent; adders' poison is under their lips.' I remembered she had been reading that psalm, and it must have mattered to her greatly to have left her quill in her Bible marking the verse."

Again, there was a small tumult in the Town House, and it was the last thing that Mary heard before, mercifully, she passed out and collapsed onto the floor.

Thou accused him falsely of plunging
the Devil's tines into thy hand . . .

**—The Remarks of Magistrate Caleb
Adams, from the Records and Files
of the Court of Assistants, Boston,
Massachusetts, 1663, Volume I**

Thirty-Six

The trial paused, but not for long. Mary's mother and father rushed to her side, and quickly she was sitting up between them, resting against her father and Benjamin Hull, while her mother was looking into her face. She had been unconscious for barely a moment.

"My darling," her mother was murmuring, "my darling."

She nodded at Hull that she was fine—or she supposed, as fine as any woman could be who was about to be hanged—but her scrivener nevertheless stood up and asked the magistrates if they might recess the proceedings until after dinner.

Adams leaned over the bench and looked at Mary, his countenance dismissive. "We have just begun, Benjamin. Dinner is hours away. Mary's eyes seem open and alert."

Mary took a breath and said, "Yes, we can proceed. I am sorry. Suddenly I felt lightheaded." She restrained herself from adding that she had been fed little but corn gruel and moldy cheese in the jail, and had subsisted mostly on the bread and meat that her parents had carried in. She stood with her father's assistance.

"Very well," said Adams, and he glanced at the men on the bench. "I have no more questions for the girl. Dost thou have any?"

"I do," said Richard Wilder. "Catherine, tell us, prithee, of specific occasions when thy mistress was cruel to thee."

The girl seemed surprised. She shook her head and replied, "She was never cruel to me. She was usually kind to me."

"Very good," said Wilder.

"And toward her husband?" asked Adams. "I want us to be sure that we have clarity."

"My mistress's evil intentions were directed at her husband, not at me."

"Didst thou witness her cruelty toward Thomas Deerfield?" Daniel Winslow asked.

"Yes: the witchcraft. The Devil's tines."

"Other than that?" pressed Wilder, perhaps Mary's lone supporter.

Catherine inhaled, and Mary wondered if she were trying to concoct a fabrication or honestly thinking long and hard on her life with the Deerfields. But if she were planning to lie, it seemed that she couldn't sew one on the spot that would withstand the rigors of reality given Thomas's size, viciousness, and unwillingness to tolerate insubordination. And so she answered, "Her cruelty, I suppose, was her pact with the Devil."

"Nothing more?"

"I stand by my words."

"And those are most powerful," Adams reassured her. "Thou mayest return to thy home, unless anyone else has additional questions."

No one did. The court was finished with Catherine, and Mary watched the girl skulk past her as she went to the stairs, but she looked up and their eyes met. Mary saw no shame there. She thought, just maybe, that she had seen sadness and regret that it had come to this, but she couldn't be sure.

❧ ❧

The constable spoke next while they waited for Goody Howland and Constance Winston. He was a portly man, reminiscent in shape of John Eliot, but he was younger and had a more bulbous nose. His hair was deep brown, but his beard was showing the first flecks of white. His name was Stalwart Thames, and Mary knew that he was aware of her husband's tippling and did not approve. But he had never brought Thomas home or seen that he was disciplined for being drink-drunk.

"Thou saw the Devil's mark in the doorframe to the house?" Adams was asking him.

"I did. It matched the image on the coin," he replied.

"How dost thou know that Mary Deerfield

carved it there?" Wilder asked. "We have neither witness nor confession."

"I agree. But here is what we do have. We have the fact that Catherine Stileman saw Mary Deerfield last autumn in the night with the Devil's tines. Mary does not dispute this. Then we have Catherine discovering the Devil's tines and a Devil's coin in Mary's apron. We have the verse from the Bible that Mary seems to have corrupted for her malignant spell. Finally, we have a letter she wrote that suggests she is contemplating self-murder, which suggests madness—which may suggest possession."

"Thou art a fine constable, Stalwart," observed Wilder. "But art thou an expert on possession?"

"No. I am grateful that I have seen little of it."

"I must admit, I am not either. And so here is an inconsistency that baffles me. Why would Mary Deerfield have wanted to summon the Devil to assist in the murder of her husband and wished to take her own life?"

"I am only telling thee what we found, sir."

Wilder nodded, his point made. Then he asked the constable whether he had ever had reason before to seek discipline for Mary Deerfield, but Mary had never run afoul of the law and so they devoted little time to this line of questioning. Even Adams had nothing to add. And so they dismissed the constable and brought forward Valentine Hill. Her scrivener had told her that he could not predict

the old man's testimony: he did not approve of his nephew and rightfully viewed any relationship he had with Mary as sacrilegious. But he was a great friend of the Burden family, and Hull assured her that her father and Valentine had spoken at length the day before, and James had pleaded on her and Henry's behalf.

Now the old fellow stood before the bench and spoke his oath.

"I thank thee for testifying," said Adams. "We know how busy thou art."

"Less busy this time of year than at others."

"Indeed," agreed the magistrate. "Tell us: hast thou ever imported the Devil's tines?"

"I have not. But, if I am going to be scrupulously honest, I do not see them as an instrument of the Dark One. I see them as forks. And as this court knows, I have good friends who have imported them," Hill said, and he nodded in a kindly fashion at her father. Her father stared down at the floorboards.

"Be that as it may, art thou comfortable admitting that people who have been seduced by Satan might impart to them a greater, more insidious use?"

"I would, but principally because the Devil is nefarious and can make evil a child's plaything if He wants."

"Very well. Thou knowest Mary Deerfield, correct?"

"Since she arrived in Boston, yes."

"What is her relationship with thy nephew, Henry Simmons?"

"As this court learned during Mary's divorce petition, he tried once to kiss her."

"It sounds as if thou dost not approve."

"I do not condone adultery."

"Of course not," said Adams. "Have the two of them seen each other since then—other than in this Town House during her divorce petition?"

"I do not know."

"But Mary has been to thy warehouse, where he works, and one time asked thee where to find him. True?"

"Yes. But she explained it was to forgive him for his transgressions. I never asked her or my nephew if she found him."

"She has been often to the wharves. Is this not correct?"

"It is."

"Her father's warehouse is there, too," Wilder observed. "Let us not forget that. I know that she has visited the harbor often throughout her entire adult life."

"Point noted, Richard," said Adams. He leaned in a little toward Valentine Hill and asked, "Is Mary resourceful in thine opinion? Headstrong?"

"She is a woman who knows her mind."

"When she was not granted her petition for

divorce, was she likely to take our 'no' as the final word?"

"What art thou suggesting?"

"Thou heard what Catherine Stileman said this morning: Mary Deerfield made a pact with the Devil to put a spell on Thomas Deerfield that would kill him, and thus free herself from her marriage to the man. We do not need thee to corroborate that—"

"I don't think I could," said Hill. "Mary is headstrong, but she is not a murderess."

"But," Adams continued, as if he had not been interrupted, "we would like to know if thou believest—before all of us and thy Lord and Savior—whether thy nephew ever again tried to lead Mary away from her marriage."

Reluctantly Hill said, shaking his head, "He may have. He, too, is rather headstrong."

"And it is this that may have given Mary the hope that she could have a life with him, once she was freed from her marriage."

Hill said nothing more. There really was nothing more for him to say.

⚓

"Have they arrived?" Caleb Adams asked the captain of the guard. "That woman from the Neck and Goody Howland?"

"They are downstairs," he replied. "I can retrieve them."

"Please do. Let's start with the one from the Neck," said Adams.

"Poor Constance," Mary whispered into Benjamin Hull's ear. "I feel bad that she has been dragged into this."

The scrivener nodded. A moment later they heard two sets of boots on the stairs, and there she was: Mary's tall friend about whom swirled all manner of gossip and innuendo. Constance smiled at her, and Mary felt an unexpected rush of confidence. The court would not have summoned Constance if they did not believe she could corroborate the charges of witchcraft—this bench was far from neutral—but Mary knew that the older woman was as smart as any of the men aligned against her.

Adams quickly established why she had been brought to the Town House, and the severity of the charges. Then he asked, "Why did Mary Deerfield seek thee out?"

"She wanted tea," said Constance.

Adams repeated his question, beginning this time with an admonishment: "Remember thou hast been sworn in and the reason why thou art here: why did Mary Deerfield meet with thee?"

"I answered thy question: we had tea."

"She could have tea in the center of the city, and while thy company might be interesting, I rather doubt—given thy lack of communion with the rest of Boston and paucity of friends—that it alone would merit the effort it takes to reach thee."

Winston had a small grin on her face and rested her gloved hands demurely before her.

"Well?" Adams continued.

"Yes?"

"I asked thee a question."

"I answered it. Was there another hidden in thy remark that I am friendless and I missed it?"

Adams started to say something, but the governor stopped him. "We are all quite sure thou hast friends," Endicott said. "When Mary came to thy home for tea, did she ask for advice?"

"She first came to see me, two years ago, in search of herbs or greens that might help her husband's seed take root in her womb. Mary Deerfield is devout, and wanted to honor our Lord by fulfilling her role as a mother."

"Didst thou suggest any?" asked the governor.

"I did. They didn't work. When I saw her this autumn and winter, I did not recommend others."

"Art thou saying," asked Adams, "that she did not ask for advice when she saw thee most recently?" He sounded incredulous.

"That is correct."

"Then what sorts of things were discussed?"

"We spoke of the weather. The change in seasons. We spoke of her desire to assist Reverend Eliot. That's what I remember."

"She did not ask for thine assistance?"

"No. I am not sure in what capacity a friendless old woman like me could help her, other than my suggestions for things she could steep or stew that might make a seed a little happier."

"She did not ask thee for information about the Devil's tines?"

"She did not," Constance answered, which Mary knew was a lie.

"She did not inquire into the sorts of spells one might cast with such an instrument and a pestle?"

"No. And if she had? I would have been at a loss. I may not spend much time here in the center of this great city, but neither am I cavorting with Satan in the woods."

"But thou wouldst know the Devil's mark if thou saw it."

She nodded. "And I would be scared. I have no desire to meet Him. Not ever. I have seen too much of His likeness here in Boston, even among the saints."

Mary saw Wilder was failing to suppress a smile. Adams saw it, too, and said, "We have established that Mary Deerfield saw thee." He looked at the other magistrates. "I think that is sufficient."

"Sufficient for what?" Wilder asked.

"Proverbs, twelve, twenty-six: 'The righteous **is** more excellent than his neighbor; but the way of the wicked seduceth them.'"

"We do not know that Constance Winston has been a bad influence on Mary Deerfield—or on anyone else, Caleb," said Wilder. "Nor is Constance on trial."

"No," he agreed. "Not yet." Then he pointed at her and continued, "We know what sort of person thou art."

"A person with hair that is white and a face well lined," she said. "In other words, the sort of person unlikely to be noticed, unless one is looking for those who are easily demonized and bullied."

"Thou art not helping thy friend's cause with such impudence," Adams hissed. "Watch thy tongue."

"I thank thee for the counsel," she said. "I will."

And with that, Adams must have felt he had impugned Mary sufficiently, and the woman was dismissed. For a fleeting second, Mary thought that Constance was going to embrace her, but her friend was too smart for that: she knew it wouldn't help and walked past her without the slightest greeting.

"Is the goodwife Beth Howland present?" Adams asked the constable.

Before he could respond, Mary heard the woman call out from the other side of the room, "Yes, sir. I'm here."

"We have questions for thee, as well."

"I am honored to answer them," she said, stepping forward. She looked prettier than usual as she was sworn in, her bodice and skirt shades of emerald and blue.

"Tell us, prithee," began Adams, "what thou

knowest of Mary Deerfield and her penchant for evil."

Mary looked at her scrivener, outraged by how Adams was choosing to begin this questioning—it was as if it was a foregone conclusion that she had been seduced by Lucifer—but even before Hull could suggest a slightly less menacing start to the examination, Wilder leaned in and said, "Caleb, thou canst not be serious."

"I am quite serious. I will not have the Devil among us."

"Prithee, think more about thy wording. Ask the goodwife a question that will not demand she respond with a treatise."

Adams snorted, but began anew. "When thou were most charitable this autumn and took in Catherine Stileman after the girl had spotted her mistress with the Devil's tines, the two of thee spoke much. True?"

"Yes."

"And what was the principal subject?"

"We had both begun to suspect that Mary Deerfield had not been ministering to Catherine's brother, who ultimately died, but was in fact endeavoring to speed his time from this world into the next."

"Thou believest she was offering Satan a soul so that He might grant her a child of her own. Is this correct?"

"It is. That woman cost us a servant."

"Didst thou continue to see Catherine after she returned to Thomas Deerfield's home?" Adams asked, oblivious to the callousness of the witness's remark. **That woman cost us a servant.** What a despicable thing to say about William Stileman's death, Mary thought, and she noted that both Wilder and Endicott looked back and forth between Adams and the goodwife as if a madman and a madwoman were having a conversation in their midst.

"I did not seek her out, but our paths crossed."

"Thou knowest Peregrine Cooke," said Daniel Winslow.

"Yes. And she lost her baby, the infant taken, in my opinion, due to the spite that exudes like sweat from the skin of Mary Deerfield. Look at how all that she touches withers and dies! She is barren and makes the world around her a desert of dry bones that do not ever rise up: my servant and Peregrine's dead baby are but two of the casualties in her wasteland."

"Indeed," agreed Adams. "I see more than coincidence here."

"And I know it has worried Peregrine greatly that while her husband has no designs on Mary Deerfield, it seems clear that Mary allows her eyes to linger too long and with lust on Jonathan Cooke," Beth volunteered.

"What precisely is the point of this revelation?" asked Wilder.

"Yes, Beth," Mary said, unable to restrain herself. "Am I a harlot or a witch? When I was here last, I stood accused of lusting after Henry Simmons. Today? It is my own son-in-law!"

She felt her scrivener's hand on her elbow, but this time her outburst was not viewed as quite so problematic. Both Wilder and Endicott were nodding. Then Wilder said, "Jonathan Cooke seems to be incapable of restraining himself when it comes to a great many vices, but today we are not investigating them."

"I was simply answering Magistrate Winslow's question about what I know of Peregrine," said Beth.

"Who dost thou believe gave Mary the coin with the Devil's mark?" Adams asked.

"I suspect it was the woman who preceded me here."

"Constance Winston?"

"Yes."

"Constance is not on trial," said the governor. "Hast thou any proof to support that allegation?"

She shook her head.

"Then didst thou ever see Mary evidence possession?" Endicott pressed.

"No, but her possession is of a more insidious sort: it is a slow poison she brings into this world, and one she hides well."

Adams nodded as if this observation was sage and insightful commentary, rather than character aspersion founded on nothing. The magistrates looked back and forth, endeavoring to see if any of them had more questions. When none did, Adams thanked the goodwife and the governor dismissed her.

After Beth Howland had left, Adams addressed Mary directly. "Mary Deerfield, I understand thou hast people thou wouldst like to speak in thy defense. Wouldst thou like to begin?"

"I would," she said, and she looked at her scrivener. They were going to start with the midwife.

I have been examined by a jury of women, including a midwife most respected by the Church, and there is upon my body no sign of the Devil.

—The Testimony of Mary Deerfield, from the Records and Files of the Court of Assistants, Boston, Massachusetts, 1663, Volume I

Thirty-Seven

Mary reminded the magistrates of one of the pronounced indignities she had endured in the jail.

"Thou wilt recall that thou sent a jury of three women to have me stripped naked and searched for the mark of the Devil," she said. "Among them was Susanna Downing, a midwife. I present her to thee."

The silver-haired midwife bowed before the men on the bench.

"Goody Downing," Mary asked, "didst thou search my skin from scalp to the soles of my bare feet?"

"We did, yes."

"And didst thou find any mark of the Devil or sign of a witch's teat?"

"No. We did not."

Adams said, "Mary, we know this. Thou needn't have brought Goody Downing back."

"I wanted to be sure that the bench heard from the midwife herself. My body is clean."

"We know that. Goody Downing, thou needn't waste any more of thy day here," Adams continued.

Mary could tell that he was annoyed, but she had made her point. At least she thought she had until Adams added, "And, Mary, simply because thou hast not yet been marked does not mean thou art not a witch or hast not signed a covenant with the Devil. Yes, if thou hast a mark, it would suggest thou art a witch; but just because thy body is clean, it does not mean thou art not one."

"But it is a factor to consider, Caleb," said Wilder.

"It is," the other magistrate agreed, but it was clear the factor mattered little to him.

"Prithee, may I add something?" the midwife asked.

"Certainly," said the Governor.

"Mary Deerfield has been present at births with me and has always been most helpful. And the babies are breathing still. I have faith that she has not been enticed by Satan."

"I am sure there are women in this city who currently are with child who do not share thy faith," said Adams. "Look at what happened to her own daughter-in-law: we have established that Mary's presence smothered the life inside Peregrine Cooke."

"Forgive me," interjected Hull. "I mean thee no disrespect, but how did we establish that?"

"The scrivener is correct, Caleb," said Wilder.

Mary thought Adams might argue, but he simply rolled his eyes. "Dost thou have anything more to add, Goody Downing?"

"No, sir."

"Thou art excused," the governor told her. He sounded tired, and his weariness frightened Mary: he was a possible ally, and he was fatigued—too old to fight on her behalf. She knew in her heart the battle was lost, but still, she couldn't help but hope for a miracle. "Who is next?"

"The Reverend John Norton," Mary told him, and the minister came forward. As he was sworn in, Mary watched how the men behind the bench greeted him so much more warmly than they had just received the midwife or, before her, such women as Goody Howland or Constance Winston or even their prize witness, Catherine Stileman.

The reverend testified how Mary never missed a Sunday service and was a devoted churchgoer. It was all she could have hoped for.

"Tell me something," said Caleb Adams. "If Mary Deerfield is devout, then how dost thou explain the presence of the Devil's tines in her apron or the fact that she was seen with another pair in the night this past autumn?"

The reverend looked at his hands, contemplating his response. Then: "Thou viewest them with more malevolence than I do, Caleb. I do not use them and I do not approve of them, but I am not inclined to see them as instruments of evil."

"But did Mary?"

"I cannot speak to that. I rather doubt it since it was her father who imported them."

"Canst thou speak to the Devil's coin? And what of the mark on the doorframe? I find that most disturbing."

"I think thou art right to be discomfited by it. By both," said the reverend. "Satan is insidious, and He is relentless. He is especially angered by our efforts here in Boston. He will do what He can to destroy our work."

"Dost thou believe this incriminates Mary Deerfield?"

"If she carved the mark in the doorframe—"

Adams slammed his hand on the bench and said, "There was a coin with the mark in her apron! John, I mean no disrespect, but consider that one incriminating fact! The coin was in Mary Deerfield's apron."

"So the girl says."

"Art thou calling Catherine Stileman a liar?"

"No. I am simply saying we have a story with two sides. I know the Mary Deerfield I see on the Sabbath and the Mary Deerfield who has chosen to view her barrenness as a blessing and to help minister to the Hawkes. That is the young woman I know," he said.

Daniel Winslow sat forward and asked, "Dost thou believe that every parishioner thou seest in church is saved?"

"Of course not. We cannot begin to know who is among the elect and who is among the damned."

"But we do know that a covenant of works is mistaken."

"We know this with certainty."

"And so, it seems to me," said Winslow, "that the fact Mary attends church and helps minister to the Hawke children may be but a ruse to conceal her base relationship with the Devil."

"Anything is possible. But Daniel? I believe also that some eventualities are more likely than others."

❧ ❧

The questioning of Reverend John Eliot proceeded in much the same way: he spoke highly of Mary's work with the Hawkes and said he hoped that she would have the chance to continue. He added that he had higher ambitions for her yet: someday soon he wanted her to join him to tutor the children of the praying Indians in the way of the Lord.

"The Lord or Satan?" Adams asked dismissively.

"Only the Lord," Eliot replied, not lowering himself to the magistrate's level by snapping back.

"Unless her saintly behavior is but a disguise to mask her covenant with the Devil," Adams said, and Mary felt her stomach turn at the nearness of the magistrate's supposition to the truth. "For all we know," he continued, "the woman taught the Hawke children for reasons that have nothing to do with returning the family to the Lord. For all we know, her motives were nefarious."

"A fair point," agreed Daniel Winslow.

And it may have been how close Adams was to the truth that led her to surprise her scrivener and her parents after Eliot was dismissed by announcing the name of the person she wanted brought next to the Town House for questioning: "For this trial to be fair and just, before I speak what may be my final remarks, I would like the captain of the guard to bring before thee my husband, Thomas Deerfield."

Behind her, Benjamin Hull reflexively murmured, "No," but it was so soft that only she and her parents heard him.

"What for?" asked Adams.

"Everyone seems to suppose that I carved the Devil's mark into the doorframe and that I was walking around with the cutlery in my apron. No one is considering the possibility that Thomas might have been commandeered by Lucifer. Perhaps he took a knife and gouged a star into the wood to welcome the Dark One; perhaps he shifted the blame to me by planting the forks in my clothing."

"Thou canst not mean that," said Adams.

"I can. I do."

"First, thou accused him falsely of plunging the Devil's tines into thy hand, and now thou hast the temerity—when the very instruments are found on thy body—"

"No," she said, cutting him off, "not on my body. In my apron when I was not even home."

"Fine," Adams said. "Fine. Thou still hast no basis for such an accusation. None! Thou tried to sully his name with thy failed divorce petition. Now thou dost seem to want to see him take the rope for thy crime. I won't have it."

She looked at Wilder, but he wouldn't meet her eyes. Nor would the governor. It was just so much easier to bully her than her husband. And in her heart she knew that Thomas wasn't in league with the Devil. Perhaps her willingness to accuse him was further proof that she herself was. But if it wasn't she herself who had carved the mark or dropped the forks in that apron pocket, it seemed it could only be Thomas or Catherine. Goody Howland hated her, but enough to see her hanged? Not likely.

"So, he will not be asked to address my accusation?" she asked.

Adams glanced at the governor, and the lead magistrate shook his head. "He will not," said John Endicott. And that was that.

Thou believest the worst of me, but seem not to consider other possibilities.

—The Testimony of Mary Deerfield, from the Records and Files of the Court of Assistants, Boston, Massachusetts, 1663, Volume I

Thirty-Eight

And so it came down to her final summation. She was tired and hungry and cold; she felt poorly from her days in the damp jail. And she was scared. Most of the men on the bench were oblivious to the reasoning of the midwife and two esteemed ministers. Nevertheless, she was not going to confess to a crime that she had not committed. Yes, perhaps, the Devil had almost recruited her; He had almost gotten her to commit murder. But, in the end, she had resisted. Besides, it was clear that the magistrates were not inclined to be charitable toward a woman as difficult as she was proving to be.

She went to the center of the great room and stood before Governor Endicott.

"Sir, I can summarize quickly because I know how busy thou art," she began. She and her scrivener had outlined her points, and she held in her hand a piece of paper with her notes. She saw her fingers were trembling. "I have been examined by a jury of women, including a midwife most respected by the church, and there is upon my body no sign of the Devil. No mark at all. Likewise, even the women who have spoken with great passion against me have seen no sign of possession. Again, none."

Behind her, someone had murmured, "Here, here!" and she took comfort in the knowledge that at least one stranger in the Town House was on her side. She continued, "Reverend Norton has spoken well of my attendance on the Sabbath. Reverend Eliot has told thee of my efforts to return the Hawke children to our Lord and Savior. I have sat in the cold in their cottage and read to them from **The New England Primer** and told them of John Rogers's sacrifice. I have shown them **Milk for Babies.** Here in Boston, I have tended to the sick, including Catherine Stileman's own brother, William.

"My accusers have suggested as a motive that I wished to kill my husband and trade him for Henry Simmons. Prithee, recall Henry's testimony when I petitioned for divorce. He said that he tried to kiss me and I resisted. Is there other evidence that I have committed adultery? I have heard none. I went to the wharves—"

"Mary, while there, thou didst ask Valentine Hill where his nephew was," Adams reminded her, interrupting.

"I did. But as Valentine told thee: I wanted but to ensure Henry that he knew he was forgiven."

"That does not seem likely to me," said Adams.

"Believest what thou like," she told him, but then she paused. She and her scrivener had agreed that she would deny Henry, which was what Henry wanted. He had sent that exact message to the jail through Benjamin Hull, urging her under no circumstances to acknowledge their relationship because it would increase dramatically the chances of a conviction. She had to protect herself; he could take care of himself, he told Hull to assure her. But now, when the word **deny** passed through her mind, she recalled Matthew, chapter 26, verse 34: Jesus informing Peter that the disciple will **deny** Him. Jesus had meant His prophecy, she believed, as a simple acknowledgment of human failing. Of weakness. But it was—and this was clear, too—an act of cowardice on the part of the apostle. One was supposed to die for his God. She thought again of John Rogers and his family and those agonizing flames. Henry Simmons was not a god, but he was a good man.

She took a breath: she would not die a coward. No. She would not add that sin to her ledger, as well. They were going to hang her; she would face the noose with her conscience clear.

"In fact, here is the truth," she said when she resumed, standing tall. "While I would have liked very much to have been granted my divorce in the fall and would have liked very much to have married Henry Simmons—if he would have me, and I will not be so presumptuous as to assume he would—I never made a compact with Lucifer. Never."

It took a beat for the crowd to digest what she was saying—that she had just confessed to an illicit desire. But after that beat, the disapprobation rained down upon her like a gale, women and men alike calling her an adulteress and a sinner, and shouting to the magistrates to hang her. The constable had to slam his pike onto the floor three times before they settled down. Only then could Mary continue: "I know not why everyone assumes that I made the mark in the doorframe. I suppose it is because of what Catherine Stileman says she found in my apron: the coin and the forks."

"The Devil's tines," Adams corrected her.

"No. Forks," she said firmly. "And I did not put them there. Nor, in the fall, did I bury a pair in the dooryard with a pestle."

"The evidence suggests otherwise, Mary," said Winslow.

"It was not me. Not in either case. And while thou hast ignored my suppositions, the fact remains that Catherine Stileman and Thomas Deerfield were as likely as me to have been responsible for the crimes for which I am wrongly accused."

"So, thou art going to compound thy sins by unjustly accusing others of witchcraft?" Adams asked, shaking his head in disgust.

"No," she replied. "But is it not the duty of this court to at least ponder long on those possibilities? For instance, I do not know whether it is because Catherine has feelings for my husband—and if she does, God help her—or because she blames me for her brother's death. But I know as well as I know my Psalter that she could have buried those forks. Likewise, the forks she claims were in my apron? It is but my word against hers, and—"

"And so thou art accusing her of witchcraft?" asked Daniel Winslow.

"I am simply observing that this is not as clear as glass. Likewise, my husband has a history of violence that suggests a heart most susceptible to the temptations of Satan."

"According to thee. We have seen no proof," said Adams.

She held up her left hand, but the magistrates as one stared at her blankly.

"My point," she said, "is that thou believest the worst of me, but seem not to consider the other possibilities. Catherine and Thomas may both be as innocent as baby lambs. Perhaps there is a third disciple of the Dark One we have not considered with appropriate gravity. But dost thou really want to have upon thy ledger the hanging death of an innocent woman?"

"That is thy sole defense?" inquired Adams. "A threat?"

"Hast thou been listening? Of course not. It is but one small part of my defense."

"'Tis not small to accuse others of witchcraft, Mary," the governor reminded her.

"I do not make such charges lightly. And I am

not charging them, let us be clear. I am only asking that the possibility be entertained. Is it not conceivable that I am the target? Thou dost view me as the raptor, when, it seems, I am far more likely the field mouse in its talons."

"Thou art no field mouse," Adams chastised her. "And Catherine Stileman is not on trial. Nor is Thomas Deerfield. Thou art. Defend thyself. Do not suppose thou canst deflect attention away from thy crimes."

The moment was moving too fast. She was unaccustomed to this sort of attention, but there was an idea dangling just beyond her reach, and she needed to grasp it. She stood there in silence for a long moment, concentrating.

"Mary?"

It was the voice of the governor.

"May I have but a minute, prithee?"

Her scrivener and her father came up beside her and started to speak, but she waved them aside.

"Mary Deerfield, hast thou anything more to say?" asked Endicott, ignoring her question.

She nodded. "I do," she answered. The gist was close, so very close. And so she resumed her defense. "There also is this. I have said that I am not the hunter, but, arguably, the hunted. I have said that Thomas or Catherine should also be asked whether they may have been seduced by the Devil. But there is still another possibility that none of thee has considered. It is one I am only considering now."

"Go on," said Wilder.

"Thou hast suggested that Thomas or Catherine was my target. I have suggested that I might be one of theirs . . ."

She paused briefly, because the puzzle was missing pieces. Still, she had to forge ahead. "But what if Thomas or Catherine was the target of someone—someone other than me? What if I am irrelevant, but a bystander, as is one of those two?"

"Thou art suggesting someone has a grievance with Catherine Stileman or Thomas Deerfield so profound that they have gone to the Devil?"

"I am. Again, it is speculation—"

"And groundless!" Adams snapped at her. "Canst thou give us one reason why someone would do such a thing? What in the name of our Lord Jesus Christ has either done to be subject to such venom from thy tongue?"

She could give no reason for Catherine. But certainly Thomas had behaved so abysmally around her that it was possible he had behaved equally badly around others. In the end, she had been unable to murder him. But might not someone else have been willing to try? A farmer he had wronged? A fellow he had met in a tavern? Someone else he had beaten?

And that was when she knew.

She knew.

It was the word **beaten.**

Yes, she was positive. The boiled apples and

raisins. Perhaps Thomas had beaten his own daughter. Or maybe Peregrine had witnessed him beating her mother. Both prospects saddened Mary. They suggested that she herself was but the continuation of Thomas Deerfield's violence. A legacy.

She considered raising up Peregrine's name to try and save herself, but she couldn't. She wouldn't. No. Not after all that woman had likely endured.

"I have committed no crimes," she said instead, rallying, her voice strong, no longer trying to hide her exasperation. It was over. So be it. She was going to die, and her fear and fury began to morph into resignation. "Sit on thy perch, gentlemen. Scowl at me and this world. I care for this life the Lord has given me, but Christ died at the hands of the unseeing, too."

"Art thou now adding heresy to thy crimes?" Adams asked, but Wilder gently touched the other magistrate's sleeve and told him, "Caleb, she has done no such thing."

"No," Mary continued. "There was no room for Christ when He first came into our world and there was no room for Him when He died. He was scorned by authority and He was crucified because He demanded that the poor and the sinful and the children and the women be"—and she took a breath as she sought and found the correct word— "respected. Respected. The lowly for whom, just like Him, there was neither esteem nor hope. We separated and came here to this wilderness, and so far we have shown only that we are as flawed and mortal here as we were across the ocean. There is no act of horror or violence of which man is not capable. My husband stuck a fork in me and thou demandeth I live with him still. Hast thou seen the idea of charity we bestow upon the heathen? Hast thou examined the accounting ledgers of how and what we trade with them? We are scoundrels. We—"

Adams banged his fist and demanded that she quiet down.

But she didn't. She looked steadfastly into Endicott's eyes, and said, "Governor, may I have but a moment more?"

He was tired, his visage beyond sadness at what loomed. Another hanging. Another dead woman on his ledger. He steepled his fingers and rested his forehead on the tips, and nodded.

"Governor, thou hanged thy predecessor's own sister-in-law. Thou art going to hang me, too. Fine. I cannot open the minds of men whose brains have doors locked shut. But, prithee, know that thou art hanging an innocent woman. My husband taunts me by insisting that my mind is but white meat. Perhaps. But it still sees the truth of thy rot and the truth of thy fears and—"

"Enough!" Adams bellowed at her. "Enough!"

The crowd was yelling, but she heard the magistrate order the constable to take hold of her, which he did, grasping her upper arms in his hands and pulling her back from the bench. She acquiesced, and Adams said to her and to the men around him, "Have we need any more evidence of possession? Have we? We just heard the Devil speak from the woman's very lips!"

Wilder looked pale, and Mary saw that her mother had collapsed into her father's arms, sobbing, and her scrivener looked rueful and lost. So did the governor. He was too old and too frail to stop this, even if it meant a second dead woman on his watch.

"Do we actually need to convene to render a verdict?" Adams said to Endicott. "Is it not clear?"

The governor closed his eyes. Then he shook his head, not disagreeing with the other magistrate, but in despair. He didn't want more blood on his hands, but more blood there would be.

"John?" asked Adams. "What dost thou say?"

The governor looked up and gazed around at the other magistrates. Most murmured or said with what they must have felt was appropriate gravitas, "Guilty." Endicott mumbled, his voice weak, that this was too complicated to rush to a verdict, and Wilder suggested that they should bring back Catherine Stileman for additional testimony and perhaps insist that Thomas Deerfield appear, too, but they were the only voices speaking on Mary's behalf and were outvoted. The majority of the court wanted to hear nothing more about this or about Mary Deerfield. She was a woman who hadn't gotten her way and had contracted with the Devil. It was simple, really, when one looked at the evidence. It was testimony to the insidious way that Satan could corrupt anyone—even this once proper young woman and the daughter of two of the city's finest saints.

And so when Caleb Adams announced that tomorrow morning she should be hanged, Mary didn't weep or fall to the floor or beg for mercy. She was sick and she was tired and she was angry . . . and she was finished. She was ready. Tomorrow when they cast the rope around her neck at their Golgotha, she, too, would commend her spirit into her Father's hands.

She said nothing to anyone, not even to her parents, as the constable and the captain of the guard led her through the jeering throng and down the steps of the Town House, and Daniel Winslow was saying something about how he hoped the Lord would have mercy on her soul.

We cannot begin to know who is among the elect and who is among the damned.

—The Testimony of Reverend John Norton, from the Records and Files of the Court of Assistants, Boston, Massachusetts, 1663, Volume I

Thirty-Nine

Mary's scrivener went home first, followed by her mother and father, leaving her alone in the jail. Her mother wanted to remain through the night, and a part of Mary wanted that, too. But the magistrates had insisted that she spend her last night on this earth alone. And so she would pray and write two last letters.

She didn't expect to sleep.

She was grateful when the magistrates relented and allowed her a candle so she could see the paper as she formed her letters with her quill. The first letter was going to be to Henry and the second would be to Peregrine. In the morning, she would give them to her father. She was confident that he would deliver them without opening them.

It was while she was praying before starting to write, asking her God for forgiveness and thanking Him for her twenty-four years of life and the love of her parents, praying as well that she would die quickly and the agony would be brief, that Spencer Pitts told her she had company. She rose from her knees as he unlocked the heavy door, and there stood Thomas.

He took off his hat and held it boyishly in front of him, as if he were courting a girl he presumed was above his station, either literally or because in some impure, cavalier fashion he esteemed too much.

"I am sorry it has come to this," he began, his tone uncharacteristically sheepish.

"I am, too."

It was awkward and strange, but mostly, she thought, because they had so little to say to each other. Here they had lived as man and wife for five years, and now her principal thought when she saw him was this: **I haven't the time for thee.**

"I regret much."

"Is that why thou appeared at the Town House today to speak on my behalf?" she asked sarcastically. "Is that why thou came to visit me so many times this week?"

He shook his head. Instead of answering, he said, "I heard thou accused me of witchcraft today."

"Not precisely. I simply observed that Catherine and thee were as likely suspects as me to have carved the Devil's mark into our doorframe."

"No one was going to believe that nonsense."

"Thou art quite right. No one did," she said. "So, thou hast come to say thou art sorry. For what? For the beatings and the cruel words?"

"I always administered to thee with love and the

hope that thou wouldst dilute thy pride with obedience."

"Fine," she said. She wasn't going to argue.

"Thy spell, Mary. Why wouldst thou try and hex me? Look how this has ended. And it couldn't have ended any other—"

"I didn't, Thomas," she said, cutting him off.

"Art thou going to insist even now, hours before thou wilt be swinging from a noose, that Catherine—"

"No."

"Then what? That it was me? It wasn't me, Mary."

"But thou were the target. Of this I am sure. I understood this only today, but I know it now as surely as I know my own face in the glass."

"Thou knowest this how?" he asked, leaning back against the damp stone. He waited. And so she did, too, unsure whether she should share with him what she had deduced, or whether she should let Peregrine try again and, perhaps, this time succeed. Thomas Deerfield deserved to die. But what would happen to Peregrine in the next life if she murdered her father? On the other hand, what would happen to her in this one if she told Thomas what she knew?

She rubbed her arms with her hands. She was cold. So very cold.

The truth was, they preached that a doctrine of

works was a fallacy, but they all believed in their hearts that evil on earth suggested one was damned. Did the magistrates suppose that a hanged witch ever wound up beside Jesus Christ in the celestial firmament? Of course not. In her mind, she heard herself informing Thomas, her lips thin, **Thine own daughter detests thee with the heat of a blacksmith's fire.** But she did not say that. She would write Peregrine, as she had planned, tell her what she believed was the truth, and then walk with her head held high to the gallows. Someday after she was gone, in the next world, perhaps, she would learn what had transpired here in Boston. She rather hoped so.

"Thou hast grown quiet," he said finally.

"I have nothing to say."

"Thy scandal has scarred me, too—and will forever."

"No," she corrected him. "We are mortal. Nothing that touches us or we touch here is forever. Even rocks are rubbed small by the river."

He chuckled dismissively. "Thou hast become a poet in thy last hours."

"Some white meat ages better than others," she said. She supposed it would be the last thing she would ever say to him. He turned, put on his hat, and left. They were man and wife, but they hadn't touched once.

᪥ ᪥

And then Spencer left, too. He said he was going home and hoped she would sleep. She finished her two letters and prayed. When she rose, her back hurt. The days in the cell had done their work.

As she stared into the blackness beyond the bars, she saw a flickering light and supposed that Spencer had not left, after all. But she heard at least two sets of footsteps, and they were moving quietly. And suddenly there stood Rebeckah Cooper and Peregrine Cooke. The women were almost lost in the dark of the jail.

"I am flattered that our farewells will be here rather than when I stand tomorrow on the scaffold," she said through the bars, "but how and why art thou here?"

Goody Cooper glanced at Peregrine and then surprised Mary by pulling out the keys to the door. She opened it, and the two of them entered the cell. Mary backed away from them reflexively, stunned. She started to ask how they had the keys and what they were doing, but Goody Cooper placed her index finger on Mary's lips, silencing her, and they each embraced Mary in turn. When they pulled apart Rebeckah said, "Thou art trembling."

"I am unsure whether it is cold or fear. It's probably a stew made of both. Thine uncle has allowed this? Spencer gave thee his keys?"

"He did."

"Do not be afraid," said Peregrine.

Mary offered a small smile. "Dost thou know my destiny when the noose has done its work?"

"My father is the Devil," she said.

The words hung there a moment, and Mary realized that the woman had spoken them before; when she looked at Goody Cooper, she understood that Peregrine had shared them with her friend.

"Thou knew?" Mary asked Rebeckah.

"Peregrine told me."

Mary gazed at her daughter-in-law. "How badly did he hurt thee, Peregrine? How badly did he hurt thy mother?"

"It was no horse that broke her neck."

"She—"

"He knew she was plotting. Thou were not the first woman in his circle to visit the likes of Constance Winston."

"And thee?"

"He never beat me. Only her. He did things to me that were worse. Far worse. Unnatural things that I told no one until this Sabbath, when I told Rebeckah."

The other woman looked at her boots, unable to meet Peregrine's eyes.

Mary reached down and handed her the letter. "My father was going to deliver it to thee tomorrow. There was enough light in the candle to write it. I believe there is enough now for thee to read it."

Peregrine nodded and unfolded the paper. As

she was reading, Rebeckah said, "Thou spoke well at the Town House."

"I did not see thee there."

"I was. I was hoping they would ask me to speak."

"I was doomed from the start."

"Before that group? Yes, Mary, I feared that was true. But I hoped and prayed," said the goodwife, and then she took Mary's hands in hers and rubbed them ferociously to warm them.

"Thou wouldst have made a fine constable," said Peregrine, when she had finished reading. She took the letter and put one corner into the flame of the candle, holding the paper so the fire could climb it, reducing it quickly to ash. She dropped the last corner on the floor, watched it burn itself out, and ground the cinders into the stone with the toe of her boot.

"My suspicions were correct?" Mary asked. "Thou planted the forks and the pestle in the ground?"

"Yes. My father was my quarry—not thee."

"And the boiled apples? Him, too?"

"That's right. I confused my pots. My father got the harmless one cooked up for thee, and thou ate the poisoned one I meant for my father. He should have died. Hannah should not have been sickened. Thank goodness she ate but a fifth."

"But the mark in the doorframe. That was not thee."

"No. That was surely thy servant girl. It was she who carved the mark and claimed to have found the Devil's tines in thy apron."

"Because—"

"Because she is afraid of thee, Mary. She wants thee gone from this world. Because, for reasons neither of us shall understand, she does indeed fancy my father. Having thee hanged as a witch accomplishes all of that."

"We should go," said Rebeckah, and Mary thought the goodwife meant that it was time for her friends to leave. But Peregrine was taking her hand and leading her from the cell.

"What art thou doing?" she asked.

"What the magistrates didn't," the woman said. "Giving thee justice."

"But Spencer—"

"My uncle is a very good man, Mary," said Rebeckah. "In the morning, he will tell the constable that he was conked soundly on his way from the jail and when he awoke, someone had taken his keys. Worry not about Spencer."

And with that they started down the corridor and toward freedom.

☙ ❧

The night air was bracing, colder than even the jail, but it was clean and fresh, and a part of Mary wanted only to follow Peregrine blindly; how extraordinary it was to her how badly she had misjudged the woman—and then, when it seemed too late to matter, come to understand her. But another part of Mary, bigger by far, wanted to know the details of the plan.

"Tell me, prithee, where art thou taking me?" she asked.

Peregrine whispered something into Rebeckah's ear, and the other woman walked briskly down the street ahead of them, and then turned toward the fine homes near the Town House. Her friend would pass the hanging platform. After she had started off, Peregrine answered, "To the **Bedmunster,** a ship that sails tomorrow for Jamaica," she said.

"Where has Rebeckah gone?"

"To fetch Henry Simmons."

"He knows what thou art doing?"

"Only that thy emancipation was being engineered. Nothing more."

She reached for Peregrine's arm. "But what will happen to thee? Dost thou plan to come with us and desert thy family?"

"Why would anyone suspect me? I will remain here. It was clear from thy letter that thou only began to see the truth of who I am and what I have been compelled to do because thou knowest my father."

"And Catherine?"

Peregrine's eyes were two round jewels in the night. "What wouldst thou like, Mary?"

"She wanted to see me hanged. She has, it seems, made her pact with the Devil."

"Then it seems to me sufficient punishment for her to spend the rest of her days in this world with my father, before joining her true master in the next," said Peregrine.

Mary smiled in a way that she hadn't in days. "Dost thou believe thy father will have her?"

"Yes," she replied. "And they deserve whatever misery they inflict upon each other. Now, we should hurry."

"I will not see my parents, will I?"

"No. Not tonight. I want thee on the ship well before sunrise, and I want to be home well before sunrise."

"Jonathan—"

"Jonathan does not dare question me. Not after all he has done. He has his own sins to answer for." They were walking quickly now, but still Peregrine had the breath to continue: "Prithee, fear not. I have faith that thou wilt see thy mother and father again. Someday."

"Someday," she repeated, and the word rocked her as if she were on the boat on the seas that so long ago had brought her here. Her smile left her, but she saw no alternative as they raced toward the waterfront. "I wish I knew how to thank thee," she added.

"I wish only that thou wilt forgive me. I should have taken thy hand and helped thee up from thy pit years ago," she said, and then she stopped, and so Mary stopped, too. She heard it now: horses. A pair.

Peregrine pulled her behind a large, round oak, as cold this time of the year as a marble column, that stood at the edge of a dooryard. There were no candles in the house's windows, but that didn't mean that someone wasn't inside watching them as they stood perfectly still behind the tree, hoping to be shielded from the road by its broad trunk.

There on horseback were Thomas and a fellow Mary didn't recognize. Was it possible that her husband had left her in her jail cell and then gone to the ordinary until it closed? Apparently, it was. The other rider spotted them behind the oak.

"Who is that? Who's there?" he asked. Like Thomas, he was a big man. "I can see thy breath."

The idea came to Mary that she had come so close and yet was, in fact, destined to die here. It was her winter yet. So be it. "I will go to them," she whispered.

"Come out!" Thomas shouted. "Show thy selves!"

Peregrine pried Mary's fingers from her arm and

shocked Mary by pulling a knife from her cloak. She walked fearlessly from behind the tree and past the first rider to Sugar, her father's horse, the knife shielded by her side.

"Peregrine?"

"Yes, 'tis me."

"Why art thou out?" Thomas asked, his tone condescending, as if he were speaking to a toddler that was stretching its leading strings. Mary recognized, even in so short a sentence, the precise enunciation he used when he was drink-drunk.

"We should both be in our beds, Father," she said.

Thomas spoke to his drinking companion. "Sam, this is my daughter. I have no idea why she is not home. I, of course, have but an empty bed. But this one? She has her gambler to warm."

"Thy bed won't be cold long, Thomas," said his friend, chuckling. "Thy servant will be thy wife."

"And my life will be much improved." Then he climbed down from Sugar. "Peregrine, I shall bring thee home. I haven't a pillion, but we can walk. Thou canst tell me what devilment thou art up to at this godless hour."

"Dost thou feel nothing about the fact thy wife will be hanged tomorrow?" Peregrine asked.

"No," he said, his voice ice. "She is the spatter at the bottom of a sick man's slop pot. I am thankful only that she was barren and brought forth no demons. The Devil can have her."

"Thy father," Sam told her, "has endured too much already at the hands of that witch."

"Come, Peregrine," Thomas commanded. "Sam, I will see thee soon enough."

"Dost thou plan to watch her swing tomorrow?" Sam asked him.

"I do not. That face is ugly enough to me while it breathes. In death? It will be a mask too vile to bear."

"Father, she is—"

Abruptly, Thomas took his daughter by the throat. "Enough!" he yelled, before calming ever so slightly. "Enough. I know thou art out tonight because thou hast plans that will wind thee in the same crater as Mary. Let me bring thee home and save thy soul."

Sam climbed off his horse, nearly stumbling he was so inebriated. Then, slurring his words, he said, "Thomas, it doesn't seem thy can manage thine own seed."

Thomas looked back and forth between his drinking companion and Peregrine, visibly insulted by the idea that he could not discipline his own daughter. And so he did what Mary knew he would do: he took the hand that was gripping the woman's throat and in a motion that was swift and awful, he backhanded her across the side of her face with it, knocking her to the ground and the knife from her hand, where it bounced like a stone on the frozen earth. He bent over and picked it up, studying it for a moment as if it were but a fallen leaf or flower he didn't recognize. Finally, he spoke: "I am going to presume thou hast this because of fears of encountering some common scoundrel in the dark, and not because thou hast plans to add patricide to thy ledger."

"Patricide? Recall what thou just said about thy wife," she responded, rubbing her cheek where he had struck her. From experience, Mary knew the flesh there was warm. "The words mark thee, too: thy face is ugly enough to me now while breathing. In death? It will be a mask too vile to bear."

Thomas had to think about what she had said, slowed by the beer he had drunk. But when its import registered, he kicked her in the side, and then Sam did, too, slamming the toe of his boot into her ribs, and even muffled by the weight of her cloak, Mary could hear clearly the sound of each thud, a thump reminiscent of the hard work of tenderizing raw meat. For the briefest of seconds, Mary wondered at Sam's complicity, how comfortable he was joining in on the beating. But he was drink-drunk and he was Thomas's friend, and that probably was all the explanation there was. He was a man; he was a harrier.

"Thou hast always been a whore. Look at what thou married," Thomas was saying.

"Kick my jaw and break my neck! Isn't that how thou killed my mother?" Peregrine hissed when her father paused his beating.

"Thou dost not believe that."

"It is the truth. And, coward thou art, thou blamed it on a horse."

"Thou art a fiend, child, a monster. Thou has a brain that is but white—"

"Meat?" asked Mary as she emerged from behind the tree.

"Mary?" He looked aghast, as if he were seeing an actual demon risen up from Hell, a monster with talons sharp as scythes. And so she became one. A winged Fury. She rushed at him, and he was so shocked by her presence here in the night and the speed of her assault that she was able to wrest his dagger from its scabbard and use both of her hands to spear him with it—a motion as fluid and violent as the crash of a wave. She plunged it deep and hard through the fabric of his coat, between his ribs and into his heart. He looked down at the hilt that protruded from his chest, but then he gazed at her as if seeing her for the first time.

"Yes, Thomas, it is I." She held up her thumb and its two nearest fingers and said, "Meet the Devil's tines." Then with that thumb and those two fingers, she twisted the pommel at the end of the handle, turning the dagger like a knob.

His knees buckled, and he crumpled at her feet and beside his own daughter.

Peregrine rolled away from him and sat up.

"I am sorry," said Mary. "But only that first he was in thy life and then in mine."

Peregrine shook her head. "Thou dost not need my forgiveness."

Sam started toward his horse, but Mary grabbed him by his coat. "Say a word ever about what thou hast seen, and I will be sure that thou dost perish the next day. Remember: they say I am a witch."

"They hang witches, Mary Deerfield," he said, but his voice was without conviction.

"But not before we—baleful and bitter—leave behind us a trail of desiccated fields and dead animals. Of babies that rot in their mothers' wombs and men such as thee who fall like stones from their mounts, their hearts cold and still."

"Thou art going to be dead in the morning," he murmured, but again his tone was fearful and weak.

"Then I will bring thee with me," Mary told him.

He might have said more. He might have attempted to climb back atop his horse. But instead he grunted and stood up straight, turning his head to see Peregrine behind him. She pulled her knife from his back and he winced, and then she slashed it across his neck, the fellow's blood geysering like a fountain. He sunk to the ground, choking, and then—with a suddenness that surprised Mary—he was gone. Peregrine wiped the blade on the sleeve of Sam's own coat.

"One hates to lose a good piece of cutlery," she said.

"And Thomas's dagger?" Mary asked, pointing at it with the toe of her boot.

"Dost thou want it?"

"No."

"Neither do I."

Peregrine took her hand and said, "Let us leave before a sentry comes upon them. Let them think it was bandits or whoever attacked Rebeckah's Uncle Spencer and set thee free."

"They will suppose it is me."

Peregrine nodded. "Perhaps. But if they deem it likely thou left Boston with two dead men in thy wake? Thou wilt be feared as most potent. They will believe that in their lifetime they were indeed present for the hour of the witch."

"A witch? No, not merely a witch. The Devil."

"Ah, the Devil Herself," said Peregrine. "We really don't know whether the Devil wears breeches or a skirt, now do we?"

Mary contemplated the idea of the Devil in the guise of a woman as they rushed to the wharves, and at one point she looked up into the sky, awed by the stars. There were just so many. She thought how she would see them again from a ship at sea in eighteen or twenty hours, the same God behind them. There were people in the world who were good and people who were evil, but most of them were some mixture of both and did what they did simply because they were mortal. And her Lord? Peregrine's Lord? He knew it all and had known it all and always would know it all. But the deliberations of His creations? Meaningless. Absolutely meaningless. Still, there was one thing of which she was certain.

"Oh, I think we do know," Mary said finally. "Yes, this may be the hour of the witch. But the Devil? He most definitely wears breeches. The Devil can only be a man."

EPILOGUE

Mary sat on the grass and bounced the child on her knees. She looked into her eyes, which were the same blue in this light as the sky on the day she had been sentenced to death, but when they were indoors could appear the color of slate. They were round in much the same way that the child's remarkably beautiful face was cherubic. When the girl's hair was longer, Mary imagined the silk ribbons she would place in it, ribbons very much like the kind Beth Howland had used in her little Sara's. Mary had named her daughter Desiree but called her Desire, after the child who had come to her in a dream—a vision—back in Boston. The girl was a year old now, and Mary's memories of New England were growing distant. So were her memories of her brief winter in Jamaica, after she and Henry had wed. She remarried as a widow— though no one in Jamaica knew she had a husband who had died, because no one knew she was the infamous Mary Deerfield from Boston.

Now Mary and Henry and Desiree were ensconced in her brother Giles's estate, while Henry built a more modest house on a tract of land that her father and Giles had conspired to give them.

There was a breeze this afternoon, and Mary could smell her brother's sheep, even though they were but a slow, rolling mass of off-white as they grazed on the far hillside. She could see one of the dogs running aimlessly in circles near the herd, and occasionally she heard the animal bark at a bird or something it spotted in the brush. In the sky, to the west, were waves of flat, fibrous clouds haloing the sun. Henry had spread a blanket on the grass, and when she looked over at him she saw that he was handing her a piece of bread. She thanked him and broke it into an even smaller piece—tiny, really—and placed it on her baby's tongue. Communion, she thought. Communion. She wasn't barren. She just wasn't meant to bear a child with Thomas.

Less often these days she wondered what the gossips were saying in Massachusetts. In one letter to her mother she had asked if they had ever found the bandits who had murdered Thomas and his drinking companion: her mother, of course, knew the rumors that Mary had taken both lives before disappearing, but Mary suspected it gave her mother great comfort that she denied anything to do with those deaths. Her mother had written back that so far no one had confessed, though some were starting to believe it must have been savages. Perhaps it was also Indians who had had something to do with her escape. Maybe it was praying Indians she had met while ministering to the Hawkes. Who

else could have smuggled in knives and behaved with such vicious disregard for human life? John Eliot had said this was unlikely, but increasingly people had come to doubt that one woman could leave such a trail of blood in her path, not even a barren one who had had the temerity to accuse her husband of such inexplicable violence.

As for Henry, there were gossips who whispered that he was with Mary, either in Rhode Island or New Haven, but his aunt and uncle defended him staunchly and said he was in Jamaica. Valentine explained that the New England climate—his word, and he knew it was a pun—did not appeal to his nephew.

It all seemed so far away, even when the weather was such that she felt a twinge in her left hand. But she was here. She was alive and she was happy. She kissed Desire again and watched as the child wrapped one small hand around her finger. That night they would eat supper at the great table in her brother's house, and without shame she would use a knife and a spoon and a fork with three glorious tines.

ACKNOWLEDGMENTS

I don't own most of the books I bought for classes when I was in college. But one set has survived four moves as an adult: those books I read for the different courses I savored about seventeenth-century America. In some cases, I saved them because I occasionally found comfort in the poetry of Anne Bradstreet. In others, it was because—always a spectacularly anxious soul—I identified with the Puritans' often desperate self-examination.

And so I want to begin by thanking Barry O'Connell and David Wills of Amherst College— the former a professor emeritus of English, the latter a professor emeritus of religion—for instilling in me a fascination with the Puritan mind.

I am deeply indebted to L. Kinvin Wroth, professor emeritus of law at Vermont Law School. We first had lunch in the summer of 2001—twenty years ago—when I reached out to him to discuss the novel I was contemplating about a Puritan woman's attempt to divorce her husband for what today we call domestic violence but in the seventeenth century was called cruelty. He pointed out to me the articles it was critical I read about seventeenth-century law and the first New England courts. He read a draft of this novel and patiently corrected my most egregious mistakes. I will always recall fondly our lunches in South Royalton.

The books I read or reread included:

Sydney E. Ahlstrom, **A Religious History of the American People** (Vol. 1)

Josiah Henry Benton, **The Story of the Old Boston Town House, 1658–1711**

Carol Berkin, **First Generations: Women in Colonial America**

Kristina Bross, **Dry Bones and Indian Sermons: Praying Indians in Colonial America**

James Deetz, **In Small Things Forgotten: The Archaeology of Early American Life**

James Deetz and Patricia Scott Deetz, **The Times of Their Lives: Life, Love, and Death in Plymouth Colony**

George Francis Dow, **Every Day Life in the Massachusetts Bay Colony**

Jonathan Edwards, **The Nature of True Virtue**

Nathaniel Hawthorne, **The Scarlet Letter**

Carol F. Karlsen, **The Devil in the Shape of a Woman**

Perry Miller, **The American Puritans: Their Prose and Poetry**

Perry Miller, **Errand into the Wilderness**

Perry Miller and Thomas H. Johnson, **The Puritans: A Sourcebook of Their Writings** (Vols. 1 and 2)

Edmund S. Morgan, **The Puritan Family**

The Norton Anthology of American Literature (Vol. 1)

Glenda Riley, **Divorce: An American Tradition**

Walter Muir Whitehall, **Boston: A Topographical History**

The following articles and essays were helpful to the construction of this novel:

Judith Areen, "Uncovering the Reformation Roots of American Marriage and Divorce Law," **Yale Journal of Law and Feminism** (Vol. 26)

Thomas G. Barnes, "Thomas Lechford and the Earliest Lawyering in Massachusetts, 1638–1641," Colonial Society of Massachusetts, publications (Vol. 62)

David C. Brown, "The Keys of the Kingdom: Excommunication in Colonial Massachusetts," **New England Quarterly** (Vol. 67, No. 4)

Zechariah Chafee, Jr., "The Suffolk County

Court and Its Jurisdiction," Colonial Society
of Massachusetts, publications (Vol. 29)

Laura Clark, "The Second Divorce in Colonial
America Happened Today in 1643,"
Smithsonianmag.com

Lauren J. Cook, "Katherine Nanny, Alias
Naylor: A Life in Puritan Boston," **Historical
Archaeology,** 1998 (Vol. 32, No. 1)

George L. Haskins, "Lay Judges: Magistrates
and Justices in Early Massachusetts,"
Colonial Society of Massachusetts, publications (Vol. 62)

Michael S. Hindus, "A Guide to the Court
Records of Early Massachusetts," Colonial
Society of Massachusetts, publications
(Vol. 62)

Catherine S. Menand, "A 'Magistracy Fit and
Necessary': A Guide to the Massachusetts
Court System," Colonial Society of
Massachusetts, publications (Vol. 62)

Elizabeth Wisner, "The Puritan Background of
the New England Poor Laws," **Social Service
Review** (Vol. 19)

And then there is the remarkable team at
Doubleday, Vintage, and Penguin Random House
Audio: Kristen Bearse, Laura Chamberlain, Todd
Doughty, Maris Dyer, John Fontana, Kelly Gildea,
Elena Hershey, Suzanne Herz, Judy Jacoby, Anna
Kaufman, Ann Kingman, Beth Lamb, James

Meader, Nora Reichard, John Pitts, Paige Smith, William Thomas, David Underwood, LuAnn Walther, and Lori Zook.

I am so grateful to my agents: Deborah Schneider, Jane Gelfman, Cathy Gleason, and Penelope Burns at Gelfman/Schneider ICM; to Brian Lipson at IPG; and to Miriam Feuerle and her associates at the Lyceum Agency. Thank you for always having my back and for the great gift of friendship, and—in the case of Deborah and Brian—serving as therapist and confidant. I couldn't do any of this without those two.

And, of course, there is Jenny Jackson, my editor for over a decade now, who is the definition of wisdom and equanimity. I can only imagine the sorts of train wrecks I would be writing were it not for her insights. She makes the books better when we are first discussing a very broad idea, and she makes them better when she is reading them line by line. She is the ultimate champion of this author and all her authors.

Finally, I am—as always—profoundly appreciative of the counsel of my lovely bride, Victoria Blewer, and our daughter, the always amazing Grace Experience. My God, those two women are patient and smart. Victoria has been reading my work since I was first amassing rejections (250 before I lost count) for short stories when I was eighteen years old, and giving me advice that is at once kind and unflinching. Grace has been sagely critiquing my novels since she was in high school—and bringing many of my characters to life as one of the very best audiobook narrators in the business.

I thank you all. Truly and humbly.

A Note About the Author

CHRIS BOHJALIAN is the #1 **New York Times** best-selling author of twenty-two books, including **The Red Lotus, Midwives,** and **The Flight Attendant,** which is an HBO Max series starring Kaley Cuoco. His other books include **The Guest Room; Close Your Eyes, Hold Hands; The Sandcastle Girls; Skeletons at the Feast;** and **The Double Bind.** His novels **Secrets of Eden, Midwives,** and **Past the Bleachers** were made into movies, and his work has been translated into more than thirty-five languages. He is also a playwright (**Wingspan** and **Midwives**). He lives in Vermont and can be found at chrisbohjalian.com or on Facebook, Instagram, Twitter, Litsy, and Goodreads, @chrisbohjalian.